The
FAVOR OF KINGS

"'From my doleful prison in the Tower, this sixth of May.'"

[Page 344.]

The
FAVOR OF KINGS

BY

MARY HASTINGS BRADLEY

ILLUSTRATED

NEW YORK AND LONDON
D. APPLETON AND COMPANY
1912

Published April, 1912

Printed in the United States of America

TO
MY MOTHER

FOREWORD

"NEVER have bright romance and black scandal been more attached to the name of lovely woman," writes a quaint and susceptible chronicler, "than to that of fair Anne Boleyn." Certainly no girl ever flashed so meteor-like above the satellites of an English court, and no woman ever went to her doom under more awful accusations.

Since fiction could not be half so amazing as the facts of Anne Boleyn's story, I have kept this novel of her fortunes true to those facts, and have gone, for their knowledge, not only to the histories written of this period, but in many cases to the sources of those histories. My endeavor has been to reveal the actual characters and the actual situations, and to use as much of the real incident and dialogue as possible. The State Papers of Henry the Eighth, his letters, foreign and domestic; the correspondence of the Spanish ambassadors, Mendoza and Chapuis, with Charles the Fifth, and the correspondence of the French court, and of the Papal agents, the old English chroniclers, Hall and Wriothesley and Cavendish, and sundry memoirs and diaries have all contributed to the material, and where the accounts have varied and the historians disputed, I have used the account which seemed the most authoritative and probable.

The only liberties I have taken with the known facts are a reference to Surrey and his love affairs when he was yet ten years too young and a use of the name Helen

vii

FOREWORD

Sackville instead of Nan Sackville to avoid a continual conjunction of Nan and Anne.

The intermingling of "you" and "thou" was the confused usage of the times, and so, too, was the occasional address of "Master" or "Mister," even to some men of title.

One of the most disputed matters is the date of Anne Boleyn's birth, and here I have followed the opinion of Brewer, Gairdiner, Lingard, and many others in accepting the year 1507. Camden gives this date, the only positive one given by an early writer, and there seems no good reason to doubt it. Friedmann, in general so excellent an authority, does so and refers to a picture at Basel bearing the inscription HR, 1530, ætatis 27, and the words, added later, Anna Regina, as being the portrait of Anne Boleyn painted by Holbein, but Mr. George Scharf has pointed out in the "Archæologia," vol. xi, p. 81, that the picture is of Anne, Queen of Hungary and Bohemia, whose age exactly tallies with the dates, and that the letters are not HR, but HB, which was the signature of three German artists of that period, one of whom, and not Holbein, executed the portrait. Also in Henry Clifford's "Life of Jane Dormer, Duchess of Feria," edited a few years ago by Father Stevenson, we are told that at the time of Anne's execution, "She was not 29 years of age," which, if the reckoning of time from the New Years was meant— there were four different ways of reckoning it then— would place Anne's birth before May 19, 1507.

But I do not wish to enter an historical controversy but only to suggest the truth of the colors of the picture I have tried to paint, and to offer the Anne Boleyn of this story, a very human girl, gay and fearless and rashly proud, as the likeness of that Anne who dared

FOREWORD

and lost so long ago and whose blood was the first of any woman's to stain an English scaffold.

I wish to acknowledge my indebtedness to the histories of Paul Friedmann, of Brewer, Gairdiner, Strickland, and Hume, and to express my gratitude to the librarians of the Bodleian Library, Oxford, for the generous use accorded of the documents and MSS. in their possession.

Also I wish to thank Miss Louisa Sewall Cheever, of Smith College, Northampton, Mass., to whose friendship and encouragement this book owes much of the inspiration for its undertaking.

MARY HASTINGS BRADLEY.

CONTENTS

CONTENTS

LIST OF ILLUSTRATIONS

THE FAVOR OF KINGS

CHAPTER I

THE QUEEN'S REFUSAL

APRIL, the deceitful minx, after promising fair weather, was sending gust after gust of rain. With wet, mocking fingers she tapped at the mullioned panes as if to flout the three exasperated young men within, booted and spurred for a ride, who were lounging in the palace hall and roundly reviling the state of things.

" Devil take it ! " groaned Norris, with a yawn that eclipsed half a well-featured countenance. " The month's a very woman for tears ! "

" A jilt — like all her sex," pronounced Wyatt, the poet.

" Will it never have done ? " Brereton grumbled, drumming on the leaded glass and staring out over the drenched gardens to the rain shrouded sweep of country beyond.

" An it does, the ways will be muddy," Norris gloomily predicted with a careful thought for his new breeches.

Wyatt opened his lips for a scoffing rejoinder, then stopped to listen. He had caught the muffled blare of a trumpet and the distant grinding of heavy doors.

" Hark," said he, " the queen is coming from mass."

Usual as the incident was, it was at least an incident, and in their tedium they paid it a more flattering attention than it generally received. Turning to face the great doors at the end of the hall, they swept off their hats, brushing back some random locks and shaking out a frill or two in preparation. They were three as fine looking young men as you would often see in a row, all between twenty-two and twenty-three years of age; Brereton big and ruddy, with a mane of golden hair the color of the massy gold chain about his neck, Norris lithe and dark, and Wyatt between the two in stature and beyond them both in a distinction of bearing and charm of feature. Youth and gay spirits and a kinship of tastes had made fast comrades of them.

In a few moments the large doors were pushed open, maneuvered by four backward moving little pages, bowing at every step to usher in the procession. Two pages came to a standstill on either side of the entrance while the other two made their crab-like way down the hall to open the opposite doors leading to the queen's apartments. Two trumpeters came next, rending the ears with a roar as they entered the hall, and then appeared the woman for whom all this ceremony took place.

She was a thick, middle-aged figure, cumbered with heavy velvet and satin damask. Lacking in the appearance of majesty, lumpy, plain featured, with the scant hair strained baldly back to be hidden under a black velvet cap, she nevertheless managed to express majesty's authority. There was a proud habit of command in the very set of the neck upon her shoulders, in the proud lines of her harsh features, in the arrogance of her eyes. She crossed the hall slowly, awkwardly, her sagging train supported by the two Spanish women who had been her life-long attendants at her alien court.

Two by two followed the English maids of honor, some with faces meekly cast down as if in pious revery, others

2

bright-eyed and alert, shooting slant beams at the three courtiers. Demure or daring, a visible self-consciousness animated them all as they passed by, all but the youngest maid of honor at the end of the line, who marched in a kind of furious oblivion. She was a slender slip of a girl, of delicate lines and vivid color. High carried head, face pale but for two crimson fires in the cheeks, dark eyes immovably forward, blazing with unguarded emotion — such a bearing arrested even young Norris's wandering gaze.

"Look at Mistress Anne," said he in wonder.

Wyatt was already looking. "She is ill-pleased," he diagnosed promptly. As cousin of the girl, he might, on that and other accounts, be considered an authority on her humors. "There is a storm brewing — God send cover to the poor wretch on whom it breaks! Anne hath a dagger behind those red lips of hers. . . . It would seem that the mass brought but scant peace to her soul."

"Mistress Anne was bent over a letter the great time," volunteered one of the small pages, who, now that the train was past, had sidled over from his post at the door to insinuate himself among the young men.

"Billet-doux during mass!" sighed the poet in mock dismay. He looked across to the doorway through which flickered the last scarlet gleam of Anne's gown. "There is some love mischief afoot — I shall give a candle to Our Lady of Good Chances that I am not in Percy of Northumberland's shoes this day."

"Ho!" said Brereton with a grunt of awakened interest. "Is Percy then —"

"My supplanter!" Wyatt laughed — the laugh of a man who turns a resolutely gay face to the world, but there was an edge to the laughter. He had worn his cousin's colors at joust and tourney since her arrival in

3

THE FAVOR OF KINGS

England from the court of France, and though he carried off the affair lightly as the customary allegiance of knight to lady, the lightness had sometimes a summoned air. "In faith only the blind can deny it," he proclaimed airily. "Henry Percy hath fallen over heels in love."

Brereton, tweaking the curls of the page, who sustained a difficult grin under the attention, looked reflective.

"That Percy hath been contracted to marry Lady Mary Talbot these three years," he said.

Wyatt shrugged airily. "Aye, three years, and women are not wine to grow dearer through keeping. And the contract, I hear, was none of Percy's making. His father made it — let his father look to it."

"You think then that Percy intends — ?"

"I think then that Percy intends," Wyatt gayly assented. "I think also that Anne intends, which is the important matter, and that my small cousin will therefore be Countess of Northumberland some fine day. I must be choosing my rhymes for the occasion."

The girl of whom he prophesied so securely had entered the chamber of the queen. It was a long, somber apartment, hung with tapestries between the panelings of carved oak, and lighted by small windows, near whose leaded panes were placed the embroidery frames where the ladies in waiting were already setting to work. Time hung heavily for young spirits in this chamber where King Henry and his gay retinue rarely entered; the days were dull repetitions of devotion and needle work and the only hint of amusement was the evening play of cards and a snatched gossip with the suite of those who came to pay their respects to the queen.

Catherine was seated before her embroidery frame

4

THE QUEEN'S REFUSAL

where the rich greens of a forest were taking shape under her skillful fingers; the ladies about her bent, half squinting in the grudging light, over their work in silence. Conversation immediately after mass was not considered indicative of a proper train of pious reflection. The youngest maid of honor had not taken her place at her frame. She was standing beside it, her eyes on the queen, her hands tensely clinched at her sides as if gripping upon some supreme resolve. Then with a swirling flutter of draperies she moved impetuously forward and fell on one knee at the queen's side.

"I crave a moment's hearing of your Majesty," she cried, and the sudden appeal of the young voice vibrated with an indecorous sensation through the calm room.

In surprise Queen Catherine looked down into the excited face of her maid of honor, and there was a brisk rustling of silks as her ladies turned to the strange sight of Anne in petition.

"How now? What have you to ask?" There was scant promise in the queen's tone and in her attitude of suspended industry.

Anne's eyes swept the attentive listeners. "Will your Grace have the goodness to hear me privily?" she besought.

The queen gave a look about the room before which her attendants discreetly lowered their lids.

"Speak out, girl," she commanded. "This is privily enough."

Anne swallowed hard. She had no illusion about the queen's feeling for her. Between them had ever rankled the antipathy of alien temperaments, and strong personal pride to which their close association had given a thousand indefinable ways of expression. But she saw no help for herself now except through the queen, and after all

5

THE FAVOR OF KINGS

Catherine was a woman and had often been a pitying one to subjects in distress. Perhaps now her pride would be gratified and her spite appeased by such humility of appeal. But it was bitterly hard to speak out and bare a sensitive heart before that curious roomful.

"Your Grace knows," she began desperately, "that in these years at court, since my return from France, I have ever served you with loyalty and devotion. If I have e'er offended it has not been from a wish of my heart's. Let me implore that out of your great charity your Highness will intervene on my poor behalf. I am in such strait fortune! The Lord Cardinal "— even through the tone of pleading that name shot a quiver of rancor —" the Lord Cardinal hath forbidden my troth to the Lord Percy of Northumberland."

Catherine's beetling brows contracted sharply. She thrust out her lower lip — an ominous sign. "Thy troth? Percy of Northumberland? What art thou raving about? What art thou to him?"

"Your Majesty, the Lord Percy has honored me with the proposal of his hand. We plighted our troth. And then the Lord Cardinal —"

"Thou hast been having secret love meetings with this Henry Percy?" Clearly the tale had not made a good beginning. Catherine had stern standards for her maids.

"I but talked with him here at times in the chamber while the Lord Cardinal was having audience with your Highness," Anne anxiously protested. "And we are plighted to marry. We waited to implore your Grace's favor until Percy could personally acquaint his father with his hopes." Catherine's expression seemed to imply that these two numbers on the prospective programme would have been better reversed. Anne read this with sinking heart as she hurried on.

6

THE QUEEN'S REFUSAL

"Then as we were waiting there came one that spied on us and hatefully betrayed us to the Lord Cardinal, in whose care and service Northumberland had been placed. And the cardinal then called him to account, who made answer that he wanted nothing so much as to marry me and be released from an old pre-contract that his father had made, three years back, with the father of Lady Mary Talbot. There are contracts made and unmade every day, as your Majesty knows, and the Lady Mary's affections were in no wise touched. But oh, for no reason that any heart can see, the Lord Cardinal forbade our love. He sent for the old Earl of Northumberland to come and oppose young Percy. Oh, your Grace, your Grace, I beg, I implore of your womanly heart to take pity on us and grant us your aid! A word from you to the cardinal, to the king, and we are free to love and marry and without that word we are undone forever. It is so little to you and to us it is all. Surely God will move you to take compassion!"

Her voice rang out through the room unmindful of the listening ladies. She had forgotten their curious eyes and ears; in her passionate need pride and reserve streamed from her like leaves in an autumn gale. She was conscious only of her peril, her fear, and her hope. Through a mist of unaccustomed tears her dark eyes sought the queen's; her lips were quivering, her heart was bounding like a hunted thing's.

Little enough emotion answered her in the queen's reply. "I trust I know my duty to God without your tongue to point it. . . . If the Lord Cardinal forbade, the Lord Cardinal had a good reason."

"Oh, 'twas a reason of hard, unchristian craft!" the girl gave tempestuously back. "He wishes to keep me unmarried that he may be ever dangling the promise of

7

my hand before my cousin, the son of Sir Piers Butler, to settle with my father the old dispute over the Ormond inheritance. The Butlers give him gifts to bring this to pass — must a girl's life wait so on juggling state craft? Oh, your Majesty —"

"Is that a seemly way to mention the Lord High Cardinal to me, girl?" Anne opened her lips but Catherine's gesture checked her speech. "You are not free, Mistress Anne, to follow with your hand where you have flung your heart. I trust I have an open mind for all who sue but I see in this nothing but the vanity of a froward maid which I have had occasion beforetimes to rebuke. Your queen hath other work than the making you Countess of Northumberland. His Gracious Majesty, the king, hath long destined you for your cousin, Sir James Butler, as a fitting union to end an old family strife. To that end you were recalled from France."

"But that is over three years ago — and still the Lord Cardinal would keep me unwed so as still to hold threat or promise over the Butlers and accept their gifts." Anne's tears were dried by her rising anger and long smothered sense of injustice. "I have been but a pawn in his game. Surely to your Majesty I may seem a woman. Why may I not marry Percy? I am of honorable lineage, the daughter of a knight, and I have brought no stain or tarnish to my name —"

"I care not to discuss your fair reputation, Mistress Anne."

A faint titter, like the rustling of a spring breeze, flew among the ladies, quickly subdued for fear of the queen's displeasure. But Catherine gave no hint of vexation towards it.

"You are a froward girl to rail at the Lord Cardinal's

THE QUEEN'S REFUSAL

policies — which are the policies of the king, your master. Would you raise your tongue against him? You have ever been too unlicensed in speech and action, mistress; take heed now and be warned by this mischance which your folly has brought upon you lest worse happen. Percy is contracted to the Lady Mary and you should have known better than to raise your eyes to his. I would do wrong to have that contract broken."

"Oh, your Highness, 'twas but a talk, a promise, between the fathers three years back. Percy and Mary do not love. 'Tis I he chooses and 'tis his happiness that is in your hands with that of mine."

"Percy is a boy and should be finding his happiness in his duty and not in stolen love tokens from silly maids. We will have no French ways here."

The Spanish woman had no love for France and it was Anne's misfortune that she had brought back from that court too much of its charm and freedom to be acceptable.

The girl's whole face was scarlet with distress, but she made one more last essay of humility.

"Ah, if your Majesty would but reflect! We would serve you all our lives in such loving gratitude —"

"Which is, in any case, your duty to your sovereign," Catherine dryly reminded her.

Then as the girl, still on her knee, fixed on her a look of strangely mingled pleading and resentment, "Rise, Mistress Anne," she commanded. "I would do wrong to interfere with the king's plans. Nay, you need speak no more. I know my duty with the aid of Heaven without your voice. I am sorry for your hopes but I cannot help you in this."

Anne rose slowly, her burning eyes never wavering from the queen's face.

9

THE FAVOR OF KINGS

"Even queens ask mercy from Heaven," she said in a low, steely tone, tense with vibrating passion. "It may be, on a future day your Majesty would not be sorry to have granted some."

"Now that speech is more like to the Mistress Anne Boleyn than your former ones," returned the other, unmoved. Again the ladies laughed, a little louder this time, and one or two whispers flew nimbly among them.

"I am what your court makes me," the girl cried in sudden outbreak, then as sharply checked herself. Not a look among the ladies was lost to her though her eyes never glanced that way. She was breathing hard, her lips set to keep them from trembling, her hands gripped fiercely under her long pointed sleeves. Every nerve in her was tingling, every pulse throbbed with shame and rage and defeat, yet she stood outwardly at ease, a slow smile curving her lips.

"I thank your Majesty for your great kindness to me. . . . I shall never forget your Grace's pity on my distress."

Her dark eyes were leashed lightning. Then she bowed low and walked slowly out of the room, her head high like a flower on its slender stalk of a neck.

Through the long halls and up the stairs she made her way with an insolent, flaunting grace for any eyes that might be spying, but when she gained her room and drew the bolt across the door, her nervous strength ebbed like a racing tide and she sunk on her knees beside the window seat and buried her face in the cushions.

CHAPTER II

A BROKEN BETROTHAL

BITTER anger at the queen, at the cardinal, at Carewe, the informer, wrung her like a physical anguish and lent venom to the loss of Percy and the defeat of their hopes. Just one word from the queen — one little word! And she would not say it! She had been glad to deny her, to taunt her. Even in that tumultuous instant Anne wondered whether the queen was aware of her own gladness. Catherine seemed to her so self-righteous, so smugly assured of her own purity of motive, that no such disturbing self-knowledge could reach her. Why should such as she have the power of life and death, the girl's wild rebellion questioned. It was all unfair, unjust, iniquitous, this scheme of life! Chivalry and justice and mercy were only words of mocking lips. There was no reality but power.

Power! She whispered it to herself chokingly. Oh, for the power of ruling her own life, of riding out with her lover forth to his country home, far from all interference and tyranny! Oh, for the power to dash aside these arrogant men and women, or to wreak on them one-hundredth of the bitterness that she was suffering now! Oh, to make them feel as she felt, to foil their hopes, crash down their plans and stab their pride as they had stabbed hers! The memory of the scene that had just been enacted stung her like a hundred tongues of fire.

11

THE FAVOR OF KINGS

She writhed under the memory, her whole body hot and angry. . . . Power! It was the desire of all the world. Money and strength and beauty and intellect were only of worth for its acquirement.

Poor Anne's tears were fast and furious as the realization of her own helplessness swept over her. What could be done? Her father, Sir Thomas Boleyn, was in excellent favor at court but she knew his affable selfishness too well to dream that he would take one step for her against the cardinal. Her brother George adored her but he had no influence to exert — and she herself had only her youth and bright eyes and gay spirits, and though these had won Percy they were powerless to destroy the barriers raised between them.

Oh, Percy, Percy! How merrily they had laughed together in the garden two nights ago, how lightly they had prophesied of that golden future waiting them, how they had dreamed and talked and kissed! What a night it had been — starry and sweet with spring, with a crescent moon, high over their shoulders, etching in silver the rosebuds about them. . . . Even then Carewe must have been lurking in the shadow of those rosebushes, playing the spy.

It was a happy, happy heart that she had carried up to bed with her and now — she pressed her hands against her aching side. It was all too horrible for belief. And she was only a helpless girl of nineteen, unfriended and alone. The slow moments dragged by, each with its weight of misery, its sting of reminder. Unheeded, a little black spaniel, subdued by this strange turbulence, had crept closer and closer to her on the window seat, watching her with anxious, puzzled eyes. At last with a worried whine, he put his head down by hers and sent his rough little grater of a tongue against her wet cheek.

A BROKEN BETROTHAL

Anne started, then her arms went round him, and her tears fell with fresh violence.

"Oh, Robin, Robin — if men had but such hearts as thine —"

But comforted a little by that dumb sympathy, she sat up and put back the loosened hair from her hot face. The note she had been reading in mass had fallen from her dress to the floor and she smoothed it out and read it again.

It was a boy's scrawl, incoherent, distraught, sent in haste by Henry Percy to announce the arrival of his father whom the cardinal had summoned. Percy was both dazed and fearful. He begged Anne to do what she could; he was obliged to keep his quarters in the cardinal's household.

Percy loved her — loved her to folly. She put her wits sharply together over that. It might yet enable him to strike some blow for their happiness or it might keep him true and waiting till times should be more favoring. Or even, so swiftly did every instinct in her rise to hope, it might be possible for him to soften his father's heart. The old earl was mighty — mighty enough, perhaps, to assuage, though never to oppose, the cardinal.

She would not yet despair. She had hoped too keenly, rejoiced too deeply, to wrench herself yet from her dream.

How much of this dream had been of Percy and how much of the future Earl of Northumberland her most candid moment could scarcely have told. Percy's good looks and merry bearing, his gay laugh and boyish, whole-souled adoration of her, and his reverence toward her girlhood — sweet at this rude, jesting court — had all moved her heart to pride and joy in him, while her haughty young head, full of girlhood's vague, glittering

13

visions, was not unready for the coronet of Northumberland.

These hopes swept away, what remained? Anne stared out unseeingly over the garden, drying its tender April green in a sudden shaft of sun, and she saw herself a small, insignificant mite in this great world in which she had meant to play so magnificent a part. Not the Countess of Northumberland now — only a thin little waiting maid to a spiteful queen, at the mercy of every whim of favor. And she had dreamed such dreams!

The seven years she had passed at the French court where she had gone as a childish maid of honor to the Princess Mary on her marriage with King Louis, passed through her mind — years of color and charm and gayety, lilt of music and light hearts and dancing feet. When the old king died and Mary ran off to marry Brandon, the Duke of Suffolk, Anne had remained under the charge of good Queen Claude and had been foremost in favor of all the three hundred girls in her train. As she shot into girlhood, her quick wit delighted in the keenness of the French and her vivid intelligence gained in character in the society of men and women who thought with clearness and talked with charm, and who veiled the dull, daily vices of humanity with such a delightful mantle of cultivation. Anne had been a young belle among her companions; at fourteen she was setting a mode in gowns, inventing dances and winning acclaim by her dancing of them; she played the lute and sang with sweetness. She amused half the women and more than half the men and when at fifteen she was recalled to England she carried a harvest of lamenting verse from susceptible young blades, which drew from her only heart free laughter. She had not learned the meaning of a sigh, and her natural regret at leaving France

A BROKEN BETROTHAL

was smothered by girlish anticipation of the joys to come in England.

English joys, however, failed most dismally of materialization. She found herself an attendant on a queen who devoted her time to mass and embroidery and her money to priests and chapels, while the king was absorbed in a distant round of hunting, gambling, beefy banqueting, and noisy revelry. The girl looked in vain for the tone, the verve, the intelligence of the French court and felt curiously alien in this damp, foggy, slow-spoken England with its Spanish queen.

But the court had not been insensible to Anne's grace and wit, and as she grew older her charm shone as much as Catherine's dark chambers permitted. Her cousin, Thomas Wyatt, fell very desperately in love with her, and at the last Christmas jousts, where he won the championship, he had crowned her Queen of Love and Beauty. Other lovers began to gather about her, idle young court rufflers who all too frequently were leaving their neglected wives in the country while they themselves sought the favor of the king.

The girl was exposed to a degree of corruption and callously accepted vice that would have been the undoing of a spirit less fine. But Anne was too vigorous for such frailty. She knew very well the form she meant her fortune to take and in Percy she had found the realization of all her dreams. And now what was before her?

At four, the ladies in waiting, seven tables of them, supped together at mess and Anne went down to face the ordeal with the unflinching courage that companioned her proud temper. She bathed her poor flushed face, powdered her suspiciously purple nose, and trusted

15

THE FAVOR OF KINGS

hopefully to the concealment of the wealth of dark hair which she wore unconfined save for a single ribbon across the brow. That hair had been another cause of friction with the queen, for Catherine, whose scant locks were combed back over a small, hard roll to form a round coif about the face and were then capped by a seven pointed affair of black velvet, had denounced the girl's flowing curls as " French wiggery." It was a curious feminine satisfaction to Anne's spirit now to shake out her hair in defiance of the queen's established fashion; and the freedom of this style accorded well with her slight, springing type and framed to striking advantage her gypsy-like face, with its sparkling eyes and drolly demure mouth.

It was a hard mouth to-night as she faced the throng, and sharp sayings slipped through it as her excitement gained from the innuendo and sly laughter about her. Behind the light sentences her tongue stung like a dagger, as Wyatt had observed, and there was often more will than wit in the retorts that came back at her from her unfriendly companions.

Of all the girls there was but one to whom Anne felt drawn and this one could scarcely be called a confidante. She was Helen Sackville, a tall, colorless girl, with a long nose and curious gray-green eyes under light lashes, a desperately un-handsome young woman, yet with a shrewd humor and a caustic wit that were meat and drink to Anne among the bland hypocrisies of the older ladies in waiting. To this girl Anne gravitated when the others were disposed about the queen's chambers for a game of écarté. Helen looked down at her with an air of quizzical amusement.

" So there is where you have been these fine moonlight nights, Mistress Anne — trysting with my Lord Percy? "

16

A BROKEN BETROTHAL

Anne nodded briefly, her nerves still tingling from an encounter with a Spanish woman who had condoled ironically with her loss of prospects. Her eyes were on the doors that were being continually opened to admit the visitors who came to pay their respects here or try a hand at the cards.

" H'm — a pretty romance," Helen commented. " We had marked you together in company but never surmised how far you had progressed. . . . Methinks you were not over civil to our Gracious Majesty this afternoon? "

Anne's features quivered ever so slightly and her head went up an inch or so. " What happened when I left? " she demanded.

" Oh, the world wagged on the same. I embroidered a deer's head and horns as long as eternity. Donna Maria read a sage book aloud on the saving of souls — Oh, it seems that the queen did make the scornful jest that you seemed in great anxiety for the wedding. The Spanish women enjoyed it."

The hot color deepened in Anne's face but she made no response. Slander was too current at court to be amazed at, but her anger registered one more incentive against the queen. The doors had opened again and on the heels of the entering courtiers came a little page in Cardinal Wolsey's scarlet livery, tricked out in gold thread and lace like a pretty popinjay. He made butterfly trips about the room, lingering now at this group, now at that, for a message or a jest, and at length he slipped over to the corner where Anne, whose eyes had never left him, stood waiting with Helen, in tense expectancy.

" What news? " she demanded in a quick whisper.

The little fellow shrugged and shook his head.

" None that is good. Never have I seen the cardinal

3   17

THE FAVOR OF KINGS

more incensed. My Lord Percy is in sore straits. There is no hope for thee, Mistress Anne." He flicked a grain of snuff off his ruffles with careful concern.

Anne wanted none of the puppet's judgments; her desperate concern was with the facts.

"Tell me what has chanced," she besought. "What said the cardinal to him?"

"Much — and all to the same music. He was wroth that Percy, who was in his care, had neither acquainted the lord, his father, nor yet the king's Majesty with the matter but must go about the choosing of a wife with as much ease and indifference as if he were a peasant or a hall boy and not the heir to one of the noblest earldoms in the kingdom. 'Hadst thou submitted this matter unto his Highness,' quoth the cardinal, 'he would have advanced thee much more and mated thee according to thy degree and honor, and so by thy wise behavior thou might have grown into his grace and favor. But now' — and his voice was terrible, mistress! —'see,' he said, 'what you have done through your willfulness. You have not only offended your father but also your loving sovereign lord and matched yourself with such a one as neither your king nor your father will consent to: — and hereof I put thee out of doubt that I will send for thy father, who, at the coming, shall either break this unadvised bargain or disinherit thee forever.' And he went on to say the king's Majesty would also complain of him, to the earl, because his Majesty had intended thee for another."

"But why," came hotly from Anne, "am I so scorned as a match for this high Percy? My mother was a Howard —"

"Aye, aye, so spake Percy to the cardinal. Poor lad," said the little page patronizingly, "he was so shaken

18

and put about he was weeping like a nervous girl. We could hear his voice through all the courtyard."

Anne uttered an impatient little sound. " But what did he say?"

" Oh, that he had not known the king's pleasure and was sorry for it, that he had held himself of good years and able to provide a convenient wife as fancy should please. And he said that though you be but a simple maid and a knight to your father, you had descended of right noble parentage, for your mother is high of the Norfolk blood and your father descended of the Earl of Ormond — Oh, the Lord Percy spoke well for you, mistress, and begged the cardinal on his knees to intercede in his behalf, and with the king, for this matter that was so dear to him that he could not forsake."

" Aye? " Anne's face was sparkling.

" Why, at that the cardinal turned round to us," went on the page, all fire and gesture in the telling, " and, ' Lo, sirs,' he quoth, ' ye may see what wisdom is in that boy's willful head. I thought that when thou heardest the king's pleasure and intent thou wouldest have put thyself wholly to the king's will.' Oh, but his voice was a terrible thing, mistress, and his face held so great a rage that Lord Percy looked everywhere but there. ' So I would, sir,' he made answer stammeringly enough, ' but in this matter I have gone so far I know not how to discharge myself and my conscience.' "

" A pious cavalier! " came in low mockery from Helen.

" He said *that?* " cried Anne.

" His very words," the page affirmed, a little sulky at being snapped off in the thread of his dramatic recital.

Ah, Percy was weakening, the girl divined. In his place she would never have weakened! That soft pli-

19

THE FAVOR OF KINGS

ability she had detected in him, that had made him so responsive to her caprices, would undo him here. His was not the stuff that stood out against tempest, she felt, and was full of rage towards him that his nature was not as hardy as her own.

Helen voiced her own thought. "You should have been the man," she murmured.

"We are indeed undone — this is the end," the girl thought with whitening lips. "Go on," she said aloud. "Was there more talk?"

"Aye, talk enough. Percy was charged that he resort no more unto thy company as he would abide the king's indignation . . . so thereupon he wrote that letter which I had no leisure to get to thee until the mass to-day."

"Has his father yet come?"

"The noble earl came at once and was long closeted with Cardinal Wolsey. And then he came out with a glass of wine in his hand and sat down on a bench which was at the end of the gallery for the use of serving men — and before us all he rated his son who stood there, cap in hand. 'Son,' he said, 'Thou hast been and always wast a proud, unthinking and licentious waster, and what comfort or pleasure shall I conceive of thee, that thus without discretion, hast misused thyself, having neither regard unto me, thy natural father, nor the king, thy sovereign lord, nor to the weal of thine own estate, but hast unadvisedly assured thyself unto her, with whom the king is with thee highly displeased, whose displeasure is intolerable for any subject to bear. His indignation were able to ruin me and my posterity utterly! But considering the lightness of thy head and the willful qualities of thy person, being a singular good lord and favorable prince, and as my Lord Cardinal does clearly excuse thee in thy light act'— the little page

20

was rolling off the long sentences with unction —' he doth lament thy folly rather than malign thee for the same. Pray God this be a sufficient admonition for thee to use thyself more wisely!' he said, and tossed off the wine and scowled round on us all and then went on to say that he did not need to make Percy his heir, as he had other boys, and he threatened to choose the most promising of these for his successor and he rolled his eyes round on us and bade us mark his words and be not sparing in telling his son of his faults."

"You are a glib parrot, Master Wygant," said Anne, and tucked a coin into his hand. "You have dealt well with big words — some day it may hap their meaning will come clearer to you. Is there no more?"

"Nay." With a bow he dropped the coin in his satin pocket. "That is all. I gave it as it was — I can remember a phrase as long as the best of them, and as for meanings — what is there that I do not know? Percy will go from court, it is said in our household, with his father in a day or two, and till then he dare not resort here. I have lingered over long now. Farewell, mistresses both."

"I, too, must be making my excuses," said Anne. "I think I shall not stay here longer."

"Her Highness's manner was not over smooth to you this evening," cautioned Helen. "It bodes you no good."

"Nor does any other sign that I can read," Anne flung back. "And I care not a whit for them all!"

When she had gained the long corridor, she did not seek at once the seclusion of her room, but made a wary way down a narrow flight to another corridor from which opened a tiny balcony. She stepped out on it and stood looking over the rose garden beneath. All the hope left in her after the interview with the queen was dead. This was the end. There was no appeal. Even had Percy been of another caliber, the matter might not have been bettered. The thing might have been made to cost him his head.

Not that the king was so hopelessly displeased; this talk of Henry's will was, she felt, but a cloak for the cardinal's designs. Wolsey's was the hand that had struck down her happiness. The girl seethed with hot, ineffectual rage against him, all the bitterer for its impotence. He was treading her coolly underfoot for a political scheme that was a small thing, too, to him, but my Lord Privy-Seal did not permit even his small concerns to go astray. If his interference had been a matter of jealousy or revenge, Anne, curiously enough, could have felt it less of an outrage, for jealousy and revenge are warm human passions that strike mercilessly in self-defense, but this cold arrogance that treated her merely as a wooden pawn to be moved hither and yon quickened her to the fiercest resentment her fiery little heart had ever thrilled with.

The moon slipped out from under a cloud and sent its soft light streaming into the garden's enclosure, making it a fairyland of ethereal light and mysterious shade. It slipped through the swaying leaves of the trees to weave fantastic, changing patterns on the grass about them, it trembled airily on the budding roses and ran, like a silver river, down the wide, box-bordered paths, to flood with its radiance the marble shaft of an old sundial in the garden's center.

It was just such a night as the one when she had last met Percy, and under all the fierce surge of her anger came stealing the pain of the nevermore. Nevermore would they meet there — it might be they would never

"Was it—could it be—Percy?"

meet again. The poignancy of such denial was strange to her, but she divined that it was but the beginning of sorrow. Memories that had suddenly become an agony enwrapped her, and an aching presentiment of grief to come.

All at once she was aware of a tall, gray-cloaked figure approaching from the shrubbery.

She caught her breath sharply, in hope and fear. Was it — could it be — Percy? In that beating second, she decided that if her lover had found his way to her and would ask her to fly with him, fly she would, and brave whatever storm might come.

The figure stepped beneath the balcony, and her hope was mercilessly dispelled. The plumed hat was swept off in a low, ironical bow, and the moonlight showed the thin, mocking features of Sir Nicholas Carewe.

"A fair evening, cousin," he called.

This was the man who had betrayed them to the cardinal, betrayed them, Anne realized, out of his own jealousy and baffled passion. "My Lord Percy is remiss," he sneered. "The lady waits."

"But never waits — for *you,* my lord," the girl gave back, her face sparkling with dangerous light before his evilly laughing eyes.

"It would be a vain hope."

"Ah, cruel! All the court knows how I have pined for you!" Anne was in a frenzy; she struck savagely at her enemy with her cool, sweet-toned disdain. The man hated her because he loved her; it was his one vulnerable point and she thrust her dagger there with a spiteful turn.

"The court has something else to talk of now, little cousin. Poor Percy — it was so sweet in the rose garden! To think he will come no more. And that coronet

THE FAVOR OF KINGS

— how suitable would it have become your fair brow. It was a shrewd disappointment, and the bitterer for being so excellently assured of the prospect. You would have been the Countess of Northumberland, and now — well, what now, little cousin?"

What now, indeed? " Doubtless your spying eyes will find out," she said bitterly.

He laughed, well pleased. " I shall find out all I want to know, rest assured."

" And you will find out many things you do not want to know," was all she could find to say.

" Art thou threatening?"

" I am promising. I shall pay thee some day." She leaned over the balcony and spoke slowly, giving each word its full weight. " Thou art a sly, scheming, black-hearted fool, Nicholas Carewe, a spying tattler, not fit to win any woman's heart, nor any glance of her eyes save in disgust, so plainly is thy black heart written on thy black face. What thou hast done thou hast done in malice and spite, like a snapping cur, and, like a snapping cur, you are not worth an honest anger; you are fit only to be kicked into the dirt and so I spurn you, and so I laugh at your antics! You have not hid your heart from me. I know its presumption well."

He stared up at her, the laugh gone from his narrowing eyes.

" I never loved thee," he said with savage emphasis.

" How you love me now!" she said slowly. " How you must have pleasured in what you saw in the rose garden — the pledges, the kisses that would never be thine. How long did you watch, cousin? Were you there when I gave him the red rose? How close did you creep?"

" Thou liest!" he told her, and angry oaths slipped

24

over his tongue. "I could choke thy piping throat between these fingers, for all the love I bear thee, Mistress Anne! I but played with thee once — thou wast not worth the game."

"Ah, it was fine play, Nicholas Carewe — but you chose another face then to match your begging words." She laughed impishly at the burning eyes that threatened her. "Thou dost not love me, then? And I yearn for thee so, dear Nicholas!" Again her wild, sweet laughter flouted him.

He was speechless a moment, then pulling himself together, made a mighty effort at his earlier mockery of manner.

"Laugh on, lady. . . . One with so excellent a future must needs be light of heart. Adieu, dear Countess of Northumberland," and with a sweeping bow he took himself away, breaking into a gay snatch of song as he went as if to drown any retort she might send after.

But Anne stood in silence, watching the tall figure and swinging coat till it melted into the shadow. If at that moment she could have chosen between the utter annihilation of Queen Catherine or Cardinal Wolsey or Nicholas Carewe, she would have been hard put to it to decide.

Then she gave a slow sigh of despair, lingering for one more look at the dreaming garden, bidding farewell, in her heart, to all that the spot had meant to her.

"Truly a fair future I have!" She acceded mockingly, with dry, brilliant, ironic eyes. "Well, it is time the Countess of Northumberland should go within!"

CHAPTER III

A ROSE AND SOME WORDS

IT was no great surprise to the court, the next day, to learn that Mistress Anne Boleyn was in disgrace and ordered back to her father's estates. The command was not wholly a cross to the girl, for the seclusion of Hever Castle appeared a haven of relief from the intolerable tongues of the court and the watching eyes that were, at their kindest, but agreeably diverted by her chagrin. She knew what stories would be told of her poor love affair; what jests made of her blighted hopes. Another girl might have fashioned of such misfortune a wreath of rue and languished beneath it in charming and romantic melancholy, but not even the notion of such a rôle occurred to Anne, and if it had, she would not have possessed the slightest idea of how to perform it. To endure pity was abominable to her, and to invite it an impossibility. By the law of her nature she might command, coax, dominate, divert, bewitch, enthrall; but implore — never! She had begged that once of the queen and she vowed now that no pressure of calamity would ever bring her to her knees again.

She was aware, too, that hers was a temperament that won but scant pity in its reverses. Enchant some as she might, she must inevitably antagonize others to enmity, and the spectacle of pride humiliated has ever its relish for all bystanders.

26

A ROSE AND SOME WORDS

Little time was wasted in packing. She and Bet, her maid, made rapid work of it, while Robin frolicked round the opened boxes in gay anticipation of an outing. Helen came to lend assistance and say farewell.

" There will be no more laughter for me now your wit is gone," she declared. " I shall grow dull and dumpy as Donna Blanche, and broider unending miles of tapestry. I shall make one of your story, with you languishing in some lofty dungeon window and a despairing knight beneath. The queen is duller every minute and the Spanish jades are sneering at your departure. . . . Shall I send you news of the court? "

" I care not." Anne folded the red gown she had worn the day before into a compact lump and whacked it down on top her others. " It may be I shall get to France soon," she muttered, " if the king will send my father on some errand there."

A knock on the door and the maid rose to admit little Mary Wyatt, the poet's sister. There was none of Helen's aloofness about this small person; she flew to Anne in a tempest of affection. " Oh, my dear, my dear, my *dear!* I came at once . . . I but heard this instant . . . I cannot tell thee how I feel. I am so grieved for thee," she said with a little sob. Her tender heart was brimming with love and loyalty to Anne, to whom she had always looked up in childish, unstinted admiration. It was dreadful to her now that this merry, triumphant heroine should suffer such eclipse and her dismay broke through the shyness that usually constrained her. " But I am sure this cannot be for long. It will all come right in time, dear Anne. And my Lord Percy is such a splendid lover. I have said but little to him but I have looked on him much. He will find a way to claim thee after all."

27

THE FAVOR OF KINGS

Anne had a sharp vision of Percy, hat in hand, before his father, while the listening servants stared.

"Aye, 'twill all blow over," she assured her chokingly. "Shed not a tear for me, Mary."

"In six months our Anne will be back with a fresh lover," Helen cheeringly predicted.

Mary looked up at her a little distrustfully. She suspected Helen of a cold heart and mocking tongue — a suspicion the young lady roundly deserved — and her romantic dreams of life-long devotion were affronted at this easy prophecy. Moreover, she was somewhat jealous of the older girl's place in Anne's affections.

"You speak as if Anne had no heart," she resented, and, "Oh, I shall miss thee so!" she burst out with a sob.

Anne turned to look at her. The little thing's eyes were red with crying; her whole aspect seemed swimming in tears and dismay. Anne wondered fleetingly what she had ever done to be so much to the young girl, yet at the same time it seemed to her that Mary's emotion was trivial and childish, crying so tempestuously at a separation from a friend, for she divined that Mary's tears were even more for this than for her sympathy for Anne. What would she do if she had lost all — all — and there was no hope — no future . . . and yet one had to keep on existing somehow and acting as usual . . . and smiling. . . .

Anne reached out and pressed Mary's hand then withdrew her own hurriedly; it seemed to her that if she yielded to this sympathy she would utterly break down. Helen's dry matter of factness was the best tonic for her now. Sharply she caught up a cloak and began folding it. It was a cloak Henry Percy had admired. She wondered if she was to face such reminders all her life.

28

A ROSE AND SOME WORDS

That afternoon Anne set forth with her brother George. They were the only two of the family between whom existed a genuine attachment. With her father Anne could claim scarcely more than an acquaintanceship, and her elder sister, Mary, obscurely married after a whispered scandal at court, was a faint and shadowy figure in her life for whom she felt only a good-natured contempt. Her mother she scarcely remembered. On her return from France she had found a stepmother installed at Hever, a competent, middle-aged housekeeper of no pretensions to birth at all, save the evident fact of existence, who got on, amiably enough, with them all.

George was a dashing, gay-humored young fellow of two and twenty, fond and proud of Anne and now disgustedly chagrined that her discomfiture should be in everyone's mouth. With brotherly candor he explained his feelings. Anne had made a most unnecessary spectacle of herself and let the whole family in for a lot of sly raillery. 'Twas said Nicholas Carewe had rhymed a ballad on the story. She should have known better than run after earl's sons, and have been content with her own station.

"And what is that station?" Anne shot mutinously into this homily, as she gathered up her last belongings.

"'Tis what I can attain to," she insisted, without waiting for his definition.

"But you attained not."

The fact was incontrovertible. Anne made no reply. The superiority of his position helped George back to good humor.

"You should have seen the lions in the way, little sister," he pointed out.

"Lions!" sniffed Anne. "Foxes rather — the lean, gray fox of the cardinal. Butcher's son that he is!"

29

Anne's rages always amused the young fellow. He began to laugh, the lines of his displeasure clearing.

"Tut, tut! Well, the butcher's son has taught you a lesson not to meddle with his lambs. Percy, they tell me, is heart broken — poor sweeting!"

"You can loose thy tongue at me, George — I can ever give thee better than thou canst send," cried the girl, "but you will leave Northumberland's name alone."

"Art thou so deep in love?"

"Aye — deeper even than thy wife with thee! . . . Nay, you need not frown. I gave you warning — leave Percy's name alone."

Boleyn's clouds never lasted long; he shrugged away the reference to his wife's notorious unfaithfulness with characteristic indifference. "Make haste, call thy maid," he advised her. "It may hap the country air will sweeten that sour tongue of thine."

All the idlers about the court had assembled to watch the departure of the disgraced maid of honor, some merely curious, others with the maliciousness that infected the air of the place. Nicholas Carewe lounged in an opposite doorway, smiling steadily across at them.

It was an ordeal the girl met with a high-held head and a sudden flow of laughter and talk. George, disdaining such feminine subterfuge, called impatiently for their horses, but as these approached, they were warned back by a blare of trumpets. The gossiping courtiers and idling servants about the courtyard all whirled to attention at the familiar cry, raised loudly by approaching ushers, "On, my lords and masters, on before; make way for my Lord's Grace."

"The chancellor comes," muttered Boleyn, with that repressed contempt that the aristocrats felt so keenly for this arrogant commoner who lorded it over them. He drew Anne aside from the doorway and into the front of the lane that had been quickly formed, between which came the approaching procession. Two high crosses of heavy silver were borne aloft, and after them two pillars of silver, and then the pursuivant at arms with a great mace of silver gilt. Alongside came the gentlemen ushers with their warning cries and then, between four footmen with gilt pollaxes, on a white mule trapped with crimson velvet and gilt, rode an imposing, proud lipped man in cardinal's robes of gorgeous satin and taffety damask, and though the April afternoon could scarcely be called chill, with a tippet of fine, sleek sable about his neck.

A low obeisance was demanded, but of all the bowing ranks Anne's salutation was the slightest; she straightened quickly and fixed her eyes on the man who had just reversed the world for her. She detested every line of that slant, one-eyed face, its unctuous satisfaction, its heavy-lidded pride, its force and craft, and cruelty and power. And when his sharp gaze fell on her in passing, she gave him back look for look, with no effort to conceal the spirit that flamed within her. In the flicker of recognition he accorded her, she detected an amused perception of her mood and bland indifference to it — what to Wolsey was the anger of a little dismissed maid of honor?

George felt the hand on his arm suddenly stiffen, and hardly had the studded oak door closed on the last of the cardinal's suite before Anne, with irrepressible passion, burst out, " An I can ever do that man a hurt, so will I, please God! "

Her voice undoubtedly carried to a nearby group or two, and in annoyance at this ridiculous exhibition her

4   31

brother felt his face grow warm. Anne's threat was as comic as the squeal of a pinched mouse. With all respect to his sister's spirit, he realized her impotence and frowned on her exaggerated speech.

"You are like to destroy him," he said dryly. "I fancy it will be some time before you can bring him to the block."

"I would almost go now myself if so be he would accompany me," she answered.

"You had better use your time to pray God for a more Christian soul, little sister," Boleyn retorted, moving impatiently to her carriage. "In the next world, I fear, the meek Saint Anne will never claim you for her own."

Hever Castle was Anne's birthplace, and aside from her welcoming now of its privacy, she felt a warm affection for the place. She loved the time-weathered gray walls that gazed back at her in motionless duplicate from the still moat, she loved the echoing stone corridors and high-ceiled rooms where she had played as a child, but most she loved the great tangled wildwood of park, where noble beech trees linked hands over broad avenues, where violets padded the brook edge with purple velvet, and silver fish hung in the clear pools, where birds sang and dun deer cropped the tender grass.

Here Anne's truant feet had often carried her from the anxious care of Madame Simonette, the governess — good Madame Simonette, who taught her such excellent French and loved her with such patient devotion — here she had spent the happiest hours of that brief childhood which she considered fast closing when she went to France in the Princess Mary's train. Here she had roamed seven years later, a little homesick for that merry France, but with a headful of shining visions of the

A ROSE AND SOME WORDS

merrier times to be at the English court. And now, those shining visions turned to mocking wraiths, she roamed here again, finding in the largeness and the sweetness of the out-of-doors some balm for the fiery grief within her, even though she winced at the reminders that those paths brought her of the girl that she used to be and the dreams that she used to dream.

There is nothing in the world more sharply despairing, more utterly without alleviating perspective than youth's first sorrow. Age and experience are too calloused with scars to feel the wound to the full; and they have known too many of life's paradoxical compensations to be bereft of all philosophy, but at nineteen the heart admits no compensations, accepts no philosophy.

Anne saw only a great blackness ahead of her. All her life, unconsciously, her imagination had been living in the future, now, the future despoiled of its secrets, she was thrown back sharply upon herself. At the first she gave way to secret, passionate outbursts of rebellion, sobbing stormily at the foot of some great beech till strength and tears were exhausted. She lived over and over again her brief love story, torturing herself with its bygone sweetness and bygone hopes and painting impossible pictures of revenge upon those who had so cruelly injured her, for revenge was the watchword of the jealous-honored times. Under the dual stress of grief and anger her unformed character was swiftly hardening.

There came a day when after one of her bitter outbursts she had the weary sanity to perceive its futility and the wisdom to enforce upon herself a resolve of endurance. She began the hard schooling to the inevitable. She accepted her disappointment, she tried to make herself realize her life as it was, as it must now

33

THE FAVOR OF KINGS

be. Her immense pride had been sufficient to mask her sorrow from the public, and she found now in herself an unsuspected fiber of hardness and endurance that enabled her to confront it steadily in private. But the venom in the wound persisted — the rankling anger against the needlessness and injustice of her suffering. She writhed at the memory of her scene with the queen. She drew ridiculous, impossible, and childish pictures of the queen herself overtaken by some inconceivable humiliation; she recalled her father's shrewd observations on the insecurities of favorites and she longed ardently to be permitted to witness the cardinal's downfall. As for Carewe it was at least a spice of satisfaction that she had flouted him.

In August Sir Thomas Boleyn, or rather now, for a year past, the Viscount Rochford, arrived unexpectedly. It was the first time father and daughter had met since Anne's disgrace and the viscount glossed over now, with his usual suavity, the real reason for her presence at Hever, complimenting her airily upon the benefit of country air to her appearance. He permitted himself the single hint that in the future it would be as well to consult him before embarking very definitely on any other matrimonial affair.

Anne was grateful for this abstinence and his hopeful assumption that there was a future for her, but she did not particularly like her father. Her young egoism resented his bland lack of interest in her as an individuality and of concern for her happiness; she and George had long since reached the conclusion that their father never looked upon his children's careers save as possible stepping stones for his own. This resolute concentration on his own interests and complete freedom from all entangling sympathies had made Rochford a courtier of

34

A ROSE AND SOME WORDS

success. He could not be denied a charm of manner —
when he wished to exercise it. Anne, in her fieriest
moments of criticism, was susceptible to pride in his deft
geniality. George had inherited the lightness of that
manner to a large extent, but not its freedom from
offense; the young man sharpened his wit with likes and
dislikes, not so violent as Anne's, but enough to win
him a cordial detestation from the quarters on which his
dislike blew.

Lord Rochford was a man of many cautions, with a
keen eye for cracks and keyholes; even in the bosom
of his family he permitted no uncomplimentary reference to the cardinal whom he affected to revere. In his
presence Anne was forced to curb her recklessness of
speech. His discretion was a continual lesson to her
in unremitting diplomacy. It was the very unremitting-
ness of this diplomacy that perhaps most earned for
itself her splendid contempt; it was one thing to wear
a mask at court, and another, and very silly thing, she
felt, to persist in wearing it at home. She wondered,
curiously, if her father tried to wear it even with himself. He took no one into the confidence of his secret
and evasive mind.

By the time of her father's return the picturesque
charm of Hever had begun to pall upon the girl's active
spirits. That first great need of hers for being alone,
for facing and conquering her grief in solitude, had
passed. She sought now, rather, to fly from it and the
thousand reminders of sorrow within her and craved
diversion restlessly. She was, it must be confessed, in
a chronic state of irritability, for when some sorrow has
drained the heart of all deep emotion it becomes, in
sensitive and highstrung natures, peculiarly susceptible
to the prick of petty wrongs and exasperations and

35

THE FAVOR OF KINGS

to the little annoyances of the day. Anne, at that period, was a burden to herself and those about her.

One day at the end of the month she returned from one of her solitary excursions in the park to find the castle in a state of activity. A company of knights had been discerned riding over the tops of a neighboring hill towards Hever and a mud-spattered serving man had brought word that King Henry and some friends, returning from a long hunting trip, desired the hospitality of Lord Rochford. Excited servants were hurrying about, bringing in fresh rushes for the floor and logs for the fireplaces, rubbing up copper and brasses and silver plate, while, from without, the groans of an ox and the frantic squealing of dying pigs testified as to the size of the evening's banquet.

Anne's spirits refused to be lifted at this general air of expectant preparation. She walked slowly through the hall, feeling herself a stranger to all this hospitable welcome, and met her father in rapid converse with the head steward. He raised his hand to detain her and, after a few moment's authoritative directions, dismissed the steward and beckoned her toward him.

" 'Tis a rare honor his Most Gracious Majesty is vouchsafing us — eh, daughter?" he smiled.

To the girl's disgusted and supremely critical perception the smile was a smirk.

" He must pass the night somewhere," she answered petulantly.

Her father chose to overlook it. " Of course — and 'tis fine fortune that sends him here, and his reverence, the Cardinal Wolsey, with him. Come, Anne, seize thy opportunity and make thy peace with the cardinal. Ask his forgiveness for entangling one of his household and entreat him to intercede for thee with the queen that

36

she may take thee back at court again. Come, now."
He smiled good-naturedly at her.

"And why do you not intercede for me?" she said
slowly.

"I? Eh, I meddle not in women's matter! And I
care never to use my influence for a thing of small importance when I may need it for a thing of greater.
This affair thou canst right, thyself. Put on thy best
habit and give us some music if we call for it and bide
thy time. The cardinal hath no grudge against thee
and if you show him you are a maid of talent he may
find a use for you in his revels."

"I will ask no favors of my Lord High Privy-Seal,"
said his daughter flatly.

Rochford sighed ever so gently, less in remonstrance
than in pious regret at the deplorable folly of youth.

"Well, well — but be on hand if thou art called for,"
he advised, and gave her a swift, sidelong glance of
calculating appraisement.

"I have a headache."

"We may find that to-night will cure it." Again he
smiled at her, and the smile made Anne curiously hot
and uncomfortable.

"A pity Mary is not at home," she muttered under
her breath.

He flashed her a glance of sharp and hostile suspicion
and turned on his heel without more parley, leaving
Anne maliciously elated at the sureness of her shot even
while she winced at the confirmation it seemed to yield.
Rumor had persistently ascribed Boleyn's assignment as
Ambassador to the Low Countries and later his appointments as treasurer of the household, steward of Tun-
bridge, keeper of Penhurst, receiver of Branstead, to
the pretty face and gentle grace of his eldest child, Mary.

THE FAVOR OF KINGS

Whatever truth lurked in the report, neither Mary nor her penniless young husband, William Carey, had reaped much of a harvest; the simple beauty's light had flickered mildly, then waned to nothingness. It had been some time now since the Careys had been seen at court; they were enjoying a full measure of connubial obscurity. Her years at court had not left Anne much surprise in which to shrink from this report, but she had been careful never to touch on it before.

Anne's perversity was harder upon her than upon the household, which seemed to miss her not at all, and the sounds of feasting and revelry that roared out from the great hall woke an excited unrest in her. Lying awake in the dark, her chin propped in her hand, listening to those tantalizing echoes of the gayety that other people were getting out of life, she decided that it was time wasted to be a woman. The Lord had clearly created the earth and the fullness thereof for man.

Moreover she reflected that her instinct to avoid the cardinal and refuse her father had cut her off from a glimpse of the young men she knew, friends of her brother, Norris or Brereton, who were undoubtedly in the king's train, and who could give her the gossip of the court — perhaps news of Henry Percy. Wyatt, she had learned, was not there.

She was awake early the next morning and, with the notion of encountering some of her acquaintances, she dressed in haste and made her way downstairs. The great hall stood empty, with only yawning serving men about. The king, she learned, was breakfasting in his chamber.

Wandering to the open door Anne peeped out at a world of blue sky and sunshine. It was a day of August's richest benignity, of full-blown sweets fresh-

A ROSE AND SOME WORDS

ened by the morning dew. The girl's spirits lifted in swift response to its joyousness and unconscious of a pair of keen eyes watching from the musician's gallery above she sped out over the drawbridge and into the park.

The place was so densely wooded that in twenty paces all glimpse of the castle was lost and only thin spirals of smoke ascending from its many chimneys into the blue above told her where it was. She was in the midst of immense beech trees, great, gnarled veterans of many season's storms, whose tangled boughs interwove a canopy of green above her. Somewhere, high overhead out of sight, a lark was singing. Her heart thrilled to the exquisite song.

A little farther on a glade opened before her, half encircled by a shallow brook bubbling between its green banks that were embroidered with the delicate blue of the crane's-bill. Anne took the brook at a leap that shook her hair into a thousand dancing tendrils and reached the object of her excursion, an old stump wreathed everywhere with a glory of scarlet ramblers. Standing on tiptoe — for Anne had ever a mind for things out of reach — she began to pull the dewy roses, making as pretty picture at the task, as man could find to look upon — a maid among her roses.

A snapped bough made her turn with a start to find that a man was indeed looking at it. He was a big, finely built man, in a rich suit that bore the marks of soil and travel. His face was ruddy; his yellow beard and somewhat scant hair shone in the sun. He made a flourish with the plumed hat he carried in one hand and smiled at her confusion.

" Flora in her bower," said he, in a resonant masterful voice.

THE FAVOR OF KINGS

Anne bowed low to her king. "Your Majesty!" was all she could find to say.

This maiden fright was in itself a flattery. Henry smiled and took the brook at a bound, landing beside her with a thud of solid weight.

"Tribute," he laughed and took a rose from her armful.

"Mars taking tribute from Flora," she ventured and saw that the flight of fancy pleased.

"What other name does Flora wear among mere mortals?"

Anne opened wide her eyes in naïve surprise. She had yet to learn something of the transient place that subjects claim in a monarch's recollection. "I haven't courtesied to him more than fifty times!" she reflected, and then consoled herself with the succeeding reflection that Henry swallowed Catherine's maids of honor in the same casual, neglectful way that he swallowed the fact of Catherine's existence.

"I am Anne Boleyn," she said.

"So? . . . I recollect thee, now. The morning sun and this nymph-like fashion of the hair had so dazzled mine eyes that I did not well perceive thee, mistress." He paused a moment while his memory evidently summed up all it knew of Anne's career and then added, "We do miss thee at court."

Anne dimpled mischievously. The opening was too much for her discretion.

"I am sure that her Gracious Majesty is disconsolate!" she replied demurely.

The king stared. Not a ghost of a smile on that small mouth; its curves were buttoned in with the sedatest of expressions but her eyes — he felt he had never glimpsed anything so blithely, drolly audacious, as Anne's eyes. His own twinkled back into them, his

"'Flora in her bower,' said he."

A ROSE AND SOME WORDS

fancy caught. He had not talked with a woman for three days and here now at hand was a pink and white slip of a girl with dancing eyes and alluring wit; small wonder he expanded his chest, posed a hand on his hip and smiled down conqueringly into that piquant little face.

"Beshrew me, but she is no judge of worth an she does not," he vowed. "Had I the felicity of thy society, fair Mistress Boleyn, I would lament a parting!"

"Troth, but I have heard the gentlemen leave the lamenting to the ladies!"

The king chuckled. "You should not believe all you hear, lady."

"So I am reminding myself, your Highness."

"Nay, but a prince's word is never to be questioned."

"I must needs take your princely word therefore."

"You are as pat as amen," he laughed, and lingered on some minutes more in aimless, light-hearted banter, leaving at last in the pleasant consciousness of having given a pretty maid an immense deal to dream about.

But Anne's dreams would have surprised him as she stood among her roses, watching the last rider in Henry's train gain the sky line on Hever Hill and then vanish from sight,— she was abusing herself most villainously for not having appealed to the king instead of the queen. Henry had seemed so pliable, so easy-natured to women, that she felt she might have touched his heart and moved him even against the cardinal. She smiled at the daring of the thought, then drew a keen breath of regret.

Too late, now. The cardinal had taken his stand, the earl had interfered, Percy had been carried away to his distant home. While an impending action might have been averted, a completed one could never be undone by any means in her power. Anne took her roses and

41

THE FAVOR OF KINGS

went back into the house, but for all her regrets for the might-have-been she felt very agreeably diverted and reënforced in her own esteem by the flattering episode.

The king rode on to Westminster, his head still running on the nymph of the morning because he had seen no more attractive nymph since to displace her. With a smile he mentioned her to Wolsey, who rode at his side.

" I have been conversing this morning with a young lady," said he, " who had the wit of an angel — and was worthy of a crown."

Wolsey's heavy lid veiled the amusement within. There were so many young ladies at Henry's court whose eloquent admiration and appreciative eyes had led Henry to the same bestowal of praise!

" It is sufficient," he remarked dryly, " if your Majesty finds her worthy of your love."

Somewhat dubiously Henry recalled the vision of a clear-eyed girl under her bower of roses. Enough of the young and innocent pride of that face remained in his memory to cause the remark, freighted with an involuntary accent of regret, " I fear she would never condescend that way."

Wolsey permitted his smile to expand. It had always been Henry's way, he noticed, to magnify the inaccessible virtue of the young lady to whom his momentary addresses were paid, thus emphasizing the glory of the conquest. His slant gaze was fixed knowingly ahead, on the waving ears of his mule. " Great princes, if they choose to play the lover, have that in their power which would mollify a heart of steel," he observed oracularly.

The particular great prince nodded agreement to this dictum which his own experience had confirmed. He was so palpably occupied with the consideration, that Wolsey, who never permitted the most trivial factor in

42

the game to escape him, inquired, "And who was this witty maid, your Majesty?"

"Rochford's daughter, Anne Boleyn."

"Anne Boleyn — she that turned young Percy's head?" Wolsey recollected. "Um — it seems he had a pretty taste since your Majesty commends it. She also hath a pretty temper according to your most gracious wife."

His Majesty grinned.

"We must have her back," thought Wolsey as they rode on, "if she can but entertain him a fortnight. Her father would rejoice . . . and his advancement is no menace to me. . . . I will speak to the queen."

When Wolsey spoke it was to some purpose. The next week saw Anne Boleyn again at court.

CHAPTER IV

A DANCE WITH A KING

ORK PLACE, or York House, the London residence of the Archbishops of York, where Wolsey maintained his almost royal — many said more than royal — pomp, was an imposing mass of buildings lying to the south of Westminster palace; one side touched on the Thames, the others, encircled by lovely gardens, were surrounded by a high wall. Wolsey had practically re-created the place since it had come into his possession, lavishly rebuilding and enlarging on every hand till he had reared a palace rivaling any of the king's, whose spacious splendor lent itself nobly to the gorgeousness of his entertainment.

On this night of September, 1526, he had planned an especially gay revel for his sovereign's diversion. The great audience chamber, where the feast was laid, approached by an impressive succession of eight rooms, was a large gallery-encircled hall, hung with finest tapestries of the Flemish looms. They were changed every week, these tapestries, so numerous was the cardinal's supply, and for this occasion he had chosen a brilliant set representing subjects from Ovid's Metamorphoses. Between each arras division massy silver sconces bore up hundreds of springing tapers, and hundreds more of them swung on gilt chandeliers from the wide beams and sparkled in broadly branching candlesticks over the gold and silver vessels on the banquet table. Giant yeomen

44

A DANCE WITH A KING

were standing with flaming torches about a huge cupboard of eight stages, to throw a frank increase of luster on the burnished, jewel-studded plate it held. Not an inch of the vast, treasure-filled hall was unillumined, and thronged with a vividly attired company, the effect was a most dazzling radiance of light and color — a kaleidoscope of brilliance dominated by the cardinal's scarlet, multiplied as that was in his flocks of velvet-coated gentlemen ushers and satin liveried underlings.

The cardinal himself did not sit down at this banquet nor attempt to maintain his wonted ceremony. It was laid magically aside in the presence of his royal guest and Wolsey turned his talents to playing the host, strolling from one table to another, all graded with the most exquisite care, and accosting everyone with that delightful blend of courtesy and intimacy he knew so well how to assume. Only an occasional turn of his eye, enforcing order on the craning throngs permitted in the gallery to observe how the great world of fashion took its pleasures, recalled the stern Judge of Chancery.

The same lavishness and display that met the eye were being repeated in each course of the banquet. Beef and lamb and pork and venison followed on each other's heels, accompanied by rich pastries, jellies, and sweetmeats of French and Spanish confection and those especially invented symbolic dishes, the fad of the hour, wrought into some artificial and allusive shape.

Red, quivering hearts of jelly languished in white bosoms of cream; poor, silenced thrushes, with a spit through their tiny hearts and a dusting of sugar on their crisply roasted backs, were the flocks of love birds that nestled around a very mealy image of Venus. And where shape or substance failed to permit any analogy, some motto or riddle was attached — generally of a kind

5   45

THE FAVOR OF KINGS

to bring a broadside of laughter from the men and a flutter of confusion from the maids.

The king, seated beneath a canopy of silk, led gustily in the laughter as in the eating and drinking, his face flushed, his cold eyes lighted with wine and excitement. Catherine of Aragon was not present. His sister, Mary, and her husband, Charles Brandon, the big, blond Duke of Suffolk, were next to him, and a cluster of his intimate friends had left their places down the table to stand laughing and talking about his chair. Henry Norris and William Brereton were there, Sir Thomas Wyatt, George Boleyn, Sir William Compton, Sir Gilbert Pickering, Sir Francis Bryan, Sir Nicholas Carewe — a roistering group of wild and heedless favorites who out-devil-may-cared the gayest, most devil-may-care young blades at court.

The feast was drawing to a close when suddenly a peal of trumpets rang through the room, stilling the tongues and drawing the gaze to a curtained doorway on each side of which the trumpeters stood. There was a hush, broken by the scrapings of benches and tables as the guests turned for a view, and then in the silence there stole softy out from behind the tapestry the music of harp and lute, and after a few bars some sweet invisible chorus of girls' voices.

> Pastance, with good company
> I love, and shall until I die;
> Grudge who will, but none deny,
> So God be pleased, this life will I,
>   For my pastance
>   Hunt, sing and dance,
>   My head is set;
>   All goodly sport,
>   Is my comfort,
>   Who shall me let?

46

A DANCE WITH A KING

"Who-o shall me let?" echoed one of the unseen sopranos in a clear and silvery voice.

This was a song that the king had composed some time before, and as the fact became recognized a fluttering of stimulated delight flew about the hall. The king himself was leaning forward in eager interest. He had a keen love for music and a keener one for his own creations; their repetition was an endless pleasure.

The tapestry curtain parted now over a file of richly gowned girls, wearing black velvet masks. They entered with a slow, dancing step, singing the second verse.

Youth must needs have dalliance,
Of good or ill some pastance;
Company me thinketh the best
All thoughts and fantasies to digest,
    For idleness
    Is chief mistress
    Of vices all;
    Then who can say
    But pass the day
    Is best of all? . . .
    Is best of all?

Drawing closer to the company the masked girls circled in and out in a fashion new to the English court, lightly, airily, gracefully as flowers in a breeze, they advanced, retreated, passed and repassed in accord with the time, forming now a star and now a crescent and now an intricate true lover's knot. They were led by a slender, black haired girl in blue silk, silver starred. A velvet cape floated from her shoulders, its points hung with tiny golden bells that gave a quaint music of their own to her dancing; long gauze sleeves now fluttered over her waving hands, now fell away from her white, upraised arms. At her ankles diamond stars were flash-

47

THE FAVOR OF KINGS

ing over the tiniest of blue velvet brodequins. The others followed imitatively after her; she led the way in buoyant, spontaneous grace, the very genius of the dance, the spirit incarnate of youth and frolic and joy in life.

From the first the king's eyes fastened upon her.

"Who is that one in blue, Wolsey?" he demanded, without turning his head, bringing his fist down upon the table to add to the applause with a heartiness that made even the solid standing cups skip.

"'Tis the young lady who invented this dance to your Grace's music," returned the cardinal who stood looking over the king's shoulder. The ghost of a sardonic smile touched his full lips — he had seen this game so often! How many little pleasure traps he had baited — and how invariably the greedy quarry bolted the bait!

"Her invention?" Henry was murmuring. His smile expanded. "Her name, man. I knew not I had such a gifted lady in my realm. Her name?"

"Methinks your Highness will find it more piquant to discover," Wolsey urbanely gave back, his smile expanding.

The men about exchanged glances and a sudden noisy wail arose. Somers, the king's jester, had been edging nearer and nearer the circle and now the squat, fat-featured fellow was making a parody of blubbering, his fists digging at his painted eyes.

"Oh, sirs, I weep — I weep for the lady's husband," he sobbed. "God give him company this week, else he is like to have lonely time of it!"

The young fellows shouted. "Only this week, sayest thou, Will?" bantered Bryan. "Nay, this unknown hath a rare grace — belike she last two!"

Henry granted the chaff a roar of laughter. "Watch her dance, lads," he cried. "Was there e'er a lighter

48

foot? Sure, Venus tiptoeing on the foam was not half so dainty!"

"'Tis your Grace's music that dances," Carewe declared.

"They would be dull feet that did not rise to it," supplemented Wyatt with his engaging smile.

"Troth, but your Highness hath ever a shrewd eye for a maid," Norris murmured, his eyes on the maskers. "I know not who she may be, though she hath a strangely known air, but she is a very Titania at her revels. Mark that fairy grace, that floating hair, and gesture of command!"

The ladies had formed in line again, hands joined, their faces to the royal table, and, slowly swaying from side to side, they commenced the last stanza.

> Company with honesty
> Is virtue — and vice to flee;
> Company is good or ill
> But every man hath his free will.
> > The best I sue
> > The worst eschew;
> > My mind shall be
> > Virtue to use;
> > Vice to refuse
> > I shall use me.

"I shall use me," rang out the little leader's silvery tones.

"Ah, Wyatt, go to school to those lines," cried Norris, but Henry did not stay to breathe the incense. He rose as the maskers concluded and made straight for the girl in blue to whom he bowed low and offered his hand to continue dancing. There were raised eyebrows and significant smiles as the courtiers streamed out on the floor after him, advancing to the other maskers. The musi-

49

cians struck swiftly into the spirited measure of the canary.

"You are tired, fair unknown?" asked the king as they circled breathlessly round and round.

"Tired — when dancing with your Highness?" she gave gayly back. Her sweet, clear voice told him nothing of her identity.

"Where got you that dance, lady?"

"From mine own head and heels, your Grace."

The king glanced from one to the other.

"It had a fair home."

A little laugh escaped her — a laugh that seemed to waken some haunting echo in his consciousness.

"Ah, now I know all that they say of your Grace is true!"

"And what say they of my Grace?"

But the small unknown was no spreader of jam. With eyes archly smiling through the peepholes of her mask, "Scandal, rank scandal, your Highness," she laughed in mingled amusement and feigned reproach.

As the dance carried them away from each other in pacings and low courtesies, Henry saw that the girl's waist was slim enough to be spanned by a man's two hands, and he noted warmly the grace with which she sank nearly to the floor and then swept upward with the springing release of a young sapling.

They came nearer, her white hand resting in his, her dark curls brushing the white satin puffs of his sleeves. She was so slight he could have caught her like a flower as a sudden boisterous impulse in him craved. What lady in all his court could she be? He racked his brains. It was curious that he should have overlooked anything like this, he pondered. Where could such pretty witchery have been hidden that it had not met his eyes?

A DANCE WITH A KING

Where had they buried a maid who had power to so enthrall a man's senses and quicken his blood? Had she — Ah, Heaven, had she *not!* — a face to match that grace and voice?

Goaded by the thought, Henry suddenly checked the dance, as they turned at the end of the hall, and bending over her, twitched the mask away. His relief was tremendous. He was staring at a brilliant vision of shining eyes and shadowy hair and cheeks glowing like roses above the sky blue of her gown. The instinctive comparison brought a recollection that he voiced with eager discovery.

"Why, 'tis the girl in the garden — Flora come to court!"

She swept him a merry courtesy.

"And finding Mars turned Jupiter," she flashed with a witching smile.

"God's truth, but Flora hath turned Venus," he cried, staring. "Sure, I said the foot of Venus was never so light." His eyes were avid. "I crave my boon, sweet Anne Boleyn," he cried and leaned over her for the kiss that man might claim at the end of his dance. He took it in full measure. It was not the customary salute, but a caress.

Shaken and excited, Anne leaned to the cool of a casement near them, tossing back the hair from her flushed face. The fervor of his kiss and the aura of royalty about him flung her into fluttering confusion.

She could not remember, after he had left her at the call of the next dance, what he had said or what she had replied. Her senses were floating on the music. The thrill of her triumph ran in her veins like wine. She was intoxicated with gayety. This was life, she thought, this was living.

51

THE FAVOR OF KINGS

Never had she been so lovely, protested Brereton and Bryan and Norris and all the other courtiers, crowding where the king had led the way. She felt the following eyes upon her, the rustle of her name on their tongues. They might say what they liked now — she was showing them what she could do when she had her chance! The gay success, the music, the praise, the laughter, were doubly sweet after her long bitterness and heartache and seclusion. It was balm to see the cardinal bending over her hand, complimenting himself on his foresight in having charged her with the direction of the dance, it was joy to watch the sinister impotence of Carewe's eyes in the background. When in feigned assurance he claimed a dance;

"Nay, I dance not with thy ilk," she flung insolently back.

"Are we not of the same ilk, *cousin?*" he emphasized.

"So may a cur be cousin to true breed."

"How hath Carewe offended?" asked Norris, as the other fell back in a speechless rage beneath a summoned grin.

"Offended? Nay, such as he have no power to *offend!*" She sent her clear tones after the departing one. "He but displeases me with his presence — his ears are overwide, his nose overlong. I like my knaves handsome."

"Mother of God, but you have no fear of making enemies!" Norris gasped, amazed.

"That I have not," she confirmed.

Norris glanced at the departing back. "That flouted cousin of thine hath a mind that harbors spite. 'Tis well you are not a man, fair lady, or you would find yourself facing a bared blade."

"I am beginning to think 'tis well myself — though for

52

a different reason," she smiled. " Yet a scant time ago, down in the country, I was well wishing myself a man."

A second time Henry came for her, and his manner was such that the court eyed and smiled and whispered in corners.

They danced almost in silence. Henry said little and looked very much. Whether she glanced up or down, Anne felt his eyes on her like two gray sparks. Once in the dance her hand rested in his and she felt it gripped with quick ardor; when her fingers would have slipped away he held them in a tighter grasp. His hand was very big and strong and hot.

She was strangely discomfited. Barter and badinage came easily to her saucy lips, she could flirt light-heartedly in three languages and exchange arrowy glances and a pair of sighs, perhaps, but from this tight, stupid handclasp she shrank distastefully. It savored of intimacy, of control. And when at the close of the dance, the king bent toward her, she vouchsafed but the scantiest of pecks and whisked back, laughing nervously.

" Nay — I have been overlong at the French court to think a lady must needs reward a cavalier for a dance — be he even a king ! " she parried.

" What said you to his Highness to bring such a stare? " whispered Wyatt, as he joined her for the next gaillard.

" What I have told thee many a time," she evaded.

" You are a belle to-night, little cousin."

" And you a poor courtier! Am I not always a belle? " she scoffed, murmuring after a pause, filled in with dancing, " Oh, this is like France again — to-night ! "

" Then France must have been all music and praise and sugarplums."

THE FAVOR OF KINGS

"I think it more my native air than this," she said seriously. "Here, to be fair, a woman must be a fool. She must eat and sleep and paint and simper and go to mass — but no more, in Heaven's name, no more! She must never read nor think nor utter a word of sense. These English are afraid of brains. They distrust themselves, that is why. Now Frenchmen are clever — they hate a dull woman."

"How they must have hated you! But am I so fearful of brain, then?"

"Thou — Oh, thou art a poet and must needs enjoy those with a mind for thy verse."

"If you would but have a mind for the poet as for his verse," he whispered, with all the gayety gone from face and voice. "Ah, Anne —"

"Wyatt, thou art a married man!" she reminded him quickly with mock solemnity, beneath which ran a quaver of real dread.

"I am thy lover, now and evermore. My marriage — 'twas a yoke foisted on an ignorant young fool! I was but seventeen — I — but I will not even speak of it. It hath been naught to me these years. You and I were childish sweethearts, Anne, and I had no sooner seen you again on your return from France, child as you were still, but that infant love sprang into manhood's strength. I love thee — I love thee, I tell thee, in every fiber, in every pulse beat. God, how I love thee!"

He had stopped abruptly where the dance had carried them, close under the musicians' gallery, and he pressed her back now into its shadow. His sudden outbreak, flashing like hidden fire through his usual nonchalance, had astonished and upset her; she tried to draw her hands from his, but his grip tightened upon them. He bent forward, his face very white, his eyes seeking hers in glowing

54

intensity. Never before, in all his devotion, had he betrayed such power of feeling.

"Cousin, you are married," she reminded him again, imploringly.

"And so you are damned if you love me?" he gave harshly back. "Come, Anne, will you not be damned for love, since we are none so certain to escape it any-way?"

It was useless to struggle for possession of her wrists; she let them lie quietly in his grasp. Her heart fluttered in sharp agitation, her eyes pleaded with him to spare them both.

"Thou dost know this is folly," she whispered. "I have told thee so oft."

"Yes, thou hast told me, but then there was another preferred by thee — and one who could offer thee his name and place. And I resigned thee to him. But since that is past and we are as we are — Anne, thou hast ever a feeling for me. Can I not kindle that spark to flame? By God, I were less than a man an I resigned thee now!"

"Tom," she said quiveringly, "thou art less than a man an thou dost *not* resign me. We have been childish comrades, as thou hast said, playing in the woods at Blickling and Hever. It is no profit now to look back and sorrow that e'er I went away or that thou hast taken another. We are indeed as we are, and I do think that there is that in thee which would secretly grieve if thy little cousin and old playfellow should yield to the poorest in thee."

Her words went to the heart of Wyatt's deepest consciousness. Beneath the callousness of the court life, beneath the veneer of his surface self, there was a delicacy and reverence that he shared with few men around

him. It was a guarded flame, shut in with light words
and cynical jests, which fed the inner fires of his poet
soul. It was the dying breath of the old chivalry, perhaps, which his muse had blown into him which made
him thrill to something of the meaning of the noble
words that habit tossed so lightly from lip to lip.

Anne had made her way past the outer self to the
secret one within. She was right — Wyatt had a love
for her as well as a passion. He let her hands slip
slowly from his and with a short, embarrassed laugh,
and eyes that looked anywhere but in hers lest she should
read their depths, " Did the French court make such a
little nun of thee? " he questioned with an uncertain
smile.

She understood it was his renunciation and a swift
tenderness filled her eyes.

With delicacy she tried to carry him back to their old
light plane of understanding. " Now I am certain that
my new gown becomes me, since it sets the young blades
quarreling and my mocking cousin to making love! "

The raillery in her voice was very unsure, and there
was a fine mist of tears on her lashes. She was
unutterably sorry for him. And she was confusedly
sorry for herself, divining dimly that if he had been a
free man on her return from France her life might have
been different.

" And the king to dancing with thee," he gave back,
a note of grimness sounding. " Remember, Anne —
Henry, too, is a married man! "

CHAPTER V

HOPE RENEWED

THE rumor that Anne had danced herself into royal favor reached the queen's chambers before Anne did the next morning. When at length the sleepy reveler made her appearance, there was an acidity of sarcasm in her reception that made it evident she had not eased her position for herself. She took an impish comfort in the thought that she had been able to annoy the arrogant queen and could irritate her yet further if she chose — for her confident youth assumed that if she really wanted the king's favor it would not be too difficult to obtain! She felt in the atmosphere about her now that report was busy whispering the same thing, and she read, too, that not a soul of them there would credit her with anything but eagerness for the opportunity.

Rather sorrily she laughed to herself while she stabbed away at her interminable tapestry, wondering how she could best pick her way through the tangle. Of the king's favor she wanted nothing at all but his good will. If he liked her a little, as a blithe, pleasing maid, then she would be given a place in the court festivities and share in the revels and masques and merrymakings that romped along outside these gray, irksome rooms; she could mingle freely in the outside world, meet new and interesting people, talk and laugh and dance with them and repeat the triumph of last night. She would be bidden, perhaps, to the king's hunts — Oh, how she yearned for the out-of-doors, the saddle and the clear call of the horn across country! Wistfully her eyes strayed to the casement, whose bull's-eyed glass gave such distortion of the scene without.

All this if the king liked her a little. If he liked her too much — and her instinct hinted uncomfortably that last night he was well on his way to it — then — why then only more trouble and vexation. She had few illusions as to the attitude of her family. She remembered the scandal — though with the next breath she assured herself that it was only scandal — about Mary, and pledged herself to be careful — Oh, so much more than careful! — and guard her saucy humor when next she met his Majesty.

But Anne's humor was as hard to bind as quicksilver. That very night his Majesty came, as was not his way, to play écarté in the queen's chambers, and when he deliberately sought out Anne with a word of added praise for last night's dance she could no more have kept from smiles and gayety than a brook can keep from bubbling down hill. The keen awareness of Catherine's eyes upon her brought a deepened flush to her face and a defiant clearness to her laugh. Let the queen hate her as she would, she thought excitedly, and the cardinal plot, she would make her way in spite of all. Of Henry's favor she would take no more than might suffice to hold open the door into the gay court world, and, once a part of it, once with an opportunity for her youth and spirit and talent, she would snatch a future for herself as fair as that the cardinal had overthrown!

With the king had come a surge of followers who usually contented themselves with paying their respects to the queen in a brief morning visit, and not one of these

HOPE RENEWED

forgot to pause by the side of the youngest maid of honor and commend her dancing and hope ardently that the court would see more of her in future.

It was noticeable, too, how cordial her family had suddenly become, how amiably the Duke of Norfolk chatted with his niece, how affectionately her dissolute little sister-in-law slipped an arm about her, how fondly her father's gaze, with such judicial pondering in its depths, rested on his daughter.

The clans were gathering, the girl thought, with cold amusement. Her face hardened. She was no puppet for them. They would see what she was made of!

As the groups pressed around her, she felt suddenly the sharp edge of paper pushed into her hand as it hung concealed beneath her flowing sleeve. Her fingers closed over it, and a few minutes later, when the chance afforded, she turned to a casement on pretext of air, and read the *billet-doux*. It was very short. There was one, it informed her, so aglow with her charm that he must have speech with her alone and that as soon as might be. When would she listen to him? It was signed Jupiter.

She felt a sudden chill reversal of spirit. Her heart hammered in foolish panic for a moment, the next it reacted in anger and disgust. So this was what men were! There was no delicacy, no *finesse,* to cloak the demand, no appreciation of the flavor of her personality, her wit, her intelligence, her frank, true youth; everything was to be gulped down in this Sultanesque assurance. The brutality of it was like a blow in the face. It stunned a moment, then, at her brother's approach, she crushed the note fiercely into her hand and rallied her wits to hide their confusion.

"So you have come complimenting, too, brother?"

she laughed, while her thoughts ran on — how should she meet this? What should she do or say? Was it possible that she had made a mistake — that there was another in love with her who had hit on that very nom-de-plume?

She raised her eyes, and straight as light, from his place across the room, the king's gaze sought her. To her excited perception there was demand in the look, an eager inquiry mingled with fatuous assurance. No, there was no mistake!

" 'Twas a monstrous pretty exhibition," George was saying. " I did not know you had it in you, Anne. I never saw a fairer dance."

" And you would all have me dance again," she gave back absently, attending to him with but one part of her mind, while the other galloped on its secret ways. What should she do? Should she write and refuse — or should she name a place and make her denial in person? She could soften it better so — perhaps. Which would least offend?

" There is no mortal sin in dancing, little sister," George replied, and she answered with a bitter memory of Percy, " There is no mortal sin in anything at court — save failure."

" Thou hast a shrewd eye, Anne; thou hast seen to the heart of the matter."

Anne laughed — a little wildly. " I am sorry for thee — thy hopes are built on sand."

" France then inclined thee for a nun's life? " he murmured, stealing an observant look at her from under his lazy lids. The excitement of her manner was not lost on him.

" Something like that another said on his own behalf last night. This court is no place for maids."

HOPE RENEWED

"Doth it shelter any?" he gave back with gay cynicism. "Not for long, little sister, no, nor true wives either. . . . Look before us. 'Tis a room packful of the fairest faces and finest names in England and is there one unsmirched in the lot? See where stands our good aunt, Norfolk's duchess, who outvies her husband in scandal, at talk with my Lady Anne Hastings, for whom Compton was cited to answer to the ecclesiastical court, and next is Suffolk, our king's brother-in-law, who hath twice committed bigamy and three times been divorced. Next is mine own honorable wife," George gave a laugh of scorn, "and next her is young Surrey playing with Sir Anthony Brown, whose lady is the fair Geraldine of Surrey's verse, and look you, there is the fair Geraldine smiling on the lady who is her husband's consolation! Lord love us, 'tis a brothel! Watch those two gallant dames vying with each other for that rake Bryan's favor! And there —" his voice sinking cautiously lower —"there is the one who prates the loudest of virtue and makes the greatest show of it — our fine queen herself. And do you not know that when she was Prince Arthur's widow, waiting for Henry to marry her and keep her Spanish dowry in his treasury, that there was such talk of her and her handsome young confessor that both courts rang with it, and she plumped down on her knees to the Spanish ambassador, entreating him to intercede with her father to have the fellow remain? Pah! She was meal under the priest's thumb — aye, even after she was Henry's wife,— if a brother's widow be ever a wife, pope or no pope! He was closer than her women till the thing smoked so that Henry kicked him forth. Virtue!" He laughed.

"I had not heard that tale," Anne answered with bitter eyes on the queen. She twisted the note nervously

6   61

in her fingers. "But you would not have my name, brother, on every fool's tongue?" she added in a voice that betrayed her emotion.

"Nay," said he, "that would I not, for I heard speech of you on a fool's tongue last night as I stood at the king's side watching you dance, and I liked it little. But this I say, Anne, whether you do ill or not, wagging tongues will ever give you the name of it, and in good sooth, since you ask me, if I must needs have the name I would have the wages, too."

The girl smiled, rather piteously. She understood perfectly the half-shamedfaced, half-brazen workings of the young fellow's mind. There was enough manhood and brotherhood in him to be proud of her pride and fair name, and not a hand would he stretch forth directly to push her to the goal where the rest of her family would all urge her, but neither would he stretch forth a hand to hold her back, and, on the whole, lumping it all in all, he would have been definitely pleased if she had taken the initiative and surrendered to the king — provided always she had brains enough to make sufficient capital out of the situation to shield her from its discredit. A very complicated thing, indeed, was young Boleyn's mind, as he lounged beside her, playing with his ruffles and smothering a yawn with his jeweled fingers.

The thought of confiding to him the secret of the note left her. She slipped the paper into her pocket.

"It is an ill world, brother," she murmured, attempting her old lightness, but the passionate revolt quivered too near the surface to be restrained. "Do you not feel in your heart how ill it is," she urged vehemently, "how warped and false and twisted? When God and the Right are on every lip and I and my Might in every life? Do you not feel its bitter wrong and irony?"

HOPE RENEWED

George looked faintly uncomfortable. He concluded that she had taken the Northumberland matter harder than he had supposed. " Such as it is, it is," said he, voicing the courtier's superficial philosophy, " and we must e'en reap our own harvest from it as we can."

" Now what do you two pouring into each other's ears? " demanded Wyatt's voice at Anne's elbow.

She gave him a quick, fluttered smile of recognition. The memory of last night's scene made her ill at ease. Wyatt, however, airy and debonair, denied by his immense composure that there was anything to be ill at ease about. Indeed, he made rather a point of meeting her eyes serenely.

" We were railing at the world," she owned with a quizzical inflection at the futility of it.

" What — at nineteen? " he smiled with the superiority of three and twenty. " Why, as worlds go, 'tis not so ill. I would liefer stay in it than try the next! "

" Who would not? — But that is not saying," Anne retorted, " that you would not find more honest company in that next."

" Truth, Tom, can you find an honest man or woman among us? " George indolently observed, cocking a disillusioned eye at the throng.

" Why as to the women "— Wyatt made a bow at Anne —" here is one of whose honesty I have hard proof "— and he smiled audaciously at the reminder — " and as for the man, are there not two of us here? "

Boleyn, rising, clapped him lightly on the shoulder. " Don't push my honesty too far, Tom, that's all," he bantered. " God knows I would tell more lies than Peter before the cock crew for a new hunting steed. My black has broken a leg and I am over heels in debt."

63

THE FAVOR OF KINGS

"Why, then, if you fail me, here comes a real example." Wyatt's tone grew suddenly serious as he watched a couple entering the doorway, a tall, fine-looking man with a sweet-faced woman on his arm. The man had the brow of a scholar, deep, kindly eyes, and a mouth that was both strong and gentle. It was Sir Thomas More and his daughter Margaret. "That is the one man at court who is neither a hypocrite nor a flatterer nor a rake, and a woman with him who is both fair and true," he pronounced.

The three stood watching the couple make their way across the crowded room, stopping every few steps for a greeting or a salutation. There was a very winning charm in More's face and manner, a fine blend of kindliness and courtliness, lightened by humor and upheld by a clean, self-respecting pride, that drew all eyes to him in peculiar friendliness and pleasure.

"Those be rare souls," Boleyn assented, with unusual gravity.

"And in high favor, too!" Wyatt commented. "The king hath shown him marvelous confidence, of late. . . . Hast heard how not three days ago he visited Sir Thomas in his garden and walked there for more than an hour with his arm about his neck? Such hath he never, to my knowledge, done to the cardinal himself."

"Aye, I heard. But Sir Thomas," said George shrewdly, "is not the man to build on such favor. When his son-in-law was speaking of the thing and complimenting him, 'Aye, son Roper,' said he, 'my lord is a good prince to me and affable, but I know that if my head would bring him a castle in France, it would shortly go.'"

"So would all ours," observed the poet with a wry grimace.

Anne looked from one to the other, then her eyes

64

"'Is he—is the king—so inconstant?'"

drifted across the room to where Henry towered above his followers.

"Is he — is the king — so inconstant?"

"Is he?" laughed her brother. Then he suddenly flashed a look at her and his tone changed. "Well, no more than the rest of his knavish sex," he amended. "Henry is but a man — no worse than all the rest of us."

"Aye, worse than all the rest of us," said Wyatt in a low tone, looking directly at Anne. "Where he smiles to-day, there will be frown to-morrow — if for no better reason than that he smiled there to-day! . . . Nothing so wearies him as the thing that he possesseth. No woman hath ever held him save for the moment between his asking and her giving. He is like the wind, blowing where it listeth, and no love, no sacrifice, no honored service restrains his veering fancy. He hath but one love — himself, and one passion — gratification."

Anne met her cousin's look with a faint little smile. She understood his warning; also she considered it largely dictated by jealousy.

The approach of the others broke up this three-cornered privacy and the conversation became general. Towards the close of the evening Anne noticed that young Weston, a handsome lad of about sixteen, attached to the king's chamber, was hovering about her with a pertinacity that denoted purpose. When a lull came in the talk she felt his hand on her sleeve.

"Hast thou no note — for Jupiter?" he whispered, bending forward smiling.

She shook her head, "I have no note."

"Well then, wilt thou not whisper where thou hast taken thought for that one to meet thee? . . . Troth, he is very eager for thee," the youth urged, "and cannot long wait. He hath sent this as an assurance —"

THE FAVOR OF KINGS

Anne's fingers felt the touch of coins through the thin silk meshes of a purse he was seeking to thrust into her clasp. She withdrew her hand instantly, tingling from the ignoble encounter. The words of rejection she had meant to phrase so tactfully came tumbling forth in reckless heat.

"Tell that one," she said fiercely under her breath, "that such a maid as I grants no interviews, accepts no such — tokens."

"But Mistress Boleyn," he protested, gripping her sleeve, "this is a command —"

"Nor obeys such commands. . . . Ah, Master Brereton," she cried, raising her voice. "I thought you were passing me by. What tale were you laughing over to little Mary Wyatt? Sure, if she listened, that may I!"

Young Weston looked uncertainly at her, in naïve perplexity. Then he took his hand from her sleeve and thrusting the purse back into his pocket he shrugged whimsically and turned away.

The silence of the ensuing days assured Anne of the king's acceptance of her refusal, however his messenger might have softened it, and lightened immensely whatever uneasiness she had in the situation. But she was wrong in reading too much acceptance into his silence. Her rebuff had piqued Henry without disheartening him of anything save immediate success. And his pique itself served to prick his caprice into desire.

Anne had made too vivid an impression to be readily effaced. She had been a new sensation — invaluable thrill in the cloying idleness of courts! — and was too precious to be lost sight of. Misled at first by the bright coquetry of her manner, and by whatever knowledge he possessed of her sister's pliant weakness, Henry, after

66

HOPE RENEWED

his first rash move, played the game with more observing wariness.

He saw to it — or the cardinal for him — that Anne was included in the court merrymaking. She danced again at a less pretentious masque at Wolsey's, she rode to hounds several times with her father and brother, and in one such way or another meetings were constantly secured with no effect of premeditation. Henry, too, dined more often with the queen than had been his custom, and, instead of leaving the table directly the meal was over as had been his invariable habit, he lingered in general talk or at cards. At these times, Henry, with his keen ability for dissimulation, betrayed no interest to mark the girl to his wife's eyes, but he was aware very distinctly of the piquant grace of her presence, and his ears, while ostensibly attending to other things, were alert for the gay melody of her voice.

He wondered immensely why he had not more especially noticed her before — but then, until the cardinal had invited her to dance at his revel, there had been no opportunity to bring her out. She had been only a thin little maid of honor, and in repose, among the more buxom beauties of the court, there had been nothing to intensely draw the eye. But the eye, when drawn, lingered irresistibly. Once feeling her spell was like once tasting a rare wine; the bouquet was unique . . . and Henry resolved to drain the cup.

He was conscious perfectly of the way she evaded him at every turn, of how dexterously she slipped away from his most pointed implications, parrying his phrases with a jest and turning back his questions with invulnerable innocence. It amused him in the beginning, sure as he was of its futility, but the tantalizing delay whetted his eagerness for her and made him impatient of such dally-

67

ing. He felt that he had granted enough to her maiden panic. She had now recovered from the first shock of his demands. He determined to have clear speech with her alone.

Anne was aware of this resolve and at first in tremendous dread of its accomplishment. She felt impatient irritation because he would not accept the denial of her every word and act but must have "no" fired plumply at him, in person, and she shrank from the firing, but since it must be done she gathered up her spirit to know how to do it best.

It was not so easy to reject a king and Henry of all kings; her refusal must be very delicately managed for to anger him was to bring disaster on her and all her family. No other course than refusal ever occurred to her even for one swift second. She was too high of pride, too maiden of spirit to surrender to such ignoble fate, however the moral atmosphere that she daily breathed, might have robbed the idea of its strangeness.

Her problem was how to extricate herself from the embarrassment of his admiration with the least damage to his pride and her own new popularity. The gay good times of the last month she had enjoyed to the full and she had not been impervious to the hint of power that her dilemma brought her. From an unconsidered girl she had become a young lady of consequence and she hated tremendously to part with the new prestige. It made her give a backward thought to the lost coronet of Northumberland, realizing more than ever the independence of a powerful position, and with the prolongation of that thought came sudden inspiration.

If — so ran her buoyant fancy — if the king could be managed and worked on, if his better feelings were appealed to and his heart touched would he not — Oh,

HOPE RENEWED

would he not, recall Percy and permit their marriage?
It was a strange solution to the affair but stranger things
had happened. There was in Henry, she divined, a love
of the show of power, a joy in the parade of kingly
benevolence, that she might play on and conjure to this
end.

It was a riotous hope. It kept her company all her
waking hours and invaded her sleep with dreams. She
saw herself and Percy reunited and the memories that
she tried to banish from her forever she now welcomed
back with open arms. To be sure her quick mind questioned whether Percy would now, after their separation
and her resentful disdain of his weakness, be to her what
her girlish fancy had first made him, but she snubbed
such questioning severely. Very likely the world would
never seem quite the same to her either, now she had
known injustice and sorrow and disappointment, but that
could not be helped. It was, in spite of all, a wonderfully fascinating world, and Percy — even if she ideal-
ized him not so much — was always Percy, her young
lover, to whom she had yielded the sweetness of her heart.
She thought of his eyes, of how the deep blue of them
kindled as they looked upon her, and of the thrill in his
voice and things that he had whispered to her in the garden, and she thought — for the first time she let herself
think — how desperately he must have been missing her
all these months. Well, she would make it up to him
when they met. When they met! The dream of it
fluttered her heart. When they met!

Her young confidence in her ability to manage Henry,
to transform the self-seeking passion of a violent man
of thirty-five into magnanimous self-denial was naïvely
touching.

CHAPTER VI

THE INTERVIEW

THE opportunity came with another entertainment that Cardinal Wolsey gave in October at York Place. There was a mask, a rather tedious bit of allegory, a solo or two by a young Italian with a seraph voice and then the company broke up to chat or dance or play cards.

The king was not present and it was whispered that he had preferred to spend the evening roistering through the town in disguise, but Anne Boleyn thought that the evening would not pass without some glimpse of him.

She was sure of it, when the cardinal, singling her out for especial attention, directed her steps from room to room, on pretext of displaying the tapestries about which he was discoursing fluently. For all his smooth speech and the mask-like urbanity of his features, the girl fancied that she detected a twinkle of contemptuous amusement in the look that slanted to her under his heavy eyelid. Her strong dislike of the man never for an instant slept; indeed it was intensified by the part she perceived that he designed her to play — a puppet to amuse the king while Wolsey conducted the state — but her dislike was coated over by her youthful assurance of adequacy to the situation. She felt that she saw through his schemes and was more than equal to them, and her vanity could not resist the pleasant flattery in this all-powerful favorite's impressive attentions to her.

THE INTERVIEW

As the two stood in the end room of a long suite, a small, odd-shaped room overlooking the Thames, Cavendish, one of the cardinal's ushers, appeared at the door, and Wolsey interrupted the history with which he was favoring Anne to take the man's whispered message.

" Pshaw!" said the cardinal. "Always some affair — though it will take but a moment. I pray you pardon me if I quit you, Mistress Boleyn? 'Tis but a moment . . ."

He was out the door and Anne was alone. Long initiated to the intrigues of court, she felt a sharp prescience of crisis, and in spite of that high confidence of her youth, her knees felt weak and her throat dry. She was obliged to remind herself urgently of her ability to meet the situation and she hummed a little tune for reassurance.

> Pastance with good company
> I love, and shall until I —

" Good even, lady."

Henry had gowned himself regally for this occasion, in cloth of silver picked out with gold; jeweled chains swung about his neck, a blazing diamond star flashed on the purple velvet of his flat, plumed cap. For a moment he filled the doorway with his splendor, then came forward into the room and shut the door behind him.

" Nay, look not so fearful, sweet Anne," he said, holding out his hands. " 'Tis not thy king, but thy lover commends himself to thee."

It had come, then. The Rubicon was crossed. Anne rose from her courtesy with a pale face.

" Nay, my *king,*" she began quickly but Henry had not come to fence longer with words.

The floodgates of his feeling had opened at sight of

71

her there, alone, wide-eyed and lovely, and the torrent poured forth. He wanted her — he was resolved to have her. He did not clothe what he was pleased to call his sentiments in imaginative garb at all. He did not reckon with denial. Love he wanted, love he would have. He was master. He would have his way.

Never in Anne's life had she come so close to such fire. She had never suspected its existence. She shrank back, appalled and giddy, in a quivering panic from that inflamed pursuit.

"I think that your Highness speaks such words in jest . . . and to prove me," she gasped, retreating. "You cannot have intent to degrade your princely self!"

Unheeding her denial, he pressed closer, closer. His arms reached to draw her from the corner where she stood at bay. Anne faced him with up-flung head and flashing eyes.

"At the court of France the king does not make love by *force!*" she cried.

It checked him as nothing else on earth could have done, for if there was one thing he disliked more than another it was any suggestion of inferiority to the polish of the French, of a lack of their *savoir-faire.* He looked with amazement at the young girl who had struck such a sure note of defiance.

"Thou hast made me mad, Sweetheart," he muttered in apology.

"I cannot talk with madmen," she flung back in a trembling voice.

"Nay, then I will be reasonable — so you do but love me!"

He laughed gayly, for though thwarted in this first rough attempt, his confidence in victory was unshaken.

THE INTERVIEW

Moments or minutes might delay it but it was only a question of time.

Equally determined on her part, the girl began to recover her self-possession. With the shifting of the contest from force to words her sense of competence returned. Her knees ceased to shake, the color surged back to her face. But her breath still came and went in fluttering excitement.

" Nay — nay, it can never be, most noble king," she cried, imploringly. " Such words on your part can be only in vain. . . . For your own noble self it cannot be — and for mine own self."

" For thy sake, sweet Anne? Dost thou not — canst thou not love me? Hast thou not made me love thee — to madness, as I said. Canst thou call back the arrows thy dark eyes have shot? "

Very unhappily, Anne was wishing to Heaven that she could.

" Nay, those eyes have belied thy cold words," he declared triumphantly. " Thou lovest me! "

It was an extremely difficult assertion to combat. Anne met it with a swift, " As my *king!* "

" Only as thy king? Hast thou no heart then for the man — for Henry Tudor, thy most humble lover? "

" As my king! " she repeated again, her eyes, steadily denying, meeting his in unfaltering courage. One white, upraised hand forbade, in its peremptory gesture, the advance he was ever on the verge of making. " More can never, never be," she went on hurriedly. " For thy sake, for thy princely sake, I would not let thee do thyself this wrong. Such — such love — is unworthy of thee . . . I would die rather than bring degradation upon thee."

Her voice rang stronger on those last words, feeling she had found the right method at last, and that the inter-

THE FAVOR OF KINGS

view, diverted from its first outbreak, was being guided
in the directions she had destined.

It struck Henry's egregious vanity that she was an unusual girl, with opinions that did her credit.

"But if I love thee, it is thy duty to minister unto the
happiness of thy king," he argued shrewdly. He was an
adept at the game of sophist.

She shook her head. "And for mine own sake it cannot be. I am of honorable lineage, your Highness, and
I would rather die than lose that which is the greatest
and best part of the dowry I shall bring my husband."

It was one of the phrases that she had prepared and
she awaited anxiously its effect. Henry was hesitating.
He had not expected so much mettle. It seemed to her
that he was weakening in his pursuit.

"Hast thou a husband then in mind?" he asked.

Here, so suddenly, was her great chance. Was it too
soon for it — the ground too unprepared? She wavered
a moment, trying to read his expression but the impetuosity of her nature hurled her forward.

"Ah, if your Grace had but truly an affection for
me!" she cried entreatingly. "If your princely heart
would but grant one kindness . . . how I would honor
and serve thee for it till the day of my death! I cannot yield my poor love to your Grace — thou art too high,
too mighty. I can only go my way — remembering, with
pride and happiness, that my king once thought me
worthy of his kindness —"

"What is this kindness?"

"'Tis —'tis but a trifle — to one as all-powerful as
your noble self, but to me, it means — it means —" she
dared not touch on her feeling for Percy but took refuge
in other motives, "it means a gift so great, so princely —
Ah, if your Highness but only *would!*"

74

THE INTERVIEW

The cry came from her heart with pitiful beseechment. The desperate sense of crisis blanched her and for a moment held back the words in her throat. Then, "Dost thou recall Percy of Northumberland?" she asked, her eyes imploringly on his.

The gathering suspicion with which Henry had followed her incoherent appeal, concentrated in a glare of such sudden, startling ferocity that instinctively she fell back a step. She had a terrifying vision of a face swarthily suffused, of gray eyes like sword points, and thick lips curling back like an animal's over white teeth.

"Thou lovest him?" he snarled.

She lied, quickly, "Ah, no — no, your Majesty. He but loves me! But —"

"I remember," he said rancorously, a step nearer her, thrusting his face forward as if to read her own, "I remember the talk of him and thee."

With a gesture she seemed to plead with him for forbearance till she could find the right words to explain:

"It would have been a marvelous good match, your Majesty," she supplicated, "and one my — my pride was set on. An enemy, a silly, love-mad cousin, spied on us and all was broken off. I would love dearly, dearly, to be revenged on that cousin — and through your Majesty's all-powerful hand! It would be a wondrous triumph. If I have found favor at all in thy sight — if indeed —"

He seemed about to speak and she broke off, her eyes beseeching him still. A slow, cunning smile spread over Henry's great face.

"There are other ways, sweet Anne, of becoming a countess, an thou dost so pine for the coronet and the double train, than by wedding that beardless boy. Moreover, his father may live many years yet and defer thy pride. . . . Speak not to me of Northumberland again, an thou dost value his head."

"Nay," she murmured faintly, while hope turned to mockery and laughed horribly within her. To have dreamed of Henry's disinterested kindness — of his better nature! Wearily she braced herself to face this destruction of her fool's paradise.

"I crave pardon for having presumed to offer my poor ambitions."

"We will find better ones for thee," he promised, now smiling again, "only be kind, Sweetheart —"

"I will rejoin my father, an your Grace give me leave," she interrupted in the composure of utter despair. "My absence will give room for talk."

A certain show of virtue Henry enjoyed, as long as he was at no time hampered by the genuine essence. He stood in doubt now, trying to read the cold little face she turned toward him. If Anne's secret hopes were mortally wounded, it appeared to the king that he, too, had not advanced his designs very far in this interview. But at least there had been an *éclaircissement* — she could not feign to misunderstand now and it only remained to ply her with assiduity.

With a vast show of respect he bent over her hand.

"I shall continue to hope," he murmured, kissing her cold fingers.

"I know not how your Highness should retain such hope," she said clearly, looking him full in the face. "Your wife I cannot be, both in respect of mine own unworthiness and also because you have a wife already — aught else I will not be."

Startled, he returned her look. Decidedly this young maid of honor had an excellent respect for herself!

"At the least, Anne, take me for thy knight and serv-

76

ant," he said, and unclasping a trinket from a dangling chain, extended it to her.

It was a gold pistol, an inch long, richly chased; the barrel, fashioned into a whistle, enclosed a set of toothpicks. About the handle twined a serpent with ruby eyes.

" A small token — but 'tis a whistle that will ever call me," he vowed.

It occurred to the girl, with ironic humor, that it was a very small token indeed; a more royal gesture would have been to have swept the diamond star from his cap. Henry had a reputation for niggardliness with his lady loves.

She turned the trinket over, with outward smiles.

" Ah, your Highness," she said over her shoulder from the threshold, " I fear this is a true omen. Look — there is a serpent in the handle ! "

CHAPTER VII

CALUMNY

IN the opinion of the court Anne was a netted bird. Her struggles were futile, her conquest but a question of time. Indeed, there were few who did not believe that the girl, gauging with rare perspicacity the soon-slaked ardor of her admirer, was but feigning to refuse to draw him on the more.

"She hath a rare prompter in her father — he hath already had experience in that quarter," was the sneer Sir Nicholas Carewe spread about the court.

Certainly Anne's denial only excited Henry to keener pursuit. From an idle diversion, the passion of a moment, Anne Boleyn became the king's engrossing thought. He coveted her more every day and every day was deeper in thrall to her young witchery, her gayety and grace, and that spiritual something that illumined all — her maiden inaccessibility.

She was as refreshing as an April morning to his jaded sense. Her sudden flashes of audacity delighted him, her verve and intelligence flattered him with the thought that here was a woman to understand him and do him justice in every talent. Her pride pleased his own. She was a fit conquest for a king.

At every mask and revel and hunt Mistress Boleyn was now included and was fair to having her head turned by the amount of attention she received. And it was here that the girl's temperament was traitor to her, for

78

CALUMNY

resolve as she might to disenchant the king from his suit, she could not keep her young blood from responding gayly to the merrymaking. Her little feet danced of themselves, her eyes sparkled, and laughter and repartee rose irresistibly to her lips.

As she was harder and harder pressed, she flung herself more and more into the revels to escape the anxieties that thickened about her. Wyatt, lately returned from a mission to France, had been adding considerably to these, for Henry's love-making stung him to jealousy and overrode his scruples. In his heart he had said farewell to Anne when she was the betrothed of Percy, but now that she was no man's betrothed, and like to becoming a man's favorite he thought he might as well be that man as another.

He courted the girl at every turn, and Anne, so well liking him, parried his courtship as best she could, while his suit and her lightness toward it and the quick public tattle about it, all roused Henry to more insistent pressure.

Altogether, when Anne faced her future, she found enough anxiety there to overcast any maiden's spirits, but Anne kept her spirits by refusing to face her future. Whatever embarrassments would ensue, whatever difficulties menace, would all be met when the time came, she told herself; meanwhile she was doing the very best that she could and meant to enjoy all of the present sweets that were permissible. Things could not go on like this forever. She would never yield, she felt with sure confidence, and by and by her persistence would weary Henry's and he would find some newer face, some fresher fancy. She did not reflect how her pride, feeding on these attentions from the court, would smart at his deflection. She merely repeated to herself that matters

79

would adjust themselves somehow, and for the present, there was certainly an excitement in all this love-making and an elation in being pointed out as the " Mistress Boleyn for whom the king is sighing." So Anne presented by no means the appearance of a damsel in distress as she sat in her room one November morning and planned costumes with Mary Wyatt and Helen Sackville.

It was rarely mild for November. The yesterday's chill and fog had been blown away by a wind in the night and the casement framed only a square of bluest sky, flecked here and there with a downy puff of white cloud.

Anne on the window seat, her profile silhouetted against the blue of that sky, was bending over a lapful of finery.

" I shall put this scarlet under the lace to show off the pattern. Think you this white, here, looks soiled? " she appealed, waving a length of tissue cloth before them.

" Nay — that silver thread in the weave often gives a cloth that cast of gray," Mary Wyatt assured her comfortably.

Anne turned to Helen whose judgment was not so apt to be hampered by a dislike of dealing pain.

" But no silver thread ever gives those round spots where some saucy varlet hath spattered grease," pronounced that young lady briskly.

" Those spots I can pleat in at this end," Anne explained. " 'Tis the effect of the whole that I want."

" It is grayish," Helen then affirmed.

This was Anne's own opinion but she proceeded now to argue the matter, hoping to convert herself.

" You do see that it is soiled because you do know that it is soiled." she debated. " To the general eyes it may appear fresher."

CALUMNY

"Was it a front for the scarlet dress?" Mary questioned.

"Aye . . . nay, it *is* soiled." Anne cast the offending tissue cloth from her in sudden decision. "I would I had a new ell of mawley cloth," she sighed. "This making new gowns out of old is wearisome."

"I think we know where our Anne could get a new ell of mawley cloth, do we not, Mary?" laughed Helen.

Little Mary Wyatt smiled back uncertainly and cast a furtive glance on a new pin on Anne's gown. Her gentle, romance loving soul forgot its allegiance to the Percy affair in the splendor of this royal suit, but she was in two minds as to how to regard it. Her innate goodness took sides with Anne's fine resistance, but she was not proof against a secret thrill at the excitement of the position; her wondering awe of her king added to her confusion. On the one hand she would have rather inclined to consider Anne a frail, persecuted heroine — a supposition Anne's mirth interfered with! — on the other she would have liked to lend her sympathies to the royal love-making and condone whatever irregularities it permitted. In any case she wondered a little at Anne's reckless air about it. She did not realize that the Anne who sat devising her scarlet gown was a different Anne from the girl who, eight months before, had sat there, packing her clothes for Hever. Something more than time had passed over her. She had acquired a very definite hardiness, a scoffing disbelief in the good intentions of life and a determination to make the most of the moment.

It would have surprised Mary to know that Anne's own thoughts, at that instant, were of that packing scene eight months ago. She had picked up a mantle, and remembered suddenly that on that day that seemed so

81

distant she had folded that mantle, in misery of heart, remembering that Percy liked it and wondering if she must face such reminders all her life. . . . It had been weeks — months — since she had remembered that Percy had liked that mantle or anything else. She had not let herself think of Percy since the conclusion of that first dismaying interview with the king. There had been many other interviews since then, some short, some long, but all in lighter vein. Anne had never dared again recur to that subject.

Now to drive away these unwelcome memories she began humming a tune and finally broke into song. A kind of burlesque chant she made of it.

> The eagle's force subdues each bird that flies —
> What metal can resist the flaming fire?
> Doth not the sun dazzle the clearest eyes,
> And melt the ice and make the frost retire?
> The hardest stones are piercèd through with tools:
> The wisest are with princes made but fools.

The chant ended in a bubbling rush of laughter. "Didst ever hear such a love verse?" Anne appealed to them, her face bright with mischief. "Remark its humility — the sweet candor of its sentiment!

> "The hardest stones are piercèd through with tools:
> The wisest are with princes made but fools."

Her laughter rang through the room. "In spite of my wisdom I am to be made but a fool, it appears! Alack a day! . . . I showed the verse to Wyatt the other day for his instruction."

"Anne, you did *not!*"

"Ah, but I did, Helen. What matter?"

"Naught to me . . . but you trust Wyatt much."

CALUMNY

" In the matter of poetry — yes."

" But if he tells the king you made sport of his lines? "

" I think my brother would not do such," said Mary with her gentle dignity, that Helen put aside with a " Pshaw — a man in love will do all."

" *I* make sport of his lines — the king's lines? " Anne interrupted, in a pretty quiver of righteous indignation. " *I* jest at what my mighty lord hath condescended to honor me with? Who dares such slander? I but showed the verse to Wyatt to teach him how a true poet should rhyme and by their surpassing excellence he knew them for the king's."

" 'Tis on the common tongue," said Helen slowly, " that you have deemed a poet's favor worth a king's."

" The common tongue is a wondrous informed thing," returned Anne amiably. " Mary, will you *not* sit on my new lace? . . . No — on the other side."

" Hast heard the news of the morning? "

" Not I — unless it is the tale of the Don Inigo de Mendoza, the new Imperial Ambassador that is coming. Or that Spain hath spited France again. I am heartily sorry for King Francis. He was so kind to me in the old days in France that I shall ever remember —"

" Keep thy sorrow for one nearer home. I know nothing of Spain and France — I but heard what chanced when the king was playing bowls."

" So? Some rank slander of me, I'll vow, by your cold twinkle."

" He was playing with thy poet and the Duke of Suffolk and Sir Francis Bryan —"

" A godly band! " murmured Anne irreverently, with upcast eyes.

" And thy king affirmed that his cast surpassed Wyatt's though clearly 'twas not so."

THE FAVOR OF KINGS

" Wyatt is a rash man to bowl better than his king. But go on."

" So you but give me chance. The king insisted, however, that his cast was the better, smiling over it, and pointing with his finger and saying, ' Wyatt, I tell thee it is *mine!* ' Then on a sudden they saw what he meant ; there was a ring upon that finger which was one of thine."

" Oh, la! " said Anne, with serene indifference. " Can a maid deny when her king asks her ring ? He had given me the pin you have all been gaping at, most honorably in the presence of my father and aunt, for my playing upon the lute — 'tis no uncommon thing for a prince to do, and he requested in exchange some token of mine to wear in the next jousting match. If *that* be all thy news, Helen —"

" Nay, the best comes . . . Wyatt but laughed at this and said in his gay way, ' And if it may like your Majesty to give me leave to measure the cast with *this* I have good hope it may yet be mine,' and he drew out from his bosom the chain and silver writing tablet thou hast so often worn."

Anne made a sound in her throat. She stopped draping her lace. " Go on," she demanded.

" Ah, now we prick our ears! " Helen smiled. " Well, then, mistress, your poet goes through a play of measuring his cast with that fine spun chain while the king stands staring, and then King Henry mutters under his breath, ' It may be so — but then I am the more deceived,' and turning on his heel, marches away with a face like thunder."

" Who told you this ? "

" Sir Francis Bryan himself. I met him on the stairs an hour after. He says if he were in Wyatt's shoes he

CALUMNY

would shake, but Wyatt only laughs and says the king dare not touch him for fear of the sorry figure he would cut. Wyatt dares more than any other man at court."

" Oh, surely the king will not touch him!" Mary Wyatt cried a little tremulously, appealing to Anne for confirmation.

" The king will not — but *I* will!" that young lady briskly assured her. " The silly, bragging — why, that tablet he snatched from me at play! It was none of my giving. I asked it back at once, but he put me off and someone else came up . . . this is what comes of being kind," she fumed, her eyes two storm centers.

" Oh, he but meant a jest," Wyatt's loving sister interceded.

Helen's contribution did not lack sly malice.

" Perhaps 'tis for the best, Anne — if 'twill rid thee of thy troublesome king!"

" Thou art a fool," said Anne rudely, and most unjustly, for a fool Helen Sackville was not.

She divined perfectly Anne's vexation at the incident, and in the days that followed, when Henry appeared almost unaware of the girl's presence and devoted himself furiously to Lady Anne Hastings or some other belle whenever he was in Anne's sight, no one knew better than Helen how keenly Anne felt that coolness and the reflected casualness of the court that had been so preoccupied with her.

Indeed, understanding Anne's pride and resentment so clearly, it was secretly amazing to Helen that the girl made no effort to reinstate herself in the king's favor. A little three-cornered *billet-doux* would have done it, or ten spoken words of explanation. But Anne gave no sign and chattered away as gayly as ever to her dimin-

85

ished circle. Wyatt she banished from it, but Norris and Brereton and Weston with his engaging boyish ways, were stanch allies. Little Mary Wyatt clung to her at every turn and the Duchess of Suffolk, the "French Queen," as the king's sister was called, often sought her companionship.

Whether Anne was genuinely relieved to be rid of the king, though inevitably stung by some of the consequences, or whether she was determined to match his silence with her own, Helen could not determine.

Of one thing, however, she was sure — Catherine and her women were blind as bats at midday. The speeches and sly insinuations that they made as soon as the rumor of Anne's disfavor gained foothold among them were enough to drive a far less quick-tempered girl back to the king in revenge.

On one morning, "'Tis a fine set of tapestries we are making for the king's chamber," Donna Maria had said to Anne. "You have been away so much of late that you have not seen these, but we think now we shall see more of you."

"The king's chamber hath one noble set already," Donna Blanche had put in, she with the moles and the squint, "but as you have discovered, mistress, he tires of one thing so soon!"

Was not that enough to provoke Anne to folly? The girl had met that thrust with her most dangerous sweetness.

"Nay, knowing his constancy to our most gracious queen, how can you say such things, Donna?" she had returned in mild rebuke.

Helen had tingled with excitement at the silence in which the speech had been received. No one had dared raise their eyes to the queen. Some day, Helen said to

CALUMNY

herself, Anne would go too far in those still rages of hers — and might she be there to see!

Helen speculated a good deal, in her shrewd, dispassionate way, on the future that might lie before such a girl as Anne. With one disastrous romance now to her credit and this sensation about the king — well, it would come hard for her to descend to an ordinary knight. It would take a peer of the realm to mate her properly, but peer or knight, where were her suitors coming from?

Most of the young men about Anne, her brother's intimates and the king's companions, were already married, and though they bore their yokes lightly and endured the marital infelicity that appeared the common lot with the nonchalant infidelity of the times, nevertheless married they remained, unless a pestilence relieved them, or a scruple as to some precontract pricked their consciences. It occurred to Helen, as it had often to Anne herself, that a maid was hardly in the way of making her fortune among them.

What, in the end, would be her fate? Would some grand passion blaze her off her feet — would she fling herself into disaster or connubial obscurity as her sister had done — would she linger on at court, eclipsed in time, by fresher sensations, pressed back into the ranks of forgotten, disappointed women? Helen shook her wise, cold head over the problem.

King Henry, in gracious chat with the new Imperial Ambassador, Mendoza, became distrait. His eyes wandered. On the other side of the hall a slim, black-haired girl in pale blue was gayly holding forth to a group of young men and women. Wyatt was there leaning towards her, and his sister and Norris and blond Brereton towering above them all. The hall was crowded, for it was a revel in honor of the New Year, but through all the buzz of talk Henry's ears could catch the high, sweet note of that girl's voice.

The conversation in which he had been engaging became most insupportably dull. It lagged, flagged,—suffered a total eclipse. Mendoza was left with a bland phrase of excuse and King Henry was across the room in front of the girl in blue. At his approach the others fell tactfully away, leaving them in a little island of space in that ocean of folk.

"Anne, thou art a witch," said the king bluntly.

"And shall your Majesty burn me at the stake?" she questioned with challenging laughter in her eyes. From her gay composure they might be resuming the relations of a moment ago, instead of near six weeks.

"'Tis I am burning, Anne."

"And why am I a witch?" she demanded hastily.

"Because I vowed to the Virgin and five saints that I would have no word with you till you had asked one of me — and here I am, vow or no vow. Naught but a witch could have brought me here."

"I thought 'twas thy two feet," she murmured, catching at any shred of banter. Her cheeks were flushed; she was playing nervously with a fine chain at her girdle. It was the chain with which Wyatt had measured his cast.

Henry saw it and frowned. "How much truth was there in that fellow's brag of thee?" he shot at her.

Proudly, steadily, her eyes looked up at him. "How much truth was there in *thy* brag of me?" she flashed audaciously back. Then a gust of laughter blew out the defiant blaze of her eyes: in her left cheek a dimple popped suddenly into being.

"I had not thought your Highness was so credulous,"

she smiled mischievously. " Heaven knows I have not found in thee so ready credence for my words! "

The last storm cloud was swept from Henry's mind; he laughed responsively, and the intolerable tedium that had afflicted him those past six weeks utterly vanished. Life again held cheer and jest. He tugged at his blond beard — a gesture of content — as his eyes twinkled down into the girl's sparkling face, and he vowed to himself that it was the loveliest face at court, the brightest-eyed, the rosiest-cheeked. With cool attention to detail even in his kindling passion, he noted the utterly absurd length of her eyelashes, the exquisite lines of her throat, and the delicate whiteness of it against the black of the velvet ribbon she wore there. And he said to himself that such a prize of flesh and spirit should fall to no one else while Henry of England called himself a man.

Aloud, he was answering her, " Nay, nor shalt thou ever find credence in me for thy words of denial."

" Nor shalt thou find credence in me for thy words of love," she returned smartly. Her words were well enough, but she said them with a saucy challenge of a glance from under her lashes, a glance unwise, imprudent in the extreme, which she knew in the giving was rank folly. Yet it slipped out from her excitement before second thought could overtake it.

Small wonder he vowed stoutly, " Nay, I shall never despair. Thou canst not make me fail."

" Nor thou me frail."

" Thou hast a poet's tongue."

" Truth, I need it to match thy Highness."

" I am glad thou ownest thou art indeed my match."

" Oh, I will own I am thy match in one thing more — in resolution ! "

" I shall o'ertop thee there — I am irresistible."

THE FAVOR OF KINGS

"And I invulnerable," proclaimed Anne. "Nay, I protest I am more impervious to the arrows of Cupid than was Achilles to the arrows of the Trojans! I have not even a heel to be pierced — my mother must have flung me headlong in the enchanted river."

Henry was delighted. He had a pretty taste for mythology himself, and he had never met a woman at his court before who could have told Achilles from a corset. An atmosphere of such culture and wit, he felt, invested the affair with spiritual dignity.

"And I again must fail thee credence," he disputed. "For where love comes out, there may love come in. Through those same eyes, by which thy shafts are launched, mayhap my shafts may enter."

Anne was at a loss. She felt the analogies were grown cumbersome, so she took refuge in laughter and the frank confession, "Nay, now, I own I am graveled for matter!"

"So shall you be out of denial e'er I am done with thee!" he vowed.

"Ah, now we are friends again!" commented Helen Sackville.

Wyatt followed her directing gaze to the hall where King Henry and Anne Boleyn were dancing a gaillard. Their hands were clasped; their eyes sought each other in merry smiles that took no note of the onlookers. Wyatt's face darkened, though he forced, next moment, a short laugh.

"What else?" he uttered.

"That is what Anne will ask of herself some day — what else?" said Helen slowly.

Wyatt turned to look at her. He found this pale, green-eyed girl a curious puzzle. He had hints, at times, of underground fire beneath her bloodlessness. Now he found the meaning of her peculiar inflection intensely disagreeable, though his love for Anne made him torture himself by dwelling on it.

"You think —" he began, then paused.

"Yes," said Helen.

"Could you not —" he began and again stopped abruptly. He had been about to ask impulsively if her influence might not have some restraint upon Anne's dangerous caprice.

Helen read the thought. "No," she said. "Not I — nor you — nor anyone. What will be, will be."

"You speak like the prologue of a masque," Wyatt muttered with frank distaste.

Helen looked at him, a queer glitter in her light eyes, and then she said one of those utterly unforeseen and uncomfortable things with which no true lady should affront a gentleman.

"How all other women bore you!"

Wyatt shot her an oblique look, but he was too sad at heart to prick his wit for any light retort. The tall girl continued to regard him in strange malice: there seemed a devil in her humor.

"Where the king hath loved," she told him, "there is always a later field — for *consolation.*"

Wyatt turned on his heel and left her.

In the corridor he bumped against Sir John Russell, who was ordering his barge.

"Eh, I am glad to have met thee — even so violently," cried the older man. "I thought you would be coming to bid me farewell."

"Farewell?"

"Have you forgot I am on my way to Rome?"

"And I am on my way to — nowhere," said the young

poet, with a laugh devoid of mirth. "May we go together?"

"Eh? Thou dost mean —?"

"May I join my way to thine?"

"Gladly, Tom, gladly. But will the king —"

"Aye, Henry will not keep me," and Wyatt's bitter laugh rang out again, to his old friend's wonderment. "He will not miss me now."

Helen, linking her arm through Anne's as they came from mass next morning, informed her, "Wyatt has gone."

Anne finished a yawn. "So much the better," she cried crossly. She was outrageously sleepy and disgusted with herself for her too gay spirits of the night before. She had had a vision, in the midnight hours, of the net that was closing round her.

"You are a strange prickle of moods," said Helen slowly. "Are you as indifferent as you seem? . . . There are ladies in this court who would give their heads to get that one."

"Are you one of them?" demanded Anne in unthinking malice. "I give you leave to try."

Bleakly Helen smiled. "Oh, I tried long ago," she said evenly. "He would have none of me."

CHAPTER VIII

THE INSULT

LIFE had not been to Catherine of Aragon wholly the triumphant thing that her young eyes had pictured it in setting forth at sixteen from her father's court, to be the wife of Prince Arthur and future queen of England. But to be sure, the opening of the affair had been joyous enough for the daughter of Ferdinand and Isabella.

On a November Sunday, in 1501, the day of Saint Erkenwald, Catherine and her boy bridegroom, two white satin-clad figures posed on a high scarlet stage, had been married by the Archbishop of Canterbury before a jubilant throng, and had then led a prodigiously fine procession to the Bishop of London's palace. Six hundred ladies followed in the young bride's train; Puebla, the Spanish Ambassador, was at her left, and at her right the young Henry, then the Duke of York, a child of ten and the prettiest little figure in the world, clad in white velvet and gold, so flaxen-haired and fair-skinned, so frank and sturdy, that a rain of blessings showered on him as he passed.

There followed a carnival week of jousts and balls; at one revel this little Henry led out his new sister to dance and footed it so warmly that he cast off his coat and danced on in his doublet. Everything was joyous welcome and acclaim. Five weeks from that reception, the young bride, with her sickly husband taken from her

93

and sent to travel for his health, and her *serviteurs* unpaid, was busy defending her jewels from her avaricious father-in-law, Henry the Seventh, and begging proper maintenance.

That April Arthur died, and two months later, a treaty providing for her marriage with the child Henry when he should be of sufficient age was drawn up, and then followed long years of waiting in an anomalous position, years of alternate ups and downs, of exasperating bickerings with her father-in-law, who doled her out a miserly allowance, and of futile appeals to her parents to protect her or demand her return.

Old Henry the Seventh had no intention at all of permitting her return, for to send her back to Spain would be to send back her dowry, already snug in his English coffers, and then, too, no more advantageous match might offer for his son; and Ferdinand of Spain had no real intention to urge that return, for every year of her retention was an added claim on Prince Henry's hand — and each ruler was shrewdly aware of the other's mind and of the other's awareness of his own mind, so that the correspondence between the English and Spanish courts exhibited some very pretty fencing indeed, and a most luminous state of clairvoyance between its ambiguous lines.

Many a time Isabella, the girl's mother, must have grieved at the loneliness and humiliating uncertainty of her daughter's position, but Isabella was a Spaniard first and a mother afterwards, and she had impressed on her child's mind, on leaving home, that her first duty in England was to Spain, and that her life must be devoted to the promotion of the Spanish interests at court and the glory of the Roman Catholic Church.

It was by way of Catherine's church that there came

THE INSULT

her great consolation in those days, young Diego Fernandez, a Franciscan monk.

It was a costly comfort, however, for Catherine was obliged to pawn her plate for the fellow, going down on her knees, as George Boleyn had so scornfully repeated, to the Spanish Ambassador to plead for his retention; moreover, the scandal of their intimacy proved a convenient pretext for Henry's postponement of a marriage for which he was in no hurry. In the end the thing was hushed up, denied, ignored, and the poor waiting widow's cause was so popular with the general public that Henry, on coming to the throne in 1509, found it excellent policy to make her his queen.

During all the years of her wifehood, pious, affectionate years, with no other scandal to ripple their steady current — save on the king's side! — Catherine had retained and increased the love of the common people, not only by her charity, for she distributed eighteen thousand ducats a year for widows and orphans, but by her pitying intercession on their behalf in times of trouble. The pardoning of four hundred boy rioters at her urgent pleadings was never forgotten by the women of London. This friendship of the people was one of the joys of her life; her little daughter, Mary, and the exercise of her religion concluded the number. Queenship and its privilege she took as a natural heritage.

The greatest grief of her life had been the loss of her boy babies who would have given England a male heir to the throne. She knew that there were not wanting those among the people, particularly among the nobles, who had ever murmured secretly against the validity of the dispensation of Pope Julius that permitted Henry to marry his brother's widow, a marriage forbidden absolutely by all religious law, and who held that the marriage

95

was unlawful and the death of every little prince a direct judgment from Heaven. A son would have justified her in the eyes of all, but time, she felt now, had done that thoroughly enough, and though she knew a haunting jealousy of the little Duke of Richmond, a son of Henry and Lady Talboys, a one-time favorite, she felt certain that Henry would never discriminate against the Princess Mary, of whom he was extremely proud. The most she had to dread from that quarter was that Henry, in one of his moments of ingenious statecraft, would, for fear of leaving a divided England behind him, undertake to wed these two. She had been bitterly disappointed when her nephew, Charles, the Emperor, had broken his youthful contract with Mary, but now she had hope that her daughter would soon be betrothed to a French prince.

For some time the king had lived apart from her and it was nearly two years since he had spoken with her alone, but she knew him thoroughly and was too aware of her own influence over him to permit the slightest break in their relations. She sent daily to inquire concerning him: she looked after his linen personally, with punctilious care, and was ever affable and obliging in his presence.

Of the rumors of divorce that had reached her, from time to time, in fact ever since she had been married, she was sincerely disdainful, too secure of her own position and power to be alarmed however her intimacy with Henry might wane. She had grown hardened, through those years, to whatever jealousy the wanderings of his capricious affections might cause, and her knowledge of the fleeting nature of these affections was a vast help to the suavity of manner she offered these rivals, and which cloaked her own secret contempt.

But for this last rival, this upstart maid of honor,

THE INSULT

Catherine had a much bitterer feeling. She had never liked Anne Boleyn, prejudiced from the start against the girl's French sympathies and gay manners, and she frowned upon her accomplishments, and never asked her to play or sing, reiterating that needlework and prayers were the proper occupations for a woman's time. She had never lost an opportunity of putting the girl in her place and had used the Percy affair as an excellent means to that end.

When at Wolsey's request — a veiled command, for she dared not offend Henry's powerful favorite — she had received the girl again in her train, she had treated her as ever with a haughty politeness which Anne's success at the dance had spiced with cold malice. It was a very prickly thorn indeed in Catherine's flesh that her husband should make a favorite of this girl even for a fleeting instant, and when the instant extended and months went by, merging autumn into winter and winter into spring, while still Anne's favor grew, Catherine's vexation strained her self-control to breaking point.

It was intolerable to see this Anne Boleyn give herself such airs, to see her sweeping forth to masque or revel, to hear of her success with the lute or song, and not be able to lift one finger to prevent it. Very promptly, back in the autumn, Catherine had demanded the girl's dismissal of Henry, and he had denied it so sharply that her worst suspicions were confirmed.

Not for a second did she believe in the innocence of Anne's conduct. She believed the girl had strained every nerve to attract the king and was now flaunting his favor in her eyes. A bitter anger used to possess the neglected wife at times as she would look at the girl bent over her embroidery or, at some assembly, in animated converse

97

with vying gallants, and the anger mounted to frenzy at the amusement in Anne's gaze when she met the glance. Catherine would set her teeth and school herself to patience, reminding herself that the end would not be long in coming and then Anne's disgrace would be before all eyes.

"How long, O Lord, how long!" she used to pray before the crucifix in her secret closet.

A damp February had been blown away by a windy March and still Anne's star ascended. The whispers about her had become talk now: there was not a scullion or lackey at court so dull as not to know where the wind sat, and not a country yokel come to sleep on the rushes of a London tavern but learned the affair, with winks and chuckles, over his first glass of ale.

It was gall and wormwood to the queen's pride, and she was all the bitterer for her enforced repression and suavity. Then one day, as she turned a corner in a corridor, she came upon Anne sallying gayly forth, hatted and gowned for the chase.

Anne swept her a magnificent courtesy intolerable in its irony. Catherine's nostrils quivered with her trembling breath as she looked down at the nodding plumes that hid, for a moment, the face of her rival from her. Anne rose, and the streaming sunshine from a casement was like candles held to display her young brilliance. Catherine was conscious of a terrible desire to strike that flaunting youth to her feet.

"You go hunting, mistress?" she said slowly, looking her up and down.

"An it please your Majesty," said Anne.

"I hear," said the queen, "that you are a shrewd huntress." Her edged tone, her continued look of plain, contemptuous insult brought the quick blood to the girl's

THE INSULT

cheek. How dared the queen look so! All the world went hunting in the king's train — there was no harm in it. The anger that unfortunately was always in Catherine's power to excite rose in her.

Catherine spoke to the woman beside her, without turning her head.

"How red she grows, Maria! . . . Doth she not blush like a *maid?*"

There were four waiting women with the queen and their quick titter emphasized the equivocation.

"Your Majesty!" slipped from Anne, her eyes ablaze.

"Why should you not blush like a maid?" went on the queen's voice, a spice of bitter amusement lightening its heavy rancor. "You are overquick at conclusions, Mistress Boleyn — you will o'erreach yourself some fair day."

She stopped, and stared again at the baited girl before her, a slow, hard, measuring stare.

"You are wondrously apparelled," she commented, "too fine for the society of the simple gentlewomen about me . . . who have paid no such price for their clothes. . . . 'Twas a clever device, those new-tangled pointed sleeves, to hide that extra finger of thine!"

The laugh that Catherine waited for came unstintedly.

Anne stretched out her left hand in full sight of them all. "'Tis a double nail, your Majesty," she corrected in dangerous calm.

"Only a nail? But that is enough! Faugh! Put thy hand down — I could never bear to look upon blemishes."

From red Anne turned to chalky white. "Oh, how dare you, how dare you!" sang through her veins. "I could make you pay for this — I *shall* make you pay! If you knew —"

Catherine, looking on her, saw nothing but a little

intrigeant for her husband's favor: she had no vision of the girl soul, intolerably humiliated, intolerably goaded, quivering on the brink of a fiery revenge. She had no notion of tremendous crisis in their lives. With the savage gusto of her outraged arrogance she flung her gibes.

" 'Tis said, your Majesty," tittered Donna Maria, her loyalty reveling in Anne's helpless fury, " that Mistress Anne must needs be clever at devising strange fashions — she hath so much about her person to conceal! "

" There is that wart, that swelling, on her neck that she must hide with her velvet ribbon," sniggered another.

" A pity she could not wear a veil altogether," laughed an emboldened third.

Anne said never a word. For once she was dumb, and Catherine fed her satisfaction with the sight of her white pallor. Then the queen made a gesture of dismissal.

" Take thy deformities to thy ride, mistress," she commanded, and Anne slipped back into the doorway with a low bow to let the royal party pass by.

Then with a bursting heart she swept forth to her hunt.

CHAPTER IX

A VISION OF A CROWN

SHE rode a white horse of Henry's gift, a spirited, beautiful creature, with whose dashing impetuosity and chafing impatience at control she was much in sympathy. To-day she gave Diana the rein and with Henry's big black at her side they shot ahead of the field of riders and raced dizzily along the way that wound from St. James' Park into Epping forest.

The speed, the motion, the whistling of the wind past her ears, was all at first that Anne was conscious of. The hard riding answered her need for violent action and the buffeting wind seemed to do her struggling and screaming for her. With her head bent forward, one hand clinging to the reins, the other holding on her flapping hat, she dashed on, tossing only a curt word to the gay questions of the king. Every spark of spirit in her was flaming in revolt at the ignominious baiting to which she had been subjected. She felt outraged, degraded; her face flamed.

All afternoon she rode furiously, obliviously following the dogs that were trailing a fine stag. It was March; the bare boughs were swelling with tender buds, the ground was soft and spongy from spring rains and the little brooks ran black and swollen in their courses. The seasons seldom made their appeal in vain to Anne; she rarely saw the out-of-doors without a lifting of her spirit to its wide horizons, but to-day, though the fiercest of her trembling anger outwore itself in her heart, she felt no balm for the wound within her. The dark eyes that were set so rigidly on the path ahead of her were in reality following the path of her life, searching its conclusions, facing its despairs. The net, that her soberest moments had seen folding about her, had closed in; she was caught, branded in the eyes of the world if not yet in her own conscience. Who of that jesting throng behind them believed in her? Who of those who called themselves her friends? Who of her family? At the best, they but thought she was playing a game, deferring her surrender, raising, perhaps, her price. Under all the sweets that she had tasted in their eager deference to her, their flattery, their vying for favor, she came now upon the venom of this thought of theirs of her, this utter disbelief in her own innocence.

Oh, fool, fool that she had been, to think that she could play with fire, could control such a situation! She remembered with a sorry smile her first naïve hope that she could bend Henry to consent to her marriage with Percy. She had not profited by that lesson — she had gone on in her absurd self-confidence, thinking she could take as she liked and reject as she liked — but the court was no place for halfway measures.

But what else could she have done, she angrily demanded of this accusing self? If she had angered Henry she would have been bundled off again into the country to yawn her head off among the kitchen maids, and there would have been no second chance for her then. She would have grown older and duller and duller and older with each succeeding year, becoming wisely proficient in making jellies and flavoring sweets for such gray-beards as her father would semi-annually bring to the place. Perhaps a fat country squire would wish to marry her.

A VISION OF A CROWN

Any girl, so she vindicated herself, would have done as she had done.

And what, after all, was it that she had done? Nothing in the world to be ashamed of! There had been nothing that the whole court might not see, indeed nothing that the whole court had not seen. She was not to blame because the court had gone on and constructed tales of what it thought it had not seen. She had been pleasant to Henry, nothing more; danced, talked, bantered, accepted a gift or two, refused steadfastly any hope of her bestowing anything in return. He at least, she thought bitterly, knew how little she had granted! She had made *him* respect her!

But what should she do? How was she to go on? Leave court? . . . In disgrace, would be on everyone's tongue. No one would believe it was of her own volition. No one would believe her such a fool as to throw away her favor for such a bubble as self-esteem. And it would be too late to save her reputation then. She felt, in helpless shame, how bespattered that was now. Her sister's scandal had urged on her own. . . . Stay on at court? . . . She could not continue like this forever. Henry was impatient: she had exhausted her wit and her spirit in keeping him at his distance. If she denied him longer he would turn against her. . . . O dear God, what a labyrinth it all was! What should she do?

She was aroused from her absorption by the abrupt ending of the hunt: the stag had escaped along a brook and the baffled dogs were puzzling up and down the sides of it. She and the king had outridden all the rest and the calls of the others' horns came to them from a distance.

Henry wound his own horn, then sprang down from the sweating black that staggered under him.

103

THE FAVOR OF KINGS

" The horses are spent," he said. " Shall we rest them here while the others come up? There are fresh relays at the lodge that should soon be brought."

Anne murmured an assent and jumped down, scarcely touching his hand. They were on high ground, in a little glade on top of a long, narrow ridge. A circle of trees half shut them in. From one side came the murmur of the unseen brook down which the stag had fled and the worrying whine of the searching dogs and on the other side, through the spaces in the trees, was a view of rolling woods and meadows, brown and gray, with here and there the purple patches of fresh plowed lands, and beyond them, where the Thames showed itself broad and blue from out under its trees, the diminished towers and spires of London were etched against the western sky.

Anne caught up the trail of her scarlet gown and began to walk back and forth restlessly in the glade. She was conscious — fully — of her folly in having outridden the rest and thus furnished fresh fuel for gossip, but she told herself defiantly that she did not care, it was too late to be fastidious!

Henry, having tethered the two steaming animals, came and joined her in her restless walking. He took off his cap, running his fingers through his damp hair. It had vanished from the top of his head, but courtiers had positively assured that this baldness added to the nobility of his forehead. Although he had been drinking to a late hour the night before there were no signs of fatigue in his floridly fresh complexion: anyone meeting for the first time that ruddy, stalwart man, youthfully exuberant, would have taken him for five or ten years under his age. A powdering of dust lay on his suit of Lincoln green and he occupied himself a moment brushing it off, with shrewdly inquiring glances at his abstracted companion.

A VISION OF A CROWN

Clearly something out of the ordinary was passing behind that frowning forehead of hers!

"Where sits thy mood, Anne?" he asked at length, leaning forward to look in her face. "Thou hast said naught but yea or nay since the beginning of the hunt. Something has displeased thee."

"That something has," she returned bruskly.

"Mayhap I can remedy the matter?" he suggested.

She laughed, then gave him a darkling glance from her clouded eyes.

"In coming to the hunt I met her Most Gracious Majesty, the queen. She said certain things to me which — I liked not."

"What things?"

Anne's pride could not bring itself to repeat the insults. "I — I care not to name them," she cried, her bosom heaving.

Henry eyed her a moment in silence. He was not sorry to have her animosity roused against his wife, seeing there a chance for himself. He had no notion how strong already was that animosity. Yet his feeling for the girl resented stiffly any scorn put upon her. He turned the matter over in his mind.

"She is jealous," he told her, with a laugh, " and with good cause, I well ween."

"Not with any cause of mine!" she disputed, and her anger and disgust broke into mutinous revolt. "I vow I shall leave this court where I have too much to endure. . . . I beg to take leave of your Grace to-morrow."

The threat shot Henry with alarm. She was absolutely capable of carrying it out if she were sufficiently roused, and it would appear that she was. The look that his small gray eyes turned upon her was one of strangely humble beseechment. She reminded him in

that moment of nothing so much as some elusive bird of
passage, a gay-plumed wanderer alighted by hazard and
half ready to take wing again. The contentment that
was generally upon him in her presence vanished before
the reminder of this insecurity. He felt how insupport-
able his court would be without her bright presence.
He felt how intolerable his life would be without the
promise of her love. He felt a surge of savage resentment against the conditions of his life. He, a king,
accounted the most powerful man in England, and he
had less freedom, less joy, than some of the meanest of
his subjects! Weighted with responsibility — in his well-
ing indignation he forgot Wolsey's vast assumption of
that same responsibility — loaded with cares, tied to a
dull, sick, ageing woman, denied a son and heir, and in
love, desperately, deeply, in love with a slip of a girl
whom he was powerless to make his own! Deceive himself as he might by drinking bouts and revels, truly his
life was not a happy one!

" Wherein have I offended? " he said to Anne, turning
this over bitterly.

Anne made no reply. She tossed back the fluttering
hair from her face with a characteristic gesture that
seemed to be tossing him and his court away also from
her thoughts.

" Am I then nothing to thee? " he said a little huskily.
He was a very different man this day from the conqueror
who had tried to clasp Anne in rough wooing at that first
interview at the cardinal's.

His voice touched Anne, swift as her nature was to
respond to any genuine affection for herself. At any
rate he loved her, he very truly loved her. She exon-
erated him from his share of the situation in which she
found herself — he had but done what any man, any

"'Anne—Sweetheart!' he said."

A VISION OF A CROWN

monarch, would have done. He was not to blame that he loved her. He had suffered for that love, in her denial of it, and in the sting of her humiliation and self-upbraiding that love and its flattering respect was a comfort she hugged close. So this curiously feminine psychology made her answer his question with a glance of disarmed friendliness that was not without a hint of sympathy.

Instantly he caught at her hand nearest him and in spite of her attempted withdrawal carried it to his lips. He felt the delicate warmth of her flesh within her loose glove.

" Anne — Sweetheart! " he said in a voice that was like a groan.

He felt her hand tremble against his lips: he kissed it hungrily a dozen times, then clasped it close, searching her face for some hint of weakness, of surrender. He met only the proud denial of her steady eyes.

" Will you never love me? " he implored.

" I will never tell thee so."

" Oh, Anne — Anne! "

She tried, a moment's pause after his crying her name, to pull away her hand but she felt it in a tighter grasp. His great fingers gripped it convulsively. She heard his quick breathing.

" God — I want thee so! " came from him. It was fiercely, piteously sincere. He had never wanted anything in his life as he wanted Anne. He had never felt for any woman such curiously mingled stirring of desire and admiration. It was the most profoundly disconcerting emotion of his experience, and its primitive force re-created in him the lost innocence and naïveté of his first youth. It would have been incredible to him at that moment that he had ever found another woman desirable. As it was he forgot that there ever had been any other woman.

Anne turned her head away, and though her hand still rested prisoned in his, she twisted her body slightly from him and stared down at the ground at her feet. She was curiously shaken by his emotion and she felt the need of being cool and in command of the situation.

"Your Grace knows what is ever between us," she said in low voice. They were on the edge of a small hollow filled with last autumn's leaves that the vanishing cover of snow had left soaked and sodden. Only the topmost leaves had been dried by the spring sun. Anne stood there stirring the mass about with her foot as if she had lost something there.

"There is nothing between us," he denied.

"Heaven hath made your Highness a king," she murmured, faintly ironic.

"And my Highness will make you a queen!"

"You have one queen already." The memory of her last passage with that queen stiffened her curving lips to an angry line.

Henry pressed closer, still gripping her hand.

"And if I did not have that queen —?" he suggested, his voice thick with implication.

Anne raised her head in a startled gesture: her widening eyes caught the fire of his. He had said to her before that if she granted him her love he would surely crown her when Catherine died, but now, now there seemed another significance in his dilated pupils! Then she felt that he was trying to test her by false suppositions and impatiently she brushed it aside.

"If — what is the good of 'if'?" she cried.

"But there is good in it. Sweetheart, an thou wilt be mine I will crown thee so surely as there is a God who hears me!" His grip of her hand hurt. "Catherine is no lawful wife of mine. . . . The pope will soon rid me of that coil."

"You mean — you mean — ?" she faltered, her eyes on his.

"I will have that marriage — which is no true marriage — annulled. Then will my throne stand free for you — for *you* — and no power on earth shall let me from sharing it with you — so you do but love me, as I have hope. Anne — darling —"

Anne leaned away from him, instinctively lowering her eyes that he might not surprise her emotion there. Fixedly she stared down at the dead leaves, conscious of physical tremors and strange tinglings that were of her mind yet of her flesh too. . . . The king's voice went on, husky, yet vibrating with its resolve.

"My throne, Anne, is for thee. I want thee as I have wanted nothing in all this life before — and I will give this life and all that I possess in it to win thee. Surely thou hast a mind for me? . . . I have been patient — I have yielded to thee — but before God I can endure this no more. I will make thee wife. I will hew a way to thee though every Spaniard in hell oppose it!"

Anne's heart stood still that moment, struck with the incredible realization that he was in actual earnest, he was not deceiving her or himself, he meant to do this amazing thing for her! And then, as she yielded herself to the temptation of that thought, her heart galloped on at a terrific rate.

"I tell thee, Anne, I will crown thee!" Henry had seen the half-frightened, half-fascinated uncertainty of the girl's expression, and his words rang with stout assurance. "Thou hast said thou wouldst be naught but wife, and wife thou shalt be — even as thy ancestress was wived by another king, Edward, my good progenitor. Thou shalt be the darlingest wife a man ever cherished, the tenderest loved queen a king ever crowned."

He heard her draw a quick breath. "Ah, thou hast not taken thought —"

"Oh, I am well advised in this. I have taken thought of the head and heart of Henry of England and he swears to thee by his kingly faith that he will give thee his throne for thy love — and that neither church nor state nor pope nor devil shall stand between him and thee — aye, and in so doing he will be ridding his conscience of the foul wrong of keeping his brother's widow to wife!" He laughed loudly and strove to draw her closer.

But she backed a step away. She felt appalled and cast a glance over her shoulder at her tethered horse as if contemplating sheer flight.

"It is too high an honor for a simple maid," she stammered. "No, no, it cannot be."

"In God's name it shall be! — By the bones of my father and the honor of my mother and the Seven Pains of our Lord and my own right royal love for thee! I say it shall be!"

"But the cardinal — the pope — the emperor —" she flung at him, "they will all be against it."

"The cardinal, the pope and the emperor will all be tools in my hands, one against the other. . . . Wolsey will devise ways to do my will in this . . . we have oft discussed it of old."

"But not for *me!*" ran Anne's agitated secret thought.

"Dare the pope deny to England's king what he hath lavished on every hand? He grants annulments as freely as Heaven doth its showers —"

"But the emp —"

"The emperor is Catherine's nephew, but will he lose

A VISION OF A CROWN

my favor for an aged aunt?" Henry scoffed, his face aglow with his assurance. "Nay, Sweet, be not so fearful. Canst thou not trust thyself to me? Lean on this arm and heart!"

Henry's words were lost to Anne in the swimming confusion of her senses. The glade seemed to whirl about her. She felt the rushing of vast wings, the elation of airy heights. To be queen — to be Queen of England! Every accent of Henry's impassioned voice beat in the truth of his intention. He would crown her queen in Catherine's place!

She was too familiar with prophecies of a divorce, or rather an annulment, to feel much shock or doubt of it, accustomed as she was to regard Catherine as an unlawful usurper, but to be herself crowned in her stead was a thought too incredible to be fully grasped. Some whispering of it had come to her with Henry's offer to make her queen after Catherine's death, but she had put this shrewdly from her as a bribe — an empty enticement. . . . But now this was real, immediate. . . .

A fierce, cruel wave of joy swept over. To be queen on Catherine's throne — Oh, what an exquisite, what an infinitely ironic retaliation! Dared she trust herself to the mad project? Dared she undertake the humbling of one queen, the crowning of another?

Aye, she dared! Her blood rushed on in faster time: with feverish recklessness it sang songs of triumph and power in her veins. There was little that wild blood would not dare!

Henry bent over her, as she stood staring past him, and as he saw her face illumined with the splendor of her vision, "Thou *wilt!*" he cried and caught her to him.

But for one more instant, even within the circle of his arm, she held him off, her hands pressed against his

III

THE FAVOR OF KINGS

breast, her head bent back while her great eyes searched his face in almost piteous entreaty.

"Thou wilt be true to me?" she besought, for in that instant there had come to her some inkling of the lonely audacity of the enterprise on which she was staking herself.

"Until I die, Sweet. . . . Until I die."

In that first moment of surrender, shaken by emotion, swept by a passionate gratitude and admiration for Henry's force, ravished with the sweets of foretasted triumphs, Anne had given no thought to the price of her dream. She was half persuaded that she was yielding to the man in yielding to the king. But in the next moment a wave of denial, a despairing certitude of her own aloofness, surged through her. She hid her face on his shoulder away from his kisses. He felt her slim body tremble in his arms and held her the closer.

Alas for the thought of Percy that crossed her mind! Must the second time bring always the inevitable comparison? She put the reminder defiantly away from her — Percy had been a boy, a helpless boy — Henry was a man, a king of men! He was bringing her a kingdom! He was daring the world and all for her — for her!

And his strength and passion, even while they frightened, held a fascination. She felt that she was loved indeed. Presently, his first turbulence over, he held her more tenderly to him, pushing the tangled hair from her forehead, which his lips ever and again pressed, and a sense of gladness in him and in his love for her stole over her again.

She saw, framed in the trees' black boughs, the distant towers of London bathed in rosy light, and before her dreaming eyes then swam a vision of the city, peopled with bowing throngs who cheered her as she passed, of eager courtiers, gallant knights and smiling ladies, of feasts and jousts and tournaments . . . vista after vista of intoxicating glory, all springing from that first incredible vision of Anne Boleyn, in robes of state, mounting over Catherine to England's throne. Anne of England!

CHAPTER X .

SECOND THOUGHTS

ANNE had little sleep that night and that little was agitated with dreams. Towards morning she fell into the heavy oblivion of exhaustion from which some chance noise roused her like an alarm. For some moments after she opened her eyes she was conscious of a curious sense of well-being. She felt as if something very delightful had happened of which her senses were already aware, the meaning of which would filter presently to her brain.

In a few moments the events of the past afternoon came over her. She was to be Queen of England! . . . With the remembrance fled the last vestige of sleepiness and also that sensation of indefinable pleasure. The undertaking, viewed in morning light, within the four walls of her dormer chamber, appeared fantastic and unreal in the extreme. The visions which had thronged her restless brain all night were as divorced from reality as the incoherent dreams that had succeeded them. It was in vain to recall the example of her illustrious ancestress, Elizabeth Woodville, or to repeat the promises of Henry. She was a prey to the irritating self-reproach of having made a fool of herself.

She wondered how Henry was feeling. She wondered if he was experiencing the reaction of the morning after. . . .

Her maid, hurrying down from the wind-racked attic

SECOND THOUGHTS

that servantdom accepted unquestioningly as its due, found her young mistress, nearly gowned, staring out absently over the gardens.

"This be more nipping than yesterday, mistress," she said, blowing on her red hands where the winter's chilblains still smarted.

"I would there were no yesterday," Anne murmured. "Bet, shall we go back to Hever now? The buds will be swelling on the trees and the tender shoots pricking through the dead leaves. Another month and the ladysmocks will be white. I should love to tend my flowers again — and sleep sound o' nights. Shall we go?"

The girl giggled nervously and cast a curious look on her young mistress.

"La, but 'tis dull in the country," she answered, a little uneasily.

"Dull? And where was that farmer lad of thine that brought thee such clear honey from his bees?"

The girl giggled again in embarrassment. "Eh, that lad — Dickon . . . what great boots he wore, mistress! And how red he got when I looked on him!"

Still laughing she went to answer a rap on the door. She was back with a small packet in her hand.

"By your leave, mistress, Master Weston bringeth this to thee, and sayeth that his master, the king, commendeth himself to thee and would know how you have passed the night."

"Well enough," returned Anne laconically.

She opened the packet slowly. Inside the wrappings was a small, charmingly wrought box of silver, fitted with lock and key, and inside the box, on a bed of white satin, flashed a sparkling pendant of rubies and diamonds. A tiny note was tucked beside it. She laid down the box and spread out the note. The king had written it in

115

haste on his awakening; he sent her his love and was most glad in that which had passed; he was impatient till he should see her again. He signed himself her entire servant, Henry.

The watching maid, making a pretense of occupation about the room, cast shrewd glances on her mistress as she read. She saw a sudden animation light Anne's face, and a smile part her lips, as Anne finally folded her note and slipped it away, and Bet made bold to approach and admire the jewel that Anne had caught up again.

"La, mistress, might I have a look? — God a mercy, how the thing shines! 'Twill become you finely. Will you put it on?" and as Anne nodded the girl eagerly fastened the slender gold chain about her neck. The pendant rested just below the little hollow of Anne's throat, and, catching the morning sun, it sparkled radiantly with a thousand flashes of light.

"How it glisters!" admired the maid, while the mistress, raising her hand glass, beamed impulsively at her image. "Why those white stones be as bright as water drops — and that big one is red as blood. Sure, it cost a mint of money. I am thinking the one who sent it thought a lot of you, mistress."

"I'm thinking he did, too, Bet," cried Anne, with a bubbling laugh, "though thou art a bold wench to name it. But there is no harm in thee. Thou thinkest, then, it becometh me right well?"

"Aye, aye, it setteth thee off grand." Into the girl's simple eyes as they rested on the jewel crept a hint of wistfulness. "It must be fine," she murmured, "to be gentlefolk and wear such a thing upon one."

"Why, I take it for no more than thou dost a new ribbon, Bet," Anne returned carelessly, though that was scarcely true. But the girl's speech had touched her

116

susceptible sympathies, and running to her drawer, she pulled out a hair ribbon of sky blue satin.

"Here is one, fresh and unbemoiled for thee," she cried, tucking it into the girl's hands. "Here, now be off with thee and bring me fresh water. Thou hast forgot thy duties for thy staring!"

When the maid, scarlet with pleasure, went out bearing her treasure, Anne stood a moment quizzically smiling.

"Belike her new bauble will bring her as much mischief as will mine," she reflected, fingering the pendant at her throat. "I hear there is a groom of the chamber in hot pursuit of the simple lass. . . . I must look to it." Then she took advantage of her solitude to read her note again. She passed the love praise in it for the last sentence: "God send that we wot of shall come to pass."

"Amen," she echoed merrily. Her spirits were risen indeed. The concrete splendor of the pendant linked all her hopes again with reality. Moreover, she reminded herself, she was not a whit worse off than she was before — if Henry could crown her, well and good; if not, no harm had been done. She would be wary and not commit herself too far. She sang as she completed her dressing the song she had made for the king's words, gayly repeating the couplet,

> Youth must needs have dalliance
> Of good or ill some pastance.

There was no more talk of returning to Hever.

At ten she dined with her aunt and uncle, the Duke and Duchess of Norfolk. The Norfolks had not particularly troubled themselves about Anne during her first days at court; their deferential courtesy now was a conquest. The old Dowager Duchess of Norfolk, of whom Anne was fond, was present; so were her father, her brother, and his wife, and Mary Wyatt, who was a sort of protégée of the old dowager duchess's.

The hour for dinner had been reached and passed and the company appeared assembled, yet no move was made toward the dining hall until a tiptoeing servant had come whispering to the master of the house. Then the Duke of Norfolk rose quickly and led the way with Anne Boleyn. In the hall they were stopped by another servant. Norfolk, receiving his message with a great show of surprise and delight, gave orders for the rearrangement of the tables and then announced to his guests that Providence had sent them a rare privilege — the king was without in his barge with Sir Henry Norris, and would do them the honor of dining with them.

Norfolk hurried off to receive his royal guest and George Boleyn leaned forward and pinched his sister's arm.

"What carrier pigeon keeps Henry informed of thy whereabouts?" he laughed, and Lord Rochford smiled at his daughter with quizzical benevolence.

"Let us hope that same carrier pigeon does not keep the court informed of the king's whereabouts to-day," tittered George's wife.

"Thou art ever zealous for the honor of our name," shot back Anne promptly, and George Boleyn laughingly advised his wife, "She hath thee there! Never match thy wits against Anne's!" while Lord Rochford shook his head ever so slightly at his daughter and murmured in her ear, "Imprudent, imprudent. Never stir a causeless strife. . . ."

As Anne sat at table, at her place down the board beside her brother and Mary Wyatt, she began to surmise shrewdly that some hint had been already dropped to her father and uncle concerning Henry's intentions. She saw that both of them were a trifle self-conscious and that their eyes often met as if for consultation as do the eyes of those who believe they hold between them a secret. As for the king, he had a distinct air of being *en famille*. Dignity was jovially relaxed; he called down the table to Anne, bidding her be ready to play and sing after the meal, and informing her of the progress of the new anthem he was composing.

Anne found herself in a state of secret and suppressed excitement. The instinct for romance of her strongly imaginative temperament eagerly seized and built upon the wonderful material the situation offered. The vision of that future crown had magically dispelled the discredit of the position in her own mind; her ultimate justification would be overwhelming. She could not help reflecting on herself — what a situation! What a career she was having! A maid of honor, young and fair, sought in marriage by her king! And what a king! Anne's eyes saw Henry now through the glorious illusion of her romance. She saw his youth, his strength, his splendor and his charm, and saw them multiplied a hundredfold. She remembered the two other kings she had seen, Louis of France, decrepit, querulous, who had taken Henry's sister in unwived wifehood, and Francis, his successor, suave and debonair, and she compared them most disadvantageously to this great, dashing Henry. She told herself that she was a most lucky maid, and compared her story to the romantic ballads that the minstrels told.

After the meal she sang, and Anne had a voice of rare loveliness. She gave them " Balow," and a new verse of Surrey's, Wyatt's youthful cousin and poetic rival, set to a tune of her own making, and then at Henry's request she began, " As ye came from the Holy Land."

At the lines, " Met you not with my true love, By the

way as you came?" Henry joined in with her, and at the stanza,

> Such a one did I meet, good sir,
>   Such an angelic face,
> Who like a nymph, like a queen, did appear
>   In her gait, in her grace,

he came out so strongly with the words, *"like a queen,"* with an intent look at Anne, who to her own chagrined confusion spoiled her accompaniment, that Norfolk and Rochford glanced involuntarily at each other, and young George Boleyn became instinctively aware of something electric in the atmosphere.

When, by tacit comprehension, the company gathered at one end of the room, leaving the king to compliment the singer alone, George drew his father aside.

"What's in the wind?" he asked carelessly. "What is new in that?" and he jerked his head toward his sister and her admirer.

Lord Rochford hesitated. He did not regard his flighty son as a safe confidant, but he shrewdly reflected that Anne would probably tell him herself anyway, and he might as well prepare his mind first and have the credit of being open. He lowered his voice cautiously.

"There is again talk of a divorce . . . between their Highnesses," he murmured as George did not comprehend. But once with the cue, the young fellow's mind was alert enough. His face showed his sudden thought.

"And do you mean there is talk of — of a successor?" he demanded incredulously.

His father nodded. "*Talk,*" he replied with peculiar emphasis. "And mind, not a word to thy wife. Norfolk and I are all that are advised — and he hath but thrown out an enigmatic hint to us this morning. Even his Eminence is not aware. Never drop a word on't."

SECOND THOUGHTS

In his turn George nodded, with vast carelessness like a man of the world. But his expression betrayed how the thing had struck him. After a pause of astonishing reflections he murmured, " Well, what think you, sir? "

" Of the divorce? Oh, that may well come to pass — Henry and Wolsey are both set towards it. . . . But as for — anything further —" he hesitated, " why, Norfolk thinks 'tis folly. The caprice will last a fortnight."

" And what do you think? "

" Why, I think 'tis folly too. And so it is. . . . But that is no reason why it may not hap," he finished with one of his delightfully whimsical smiles.

They were both silent a moment, casting covert glances at the pair by the window.

" Anne is a — a clever girl," said her brother in a shaken voice.

" Clever, yes," returned the father in cool appraisement, " but too hot — too hot! She will out at him some day as at an uncrowned head. . . . And she makes enemies."

" Yet 'tis that very spirit that wins him," the younger man mused.

" Too hot — too hot," Rochford repeated. " Build not on't. I do not. Then when 'tis shattered will we be not cast down."

" I have seen Wolsey," Henry was informing Anne.

" Your Grace is prompt."

" My Grace is eager," he gave back, pressing her hand. " I count a day too long."

Shyly she returned the pressure. " And what said my Lord Cardinal? "

" He is of my mind entirely, and he is full of wise devisings. . . . I did not acquaint him with the dearest part of my secret matter," Henry added meaningly. " We will let that come later. His business is to clear the throne — mine to fill it."

Anne drew back her hand. So he had not dared the cardinal's disapproval! She felt a quick renewal of her old spite against Wolsey as she divined how strong his opposition would be to any marriage between her and the king, however lightly he might pass over the talk of it now when it was out of the question. And this very incident was revealing to her the extent of the cardinal's influence over the king.

A shadow crossed her face that Henry, always clairvoyant when his vanity was involved, was quick to interpret. Eager to play the ruler in her eyes, " Oh, I have let fall sufficient hint to advise him of my will," he declared pompously, " but it is not needful that a servant should know all his master's mind."

" Then, perchance, I am myself not fully aware of your Grace's? " Anne flashed back petulantly. That shining vision of her all-powerful royal wooer had suffered an unexpected eclipse — she felt uncomfortably that he suggested a plotting schoolboy circumventing an awe-inspiring master!

" Nay, Sweet — with you am not I the servant and you the mistress? " Henry reproached, leaning closer to her and smiling into her clouded eyes. The warmth of his words, the eager importunity that every inflection, every glance expressed sent all her doubts whisking again. If the cardinal were strong, she would be stronger, she that had weapons that no cardinal could wield! Her confidence touched her lips again with smiles, and she gave her head an impudent cock-sure little tilt like a braggart robin, as she laughed, " Troth, I know not what sort of servant your Grace may prove! I think I will but take you on trial."

SECOND THOUGHTS

" My love hath no fear of any trials you may impose!"

" Then I impose that you do *not* grip my hands like that when all my kinsfolk are peeping over their shoulders at us! . . . Do you not know they will be saying ill of me?"

" Not for long, darling," he promised. " List, this is how we have devised the matter. Wolsey, as Archbishop of York, together with the Archbishop of Canterbury, will hold a secret sitting of the ecclesiastical court. They will summon me before it for living with my brother's widow. I will defend myself — exceedingly ill "— his eyes twinkled knowingly —" and they will pronounce sentence against us, declaring the marriage to be no marriage, as indeed it hath never been one, and impose some penalty to which I will say right hearty amen. We will then live apart for a time to avoid scandal and then, why then, little Sweeting, we are free to love and wed! Is it not bravely resolved?"

Excitement was shining like a lamp in the girl's face.

" And when will this come to pass?" she questioned.

Her lover tweaked a straying curl. " This head is then impatient for the crown?"

She laughed in irrepressible pleasure and confusion at the thrill that his words of crowning sent through her.

" For my part, I would God that it were the morrow," he declared, " but there is yet need for caution while the French Ambassador is here and the negotiations for Mary's hand not yet concluded. We must do naught to injure her position till that is done. Not," he added defensively, " that her position will be in any wise touched, for her rights shall be maintained." He was silent a moment, and Anne felt how strange and remote that past of his seemed now to her. She had visualized him so intensely as her lover that it was a shock to remember

123

that he was still the public husband of another and the father of a little girl of eleven. His life with Catherine seemed very distant and unreal. So, too, did her passages with Percy. She reflected that life was a very curious experience — that is one part of her brain, the very smallest part, was reflecting that. All the rest of her was waiting, tinglingly expectant, for Henry to name a time when all these remarkable proceedings were to begin.

"Once Mary is betrothed," he continued, "there will be naught to let us. And, look you, the betrothal itself giveth us a good pretext for the inquiry, for we can say that the French threw such doubt of Mary's position, owing to the circumstance of her mother's marriage, that the archbishops were moved to clear the matter. . . . By April Wolsey promises that we shall be at it."

April — and it was March already!

CHAPTER XI

AN INOPPORTUNE EVENT

HOWEVER, it was May, before the two arch-bishops felt that the time was ripe for that secret tribunal of theirs. The treaty with the French had been signed and the Princess Mary was betrothed to marry either King Francis himself, or his second son, and enough of the nobles of the court had been sounded on the subject of the divorce, " The king's secret matter," as it was whispered, to give assurance of their support. Not a man of them, even if he had a notion that Anne had aught to do with the strength of the king's desire for his freedom, believed for a moment that she would actually profit by it.

Cardinal Wolsey, from his long experience of his ruler's caprices, was more thoroughly incredulous than any. He did not doubt that Henry cherished some random and fervid intention of making the girl his queen but by the time he could be able to do so he would have forgotten the color of her eyes. Anne was still a pawn in the game. She would serve to keep the king amused and if she pricked him towards freedom, in a humorous spurt of feminine grasping at the moon, why she was still serving Wolsey's ends, for with Henry free there would be a fine opportunity for the cardinal to make a good match for him and win a generous recompense in the making. The French would be very glad to marry off a princess to the king of England. They would pay Wol-

THE FAVOR OF KINGS

sey a handsome price if he brought about such a marriage and the price that the cardinal's secret dreams were harboring was nothing less than French help in making himself the next pope. There was always, Wolsey had asserted, one more rung in the ladder of ambition but he himself had approached the topmost rung of his. The Papacy! Pope Clement was ill and failing . . . why not the Cardinal of England as well as another? With the aid of France the thing was not at all impossible. The son of the Ipswich butcher, the petty scribe of Nanfan and Fox, had scaled more difficult pinnacles than that!

But all this of course was for the future. For the present the annulment of the marriage must be brought about.

So Wolsey went to work, laughing in his sleeve at the hopes he saw stirring in Anne Boleyn's mind, and reflecting for the thousandth time what simple tools the passions of other men were to one who was beyond them. Wolsey had but one passion, advancement, and its watchword had ever been concentration. The loves and desires and weaknesses that distracted others from their goals were like children's playthings to his thoughts. Only once had a woman seriously entered his life and she had been so soon hidden from him in the mist of death that the experience appeared a fleeting illusion. He remembered that he had cried in secret over her dead body. He recalled the fact now with a species of ironical wonder. There had been plenty of other women that he had amused himself with in those youthful carousals in which he had played boon companion to a roistering king — he had two daughters now shrouded in a convent in the north and a son in Paris to whom he had granted rich English benefices — but these other women were like

AN INOPPORTUNE EVENT

shadows thrown on a screen. Impossible to conceive of one of that sex agitating him for an instant! He had a profound contempt for femininity as irrational, wayward, capricious, undone by compassion and vanity and amiable scruples.

The seventeenth of May was the fateful day when his Eminence, the Archbishop of York, and Warham, Archbishop of Canterbury, held secretly a court at Westminster, beginning proceedings against their king for his scandalous relations with the widow of his late brother. Three days later the court met again and again three days after that. In the meantime, the two archbishops, feeling their authority a little shakily insufficient to decide so far-reaching a matter, had the question put to the most learned bishops of England as to whether a man might validly marry his brother's widow or not with a dispensation from the pope. Either the bishops were more dense or more independent than the archbishops had foreseen for the majority of them came out with a plump statement that a man might do so with perfect validity, providing he had that papal dispensation. This made it extremely difficult for the archbishops to decide as Henry demanded, and then, if they did so, they pointed out that Catherine would still have left the right of appeal to the pope. It would be wise, Wolsey insisted to his angry sovereign, to sound the pope first, and make sure that he would abide by the king's wishes.

Henry grumbled and protested. It was incredible that the pope should ultimately deny him and he did not want any delay, he wanted the archbishops to go ahead. Wolsey repeated how ineffectual any decision of theirs would be without papal authority and urged a secret messenger to the Vatican.

THE FAVOR OF KINGS

And then, one rainy morning, a bespattered courier rode a staggering horse to the gates of Richmond palace with urgent tidings for the king. The emperor's troops had entered and sacked Rome and the pope was shut up a prisoner in his own castle of Saint Angelo.

It was a complication for Europe generally, but Henry's first furious thought was not of political situations. He was realizing bitterly that this was no moment to ask an imprisoned pope for a judgment against the aunt of his besieger.

"God's blood, but I think that Spain and the devil are leagued to thwart me," he stormed. "Why in the name of all that's damned should Spain and the Vatican have been at odds at this moment? . . . May hell receive them all!" Savagely he kicked the spaniel that leaped to fawn upon him and sent a plate of Spanish luster ware crashing to the floor. A quaking page was sent scurrying in haste for the cardinal.

Henry was in no better humor when he had conferred with him — if his tumultuous outbreak of imprecations can be called a conference. His brow was black when he strode out to the chamber where his attendants were idling.

"He bursts with thunder," was Norris's hurried aside to Brereton. Both young courtiers were by now in the king's confidence and enthusiastic supporters of Anne and the divorce.

"Well, sirs?" growled Henry with a general air of challenge.

Norris dashed valiantly into the work of consolation. "Sure from thy Highness's visage, methinks that his Eminence hath brought small comfort," he ventured.

"Comfort?" uttered Henry between his teeth, with a ferocious glare. Anne would scarcely have recognized his face. " His word is wait — wait — wait! The time is out of joint — have patience for a few months — *months,*" he ejaculated ferociously, " when weeks are too long! I could wring the neck of that wry-faced loon that brought me this news. . . . Months!"

" Methinks your Highness puts too black a complexion on the matter," Norris smoothly presented. " Or that his Eminence is too restrained by his most usual caution. He thinketh the pope will not decide for thee? Now it may hap that he will be all the more eager to decide for thee and against his besieger, the emperor."

" Thou art a fool, Norris. The pope will not aid England unless England aid the pope, and we cannot take the field against the emperor. France would at once throw in with him. Why Spain hath Clement by the very beard: he is shut up in Saint Angelo and the Imperial troops are ravaging the city, despoiling monastery and convents, looting rich shrines and making sport with nuns. . . . 'Tis a scandal to Christendom. . . . Besides Clement is a craven. He quakes for his own miserable remnant of life. Our envoy had speech with one of the men shut in Saint Angelo with him, Cellini, that artificer who was at the court of France a while anon, and this Benvenuto Cellini saith that Clement is ever on his knees, in groveling petition. . . . He would not dare offend the emperor."

" The matter, your Highness, hath not gone so far as pope and emperor yet," Brereton asserted, " nor need it ever. England hath priests to attend to England's conscience at home. Let them decide."

" Hath not the pope ever final appeal, thou idiot?" Henry thundered.

Brereton only blinked stolidly. " So should it not be," he muttered.

THE FAVOR OF KINGS

" Sooth, it's a fact that the matter hath not yet reached pope or emperor," Norris declared. " Who knoweth that her Highness will appeal? She is as yet in ignorance —"

" Ignorance! " snorted the king. " I tell thee the devil is in league with all Spaniards and that I have very blabbers about my person! Wolsey hath learned that the very day after the first sitting of the court at Westminster, Mendoza, the Imperial Ambassador, was full informed. The man who told Mendoza was from the queen's suite. From where she got it I know not — but if I caught the gab-mouth —! The news will be half over Spain by now."

" And yet that doth not prove that the queen will appeal," Norris made hold to insist. " Doth not her Highness value your princely favor more than all else? And when she learneth thy will towards her will she not submit herself to thy pleasure? What good thing will she obtain by thwarting your Highness in this? She is a lady of devout mind and leaneth toward a quiet life. She knoweth that thy royal self is a very lion when roused. Will she not shrink from incurring thy anger? . . . Troth, the matter does not look as black to me as it is painted! "

Henry's humor changed with its characteristic abruptness. His scowl relaxed, his small eyes twinkled and he gave Norris a sudden buffet on the shoulder that sent him staggering

" Od's bodkins, man, but thou hast a head on thee after all! " he proclaimed. " I am more than half persuaded thou art right. England need not pull such a long face. . . . Come, one of you off to Mistress Boleyn and bring her this news with my greetings. I, myself, will shortly follow."

CHAPTER XII

A ROYAL TÊTE-À-TÊTE

THE words of Norris about Queen Catherine made a strong impression upon Henry. Accustomed to a slavish compliance in all his whims it was really impossible for him to conceive of protracted denial. It seemed to him that the simplest way to cut the knot was to wring from Catherine an agreement to the proceedings.

She was a religious woman. Very good! Then if he pressed the point that his conscience felt their union to be one of mortal sin there would be nothing for her and her religion to do but acquiesce. Delightfully simple and sensible!

Therefore, when three more weeks went by and Wolsey still balked at continuing proceedings in the present uncertainty of ecclesiastical conditions, Henry presented himself at Catherine's chambers requesting a private conversation.

In a flutter her ladies rose from their embroidery and retired into an inner chamber, and for the first time in over two years the husband and wife were alone together. Catherine made a quick step toward him, caught and raised his hand to her lips.

"Good, my lord, 'tis many a day since I have been so rejoiced," she told him. "I beg your Grace to be seated — this chair, here, hath been thy favorite of old."

Henry ignored that chair and took another. With a

rustle of her bulky draperies Catherine seated herself opposite. Abruptly he began.

"Thou canst not be ignorant of what brings me here."

"Nay, I have too long known thy kindness of heart to be ignorant of it," his wife returned with celerity. "I have known thou wouldst not leave me too long without thy favor."

This was not the opening that Henry desired and he cast about for another.

"I see," with a nod at the ebony rosary dangling at her girdle, "thou art ever at thy devotions."

"My prayers for your Grace's welfare rise continually," she replied, her fingers nervously entwining in the rosary.

He eyed her a moment contemplatively. His look was mild.

"I, too, have been oft at prayer of late," he continued, "and it hath come over me that my conscience is not clear toward Heaven. I have felt a strong conviction of sin."

For one incredible instant of sparkling hope she believed that he was in earnest and that he referred to Anne. Ah, that was over then! She had known it would not endure. . . . But coming so suddenly . . . after such reports . . .

"Your Grace!" she murmured in a trembling voice.

"And in this scruple I have not been alone. It may have come to your ears that my archbishops —"

Her hope was over. She saw in an instant the part he had come to play. She set her lips, the muscles of her mouth twitching.

"I know not to what scruple your Highness refers."

"Then is thy conscience duller than mine, for I have long felt that in our union there was mortal sin."

A ROYAL TÊTE-À-TÊTE

"*Long* felt —?" she uttered quiveringly.

He had come prepared for some reproaches and swept promptly over them. "Aye . . . thou and I have contracted no true wedlock."

"Thou sayest this to me, to me, my lord?" she interrupted harshly. He saw her beetling brows stiffen and contract and the sharp ridge between them deepen. He noticed with distaste how thick and fat her features were become and what hairs her moles carried. Truly, it was effrontery in the woman to consider herself now a mate for him!

"I have heard rumors of this — this thing," she went on riding over his beginnings of another speech, "but I would not insult your royal self by crediting them. . . . And now thou sayest this to me!" Her voice shook. It was evident that in spite of what preparation she had she was exceedingly upset. Recovering herself, she went on in a firmer tone, "I think your Highness cannot be in earnest."

"My good Catherine," said Henry, leaning forward, his eyes keenly on hers, "I am very much in earnest. . . . I am grieved to grieve thee, but we have come to a parting of our ways. We have offended against Heaven and Heaven hath sent such a sense of its displeasure upon my soul that I can no more endure it. And knowing thy religious mind, I cannot but feel that something of the kind hath come to thee in secret which thou hast hidden for fear of paining me. But let us now be open. Let us own our sin and separate —"

She made a choking sound in her throat. For an instant it was impossible for her to get a word out, then they came with a rush.

"For eighteen years," she gasped, "I have been loyal wife and true to your Highness and is there now talk of questioning my honor as a wife and my title as a queen? Truly, I think your Grace raves, you cannot mean this thing! Bethink yourself! I have been your wife these eighteen years. I have borne thy children —"

"But no sons have lived. Therein hath Heaven punished us," put in Henry calmly.

Her features stiffened. "I do think that my conscience lives so near Heaven as your Grace's and I find in that grief no punishment for sin, but only a trial for us to undergo. And it may indeed be a mercy in disguise. For where would your Highness find a fairer heir than in the Princess Mary? And indeed your Grace was not wont to look upon our old griefs in such cruel wise. It was not always so. Hast thou forgot those years — those years — ?"

The composed, slightly bored face of the man opposite her told her that he had indeed forgotten those years. All that had been husband in him had vanished utterly. It was incredible to her to think that she had once been his bride, that they had once mingled their tears over a dead son. He sat there, exuberant in youth and strength, wrapt in a world of his own, eager with its desires. She felt herself suddenly forlorn and old and helpless, unable to sway him in the slightest fashion. A terrible sob shook her; she forced it back but the hot tears filled her eyes and ran slowly down her cheeks. It seemed to Henry that she was weakening.

"You excite yourself — come, Catherine. Look at this thing in reason," he said persuasively. "It is not so terrible as thou thinkest. What to thee are the cares of court? Thy mind is on higher things; thou art for reflection and meditation and pious deeds. Choose thou some other residence and thou canst spend thy days as thou wilt — aye, and be happier so than now. Thou hast always been loving and careful of my conscience's welfare and it should not plague thee now to yield thy place when thou canst no longer minister to my happiness . . ." It seemed to him as he spoke that he was uttering only the most reasonable truths. "The years have come between us. Thou hast but six more than I but with thy Southern nature 'tis twice six. Thou hast come to the time when retirement is but natural —"

More and more her emotion had been mastering her during the course of this singular speech and at that last reference to her age she burst into wild sobbing, her face in her hands, her bulky body rocking piteously to and fro.

Henry got up and took a restless turn or two about the room. He spoke to her but his voice was lost in her sobs. When she seemed quieter he began again insistently on his arguments, pressing her to name a place of retirement, and her distress broke out afresh.

"No — no — no!" she iterated convulsively, shaking her head violently.

Beyond that, he presently decided, there was nothing to be got out of her. He caught up his cap, which he had tossed on a table over her open breviary, turned it about a moment or so, irresolutely in his hand, eyeing her bent head half pugnaciously, half discomfited.

Then he clapped on his cap and bade her farewell. "There is no need to take this so hard," he pointed out. "It is all being done for the best. Have no uneasiness. . . . And Catherine, look to it that thou keepest this to thyself — wilt thou not?"

Only her convulsive weeping answered that last bland request.

CHAPTER XIII

THE CARDINAL'S ENLIGHTENMENT

IT was the last day of September, 1527. The country was still green with the abundance of a lush summer but there was autumn in the chill air and the tug of the wind and the streamers of long gray cloud in the sky.

Cardinal Wolsey, fresh from the milder airs and brighter sun of France, found the crispness too penetrating and drew his mantle closer and wrapped his sables more tightly about his throat, as, at the head of a long train of retainers, he rode along the highway, on the last stage of his journey from Dover to London. His thoughts, that had been running backwards more often than forwards, dwelling in agreeable retrospect upon the pleasant honors shown him in France, forsook their musings, as he neared the town and concentrated upon the conditions that he might expect to find there.

Anne was still in favor. That he knew from his last messages from Henry, and it gave his reflections a tinge of uneasiness now as he recalled that in discussing Henry's prospective freedom with King Francis he had somewhat too assuredly hinted at a French alliance, mentioned in fact, the king's sister, the Duchess of Alençon. Francis had certainly understood that he was Henry's mouthpiece. . . . However, it would be months before the divorce could be obtained and by then Anne's star would be set. It was probably now on the wane.

THE ENLIGHTENMENT

The league with France against the emperor, which had been the object of Wolsey's journey, had been most successfully accomplished. Henry would be pleased, if he could spare enough thoughts from his divorce to be interested in anything else. It was unfortunate that Henry was still so set on that divorce as not to wait for the most expedient way. Certainly an appeal to the pope, still the prisoner of Charles, was not the best way! But Henry had decided that it was, and after Wolsey's departure had sent old Doctor Knight, his first secretary, to try to make his way to the pope. Wolsey had had an interview with Knight in Compiègne and mentally condemned him as totally unfit for the fine *finesse* of the affair but he had no authority to prevent the fellow's leaving on the king's errand. Well, perhaps it was for the best, as it would show Henry the folly of trying to take things in his own hands, Wolsey decided, dismissing the affair with a shrug. And by to-morrow Anne Boleyn might be enduring the sneers of some victorious rival.

The court was at Richmond and as the cardinal entered the great gate and looked across the gardens to the pleasant, ruddy façade of the palace, his three months absence made him survey the view with the critical eyes of a newcomer. His feeling for elegance, reënforced by his recent French standards, condemned the gardens as too small, too informal and confused, and the palace, he felt, lacked impressiveness and force. Some building was going on in the west wing and Wolsey's thoughts sped to the colleges that he was having erected at Ipswich and at Oxford and he wondered how long it would be before he would be able to go there and observe the progress that had been made. These colleges of his were the affections of his heart; he lavished on them the care, the dreams, the hopes, that other men put into their families. He had brought back with him some beautiful patterns of embroidery to serve as models for the copes his scholars were to wear at Cardinal's College at Oxford, and he had a vision of stately edifices, sun-flooded quadrangles, and richly-gowned students passing to and fro under Gothic doorways into splendid halls, and passing out, by and by, into the world, as finely mannered scholars, courteous of bearing and ripe of judgment . . . England had need of them.

He had halted now before the palace gates and his ushers were about him to assist in dismounting. The house servants, that the sound of his warning trumpets had brought streaming out from the palace, formed a respectful lane for his passage, and the Dukes of Suffolk and of Norfolk hastened to greet him. The cardinal stood in chat with them while he sent Cavendish, one of his ushers, to acquaint the king of his arrival, for it was always Henry's custom to receive him in a private room for their confidential talk.

Cavendish returned and stood on the outskirts of the little group.

" Well, sir ? " said the cardinal over his shoulder.

" The king, your Eminence," reported the usher, " is in the great hall."

" Alone ? " the cardinal wondered.

The usher stammered. He looked pitiably bewildered. " Nay — nay — there —"

" Didst give him my message ? " his master curtly demanded.

" Aye, your Eminence, that I did. He was sitting there in the hall with many about him. ' Where is the Lord Cardinal to come ? ' said I, and at that up spake Mistress Boleyn, who was sitting at the king's side,

THE ENLIGHTENMENT

' Where else,' quoth she, ' should the cardinal come but where the king is?' and although I waited, struck with wonder at her, the king but confirmed the lady and so — and — so —" the fellow's voluble report trailed off into uncertainty.

" As his Highness wills," returned Wolsey suavely. His air was one of indifferent acceptance, but from his single and piercing eye he gave his hapless usher a glance that made him blench.

Bowing to the dukes, he moved with a dignified and stately tread into the hall but beneath this simulacrum of proud composure the inner man experienced violent and savage emotion. That such a message should be sent to him! And sent by a woman, a dangling favorite, a little maid of honor he himself had thrown into the king's way! He felt a pricking and tingling sensation over his entire body. And then something curiously cold, something that was not anger nor humiliation, something that he never felt in all these long, superbly confident years, seemed to creep up and down his veins with chill suggestion. It was fear . . . only for a moment, but that moment made his throat dry. Then, in an instant, it was gone, and he knew an anger the deadlier for that weak surrender. " The little fool shall pay," he thought grimly, knowing how those two dukes, small, dark Norfolk and big, blond Suffolk, both outwardly his friends and inwardly his bitterest foes, must have enjoyed that moment.

But now, knowing that immediate submission was the only route to regain Henry's favor — intolerable that it was that he should have to regain that favor! — he played his difficult rôle with outward ease and courtesy.

But imperturbable as was his mask of expression, it was not hard for Anne to divine his thoughts and she

139

took a wayward pleasure in pricking him yet more with her malice.

She interrupted his first few sentences to crave Henry for a cushion at his hand; she twined one of her long dark curls over her thumb into a circle and then slipped it, ring-fashion over Henry's finger; she played a dozen youthful impertinent tricks, doubly harassing to the smoldering man before her from the doting pleasure that Henry took in her every word and act.

"However," as Wolsey reflected to himself that evening as he sat in his chamber warming before a genial fire the body that the physical exertions and the mental revolutions of the day had left exhausted, "passion is a very transient thing."

Aloud he said to the only creature on earth to whom he ever addressed a disinterestedly confidential word, "Mistress Boleyn hath more wit under the hair of hers than I credited." He spoke to Patch, his fool, a long, loose-limbed fellow, with a comic, wide-eared face, who sat now at his feet, looking up at him with eyes as idolatrous as a woman's. "In my absence she hath twined round him." He reflected that he himself, in the days when Catherine had been a consideration in her husband's life, had then taken advantage of her absence in the same way, to tighten his hold on Henry. "The wheel turns," he thought.

"Eh, master, she leads him by the beard," the jester said. "She hath a merry life."

After a time, Patch, watching, saw his master's face relax and a smile, infinitely sagacious, infinitely malicious, wrinkle the corners of his full mouth.

"But he tires — he tires, Patch," he murmured. "How many times have I seen —! She hath lasted long but he will cloy of her. And when he does — when he does — then will I —" The glare of his single eye completed that menace.

However, since the cloying process had not yet commenced, Wolsey hastened to reconcile himself at once with the reigning divinity and assure the lovers of his eagerness to serve their interests. He was admitted again to private audiences with the old time show of favor, but the old time empire over the king's mind was distinctly over.

Warned by that interview in the great hall, Wolsey looked at Anne with more attentive eyes. His easy, tolerant contempt for her as a light, capricious woman-creature, a clever tool to his hand, was gone; in its place stirred sharp dislike and a faint touch, if possible, of respect. She had mettle, she had will, she had insight — but she was untrained, inexpert, passionate. So he summed her in his mind while a faint foreboding grew in him as he realized how largely he had committed himself to France in favor of that alliance with Henry. However, he meant to strain every nerve to bring that alliance to pass; it was needful for his own credit and for his papal ambitions, and he concluded sagely that the best way to make his hopes a possibility was to make the divorce an impossibility until Anne's influence waned.

It would be easy enough, he reflected, to assure her of his anxiety to obtain this divorce for them, since a good deal of time must inevitably elapse and a good deal of water flow under the bridges before a decision could be obtained. And the time was his friend, not hers.

After that first saucy exhibition of her power, Anne was quite ready to be conciliated. She had, under all her antagonism to the man, a profound respect for the quality of mind that had so impressed itself on England.

THE FAVOR OF KINGS

In the months of his absence her eyes became somewhat open to the tangled difficulties of administration and her mounting sense of Henry's character discerned that however boldly his will-to-have might grasp at its desire he lacked the perspicacity and undeviating diplomacy to achieve his own ends.

" So we and my Lord Cardinal are thick as thieves? " laughed George Boleyn one morning as he played with her spaniel in her chamber, for now Anne, released from her long-nominal attendance on the queen, had a fine suite at her disposal next to her father and her aunt and uncle. " We smile, we cozen, we scribble *billet-doux* — eh, sister? "

Anne nodded with a droll grimace. She was at her writing table, a quill in her hand. " Boon companions," said she. " I am writing now to thank him for a dish of carps sent from his table. . . . And they were very good carps, too."

" The tale of his reception hath gone the rounds of London. There is a ballad made upon it."

" ' And where shall we see the king? ' quoth she,
'But in the great hall where the king and I be!'

. . . It must have been a shrewd shock to him."

" It was," the young lady affirmed serenely. " He turned the color of an over-cooked plum tart."

George laughed, tweaking the spaniel's ears, who retired growling only to rush again with little joyful barks on his tormentor. " And after that, think you, he will use his wits to crown you? "

" Need's must — there is no other way out for him. He is eager enough in our service, and troth, I think we need him. . . . And, by the way, brother, if he should say aught to you of Knight's instructions, the real instructions, I mean, look you that you confirm him that they were given to Knight *after* he had left Wolsey at Compiègne."

"Eh? So you've told Wolsey what were Knight's real errands?"

"Sith he's to help us he must know the facts." Anne signed her name to her note with a flourish.

"Yes, to that . . . but why," he lazily wondered, " do you tell him that Knight had those instructions *after* Compiègne? Why not the truth — that these were indeed his instructions all the time only that Henry wished them secret from all, and so Knight disguised them when he talked with the cardinal at Compiègne."

Anne's face darkened. She hesitated and then, "Henry's caution," she said shortly. "He does not want the cardinal to know that he was not frank with him at first."

"Is he the king's master?" George questioned with ironic eyebrows.

Anne herself had the same disdain for Henry's subterfuge with his minister but she did not choose to disparage her lover to her brother and made no answer. Some tangled worsteds gave her a pretense of occupation and she bent over them awhile, idly straightening the skeins while her brother continued his lazy romping with Robin on the casement seat. In the year the relation between those two had subtly changed. Anne had ceased to look up to her brother as a member of a privileged and envied class in the gay court world: she had become a member of that world herself and a much more important one, and so, although he retained, to be sure, the inestimable and permanent advantage of his sex, they met on terms whose slight inequality were in her favor. George was immensely proud of his sister and dominated by her more adventurous spirit.

" 'Tis well we told the cardinal when we did," owned Anne at last in a slightly troubled voice. " He thinketh we were ill-advised in what we sent Knight to ask, and so we have sent father's chaplain post haste to overtake the doctor before he can win to the pope."

" What, Barlow? Well, he's a sagacious dog. But ill-advised in what?"

" Wolsey thinks that we were asking too much. Knight was to seek a dispensation, you know, for Henry to marry again, without waiting for the other marriage to be set aside. The second marriage would itself be a setting of the first aside, and yet," Anne pointed out dubiously, " it appeareth as bigamy."

" What o' that? Hath not the king's own brother-in-law twice committed bigamy and been three times divorced? Sure his Holiness might allow the king himself one little leniency in the matter."

" Wolsey says that he would never consent — he would never consent as things be. He says that Christendom would cry against it — and in truth I am not so eager to rush into this bigamy thing myself, but I could not well deny — no, we must rid ourselves of the first marriage first. We *were* hasty and ill-advised. Barlow is to tell Knight to ask the pope to have the whole matter left to a legatine court in England and then to win from him a dispensation for Henry to remarry if the divorce is granted."

" But if it's granted, why needs he a dispensation?"

Anne bent her head over her work. " The dispensation is for him to marry one within the prohibited degrees of affinity," she answered in a lower voice. She felt the glow of a blush in her cheek and wished to hide it from her brother. Since Henry had given those instructions she could have no more doubts as to that past of his with her sister Mary which brought them within the outer degree of prohibited affinities.

George stared, and then loudly laughed, "Ho — it is a coil! He asks for a divorce from one woman because she is within the prohibited degrees on one count and in the same breath he asks marriage with another within those same degrees on another count. 'Tis a good jest — I vow, 'tis a good jest!"

He was so accustomed to Anne's gay humor that he was amazed when she lifted a scarlet face to flash an angry look at him.

"You may e'en keep your jests to yourself," she snapped.

He was ingenuously puzzled, then he stooped over the dog to hide a smile. "Jealous," he said knowingly to himself. He had no glimmering of the outraged delicacy that still struggled in the girl's soul against the callous corruption of the world about her.

"Why, that should be no hard matter," he observed. "Look you, Emmanuel of Portugal wed first Catherine's sister, Isabel, and next the sister Maria, and next Eleanor, the niece of his first two wives, all under dispensation, and under more dispensation Charles, the emperor, married his cousin." After a moment he said carelessly, "Hast thou heard aught from Wyatt?"

"Now how could I hear from Wyatt?"

"Methought he might have penned thee some verse from his prison cell. . . . Do you know what ransom the Imperial troops are asking for him?"

Anne shook her head.

"Three thousand ducats. Three — thousand — ducats! And his poor family has squeezed their estate near

dry to pay for their last liveries. Troth, but he was a
fool to go careering about Italy when the invaders were
looking for prisoners! . . . Do you think Henry will
make up the sum?"

She frowned, then meeting his mischievous glance, she
laughed outright.

"That he will not. He loveth Wyatt for himself —
but he loveth him not for me. He believeth that I never
cared for him, yet he believeth it not. He trusteth me
in all things, yet he trusteth me not in this."

"And small wonder. An I were a woman I would
ne'er be January when Wyatt woed."

"I have been January so oft it hath become a habit
to my mood," Anne vowed. "But of this ransom —"
She rose impulsively and unlocked a cupboard in the
room from which she drew the silver box that had contained Henry's early gift of a pendant. Unlocking that,
she emptied its stores of gold pieces in her hand and gave
them to her brother.

"Add this to the sum, but as coming from you," she
cautioned. "There is no need to ruffle Henry on this
but if the sum be not made up then will I ask him for
more, ruffle him or no. . . . Poor cousin. I fear he is
faring ill in some Italian cell."

"Mayhap a cat will bring him a pigeon each day, as
did that famous cat to his father when he was in the
Tower," George suggested lightly, pocketing the coins.
"No wonder the Wyatts do honor to the cat. . . . Oh,
Tom will win back to us safe enough, never fear. He
hath this likeness to a cat that he falleth ever on his
feet! . . . He will be mazed at all that hath happed in
England since he left."

"I may be queen e'er he returns," Anne declared with
a look that revealed the tingling eagerness within her.

THE ENLIGHTENMENT

George returned the look, struck to an expression of that amazement that she often aroused in him.

" God's truth! but you are monstrous sure of being queen, little sister! "

" Why so I am," she declared, her eyes glowing with high confidence, her lips edged with laughter, " so I am, an I do not have the smallpox — or lose a front tooth! "

CHAPTER XIV

THE PESTILENCE

THAT was in November and no result could be expected from Knight for two months or more. Those months seemed long to Henry's impatience and to Anne's, but after all when two people are in love — even when one of them is only in love with love — the time is not tedious. And they had every resource of amusement.

Anne found her position tremendously exciting. She lived in that excitement, slept, ate, talked, danced in it. Henry was her shadow. There was no pretense now of concealment; everyone knew she expected to be made queen, and whether the courtiers believed in her success or not, they treated her with the deference due to one already crowned. She breathed an atmosphere of adulation. Even her confessor, when she owned to him that she felt her bearing over-proud, declared to her that he had never found the grace of humility so sweetly flourishing in any female character. For the confessor, too, had his ambitions. He wanted to be the confessor of a queen.

Everywhere Anne carried herself with blithe assurance. From her air with Henry she might have been the queen and he the consort. Her gowns and jewels were paid for out of the privy purse. She moved, a bright, spectacular figure, across each day's stage of petty drama, gay, alluring, audaciously confident. At the

THE PESTILENCE

Christmas revels she and Henry whispered together that before the next Yule-tide she would be his wife and queen.

In January she suffered a sharp reversal of spirit. The documents which Knight had obtained from the pope, whom he had seen after his escape to Orvieto, were forwarded by special courier and were found not to have been worth the pain of writing, for by an ingeniously inserted word or two Clement had contrived to make the commission of no effect. Whatever the English court might decide, permission to appeal to the pope was still left, and the fact that Clement retained this right pointed that he intended to exercise it.

Balked and chagrined, Henry made life thoroughly unpleasant for those around him, and Anne wreaked part of her chagrin upon him by leaving court for Hever. It was a triumph for Wolsey, for it sustained his objections to Knight, and the cardinal made haste now to bestir himself in the royal cause, sending his own chief secretary, Dr. Stephen Gardiner, and Dr. Edward Foxe of the Royal Chapel, hurrying to the pope with twofold instructions. They were to urge him to give to Wolsey and to some other legate such authority as would enable them to pronounce a final judgment in the case, and they were to dispel any prejudices the pope might be entertaining against the lady whom the indiscreet Knight had allowed him to learn was Catherine's chosen successor.

Anne smiled when at Hever — the two emissaries stopped there to display their instructions — she read in the cardinal's fine hand of her, " excellent virtuous qualities, the purity of her life, her soberness, chasteness, meekness, humility, wisdom, descent right noble and high through regal blood, and education in all good and laudable qualities and manners! " Truly, a great change had come over the times since she had been cast aside as too trifling for the bride of an earl's son!

Great stress was laid, in Wolsey's appeal, upon the urgent need of England for a prince and heir. The need was great, for no woman had reigned upon its throne, and if the kingdom was left without a direct male heir it would be torn between rival claims. The Princess Mary's succession would be most certainly disputed by the Duke of Richmond, by James the Fifth of Scotland, son of Henry's eldest sister, Margaret, by the Greys, inheriting through his second sister, Mary, and by the Marquis of Exeter, grandson of Edward the Fourth; and there were others, too, who would press what claims they possessed if the chance offered. A formidable array of perils!

Anne, when she read this, was shrouded in far-reaching dreams. She felt the house of her hopes was built upon a rock for she had the strongest of political necessities to back her. It should be clear to the most blinded that it was better for an old woman to be displaced than for the kingdom to run red with the blood of another civil war.

The raw, wet February of 1528 kept England shivering a month long; a windy March swept over the land and it was April before word came from the two emissaries, and then a special messenger reported that after lengthy struggles with Clement they were obtaining all the king desired. Anne, in high feather, carried her head higher than ever and Henry's rollicking good humor made the court a carnival.

When Foxe himself arrived in May, bearing the commission from the pope which appointed the case to be tried in England before Cardinal Wolsey and Cardinal

THE PESTILENCE

Campeggio, Henry and Anne kept him with them the day long, making merry over the news, and when he left them, late at night, he was ordered to go at once to Durham Place in the Strand, where Wolsey was, and show him the commission.

"How now, Wolsey?" was Henry's cheery greeting, next morning. "Is it not well done?"

The cardinal hesitated and in that instant Henry's good-humored challenge changed to something of belligerency.

"Aye, your Grace, 'tis well — as far as it goes," the cardinal said slowly.

"As far as — what flaws do you pick? Could a man better advised toward England be chosen than this Cardinal Campeggio? And he is ordered to hasten here next month. Marry, if the pope does not intend to decide in my favor why permits he to have the case opened at all?"

"Perchance his Eminence hath found some reason for further delay," came from Anne Boleyn in dangerously silken tones.

Again there ran through the man before them that prickling current of dread. He felt how precarious, for all his care, was his footing among these pitfalls. How they turned on him at the first hint of denial! Was he to blame that Foxe had not brought a strong enough commission? True the permission to have the case tried by the legates in England was granted, but there was no definite, only an implicit, surrender of final authority to that court, and Wolsey's trained mind saw that, as in Knight's documents, though more subtly covered, the appeal to Rome was still open. But his caution, aroused by the revelation of their manner, closed his lips. He answered smoothly, "No more delay — nay. I am but so zealous in the cause that I would not leave room for

151

disaster to creep in. Let the legate come with all speed and let him bring with him a decretal to define the law as we are to judge it. Without some definition we have room for confusion of opinion."

"A decretal, by all means," the king cried in a voice of relief, yet tinged with impatience as if yielding a point to his minister's caprice. "Write to Gardiner for it and have him press ever for the legate's speedy departure."

"Your Grace's will be done," Wolsey assured him. "Truly now is my heart much lightened."

But as the cardinal rode back to Durham Place on his white mule, the trumpeters blaring before him and the silver crosses borne aloft, it was not a light heart that beat in his bosom. Care had tightened her clutch of him. He had not dared tell Henry the truth and brave his displeasure. Henry would choose to believe that Wolsey feigned dissatisfaction because he wished delay and Anne, in her heart, was suspicious of him, for all her surface amiability. What instant antagonism she had betrayed! And how set were the pair of them on their absurd union! The statesman sighed as he reflected that after all other men's passions were not the pliant things he had considered them. Why, in the devil's name, did Henry not tire of her? . . . Could no one devise a way —?

A few weeks later it appeared as if Providence itself had devised a way of disposing of the young lady. For the sweating sickness, as the epidemic was named from its manner of attack, which had been ravaging the congested portions of the city and routing the priests at all hours to hear the confessions of dying lips and administer last rites to those who had been in health that morning, grew more audacious, and reaching from quarter to quarter, invaded even the sanctity of the palace itself. And one of its first victims at Greenwich was a little maid in Anne's service.

The alarm spread quickly. Court was broken up. The king prepared to retire to Waltham and Anne made ready for Hever. The halls were filled with excited courtiers bustling about with orders for departure. Everything was tumult and hurry. Strong men, careless and lusty livers, who could beard an enemy with a jest, were thrown into quaking confusion by this unseen foe who stole among them like a thief in the night, laying its cold and compelling hand on rich and poor alike.

"The infection — a maid of Mistress Boleyn's hath fallen ill," was on all lips.

When that news reached the north wing of the palace a grim-visaged woman went down on her knees before her crucifix in silent prayer. Her lips moved but none of her attendants heard the words that rose to them; they had no need for their own hearts knew them.

Wolsey said no prayers — he kept those for public custom — but the hope that shot up in him beat in his heart like a caged bird against the bars. How pat Anne's death would fall!

A week later came the news that she was lying dangerously ill at Hever.

"But you may place your last ducat on Anne Boleyn," Henry Norris gayly announced to the circle of his intimates one July morning at Hunsdon, where the king had removed in his flight from the infection. "The lass hath a genius for victories — she hath snatched one now from the very circumstance that was to defeat her. . . . When she fell sick, Lord! what a Spanish crowing there was, and what a quaking in our camp!

12   153

Not only the girl was down, but her father, too. The hand of God, says that woman of the queen's, the one with the squint. Why, even if Anne died not of the sickness, 'twas said the separation from Henry would wean him from her, and that her looks would be damaged. Wean him from her? He is madder than ever — he is a caged lion. He sent Butts, his own physician post haste — a man we had not thought he would let from his own side in these times of danger, and kept a courier wearing out horses on the road between Hunsdon and Hever. Why, if the lady needed a device to fan that flame of his, she could have found none shrewder than this same sweating sickness."

" And in truth . . . it hath not damaged her looks? " big Brereton put in, with odd hesitancy.

" Damaged them ! " Norris laughed. " When I laid eyes on her, three days since, I vowed I had never found her so killing. A thought pale, perhaps, but a lovely paleness. Zounds, man, you need not look so relieved — 'tis not for you that those looks bloom ! " and Norris, still laughing, dealt Brereton a rollicking thrust in the ribs.

" Come, come — drive it not home," Bryan gayly interposed. " Have ye not seen how full of sighs this great ruffler hath grown ! He hath neglected his dress — he hath not worn a new rig for a fortnight — and goes about scribbling little verse full of eyes and cries, and heart and dart. Why, his case is as plain as the nose on his face ! "

" Which you will do well to leave alone or your own poor nob will be tweaked to some bigness," Brereton promised, joining in the mirth at his expense, but with a self-conscious note of constraint that brought Norris's eyes alertly to him.

THE PESTILENCE

"By the Book, Francis, now you speak on't, I think 'tis so," he cried, smacking his leg. "Our Brereton is changed. He hath not cozened a countess nor betrayed a country wench for a month long to my certain knowledge. Sure I thought 'twas the fear of the pestilence upon him bidding him clean his soul, but now I see with another pair of eyes."

"You will need another pair if you keep on, for I will black your present out of all seeing," grinned the big fellow, but his grin was stiff. "This is no kind of talk for king's men."

"Sure we'd all be burnt for sacrilege for mentioning you in the same breath with the lady," Bryan declared.

"It is very good talk for king's men," Norris insisted. "If the pope prove obdurate the king may have his uses for thee . . . so complaisant a husband as thou wouldst be —" He dodged the gauntlet that Brereton sent hurling at him.

"You're a crow's nest of foul-tongued profligates," proclaimed the victim of their jests, "and I will have no more of you," and with a vast assumption of indifference he took himself off.

"Seek out George — doubtless in his society you will find some family flavor of the divinity!" Bryan roared after him.

"I'll keep the gloves for the three shillings you owe me on that cock fight," Norris used his full lungs to add.

Then, still chuckling, he turned to Bryan, "By Heaven, there is something in it — think you not? The man was touched!"

"Naught likelier," Bryan carelessly assented. "But he is a wise fellow — he is not like to beard his sovereign,

155

as did Wyatt, for the lady's favor. Have you heard more news of Wyatt?"

"None but the same. He escaped before his ransom was paid, so he hath saved his friends three thousand ducats, for which God be praised! He is probably making the best way he can out of that unlucky Italy."

CHAPTER XV

IN HEVER CASTLE

THE sound of a horn rang through the clear country air, and Anne, flying to the casement, glimpsed on the top of Hever Hill, a gallant figure on horseback against the summer sky. A moment he remained poised there, then dashed down the hillside and entered the cover of the adjoining woods. Anne lingered at the casement till she saw a little group of outridden retainers appear in turn upon the hilltop, and then she darted to her mirror in a pell-mell of excitement. She had not seen Henry since her illness, for in spite of his lover's anxiety, his terror of sickness had kept him away, and she had not expected him for a full ten days yet. Now in another minute he would be knocking at the gates!

" I look a fright — my hair is all undone," she told herself in dismay, struggling out of her brown dress into one of a soft rose-color. " Bet — Bet — where art thou? Come here,— no, run and tell my father that the king is come — I saw him from the casement. Bid him receive him below — I will be down. No, I will not be down — I will be in the library. Let him have his drinks ere he come up . . . that will give me the more time. I am a fright. . . . And send me Mary Wyatt to do this gown — Why must the fashion be that a woman must needs be an eel to hook her dress? . . . I am as nervous as a witch before her stake," she laughed to

157

herself as her hands shook in brushing back the heavy hair that swept over her shoulders. "Will he think me changed? . . . It seemeth a year since we have met."

A thunderous knocking at the gates put an end to her soliloquy. Laying down her hand glass with a little *moue* at the white face she saw therein, she slipped out from her room and down the passageway to the great library. It was a fine room, paneled in dark, rich oak. A small musicians' gallery ran across one end; a fireplace, overhung by a deer's head with branching horns, was at the other. Along the sides were some grim-faced portraits, mostly of Anne's own mother's family, the Howards, and a tapestry or two, while the books and manuscripts that gave the room its name were ranged in shelves and cupboards along the walls. Towards the east two double casements, their leaded panes medallioned with armorial bearings, filled the library with soft summer light. Anne sat down on the seat before one of them, listening to the uproar of voices before — it sounded like an uproar in the stillness of the old castle — then she heard the quick sound of feet taking the stairs three steps at a time. Henry had not lingered over his greetings and his drink.

She rose to meet him, her hands half stretched out, and the next instant he had dashed like a whirlwind into the room and caught her to his breast.

"Anne — little Anne!" he whispered huskily. "Little Sweeting — my pretty rose. . . . It hath been a year —" He released her only to have her face where he might cover it with kisses. Then he held her off to gaze at her and in the gazing realized again the menace of her illness. She was so slight, so fragile! It seemed as if a breath could blow her away. Her dark eyes

158

looked tremendous in her thin face. He caught her to
him again with a sigh that was half a groan.

" If you had died — before you were mine ! " he cried.

" When I am yours you will then be ready to part with
me ? " the girl gave quickly back, with an attempt to
release herself.

" Nay — you are too keen —" he kissed her lips to
silence. She felt his tremble on hers and realized afresh
with a sense of happy power the strength of his passion
for her. She pressed her cheek against his great arm
with a thrill of proud possession. Her big Henry ! Her
king and lover !

He drew her to the casement, and with his arm about
her and her head against his shoulder, they sat in that
indescribable content, that oblivion of time and the world,
that is peculiar to the state of lovers.

Through the open casement floated the warm breath
of July, rich with unthrifty sweets ; the birds from the
forest sang shrilly clear. The castle was very still. The
bark of a dog and his splashings in the moat, and the
hollow stamp of a horse in the stables, sounded remote
and far away. Idly they rested there, now regarding
each other, now the square of sky and wood that the
casement framed. Their talk was desultory. Now he
told her of the progress he was making with his book,
which he was writing in favor of the divorce, now he
enumerated the remedies and precautions he had taken
against the infection — eventually abating,— but mostly
the talk ran of his love for her and of the pain her
absence had been.

" You will always love me so ? " Anne murmured —
'twas perhaps the dozenth time — and for the dozenth
time her lover answered, his kiss on her lips, " Till death
take all loving from me."

This time she did not content herself with the vow.

"Nay," she persisted, "will you always look on me with such kind eyes? Shall I be worth the trouble and vexation you incur in making me your queen? . . . 'Tis a very high estate to which you are raising me. I grow dizzy when even my thoughts reach it. At times I think it cannot really be. . . . Will you ne'er regret — ne'er look back — ne'er wish you had chosen to crown a more regal brow than poor Anne Boleyn's?"

He kissed the brow. "There is none more regal . . . none more fair."

"But when I am no longer fair?" In her eyes rested a sudden shadow — a thought of Catherine's lot — but only as fleetly and lightly as a cloud shadow on a brook. He had never loved Catherine! He had sworn it to her.

"Thou wilt always be fair."

"So I think myself," she owned with her soft laugh, "for I cannot think of myself — or of thyself — as ever old and gray. Just as those who sat in this room before us, I dare say, could never think of themselves as growing old and going forth. Poor souls! . . . But some day — some day, even I — And thou wilt never love anyone else?"

"How can I, when I have given all to you?"

"Nay, but bethink thee, Henry, will you ever and forever love me so? I have been wondering much since I have been ill and alone. Speak me true, for if thou wilt change, if thou art not sure, then were it better to end all now. . . . We will not try to live our dream."

"While I have breath left to kiss thee, darling, God, He knoweth how I shall cherish thee. Never a lady was loved as thou art, Anne. . . . Why, Sweet, what aileth thee to question so coldly?"

"I know not — I never was so happy before, and yet

IN HEVER CASTLE

I fear I know not what. How will this end? . . . They will all hate me when you make me queen."

" My subjects love where I love."

" Ah, they will be jealous of me, under all their flattery to me, and many hands will reach up to pull me down. And if I lose thy love — women have warned me that thou art a fickle lover, my king! "

" I have never loved thee before."

She lifted her lips for him to kiss, in marvelous content.

Presently, " How little we know," she murmured, her eyes roving idly about the great hall, already filling with the shadows of the declining day, " How little I dreamed, as I roamed a child about this place, that here I should some day sit with my king! "

" God had his destiny for thee," said Henry piously.

Her upturning eyes found no answering twinkle in his own. It was one of those moments that tickled her with his lack of humor. . . . She wondered, half quizzical, half mutinous, whether God had had His destiny for her sister Mary also, and concluded that her own individual wits had more to do with the assurance of her prospects than Providence.

Aloud she acquiesced, in vast gravity, " Sure He works wonders," and then, with her irrepressible laugh, " but oh, that it would please Him to perform with greater speed."

Henry stirred restively.

" If He would but incline the pope now to see His hand in this, and the queen to bow to Heaven's will! "

" The devil's in the woman to thwart me thus," Henry growled under his breath.

" If she would but submit — as she makes such outward protestation of doing! — to your Grace's will for her,

and retire, as Queen Dowager, to some estate. Then
she could live her life and you yours — and how happy
we could be!"

A genuine sense of grievance sharpened Anne's tone.
She felt that Catherine's attitude was unreasonable. The
woman had lived the best part of her life; now let her
bow to unchangeable conditions, make her bargain with
circumstances and get the most out of her remaining
years. She professed to love retirement and prayer.
Very good, let her retire and pray! . . . England's throne
had never been hers by right — she had been lucky to
be allowed on it so long.

"She can delay — she cannot stop me," Henry muttered. His scowl was vicious.

To banish the cloud she had raised, "How little I
dreamed," Anne recurred, "when you found me gathering flowers — two years ago — that when I gave thee that
rose —"

"Thou wouldst be giving thy heart? . . . When did
you first begin to love me, darling?"

She paused a moment, honestly wondering. She was
conscious of a much deeper tenderness for him now than
she had ever known. When had the change come about?
. . . Her woman's instinct to give pleasure led to a sweet
mendacity.

"That instant, I think, though I knew it not. . . . I
remember, when I watched thee ride away, I thought —"

"What didst thou think —?" as she paused.

She recalled too well, and an ironic smile hovered on
the curled edges of her lips. How far away Percy
seemed now!

"I thought — I wished I had known thee before," she
replied with misleading truth.

"Aye, and I, also. I had speech with Wolsey when

IN HEVER CASTLE

I rode back, and I do remember I told him I had met with a maid worth a crown." Henry paused over the significance of it.

" What said Wolsey? "

" He said — well, he judged it enough if I found you worthy of my love."

" Insooth! . . . And was it at thy will the cardinal requested the queen to recall me? "

" Nay," slipped from Henry before his second thought that a yes would be more lover-like, could overtake it. Anxious ever for the best impression, he amended, " Not at my spoken command, that is. But I let fall such hints —"

She smiled a dutiful gratitude, while she disbelieved. His nay had been honest, she divined; he had admired and forgotten, while Wolsey had remembered and flung her again in the king's path. Clearer than ever she understood the part that pitiless maker of destinies had meant her to play. Well, she had paid him out for that!

" But when I saw thee at the dance," said Henry, and his eyes kindled at the memory, " then, Sweet, I felt I must have thee for my own or ne'er know happiness again. 'Tis beauty's flower, I thought, and shall one pluck this save the king? . . . Oh, I loved thee, Anne, I loved thee from that moment. I knew not then how cruel you could be," he added in plaintive chiding.

" An you call virtue cruel! " she returned, with that little set of the lips he knew so well.

" Is it not cruel when I perish from it? "

She leaned away from his tightening embrace, knowing how swiftly her lover's deference might slip back into demand if her spirit failed.

> Virtue to choose,
> Vice to refuse,

she sang mischievously to him from that song of his own to which he had first seen her dance.

"I but follow your grace's counsel!"

The afternoon wore on. The west was stained with saffron and rose before Henry had forced himself to take leave of that slender girl whose laughing eyes and petulant lips were more than all his world to him. At last he tore himself away and Anne lingered on the casement seat watching for that final glimpse of his figure on Hever Hill. She saw him turn and blow his horn, and then he galloped on out of sight with the little group of riders at his heels.

Paler and paler grew the sunset; dimmer and dimmer the shadowy forest. A lilac veil seemed drawn over the world. The bird songs had sunk to quiet; only here and there from the leafage came a last call to the nest. A hoarse croaking of frogs boomed out from the moat; from a pool in the forest came a faint answer softened by distance to harmony.

Anne lay dreaming at the window her rare, vivid day dreams. Across her mind swept a procession of brilliant pictures. . . . One insistently recurred — a great hall, the hall of Westminster, filled with applauding multitudes, echoing with music's note . . . and before all that multitude, up the steps to the throne, led by a kingly hand, mounted Anne Boleyn in regal robes. . . . They would be gold and white, she decided joyously — or else scarlet tissue . . . with ermine fur and gems. She saw other gatherings, masks, revels, receptions for ambassadors and foreign kings who would bow before her as she received them with her husband. . . . She saw herself dancing triumphant down the years — till sedater days brought their dignity upon her and she stood, a charming matron, at the marriage of her son, the heir of England, to some princess of France — her son, the heir of England, the king to be!

"Art here, Anne?" the voice of her stepmother broke in on her dreaming.

"Here, mother . . . just wondering what robes I shall wear at my coronation. White and gold or scarlet, think you?"

"I think thou art a random talking maid." The stepmother endeavored to infuse some severity into her tone. She was secretly uneasy at Anne's aspirations, and divided between a nervous apprehension and a flattering delight. It was difficult for her to become accustomed to such sudden accession to greatness in her wayward stepdaughter.

"Coronation, indeed!" she brought out, entering the room and closing the door carefully behind her, her big bunch of keys clattering at her girdle, "your father would smoke to hear you crying it out thus. . . . Tell me in truth, Anne, is your mind serious in all this? Do you fully expect to be queen in your mistress's stead?"

"My mistress!" Anne curled her lips mockingly. "I expect to be hers, if the pope will but ease Henry of that yoke. And 'twill not be long now."

The Countess of Rochford stood looking with troubled, searching eyes, as if to read this baffling spirit to its depths. Then, with a sigh, she sank on the window seat beside the girl.

"You were ever a froward girl — it may be," she owned, "but I could not believe such things would come to pass if I had not the king's presence here under my own eyes and all your goings on in London back of it. The little thing I washed and tended when your own good mother was alive — how she doted on you, poor

THE FAVOR OF KINGS

lady! She would be amazed to see this day — to think
of you to be queen — to wear a crown — to sit on a
throne! . . . Nay, nay, that can never be!" the good
woman broke off to declare, grown quite positive of it as
her mind had conjured up that concrete picture of
crowned royalty on its pinnacle. "It can never be.
Queenship is not for a simple maid. 'Tis a dangerous
path you are in, as full of snares as a wood of brambles.
Thou wast ever a shrewd lass — be warned while there
is yet time and let it all go by."

Anne laughed shortly. "What shall I then do,
mother? Go back as maid to Catherine? Sit at the
Spaniard's feet?"

The stepmother sighed, with a covert turn of her
eyes on Anne. At last she brought out, "Hearest thou
naught from Henry Percy?"

"Less than naught."

"Yet — dost thou not think he would devise some
means to aid thee?"

"Aye, Percy is full of brave devisings!" Again Anne
laughed. "Why hast thou not heard that he is already
married to Mary Talbot? His father saw to that before
he died and left him earl."

The elder woman sighed again, turning the situation
over in her mind.

"Thou dost not seem to believe that I am to be queen,
mother?"

The countess shook her head. "It may be — I know
not of such things — but I fear —"

"You fear —?"

"No good from it all, dearie."

"Nay, if I am crowned what ill can there be? But
tell me, tell me true, what dost my father think in this
matter?"

IN HEVER CASTLE

"You should know; you have his counsels more than
I."

"I know his counsels — I ask what you guess his mind
to be in the matter."

"His mind is a very secret thing," said the wife simply.
"But I know he thinks you do attempt too much, and
that you had best take what is in your grasp."

"He will play none but the safe game," the daughter
murmured, "but I would grasp at the sun, though it
burned."

"Aye," assented Lady Boleyn, and then irrelevantly,
"A pity Wyatt was so young wed."

Anne arched her brows in raillery. "Still at that,
mother? Why, so I think myself, but I have no heart
to wish his poor lady any ill. She has a lonely lot, but
if she would marry a boy of seventeen —"

"He was but a foolish lad, and the parents made the
match. I am sorry for Wyatt. There is better stuff
in him than in that other cousin of thine, that rake,
Bryan. Is he still abroad?"

"He hath not yet gone. Oh, you mean Wyatt. I
thought you still spoke of Bryan, for the king purposes
to send him as envoy to meet the coming legate, Campeggio. Yes, Wyatt is still abroad."

"Hast thou heard from him?"

"No, and to what purpose an I did? Nay, nay, mother,
there may be husbands enough at court, but none for
me — Henry would have their heads for it! And I cannot go back now, I will not, when all eyes have been
drawn to me. Shall I fall back now and bear the jeers
and laughter, aye, and the ill names they call me? There
is no other way for me now — I must go on, I must win,
or I shall die shamed!"

Then, as if regretting the urgency her speech betrayed,

she added with assumed lightness, " Master Tyndall's Scriptures prophesy ill to him that layeth his hand to the plough and taketh it back."

" Anne — Anne — thou hast not read the work of that accursed heretic ! " Lady Boleyn crossed herself in alarm. " They say the devil opens his veins for black blood for him to write with ! "

" Vastly obliging of him," the girl scoffed. " But the Bible that I saw, mother, was in good German ink." Then to dispell the anxious alarm she saw gathering on the older woman's countenance, " Nay, look not so ill. 'Tis a good book, the story of our Lord and Saviour. There is no evil in it."

" But 'tis forbidden to be read. The Church hath laid its holy ban on it. There were two men burnt on All Saints for such reading — and Master Holworthy of our village was brought before the Council and heavily fined because of the accusation that he had sheltered it."

" How soon, think you, Henry will pile up the fagots for me ? "

Her stepmother shuddered. " Talk not on't, my flesh pricks as if someone stepped across my grave. Bethink you of your soul, girl. These be matters for priests to decide."

" Why be they ? What is a priest to tell me what I must and what I must not read ? A priest is but petti-coated man whom you would not trust with your kitchen wench. Have I not a soul as clean and a brain as shrewd as a priest ? Can I not see with as good eyes, think with as keen wits, feel with as fine sensibilities ? As for that, am I not as good as a bishop myself — right reverend female bishop of the Catholic Church, for Wolsey hath made over the revenues of Durham to me."

" But priests have taken holy orders —"

"Holy orders given of men. Thou art not still so simple down in the country as to believe a man's soul is white because his head is shaven? I tell thee priests are man-made things who stand between us and heaven to collect toll for pointing us on our way. There are no words of priests in that New Testament — I tell thee, it is a good book, the story of our Lord's birth and passion and the salvation that He left for our souls. Why should I be forbidden to read that?"

"Anne — Anne —"

But Lady Boleyn's shocked protests were powerless to check the girl's vivid earnestness. She leaned forward, her eyes aglow with a steady light her mother had never seen burn there.

"It is the vilest wrong," she said passionately, "to keep that book from the people — a book that would do their hearts more honest good than all the chanted masses — though a mass is a lovely thing. But I will tell thee something else, mother, the wherefore that I think the priests do deny this book, there is no word of them nor of the pope himself in it. That came later, in the works of the Holy Fathers, but it is in my mind that there are other ways to heaven than with Saint Peter's keys. The Lord, when he was on earth, dealt with the people himself, and through no triple-crowned mediators. 'Tis a shrewd thing, the Papacy, and 'tis shrewd for it to forbid any book that would make a man think for himself and not through any priest's shaved head."

"Ah, heavens, what talk! Could the priests but hear you now, you would be excommunicated!"

"That is what my good aunt, Lady Norfolk, says I will be anyway if I keep on with this marriage. In her heart she is against me and a Queen Catherine woman. Eh, I will sit above her at the board yet!" Anne prophesied, then returned to her attack. "Why, mother, doth not the pope read the Scriptures? Are they not holy? Why then are they evil for me? I —"

"But if it is known that you read them —"

"It is known," Anne brought triumphantly out. "Sure, 'tis known to the cardinal himself, and much good did it do him! I gave my book to one of my ladies, Mistress Gaynesford, to read, and she paid so much heed to it that morning and so little to Zouch, that was her sweetheart, that he snatched the book from her in play and carried it off. Then at mass, being dull, he opened it and began to read and became so lost to all around him that he was forgetting to go out when mass was done, and a priest came softly up and snatched the book away. And to clear himself the frightened fellow told from where he had it, and the priest ran post haste to the cardinal, and the cardinal, God wot, gave thanks and was in a heaven of anticipation. He meant to denounce me to Henry, to slyly insinuate concerning my secret Lutheran tendencies — but I was before him!" Anne laughed maliciously. "As soon as I heard from Zouch what had befell, I sent for Henry, and with great indignation related how my book had been taken away, a book, I told him, that was worthy of the highest, and on which I wanted his princely opinion, and I denounced the cardinal for hiding such a rare book from his king. And Henry sent to the cardinal and the book came back and his Eminence's most humble apologies for the frowardness of the priest. Ah, well do I read that cardinal. He would have undone me there, but I was too quick for him. I let him have no hand in the making up of Henry's mind!"

"But, Anne — Anne —!" Lady Boleyn could only protest, "what risks you run — and all for reading a book!

IN HEVER CASTLE

Sure, if that matter had been reported differently to his Highness, it might have been made to cost you his favor, I fear."

" And wasn't that just what you were advising me to lose, a minute agone? " Anne thrust home.

" But not with danger —"

" Nay, mother, never fear for me. I can take care of Anne Boleyn. And as for this burning men for reading of our Saviour, why it is an accursed and evil thing. I saw a man burnt once — I was riding and came suddenly upon the place. He was old and white-haired and feeble, but he had such spirit . . . such spirit. He cried to his God in such a strong voice — even with the flames licking his lips and his cheeks falling in ash. . . . Oh, it was terrible! I could not sleep nights! And his wife and children, poor souls, stood sobbing there — Ah, if *I* could not sleep, what nights they must have had. *What nights!"* Anne's voice broke suddenly. The tears overran her eyes. She turned her head sharply and looked out the window to hide them from her stepmother.

" There, there," that good woman said soothingly, " you are weak yet from your fever. You see it is a book that does no good if it brings such things to pass. . . ." And then hastily she sought a safer topic.

" Didst say that Francis Bryan is to be sent to Europe? "

" Aye," said Anne, her voice still shaky, " he is to meet Campeggio, the Italian legate, in France. 'Tis for a courtesy and also to hurry him along. I doubt not the pope hath given him orders to linger all he may by the wayside, but Bryan will change all that. . . . Ah, if only —"

She broke off. She did not wish even her mother to see into the depths of her anxious impatience.

THE FAVOR OF KINGS

The countess sat silent, absently smoothing a tapestry cushion. Presently she murmured, "Your father says she will never accept an English judgment. She will appeal to Rome."

"The pope hath promised to let Wolsey and Campeggio decide."

This time it was the mother who had her fling at Rome. "Popes and foxes have ever two holes to a burrow," she quoted. "Yet she may appeal but in vain. Charles may not press her cause, for he has little to gain from it. She is no young maid. Let me think — she must be forty-three now. 'Tis hard on a woman that age to have her place and name taken from her," she sighed half to herself.

Anne flashed a resentful look at her through the dusk about them.

"Think you she is Henry's lawful wife?"

"La, how should I tell? I heard many murmur when he married her, but then he had a dispensation — and after so many years of being taken as lawful — Eh, but I think she did wrong to wed him in the first place, and now see what hath come upon her for it! Heaven hath punished her hard. If she had only had a son, though. . . . I mind how anxious they were to have one, and then that first child — was it a girl or a boy, now? A boy, I think — was born dead. Few enough knew of that mishap at the time, and 'twas hustled away like a pauper's brat for fear folks would say that it was the judgment of Heaven upon them. The outcry, your father says, was great at court against the marriage, though 'twas ever popular with the people. The story of the child got out, though. They had written their hopes to the King of Spain, or rather that Friar Diego, the queen's confessor, had. Catherine was under his thumb, and Henry was so easy-going and complaisant that either he did not or he would not see. However, at last he —"

"Yes, I know," cut in Anne. "He drove him out. But what about the king of Spain?"

"'Twas some time before the poor lady had the heart to write her father of the disappointment. Everything in England was hushed and secret; no man durst speak of it, and few indeed knew aught for a fact. Catherine was up and about, at table and tournament, though she leaned on her chair and looked like very death. . . . And 'twas the same over again with the second child, only more mystery and play acting and pretense. The poor wee corpse was flung in the river at night, and if ever a word of God was spoken over it was spoken by that black-hearted priest Diego, who was closer to the queen than her woman, being a torch of scandal for the court and a pit for her own feet."

Anne rushed in amid this tangling of figures.

"How many children were there in all?"

"Am I not telling you? One and two dead, and then a live boy — bells ringing and bonfires in the streets and priests and acolytes marching with pyx and cross and singing matins to all the people: 'A prince is born this day! A prince has come into the world! Peace on earth, good will to men!'"

Anne was stirred with a quick thrill. "So will they sing for my son," her heart whispered to itself.

"I mind the words well. 'Twas before I was married to your father and Betsy Trimble and I stood out in the village street to see them pass —"

"How long did it live?"

"Was I not telling you? How can a body talk, Anne, when you are clipping your questions at 'em? You were the same as a young one when I was for telling you anything. . . . How long did it live? Oh, a matter of weeks. 'Twas the New Year it was born — the New Year 1511, since you count time from the New Year, though I like better myself the old way of reckoning from our Lady's Day. But this is an age that is for new-fangled things. Well, it was born the New Year and gone in February. They had not two months' comfort of it — after the king had gone on a pilgrimage and all! He went to Our Lady of the Gray Friars at Walsingham, a shrine second only to Saint Thomas of Canterbury, and the better for this cause as Our Lady was a guardian of young mothers. At Barsham he halted and took off his boots and hose and walked barefoot to Walsingham, but all to no good, dearie. The punishment was on them and in a few weeks the young thing died. And the next was only born to die, and the next was born dead — or was it the other way about? — and everyone at court murmuring that England was without an heir, and wondering when the king would put away that woman and take a lawful wife."

"What made him keep her?"

"Oh, 'tis not so easy putting away queens, though your foolish head may now think so. And Catherine was not then so ill to look upon, a big, broad, red-haired woman. They say she is as gray as a rat now, but you can scarce see her hair under that cap. Then, too, Henry has the Tudor stubbornness — he will not own that he has done ill unless there is something he desires to gain by that owning. . . . And I dare say they continued to have hopes — and then the Princess Mary was born and lived and that was something!"

"Too much!" Anne frowned sharply. The day that she had left Greenwich she had passed the Princess Mary in the halls, and the child, darting on her a look of hate from her wise, unchildlike eyes, had cried out in the hearing of all, " Good riddance — six-fingered scum! "

" Eh? Well, that was something, as I said, but not enough to show that Heaven's curse was lifted."

" Perchance I am the fulfillment of that curse," Anne mocked, still frowning.

Lady Boleyn sighed in unconscious sympathy. " A sharp fulfillment to the poor lady."

" Why, mother, do you pity her? You have called her hard names in my hearing as a child, and wished her down from a throne where she brought only disaster."

" Aye — I know, but —" the older woman hesitated. The age in her was in unconscious league with the age in Catherine against this ascending youth. Then she apologized for her weakness. " Truth she may have no right thereon, but Henry took her for wife and she hath been there so long —"

" A long enough wrong makes a right then? You waste your pity for the Spaniard gives none in return. She had no heart for my need."

" What need? . . . When did she refuse thee? "

" Oh, a long time since." Anne was half repentant of having spoken, but her bitterness drove her on. " I never told thee, but when the cardinal stood between me and Henry Percy, I asked of the queen — Oh, why should I fence? I begged on my knees before them all to have her help me. . . . She said she had other duties than to make me the Countess of Northumberland. It was a pretty jest and pleased her ladies well. . . . I shall remind her of that jest some day — it were a pity to let so excellent an answer be forgotten." There was an edge under the silk of Anne's soft voice that made her stepmother look at her with a feeling in which there was something like to fear. She felt as if the young creature beside her with the dangerously glowing eyes and twitching nostrils was another than the girl she had known, a strange, ardent creature, imperious, unfathomable, capable of unforeseen caprice, mating herself to high destinies. She felt a passing thrill of wonder at her . . . the next instant this alien vision of her stepdaughter was swept away, and she saw her as her own dear girl smarting with the memory of her wrongs and her hand went out to her in involuntary sympathy and love.

"She is a hard woman — she would have done well to make thee Countess of Northumberland!" she cried, every vestige of sympathy for Catherine swept away by her memory of Anne's grief.

Anne gave her hand a warm, quick squeeze, then rose with an unsteady little laugh.

"'Tis dark as midnight — I have talked myself aweary. . . . Countess of Northumberland?" she repeated, her voice grown light and exultant. "Nay, Queen of England is a vastly better title!"

CHAPTER XVI

THE QUEEN SPEAKS

I'N August wrote the French Ambassador, Du Bellai, to his king: " Mademoiselle has at last returned to court and I believe the king to be so infatuated with her that God alone could abate his madness."

Henry's passion was the theme and wonder of the court. Anne was lodged in a splendid suite next to his, and not a courtier that vied for royal favor but came to Anne's rooms daily, as in the old, the very old days, other courtiers had come to the queen's. She was the cynosure of eyes, the theme of tongues, and the hope, the eager, urgent hope of her kinsfolk.

The younger courtiers, her brother's set, the idle, jolly rufflers of fashion, spending their all upon their backs, who roistered about Henry night and day, were hand in glove for her, lauding her to the skies, reveling in the merriment she brought, captivated in stout earnest by her charm. In the older set, those who were eager for the cardinal's overthrow were hopeful of bringing it about through Anne and so leagued themselves with Norfolk, her uncle, and Rochford, her father. There were others, like Sir Thomas More, that stood aloof from the participants, the outwardly courteous, inexpressive onlookers, and still others, who were, either in secret or in public, adherents of Catherine and the interests she represented, but these last were few in number and had no place in the riotous merrymaking that surrounded the person of the king.

Anne had been hitherto most tantalizing in absenting herself from court, in caprices that were intuitive wisdom, but it had been no part of her design to be away at the arrival of the legate, Campeggio, and when Wolsey urged the disadvantageousness of her presence at that time and Henry, for once, held with him, " she smoked," as Carewe succinctly reported, and announced in dudgeon that as she had been sent to Hever, at Hever she would remain, and maintained an attitude of petulant resentment that Henry was at some trouble to mollify by frequent messages and expensive presents.

In September of that year 1528 he was able to write her: " The legate, which we most desire, arrived at Paris on Sunday last, and I trust next Monday to hear of his arrival at Calais; then I trust awhile after to enjoy that which I have so long longed for, to God's pleasure and both our comfort.

" No more to you at present, mine own darling, for lack of time, but that I would you were in my arms and I in yours, for I think it long since I kissed you."

The time proved longer than Henry's ardor desired, for it was weeks before the ailing and gouty Italian arrived in London.

He had brought with him the commission which entrusted the decision of the annulment to himself and to Wolsey, and which promised that the pope would not revoke those powers, and he had also brought that for which Wolsey had pressed, a decretal defining the law in the case in a manner so favorable to the king that the matter appeared judged beforehand. But this decretal had been wrung from the pope and now that another turn of his variable fortunes placed him more than ever at the mercy of the emperor and the emperor was proving generous, he was less inclined to commit himself and he had sent message after message to Campeggio, forbidding him to show the document to any save the king and Wolsey, or to reveal its contents. Moreover, he was to dissuade the king, if possible, or persuade the queen to enter a convent; failing this, to delay the opening of the trial.

Poor Campeggio! After two private audiences with the king, wherein Henry had plied him for continuous hours with all the arguments that his natural shrewdness and his knowledge of law and theology had arrayed, the luckless legate wrote the pope that, " The king is better versed in the matter than a great theologian or jurist, and if an angel descended from heaven he would be unable to convince him of the validity of the marriage."

Henry having proved unyielding, the other alternative was the queen. Could she be induced to enter the life of religion?

She could and would, Henry opined, delighted at Campeggio's aid in the matter, and for inducement he piled concession on concession. The title of Queen Dowager would be given her, and all her dowry and belongings; the Princess Mary — failing a legitimate male heir — would be heiress to the crown, and nothing would be required of Catherine but the conventional vow of chastity. She would be free as air to do what she pleased.

A wise woman would have accepted the offer, but Catherine never for a second considered it. Compromise was absolutely foreign to her and while she might not be shrewd enough to strike a way through her difficulties she had a terrible, bulldog tenacity in clinging to her resolve. Never did she confront the possibility of defeat. The imagination which sustained Anne by lifting her eyes

THE FAVOR OF KINGS

to the goal ahead, was met in Catherine by a want of imagination which robbed the combat of the paralyzing terror of disaster. She shut her eyes and held on.

It is to be surmised that somewhat in Campeggio stirred sympathy for Henry during his private interview with the queen, one gray October morning. Catherine was rock and iron and tempest. She would die, as she lived, a wife, she flung to all his pleadings of concession.

Her stiff-robed bulk filled the great carved chair in which she sat; there was immobility in her attitude and in the rigid lines of her proud features. Every art and eloquence in his possession Campeggio tried in vain — in vain, too, his attempted exercise of priestly influence and authority.

" But may your Majesty not see God's hand in this? " he suavely suggested. " Is it not your duty to submit yourself to His will and accept the trial He has laid upon you? "

" Ha! " said Catherine scornfully in her throat.

To the warning, in a sterner voice, that the sentence might be against her and submission become a necessity, not a merit, she blazed her defiance.

" Let a sentence be given, and if He be against me, I shall be free to do as I like, even as my husband will."

The cardinal raised his hand in deprecation, a delicate, priestly hand, with choice lace falling back from the wrist.

" But thy child," he gently rebuked. " The fate of the Princess Mary is in thy hands. Wilt thou wreck it in attempting to thwart the king? "

" Is it wrecking my daughter's name, to keep her mother's name and marriage sacred? " Catherine flung at him.

" The Princess Mary's position is now beyond dispute,

and will be harmed not by your retirement. But if you anger the king he will vent his displeasure on her."

" He will not — he dare not. She is his only daughter and heiress of England, and to permit him to marry again would be to raise rivals to her claim."

" It is rivaled now in the person of the young Duke of Richmond. England hath great need of a rightful male heir."

" None would be rightful but my child. That scum of Lady Talboys is naught to us. The Princess Mary's title is sure."

" That will it not be long," the man warned her gravely, " if you refuse to make terms with the king. He is ill to trifle with. And is it such a hardship that is asked? Your own honor, the honor of your daughter, would be in no wise injured were you to enter the life of religion, and naught but the vow of chastity would be required in the matter. You would be free to reside at any of the palaces that you wished, you would be in full possession of your estates and dowry, and you would have the wardship of your beloved daughter, and the title of Queen Dowager. In that you would be following the honored example of a queen of France. I cannot too strongly counsel your Grace to accept, and I bring the advice of the Holy Father to the same end, and the secret wish of your nephew, the emperor. Is it not a duty laid on your soul not to cause dissension between the Holy See and England? With no sacrifice on your part, for you would but be conceding what is no longer yours, the person of the king, you would be ensuring the continual peace of yourself and your daughter and the welfare of the realm. You would win the Holy Father's most tender benediction, a true daughter in Christ. So now when you refuse this duty you do wrong —"

THE FAVOR OF KINGS

"I do wrong — I? . . . Oh, you men, you are all of a piece! What right, what reason is on your side! Am I the king's wife or am I not? If I am not, how can Mary be Princess of England? Did not the king feign that the Bishop of Tarbes inquired into her legitimacy on her betrothal to the French prince? How long would her position be honored if I swallowed this insult? First I would go, then my child! And what hurt can she fear from her mother's proving her own right and legitimacy?"

"But perchance —" Campeggio ventured very significantly, "perchance it should not be proved? If your Grace's contention was not accepted? Then would the princess be disproved heiress without in —"

A rattle of angry words drowned his speech. Catherine was leaning forward in her chair, her hands gripping its arms, her face twitching with the wrath that was vibrant in her voice.

"My contentions not accepted? My rights as an honest woman and a queen denied in the face of God and His Justice? Who would do this thing, my lord? Would you? Would your master, the pope? Never will I believe such infamy of an agent of God's! 'Twas a former pope's dispensation married us: if that prove now at fault, what security will hereafter be placed in any papal bull? There is no law in Heaven or earth that can unmarry me from Henry and no power that will force me to yield one jot of my right though I were broken on the wheel! Can you face these words, my lord legate, can you deny me the truth? — Ah, you men, how you patter and shuffle and lie to reach your ends, yet crave ever a fair appearance, however foul the secret mire you wallow in! I am sickened with this talk of sin and conscience — do I not know Henry's conscience? I have

THE QUEEN SPEAKS

been his wife for nineteen years and I know and you
know that he is a man to be fed and flattered, with no
scruple save to make a show with, and no law save the
limit of his power. You know and I know that his
infamy flaunts through this palace, whose shame is hanging over England like a curse —"

"Madame!" Again the upraised, feeble hand.
"Doubtless — in hopes of a succession —"

"The succession!" Never had the Italian heard
fiercer scorn than was flung into those two words. "The
succession — of Mistress Anne Boleyn! Oh, worthy
dam — Oh, worthy heritors of a crown! I know the
lady, my lord, she was maid to me till I sent her packing
for a low wanton intrigue with Henry Percy — a saucy,
upstart, scheming jade, who has been love to Thomas
Wyatt, a poet rake, these many years, whose favors are
every courtier's for the asking — or the paying! — a sly,
black-eyed, double-fingered hussy who hath bewitched
Henry Tudor with the arts the devil, her master, doth
lend her! And this is the woman you would put on
the throne of England! Oh, she would soon have you
and your kind overboard — a loose-tongued, free-think-
ing Lutheran —"

"Your Highness! Your Highness!"

"Spare your words. I know your heart, you are all
men together. What is there in a man that makes him
so like a devil? . . . No, no, I do not mean you, my Lord
Cardinal; you may mean only kindness, indeed I trust
you do, but I have been so embittered with the man
Wolsey, whose falsity and ambitions I will cast into his
teeth an he come beseeching me again to throw my fair
name into the mire to cushion his pathway! . . . I know
the man. . . . You are not he — but you are all men.
You hang together — you condone each other's vices —

183

you veil each other's crimes. An' a woman — good God, let a woman but glance so fleetingly aside and what a stone throwing is there! All your hands against her. . . . What, my lord, are all your arguments to me? Are they for the right, the justice of the cause? Not one! 'Tis all for expediency and prudence. It is, 'Bethink you, Madame, of the Princess Mary and anger not the king,' and, 'Softly, lady, let the king have his way. Consider how much he yearneth towards this new — wife — and go you to a convent and pray God bless the union.' And, 'True, your Majesty, you are the king's wife and the crown is yours, but your head has grown gray under it — put it on a fairer brow, do not trouble to defend yourself when they call you no wife and your marriage a deadly sin — it will stir up strife and embarrass the pope and annoy Charles and disappoint Henry. All other men are freed when their old wives cloy. 'Tis the way of the world. Let thy honor, thy daughter's honor, go —'tis for the best —'twill please the king!'"

Campeggio did not meet her eyes, he was staring out the window on the blue, wind-ruffled Thames: the wrinkles on his face looked deep and sunken. Then he turned to her and his hands, with Italian expressiveness, went out in a gesture of deprecating admission.

"My dear lady," he said in his softly ironic tones, "this is Life."

But there was no response in Catherine to such philosophizing; she had no intellectual interest in the generalization.

"Neither the realm nor the greatest punishment," she said, speaking more quietly, though with breath shortened by passion, "nor even being torn limb from limb shall alter me in this, and if after death I were to return, I would die again and yet again, rather than give way."

CHAPTER XVII

A TRAGIC FARCE

THE great Hall of Blackfriars was the theater selected for gaping England to witness upon a June day, 1529, the novel spectacle of its king and queen debating in open court the validity of their marriage. The pope had wished the inquiry private, but Henry's theatric taste made him stage it with splendor, and his thirst for popularity inspired him to take the people into his confidence to try and win them by a personal appeal.

The hall had been most sumptuously fitted up for its farce of justice, with the two legates in their scarlet robes in chairs draped with cloth of gold on a raised platform, and with the king and queen, amid more golden drapings and canopies, raised on either side of them, and the Archbishop of Canterbury and his bishops and the counselors for the king and queen in front, while all about the sides of the hall were packed the peers and members of court, the officials, the clergy, and all the commoners who could effect an entrance.

Back among them, shrouded in a veil, was a girl whose delicate features, sharpened with eager suspense, took on the irony of derision as the sentences of the king's address rang out, declaring the anxiety of the royal conscience and the pious resolve to continue no longer in the mortal sin of an unholy wedlock. Not so would she have postured!

THE FAVOR OF KINGS

The Dowager Duchess of Norfolk beside her. nodded her understanding of Anne's thought.

"Appeal to men and they will turn against you — carry all with a high hand and they clap you to the skies for valiance," she whispered. "The world loves its conquerors."

"Amen," grunted big Brereton, who, with Norris, pressed close to them in the throng. "This clatter of priests' tongues deafens me!"

"Priests' tongues!" sniffed the old duchess. "Nay, it hath gone further than priests — all England is wagging. Not a toothless grandam in her chimney corner but hath her opinion on whether the king be rightfully married or not, not a dog-faced peasant but knows the opinion of Heaven in the matter."

"Heaven's will is clear enough," Anne gave back. "'Tis but the opinion of those slant-eyed foxes that *I* crave!"

It had been a time of fretting impatience for Anne. In December she had returned to court, where Suffolk House was given for her establishment, and though she had every assurance of success, from the sight of the pope's commission granting power to Wolsey and Campeggio to try the case, and promising not to revoke that authority, to Henry's account of the decretal that defined the law in his favor, fairly prejudging the case, yet a haunting fear possessed her of some blow in the dark.

There had been too much delay. She did not trust that pope: it was whispered that Catherine had private assurances from the emperor that nothing would be done against her, and Anne was more than convinced that Pope Clement was lying impartially to both sides, cozening them in desperate opportunism till he could see which of

the alternate dangers threatening him from emperor and
king would be ultimately the least perilous. It was perfectly realized that neither the validity of the dispensation,
nor the justice of Catherine's claims, nor England's urgent
political necessities were taken into his consideration for
one instant.

But now, though maddeningly postponed, the trial had
opened and it dragged its weary length of formalities
along, according to its preconceived plan, until unexpectedly, on the conclusion of Wolsey's address, Catherine
of Aragon rose suddenly from her seat.

Deliberately she circled the legates and bishops, in a
hall grown so still that the creakings of her stiff silk were
audible in the farthest corners, and when approached to
the king's chair she went down on her two knees before
him, reaching up with clasped hands and pouring out a
loud and passionate appeal.

"The *poseuse!*" muttered the old duchess, but that
the poor queen was not reciting a set speech for spectacular effect but was laboring with an almost uncontrollable
distress was evident from the curious fact that she spoke
in almost broken English, as if her tongue had forgotten
the habits of so many years and slipped back into the
accents with which she had first expressed herself in
her husband's language.

It was a wild and piteous harangue that she poured
forth.

"Your Highness hath declared that it is your desire
that this marriage shall be proved valid," she was reminding the king — and indeed Henry, in one of his many
posturings before the Council, had acquitted himself of
that very declaration in order to establish his perfect
impartiality in the matter —"and have declared your
great love for my person and have stated that were you

free to choose you would liefer marry me than any
woman in your realm, so then by all the loves that have
ever been between us, for the love of God, for my honor,
and for that of our daughter and yourself, let me have
justice and right. Have pity on me, a poor, lone woman
and a stranger, without a trusty friend or impartial ad-
viser, flying to you as the head of justice in this realm.
Alas, how have I offended you, that you should seek to
put me away? Have I ever attempted to do anything
against your will and pleasure? . . . I take God and all
the world to witness that I have ever been to you a true,
humble, and obedient wife, ever conforming to your will
and pleasure, never showing ill-temper or discontent by
word or look, but always pleased with all things in which
you showed delight, and loving all whom you loved, for
your sake alone, whether they were my friends or my
enemies."

"La, la, what love she hath shed!" muttered the
duchess, but Anne did not hear; she was leaning forward,
her lips parted, her eyes big and dark. She was thinking
of the time that she had knelt to Catherine. . . .

Henry had risen from his seat and bent over the queen,
trying to raise her from her knees, but her hands repulsed
him; she went on, beginning to sob, but still speaking
loudly for all to hear.

"For twenty years I have been a true wife to you,
and by me you have had several children, though it has
pleased God to call them out of this world, which is no
fault of mine: and when you had me at the first, I take
God to judge whether I was a very maid, and whether
it be true or not I put it to your conscience."

The dowager duchess shook her head vehemently.
"Tut-tut-tut," she clucked between her teeth. "She may
vow so, but some seven and twenty years ago the whole

court was whispering Prince Arthur's boasts to the very contrary. He was a sick young husband, but husband he was. . . . And then there was that matter of the priest —"

" Which may have been but slander," Anne gave back in an undertone, amazed herself at the impulse that prompted her to the queen's defense. " They may have loved — but not to ill doing."

" Slander ! " shrugged the old lady expressively. Her nose lifted in disdain of such absurd sentiment. " When everyone knew —"

" Everyone knows many a thing now that is not true," Anne muttered and the old duchess, suddenly divining the impulse of the girl's denial, reached out and patted her hand smilingly.

" We know thou art as innocent as a field flower," she whispered, " else," and she chuckled incorrigibly, " Henry would not be so hot after thee."

Through this rapid interchange of murmurs Anne had been listening to the impassioned tones of the kneeling queen. " If any just cause or impediment can be alleged against me," Catherine was declaring, " I am well contented to depart to my great shame and dishonor, but if there be none, I here most humbly beseech you to let me receive justice at your hand." Raising her voice, till it carried to the pressing listeners blocking the wide-open doors and filling the hall beyond, she went on to urge that she could not expect justice from English subjects or an English court, " and, therefore," she added, " I most humbly entreat you, as a charity for the love of God, to allow me to prosecute my appeal in Rome before the common Father of all Christians."

She started to rise, and the king sprang forward to assist her. Bowing, she turned away, but instead of passing about the bishops again to her seat she motioned to Griffeths, her general receiver, to present his arm for her to lean upon, and then directed her way forward, out of the court.

Quickly the king beckoned to the crier and commanded him to order her, in the king's name, to return.

"Queen Catherine of England, come into court — Catherine of England, come into court," roared the crier's voice, and Griffeths, pausing irresolutely, whispered. "Madame, you are called!"

He felt the agitated trembling of her heavy body as she pressed forward.

"On, on, it maketh no matter," she answered fiercely, the tears her excitement could not control, perhaps did not wish to control, raining down her cheeks.

Again the crier shouted her name, and Griffeths, in two minds, would have hung back.

"On, sir," she commanded, " it maketh no matter, for it is no indifferent court to me. . . . I will not tarry," and she swept resolutely from sight, her ladies hurrying to rejoin her at the entrance.

There was a tremendous stir all through the hall, a rustling of tongues and clothes as people turned and whispered to each other, gesturing, expostulating, demurring . . . everywhere there were clustered heads and curious eyes slanted at the king. . . . Henry felt the sudden current against him. Catherine had made a powerful impression. With his eagerness to be with the popular tide of feeling, and his thin-skinned inability to permit himself to be for a moment thought of as being in the wrong, Henry sprang excitedly to his feet, and addressed the court in feeling tones of sympathy.

" Forasmuch as the queen is gone, I will in her absence declare unto you all, my lords, she hath been to me as true, as obedient and as conformable a wife as I could in my fancy wish or desire. She hath all the virtuous qualities that a woman of her quality, or of any lower rank, ought to possess!"

Did there come to Anne Boleyn in that moment some swift insight into the character of the man to whom she was yielding her life, staking all her future upon? . . . If it did, it was gone in the moment before the answering reassurance of self-confidence! She shut her foolish eyes to his shallow instability, his callous insincerity, thinking that these lies, these posturings, these tricky machinations would always be for the others about him: for her, who held his heart, the innate sincerity of his love! But her cheeks flamed that he should, as she felt, degrade himself by those protestations that hoodwinked nobody and but revealed his thirsty craving for appro- bation — not so would she have played the ruler!

But there did come to the girl that night, as she tossed restlessly, far from sleep, a haunting perception of the pitiableness of that woman, old and haggard, weeping at the feet of her husband. She closed her heart against that pity; she flouted it with the memory of Catherine's old insults to her, but it persisted, sharp and discom- forting, setting deeper currents of thought stirring in her, new questions knocking at her brain. . . .

At last, turning at bay against the tracking doubts that pressed upon her, she faced the thought. Was Catherine right? Was she?

Canon law forbade the marriage — but Henry had been willing to oppose canon law with a pope's dispensation, those twenty years ago, she reminded herself, endeavor- ing, with new largeness of character, to slip away from the distortions of her pride, her ambitions and her hates, and to be fair to the enemy whom even to think of was to make the blood quicken in her veins. But her thoughts circled swiftly back to her justifications. Henry had been willing to accept her as wife for a particular result — an heir for England. It had failed and Catherine would now never realize that hope. If such had been the case when he married her he could have put her away at once; why then, not now? Catherine had staked herself upon a chance which had gone against her — she should take the fortunes of war with a positive gratitude for the generous terms of her dismissal, instead of haggling wretchedly for the validity of that dispensation!

It pierced Anne's consciousness that she was playing a strangely significant part in England's history; she had precipitated a crisis, political, religious, whose far-reaching effects she could not begin to foresee. There were large things at stake — the right of trial of English cases by English courts, the lessening of the papal grasp. A perception flittered vaguely across her of being a tool in the hands of forces greater than she divined, forces waging a persistent and inevitable war . . . the perception faded and she saw herself, from a different angle of vision, as a person of deep importance, of vast potential power.

What could she not do, she who had England's king at her beck and call! There came to her a larger vision of the possibilities of her position than she had at first conceived of and she saw herself abolishing abuses, protecting heretics, encouraging education and all true feeling in religion. . . .

By morning, when sleep at last came to her, she had forgotten in her enthusiasm for the good that her reign would bring, the immediate devastation of the discarded woman, kneeling before the husband of twenty years.

CHAPTER XVIII

THE LAW'S DELAYS

THE tedious delays which made the case drag on interminably through June and through July had daily tightened that knot of tension in Anne's breast, and deepened the weight of her secret burden of foreboding.

There was the pope's written word to let these legates decide and there was the secret decretal defining a favorable law; it was incredible that Clement would recede from all he had promised England, but yet — but yet —

So that when Anne saw the king's face, as he burst in the door of her apartments on the day set for concluding the trial, although her heart gave a terrible, sick drop of dismay, she had nevertheless a cold sense of having all along expected this very thing and her manner was strangely quiet.

"It is — against us?" she asked, white to the lips.

"It is *nothing!*" Henry answered with a roar of anger. "It is nothing — nothing — nothing! No sentence at all is given — the court is prorogued — prorogued to October because that is the custom of the courts at Rome!"

His fury was immense. The veins swelled in his neck, his skin burned, his lips curled back over his teeth in the snarl of an infuriated beast as he poured out an astounding stream of profanity and invective. Anne put her cold hand calmingly in his; it was at least better

than the opposing judgment her worst fears had anticipated.

"Tell me all," she asked.

Suffolk, red-faced with anger, had followed in his
brother-in-law's wake, and they told her, roundly cursing
as they revived the scene, how when the king's proctor
had demanded sentence, Campeggio had arisen and in
smooth Latin announced that the court was prorogued,
for it was then the time of vacation in Rome and there
would be no further sitting till October.

"Wolsey sitting grinning by," flung out Suffolk, which
was not a truth, for Wolsey's features had worn a mask-
like fixity, "and I struck the table a slap under his
hawk's nose and let fly, 'Now I see the old-said saw is
true, that there was never legate nor cardinal that did
good in England!'"

"How answered he?" demanded Henry. "I left—"

Suffolk's red face grew a shade redder though he
shrugged with immense disdain. "That I was not the
one to say it."

At another, less furious, moment Henry might have
grinned at the aptness of the reminder, for long ago,
when Charles Brandon had rashly eloped with the king's
sister, on the death of her French husband, making her
his third, or perchance his fourth wife — none were quite
sure! — it had indeed been Wolsey who had made peace
between Suffolk and his angry king, and again, later,
when Suffolk had disbanded the army without leave,
Henry's rage might have cost him his head but for the
cardinal's intervention, but the king was in no mood now
to join with Wolsey in these reminders of benefits forgot.

"His damned arrogance!" Suffolk was uttering between his teeth. "The butcher's son — to toss that in
my face! He hath outwitted us—"

THE LAW'S DELAYS

" October," Anne was desolately repeating.

" October! " Henry ground out. " There will be a new trick turned ere then. I see that Clement means to fail me."

Suffolk suddenly stopped his angry growling. " Well, sire, I will out and see what is being done. I leave you in fair hands,"— a half smile touched his surly face as he glanced at Anne —" belike you be in better mood when we meet. For me there is no such solace."

" And yet my solace is my torment," Henry muttered, with a look at the girl he had hoped to make his wife ere that October came. " Oh, to be flouted so! " he burst out as the door shut upon the duke. " To be cheated by those lying Italians —"

" Italians? " mocked Anne, with ironic emphasis. " Oh, never say *Wolsey* to me again! "

Suddenly Henry crossed the room and caught the girl in a grip of rough passion.

" They cannot balk me of all, Anne," he said hoarsely. " They cannot cheat me of thee, if thou art indeed mine own. I am sick unto death of nays and coldness — come, be mine. Be mine and end this torment of delay! "

" Aye, end it an thou wilt," she cried, and the ringing challenge of her voice roused wonder and stayed his clasp.

" Marry me! " she flashed imperiously at him.

" Troth an I could —"

" An thou *couldst!* If you and Catherine are not wed what is to let? Is there no priest in England bold enough to do his master's will? "

Backwards in the circle of his arms she leaned, her uplifted face blazing its reckless challenge into his.

" Art Hal of England or Clement's man? " she taunted.

195

THE FAVOR OF KINGS

For an instant his eyes caught fire from hers but the straw flame flickered and she saw gray calculation fog his gaze.

"'Tis a matter of state — the time is out of joint —"

"Marry me!" she flung insistently into his hesitant mutterings, and again, "Marry me," she breathed, drawing closer, her back-tipped face a lure for love.

"I will," he groaned, "so thou but love me now. At the first chance . . . when this hot outcry has cooled."

Like a whirlwind she was out of his arms and away from him.

"*When* and *by-and-by* and *at the first chance,*" she derided in mocking fury. "Oh, God give me patience to wait till my hairs are gray! Troth I need it with such a lag o' love as thou! . . . Where are thy vows now? 'Anne, I will crown thee — Anne, I will make thee queen!'" she mouthed back at him. "And what hast thou done? . . . I am the laughter of the court. I am held for thy light of love —"

"So would you be in truth an your heart were indeed mine," he tossed back, smarting.

"So now you throw my virtue in my teeth! . . . Were I otherwise I'd not be worth the wiving! . . . Well, I am done with all this. I know enough from more. I am wasting my youth and my fame in a wild goose chase but now I stop. I leave the court, I give up all pretensions to your Too-High and Mighty Majesty and cleave unto my own low estate where I pray you let me rest. . . . This is the end for us."

"Anne, thou art mad."

"Nay, my madness is over."

"Anne —"

"Touch me not. I am not thy betrothed."

"Unsay that, Anne, unsay that. I will not give thee

THE LAW'S DELAYS

up. Thou art my very life — my wife that shall be — queen of all my realm —"

She sank down on a chair and covered her face with her hands.

"Am I?" she sobbed in a storm of tears. "Am I? . . . Or am I only a mock of time, a fool of fortune, dizzy with a dream?"

He knelt beside her pouring out wild words and oaths and vows of love and presently, her fury spent with its own violence, she let herself be wooed and won from her mad mood.

"Belike I shall be thine," she said wearily, sopping her eyes with her wet handkerchief, "but it hath the look of a long wooing. And I am fair graveled for patience."

"And I the more so," he chafed unhappily.

"Yet you will not wed me and dare all," ran her secret bitterness but she did not speak it out again. She had taken the measure of her present power and for pride's sake was now silent while he talked eagerly, trying to build up again her hopes and faith. Many a knight, he urged, had fought for years to win his true love and he would do no less and she must trust his courage and his love, and as his ardent words played on her pride and vanity her despair ebbed and the net of her situation closed about her again. For after all, what else was there now in life for her, what could she do but trust in him and go on? Impossible for her proud spirit to renounce its dream!

And so, with abrupt change of mood, she roused from huddling in her chair, and shook the black curls over her tear-stained face.

"Sith you are so resolved on my poor self, Hal, I can not say you nay," she cried, "but let us be up and out of London town. I am sick of the hot streets and of

197

quibbling courts; let us be done with all and out into the green wood with the cool wind in our faces and the waving trees about."

" In Heaven's name, yes," the king concurred, and that night his gentlemen and Anne's ladies began hastily to pack for the excursion.

They were at Grafton, after an idyllic sojourn at Woodstock, fair Rosamond's bower, when Cardinal Campeggio, escorted by Wolsey, arrived to bid the king farewell.

It was September, and the months which had elapsed had completely shattered any remnant of hope which Henry might have retained that his Holy Father meant to fulfill his pledges or arrange, in any favorable way, the matrimonial difficulty. In bland oblivion of every promise Clement had yielded to the emperor's urgings and annulled the legate's powers, revoked the cause to Rome, and cited both Catherine and Henry to appear before him — a choice predicament for a king of England!

It was not hard to see on whose head Henry's displeasure was falling. For when the two cardinals arrived at Grafton, there were no lodgings provided for the Lord Chancellor of England and he was indebted to Henry Norris's kindliness for a place to change his garments for supper, while the neighborhood was searched for rooms for the night. Yet so unforeseen were the disconcerting reactions of King Henry's moods, that though the betting was five to one on Wolsey's immediate disgrace, the king received him most graciously, and taking him by the hand, led him to a window in private talk with all the old time show of intimacy.

And although once the king's voice was heard in sharp question over a paper, saying, " How can that be? Is not this your hand?" yet the talk concluded so amiably with a reappointment for the evening that the Boleyn faction took swift alarm. Sharp warnings were whispered Anne to stiffen Henry against his former favorite and when the king joined her at supper she treated him to a petulant dispute.

" Is it not a marvelous thing, sire," she demanded with a provoked laugh, " to consider what debt and danger the cardinal hath brought upon you with all your subjects? "

Henry drained his cup and wiped his beard. " How so, Sweetheart? "

" Forsooth, there is not a man worth five pounds but he hath indebted you unto him," she gave back, referring to a recent loan which had set the people all by the ears.

" Well, well," said Henry temperately, " as for that there is no blame in him for I know that matter better than you or any other."

" Nay, sir," said Anne, her color rising, " besides all that, what things hath he wrought within this realm to your great slander and dishonor! There is never a nobleman but if he had done half so much but were well worthy to lose his head! If my Lord of Suffolk, my Lord of Norfolk, my lord my father, or any other noble person had done much less than he they should have lost their heads ere this! "

Henry smiled into the excited face. " Why then I perceive you are not the cardinal's friend."

" Forsooth, *I* have no cause! . . . Nor have any others that loveth your Grace, if ye consider well his doings." She paused and then with a short laugh, " His *friend!* "

When Henry, only superficially impressed, had gone off to his appointment, she remained angrily ruminative. She feared Wolsey as she feared none other in the world, and when she learned that he was to remain for a meeting of the Council in the morning and not depart with Campeggio till afternoon, it did not need her father's anxieties to prick her to action.

Breakfast at Grafton was at the hour of six and it was the king's custom to take it in the Boleyn apartments. That morning Anne sent for him earlier than usual and he found her in a riding suit of Lincoln green, a cocked hat already perched on her flying hair.

" Prithee eat in haste and let us away," she cried, smiling and waving him to the table. " I can hardly wait. The day calls me and it is in my mind to see that stretch of land that you destine for a park."

It was difficult to demur in the face of that radiant expectation but he shook his head at her. " The Council sits."

" La, sir, but you are not the Council! You are the king and surely are free to ride it out over the green country with such a nice young maid as I ? " She dimpled mischievously and pushed the honey and venison towards him.

" Nay, not free in conscience," he said with open regret, for Anne was sweetly lovely as she sat there smiling at him, and the country looked very fresh and fair as he glanced through the open casement. It had rained in the night and every leaf and grass blade held its shining drop of water. The air and sky looked fresh washed and sparkling, the breeze blew gently, and in the east the colors of sunrise still shimmered in paling rose and saffron. It was undeniably a morning on which to be up and away — but there was the Council to see — and Wolsey —

" We must wait, Sweet, till afternoon."

" Nay, your Council knows your Grace's will; they will

see it done in all matters," Anne protested, a little upright line deepening between her arched brows. But she banished it with a sudden smile.

"Oh, very well," she laughed lightly, "since your Grace can liefer part from me than that Council."

"'Tis not alone the Council but Wolsey —" he paused, fearing the name would win an outburst from her.

"It mattereth not." She went on eating, with an apparently absorbed but most dainty interest in her viands. Then she pushed back her plate, beginning to hum a gay little tune under her breath.

> Pastance with good company
> I love, and shall —

"Right after dinner," promised Henry.

She jumped lightly to her feet. "At dinner I shall be many, many miles away."

"What foolery is this?"

"Very true foolery."

"Where are you going?"

"As far as my horse can carry me on the way to Blickling."

"Prithee, be sober," Henry frowned. The young lady smiled.

"I am as sober as an anchorite in the desert, dear my lord."

"You have it in your mind to leave this place — and me?"

"I think, sire, you would not account it much loss," she gave back with a flash of defiance in her eyes.

He stared, then left the table to approach her but she put out a protesting hand. "Nay, I am in no mood for being cozened."

"Cozened? What spell is on thee?"

THE FAVOR OF KINGS

"A very woeful one. I am persuaded that the presence of Anne Boleyn is a matter of indifference to thee and I am minded to remove it. Perchance there are others more appreciative."

"Indifferent," he said, half angry, yet trying to smile at her in blandishment, "now, Anne, thou art mad as a March hare. What bee is buzzing in thee? Thou art but in jest."

"I am glad your Grace is so well advised of my humors."

She crossed the room to the door that opened into her chamber.

"I crave your Highness to excuse me — I have some orders to give."

"Anne, come hither, I tell thee."

She turned towards him, making no motion to approach, but offering him a vastly engaging and roguish face to gaze upon.

"What makes you think I am indifferent?"

She puckered her lips. "Faith, when a knight refuses his lady's company to her face and that for no reason at all save a musty Council —"

"And thou wouldst really leave me so?" He attempted sternness but there was an uncontrollable panic in his tone. "To fly at such a tangent when I —"

"Was but jesting, Harry, was but jesting," she supplied quickly as he hung fire, and running to him, she caught his coat by her two hands, smiling up into his face in bewitching confidence of the kiss that he instantly pressed on her warm lips.

"I was but jesting," he echoed, their laughter mingling, and he continued to kiss, not her lips only, but her soft brow, her eyes, her scented hair. "You knew I could not gainsay thee, little witch."

THE LAW'S DELAYS

And so, some minutes later, when Cardinal Wolsey rode hurrying into the courtyard at Grafton — for the lodging he had found for the night was three miles distant — he had the pleasure of seeing the king lifting a light figure into the saddle and then swing quickly on his own horse. The cardinal almost tumbled in his eagerness to dismount, and hurried to kneel at the stirrup where Henry was feeling for the right brace. Smilingly the king greeted him and waved him one side. " I can tarry not — another time," he called, and putting spurs to his horse dashed out after the girl who had already given rein to her mount.

Wolsey stood and gazed after, forgetting the gaping onlookers in the intense premonition of disaster that came upon him. He saw Anne, light as a fairy on her white horse, her black hair blowing like a pennant about her, against a sky of blue that seemed to deepen as he gazed; a fleeting, eluding phantom of delight after which the king was spurring his black in furious haste. And as the ageing man watched, his heart sank in heavier and heavier dejection. He had ridden with Henry on many a mad quest . . . but now his usefulness was over . . . Henry rode alone. And it had been his own hand that baited the trap.

The Duke of Suffolk advanced from the castle to greet him and Wolsey turned with a summoned smile.

" How fair the picture," he said, waving his hand at the two bright riders against the blue, and he turned again to watch them out of sight. He had a momentary feeling that he should never see his king again.

CHAPTER XIX

A FAREWELL TO GREATNESS

BUT Henry had one more service that his minister might perform. If that decretal could be wrested from Campeggio, Wolsey could reopen the legatine court — for the commission was made out to the legates separately or jointly — and once in possession of the pontiff's written promise not to revoke the legatine authority, Wolsey could pronounce a favorable judgment in the case.

"As he should long since have done," Anne heatedly declared. "Two years ago he could have pronounced the verdict quietly and with small talk, and when it was done, those who are eager now to prevent would have hesitated to try and undo. But no, he 'durst not,' he dallied, he appealed to Rome, he noised it abroad, he let Catherine rouse Charles and Charles command the pope, and then he fathered that treachery of a legatine court with its lying commissions and secret decretals. And how hath it all gone? The commission was made out with his name first but he lets Campeggio supersede him so the Italian can lag in calling the court and then prorogue it — tell me not Wolsey was unknowing from the beginning of what was coming! And all the while the decretal remained with Campeggio — Wolsey could have begged it of him for he trusted Wolsey and with good reason! If this be his best, give me another's worst!"

A FAREWELL TO GREATNESS

"If that decretal be found he shall mend that best!"
Henry promised.

But the decretal was not found, although the English
customs officials searched the protesting legate most thoroughly; and the sudden puff of hope that had flickered
before the two lovers was swiftly extinguished and left
Henry cold with vindictive wrath.

"That was Wolsey's last chance," he said grimly.
"Now they can be at him."

They were at him then, like dogs about a wolf. All
the enemies whom the cardinal's long, arrogant years
had embittered, men he had humbled, men he had injured, men whose relatives he had sent to the block, men
whose pride and ambition had seethed against his power,
bared their fangs at him and struck. Nobles and officials for once made common cause against him and ere
the king's humor could change they closed hungrily
round their victim. The very day the messenger brought
the king his disappointing news, the king's attorney drew
up articles against the cardinal for infringement of the
Act of Præmunire.

Wolsey had foreboded disaster ever since the close of
that legatine court, but always he hoped against hope, so
incredible it was to conceive of himself as overtaken by
absolute disgrace. If only he could see the king again!
He had waited for that chance in agonized suspense,
but the Boleyn faction had seen to the continuation of
those hunting excursions about the country with Anne,
and Wolsey had not looked upon his sovereign since the
morning at Grafton when he had watched him dash off
so blithely after his eluding lady.

He knew that without the king's favor he was defenseless before his enemies. He saw himself ringed in

by so many daggers of hate, pointed at him by those men who had endured his arrogant exactions in the king's name with such forced suavity, and back of them lowered the bitter animosity of all England who saw in him the very embodiment of the loathed ecclesiastical abuses. As cardinal and chancellor he had controlled the patronage of the realm and his power had stretched over all like a web; in every county and diocese his spider-like officials were collecting tithes and tolls, and to this enormous accretion of wealth foreign princes had been eager to add pension after pension to enlist his influence. He had known, of course, that this gigantic web had been spun with the single thread of the king's favor, but he had believed himself indispensable to the king until the dark-eyed girl had crossed their paths, and from the bottom of his terror-stricken soul he cursed the cool pride of her character which had undone him.

It was possible for him to defend himself with the simple truth that everything he had done, as legate, in violation of the Act of Præmunire which forbade the exercise of the power of any agent of the pope in England, had been entirely at the king's desire, but Wolsey understood the temper of his master too well to attempt a defense. To thwart Henry when he was provoked was to draw the whole force of his wrath; the wisest course was to bow to the storm and throw one's self upon the royal mercy.

Wolsey knew English justice far too thoroughly to believe that any defense would be strong enough to protect him. If he was to be ruined, ruined he would be; if Præmunire failed, the court was packed with men, who, at the king's whisper, would manufacture enough evidence of treason, furnishing names and dates, to send his head spinning. There was no help for him if the

A FAREWELL TO GREATNESS

king's favor failed, and at the king's order he yielded
the Great Seal, he pleaded guilty, he surrendered his
goods.

There are moments in life of such dramatic contrasts
that even the dullest vision sees something of their
poignancy. And in that moment when the disgraced
cardinal stood taking what was like to be his last leave
of York House there was a quality so vivid that the very
yeomen, the thick-headed giants who on feast nights
stood with upraised torches, illuminating and guarding
his golden treasures, now piling those treasures out on
tables, were thrilled with an inarticulate emotion. It
was not grief; they had neither affection nor anxiety for
their master who had been a fearful power, remote and
awe-inspiring; if anything they felt a pleasurable excitement in the stir of events and coarse humanity's careless
exulting that one who was high was now low, but at that
moment it was not excitement nor curiosity that stirred
them but a vague perception of the greatness of the
tragedy.

The cardinal was passing slowly, silently, through the
great rooms of his palace. At his order, all the riches
it contained had been brought out and displayed in the
expectation of the king's coming to take possession.
The halls of the gallery were hung with cloths of silver
and gold; the long tables down its length were laden with
whole pieces of silk of every color and quality, velvets,
satins, grograms, and taffetas; of fine linen alone there
were one thousand pieces. The prodigality of the display astonished even those of the household who were
acquainted with the cardinal's possessions.

On one side of the gallery were hung the rich suits
and copes that he had provided for his colleges at

THE FAVOR OF KINGS

Ipswich and Oxford and it was here that the cardinal paused and the longest lingered in his slow progress.

As he gazed, the rigidity which had frozen his features into a death-like mask, seemed to weaken; a violent twitching in his left cheek suddenly commenced but it was his only show of the profound and overwhelming emotion within. He was taking leave of the labors and achievements of a whole life. He had not yet given himself utterly to despair; he sustained his courage with the hope of regaining the king's grace, but he could not deceive himself into imagining that he would ever regain it to his former extent. The richness which he was surrendering would never again be his. These copes would never be worn by his scholars. That great Cardinals' College at Oxford would never be completed by him; his vision of stately stone walls and towering belfries, of sunlit quadrangles and oak beamed halls filled with England's choicest youth would not be for his eyes to gaze on.

A gust of anger seethed through the man as he thought of the men who would take advantage of his fall to enrich themselves and possess in turn the powers he had wielded. He despised them. They were a horde of pleasure seekers, incapable of laying one stone for the glory of England, or adding one jot to the learning within her borders. Whatever men might say of him, he thought with a stiffening of his pride, he had risen to great heights, he had borne great cares, he had supported high ambitions. He had had a vision of England's future welfare, of fine colleges and scholarly men and wise minded administrators — if only it had been given to him to follow this vision unimpeded! But, O God! how he had been thwarted and baffled, what circuitous routes he had traveled, what ends he had served! And all that he had done was undone, or like to it and England was left — to whom? He pitied England intensely in that moment. And in the next he was kindled with an immense passion against the absurd injustice, the capricious unreason of events. On what pitiful threads of whim and spite hang tragic destinies! What a random passion had overthrown in petulant resentment the unremitting toil of an unwearying intelligence!

As he stood there he was struck with a sudden memory of a scene that had never before recurred to him save in amusement — the challenge that had been flashed him, one long ago morning at the palace door, from the angry eyes of a disgraced maid of honor. He had lived to see that same maid of honor's strange elevation to power; he had lived to see the menace of those eyes fulfilled. And he remembered the morning when young Henry Percy had poured out his boy's tale of passion and begged to be allowed to marry this maid. Curious, that if he had consented —

He wrenched himself from the unprofitable thoughts and passed on down the gallery. On the thresholds of the gilt chamber and the council chamber he paused in turn, casting a mechanical eye on the tables laden with his precious plate. There were services of silver, richly chased, but the greater part was gold, such gold as few kings could boast, elaborately wrought and often set with many gems. The officials of the household stood guarding these wares and on each table was a book listing the plate and its weight. All was in order for the new occupant.

How many times Wolsey had seen that plate outspread at banquets; how many times he had strolled from table to table of his guests! He felt the pain of these remembrances with its prophecy of future anguish, but now he had steeled himself to endure, to maintain an appearance of proud calm, and only that twitching left cheek, the shrunken eye and the dry, blenched skin that told of sleepless nights, revealed to the onlookers through what a furnace of human despair the man was passing.

There was nothing more to be done; every arrangement had been hastily made for his departure and now all that remained was to betake himself from this place of his past power. But as he moved to that door of York House that gave upon the Thames his footsteps dragged.

At the door he paused and waved sharply back the man who had been in the custom of carrying before him the second cross of silver, the cross which was the symbol of his fateful legatine power.

"But one cross," he commanded, and to the knot of household officials standing about, his pent-up despair vented itself in the bitter confession, "God wot, I would I had never borne more!"

The treasurer of the household stepped a little forward, his light blue eyes glistening.

"I am sorry for your Grace," he said, "for I hear you are to go straight to the Tower!"

Wolsey stopped short. The twitching in his cheek became violent. "Is that the best comfort you can give your master in adversity?" burst from him and his voice sounded hollow and querulous like the voice of an old man. He shot an angry look at Gascoigne and the greedy, curious excitement of the man made him draw himself up with a return to his old haughtiness. Dryly he commented, "It hath always been your inclination to be light of credit, and much lighter in respecting of lies. . . . I would you should know, Sir William, and all those reporters, too," and his eyes swept the crowd on his heels who fell back abashed, " that it is untrue, for I have never deserved to come there."

After a moment he added with deliberate calm, " Although it hath pleased the king to take my house ready furnished for his pleasure, yet at this time I would have all the world to know that I have nothing but what is of right from him, and of him I have received all that I have. It is therefore convenient and reason to tender the same unto him again."

With high held head he descended the steps and passed through the opened doors into the waiting barge. As he took his seat he cast a casual look about and those with him saw him give an uncontrolled start. He had found himself the cynosure of a million eyes. Both banks of the Thames were lined with people, crowding, tense, expectant people, and on the river more than a thousand barges were laden down with more people, all with their faces strained towards him, their eyes alight to witness his disgrace. They must have been gathering before daybreak. . . . They must for hours have been standing patiently in place for that one precious glimpse of his departure. He felt a shudder run through him; his throat was dry. The simple sight of those people, those waiting, feasting eyes, affected him as unpleasantly as a brandished ax. He knew the thumping blood reversals of a caged hare seeing a hound outside its bars. They could not get at him, theirs were not the hands that were able to drag him down, they were but the little men he had offended, whose houses he had seized to enlarge his garden, whose relatives he had impaled for deer stealing; the bars were stout between him and them but the fact of their enmity was there, their eagerness to be at him, their promise to destroy him if he fell amongst them.

THE FAVOR OF KINGS

He tried to dismiss those staring crowds from his mind as his barge made its slow way down the river; he tried to put away that notion of their enmity and call them merely curious, the vulgar gluttons of events, but when he raised his head and met those eyes he found more than curiosity there. His eye was caught by one face in particular — a woman's face, white and starved, with eyes like caverns. There was such fixity of hate in her haggardness that he felt as if he had seen an ever-burning fire. He wondered who she was, what thing had given her that look.

He could not banish it from his mind, it took possession of him with the intensity of a tormenting enigma. And then quite suddenly it came over him. The sight of a little boy precariously balancing on a barge gave him the clue. . . . He recalled that a year or so gone by, two little boys had been busy casting down a gutter some rubbish that the rain had swept there. A laquay of the Viscount de Touraine had complained that he had been hit by a piece of it, and the French lords had taken the matter up and Wolsey had had the whole family of the offenders arrested. He had kept the father and mother and relatives and servants in jail for six weeks, as a warning; the boys themselves had been committed to the Tower. One of them died there and he dimly recalled now that there was something said about the other's having been lamed by ill-usage. Someone had made a sentimental plea to Anne about him and she had brought about his release. It was a low family — they were not worth troubling about, and yet the eyes of that mother, for he identified the haggard woman as the mother, seemed to pierce him with baleful portent, shrug it off as he might with a " Pah! Gutterscum! "

His barge had reached the Tower now and as it did

A FAREWELL TO GREATNESS

not halt there but proceeded on its way to Putney a sudden deep-throated cry came up from the mob, swelling louder and louder in its disappointment like a clamor of disappointed hounds.

The cardinal smiled disdainfully. He would live to be revenged on them yet, he told himself. But he told himself wearily. He felt old and jaded. There was so much to be done all over again — all over again.

CHAPTER XX

LADY ANNE ROCHFORD

ANNE caught her breath with delight at the first glance about York Place. She had anticipated treasure, but not such profusion as this!

With a little dancing step she left the king's side — the king and her mother and Henry Norris had come secretly by barge from Greenwich one bright October morning to inspect this palace — and flew to the nearest table heaped with its rainbow hued silks.

"Oh, *mother!*" she cried out, holding up a piece of embroidered golden tissue, as impalpable and radiant as sunshine, in such a feminine ecstasy that all three of her companions burst out laughing.

"Marry, I have had no new robes for a month," she defended herself prettily.

"There are robes for thee there, Sweetheart, for all years," Henry promised, while he turned with an equal eagerness to the tables of gold and silver plate.

"By the mass!" he ejaculated, staring at the glittering covers, and Norris gave a soft whistle of amazement. "In sooth here are trenchers fit and enough for heaven and all its angels. Odd's bodkins, but one had no need to dine off pewter in this house!"

"This satin — this scarlet satin!" admired Anne, draping a lustrous fold of it over her outstretched arm. "Didst ever see such luster? I shall have a gown of it! . . . Oh, and this velvet so tawny color — look, mother! — I shall have *that*. And see this lace! 'Tis point de Venise — it would go richly with the velvet. . . . There is another piece of it — there, mother, hand it here. . . . See now, sire," and she was across the room to the king, the lace in her hands. "Come and see the stuff for my next gown. Oh, *Harry!*" she whispered excitedly, "is it not glorious? Didst ever see such a riot of riches?"

"The plate, Anne — you've not regarded a piece. See this." Henry had a great platter in his hand, wrought about its borders with figures of the chase; the boar had eyes of twinkling rubies and tusks of pearls. "A quaint device, eh? And there's a drinking cup here — where is it — ?"

"This, your Grace?" offered Norris.

"That? No, the other. Here, Anne, see the cunning figures of the support. Here be three women, three Graces, holding the cup —"

"Then I shall take it away from you, sire — one woman is quite enough for you."

"She is the three Graces in one — and the nine Muses to boot," he declared. "So this is a fitting cup for thee — thou shalt have it."

"Ah, many thanks," Anne returned carelessly. She was back already at the table of silks where a vivid grogram of Tudor green had caught her eyes.

"It will make fine sleeve ties for the tawny velvet," she declared, already conjuring up a vision of the gown to be while her mother fingered linen sheeting. "I will have the sleeves puffed with this white tissue here and tied with this green, and I will wear emeralds with it — hast found me some emeralds?" she flashed, darting back to her lover's side. "I am planning a green gown, oh, a green and tawny gold vision of a gown, and I would wear some green stones about my neck with it."

Henry smiled down into the eager, upturned face: Anne was like a happy confident child, secure in its own audacity, confident of its alluring charm. Her cheeks were flushed, her eyes were very bright.

"Thou shalt have emeralds for thy neck and thy head and thy fingers and to sew all over thy gown," he promised royally. "Come now and go over the palace and thou shalt select the finest suite of chambers for thine own," and laughing like two children they were off, the smiling Norris and awe-stricken stepmother following in their wake.

The gown of velvet, a rich, tawny golden, the front and sleeves slashed and puffed with white tissue and the bodice studded with emeralds was finished in time for the banquet given in Anne's honor on December ninth, 1529. It was to mark her elevation in rank, for on the preceding day her father had become the Earl of Wiltshire and Ormond and she the Lady Anne Rochford. The Rochford instead of Boleyn was Henry's suggestion, for he suspected uncomfortably that her grandfather, old Boleyn, the mercer, was too well remembered in London, and he had men at work already constructing a most elaborate pedigree for his future wife.

The banquet was the first entertainment in York House, now rechristened Whitehall, since its new occupancy and to avoid any disparaging comparisons with its former state Henry had given the most lavish orders in every direction. The cooks were to excel the old régime in every way; the finest of wines were to be used, the choicest viands, the richest plate.

It was a matter of surprise to the entering guests to see that at the table of state under the royal canopy,

"'This satin—this scarlet satin!' admired Anne."

16

were places laid for two. Queen Catherine was at Greenwich — at least it had been thought so — what then was the meaning of this?

"By Heaven, sir, I know not!" returned the Duke of Suffolk to Carewe's question. "It cannot be that the king will place anyone over the head of my wife, his sister!"

That was exactly what Henry was doing. That was the meaning of Anne's triumphant graces, her air of imperious confidence. For Henry, bowing over her hand, led her above all his kin of blood royal, to the place beside him, dedicated to the queen of England, and as he did so he looked about on the spectators with an open smile.

"There is nothing wanting but to have the lovers exchange rings," Chapuis, the proud Spanish Ambassador, muttered to his neighbor.

There was indeed no pretense of concealment between Henry and Anne. The girl gazed haughtily about the room with the air of one already crowned. As her glances traveled down the long tables past the rows of faces turned her way in such eager attention and surprise, it seemed to her that her vision was already realized. Here she sat, in royal state at the king's side, the cynosure of eyes, the theme of tongues, nothing wanting to her glory but the actual pressure of the crown upon her brow! And yet, at her proud thought, her heart contracted in involuntary pain. That *actual* pressure! But it would come, she told herself confidently. Fate could not balk them forever. Why the next week her father was to be on his way to Europe to confer with the pope and the emperor who would be together there for the emperor's crowning, and from that soothing conference Henry hoped that all their difficulties would be smoothed over. He was still persuaded that it was the many false reports of him and Anne which had prejudiced the mind of emperor and pope alike. It was still incredible to him that anyone aware of the actual condition of affairs would persist in thwarting him. . . . And in the meantime no queen of royal blood had ever received more homage at her court than Anne Boleyn! So she thought as her gaze roved proudly about the hall; then her attention suddenly fixed. Beside the vixen pettiness of her brother George's wife a young man, dark and handsome, was staring at her with a peculiarly piercing and somber regard.

Wyatt had been rarely at court since his return from Italy, preferring to occupy himself with a post at Calais. She had not known now that he was to be here, and in childish delight that he should be seeing her in all her glory she smiled gayly at him. The man's answering recognition was a mere effort of the lips; his face was set, his eyes resting on hers in gloomy intentness.

Poor Wyatt — of course he could not fail to be most love-sad when he saw this great distance between them ending whatever secret hopes he nursed, Anne thought, according him a thrill of pity that was not without its subtle share of satisfaction.

" How like you our new queen? Is she not royally caparisoned?" the wanton wife of George Boleyn was whispering into Wyatt's ear.

" Most royally."

From under her drooping lids she shot a glance of sly spite.

" Marry, she is queen in all but crown and wife in all but name," she laughed maliciously and as his look turned sharply upon her, " Oh, la, la! What is the use of pretending otherwise, when they make no such pretense?" she scoffed. "Who would break a lance for virtue? 'Tis an outworn fashion with us — sure a maid would take shame to be such when she had passed a year at court!"

"Such maids are no new thing."

She shrugged lightly at his pointed reference to her loose gayeties, but her malice quickened. Leaning closer she murmured in mock commiseration, "Poor Master Wyatt! Is it so hard a sight to see another possess our old time love?"

To show anger was but to let her see the sparks her blow had struck. Wyatt laughed in affected negligence. "I know not the answer to that so well as thou. I hear," he thrust, smiling, "that there are strange holes in thy nets!"

But though he came off victor from that clash, he bore a bitter wound deep within his heart. She had pressed home to him the common talk of Anne. He had kept away from court since his return, away from sound and sight of her, refusing to admit to himself that he credited those light reports of her, but refusing to torture himself with the sight of her strange circumstances. This banquet had somehow drawn him. And now that he was there, back in the polluted air of scandals and intrigue, it became impossible for him to keep up longer this pretense with himself. Anne innocent! He said it to his secret soul in disdain, and the deep gaze which Anne found so pitiably sad held a dark scorn for the sight of her there in her royal masquerade. He was pierced with a sorrow that was not for the loss of her alone, but for the loss of that which had been the soul of her. To him she had been maidenhood and youth and spring; all the delicate inspiring purities of life.

THE FAVOR OF KINGS

He had not known before how very high he had held her until he saw her so fallen from that place of worship.

He looked at her now, jeweled and gauded till her slender body was like the glittering image of some idol, coquetting airily with the king beside her. At first glance Henry was handsome, high of color, gay of bearing, at the next Wyatt was struck with a strange pain, that was not the pain of jealousy: Henry was growing very heavy: his full lips were fuller, his neck wrinkled in fat creases above his collar; there was something gross and Sultanesque to the poet's eye in his great bulk of enamored flesh. And on the other hand of Anne, standing behind her chair in smiling converse, were her father and uncle, suave images of insincerity, assiduously grimacing upon her, and at the sight Wyatt's heart filled with yet heavier dejection. Those elegants were like vultures feeding on her youth, he thought, in bitter clarity of vision. What destinies she was making, what destiny was making her! He had never thought before of Anne as over-young and helpless: her high spirit and audacity had seemed to justify her own confidence of caring for herself, but now she seemed to him like some puppet dancing to wires that others pulled. For all her heavy robes of state, her jewels, her air of command, he saw the girl in her as he had never seen it when she was yet younger; the flushed face that smiled so proudly under the drift of dark hair was a child's face, its woman soul unwakened, its eyes smiling in a dream, unopened to the abyss ahead. Did she, in truth, expect to be crowned? . . . His heart ached for her and the price her young ignorance had paid.

It was the middle of the evening before he went to ask her for a dance.

LADY ANNE ROCHFORD

"Will it please thee, Lady Anne," he asked with a forced smile, "to consort for a time with thy own kin?"

Sir Nicholas Carewe, who was of the group about the girl, remarked, as Anne consented, "The Lady Anne is not one who doth forget her own kin in her elevation."

"Flatterer!" scoffed Anne, as she accepted Wyatt's arm. He murmured, in frank surprise, "I thought you had no liking for Carewe?"

"Nor have I now," she returned carelessly. "Therefore I like to see him crave my favor."

"But you have said he was your enemy —"

"What harm can he do me now?" Anne drew herself up with assurance. Then she spoiled her regal air by tossing her head very girlishly. "Nay, I have taught him his lesson and the teaching amused me — he asks now but the chance to serve me."

Wyatt made no answer.

Anne flashed him a petulant glance; this was a strangely disappointing greeting. He had not complimented her on the events of the evening, had made no mention of her high estate. Somewhat piqued, she too was silent, dancing in gliding step to the slow music, till they passed a group of men staring from the side wall. Then she could not forbear to whisper, "Glance at Suffolk — how he glowers at me!"

"I think that thou hast made some very dangerous enemies, this evening, Lady Anne," said Wyatt very soberly.

"Dangerous?" she laughed. "He may as well stomach it now as any other time!"

"Thou art so sure then of being — queen?"

"Dost thou doubt?"

"I have learned that naught is sure but death and grief."

THE FAVOR OF KINGS

She shrugged. "You speak like a schoolmaster, Wyatt."

"I fear my tongue hath been too long from court."

"I fear it has!" she informed him airily.

Again a pause. His thoughts were of an incredible bitterness. To be beside her so, clasping her hand, feeling the young warmth of her life, knowing she was another's. . . . He spoke suddenly, without premeditation. "It hath been long since I danced with thee."

"You have preferred Calais."

"And longer," he went on, "since that first dance with thee at court — do you recall? It was in this very hall. . . . You wore a gown of blue. Also," he added grimly, "you bade me remember that I was a married man!"

She frowned swiftly at the implication, and her flushed cheeks felt a yet warmer color, while she was angry at herself for feeling it. He was insolent.

"It's a pity," he added, "that *I* did not feel a scruple of conscience —"

He could not have told why he spoke so: some demon of jealousy and despair pricked him on, to try and goad, to see what sensitive flesh in her could yet shrink before a touch of shame. . . . She only laughed, a cold, scornful little laugh in which he felt the artificial note.

They finished the dance in silence. He did not again approach her. He lingered on, talking, eating and drinking with his old companions, listening to their ribald jests, answering he knew not what, and watching, furtively under his air of indifference, the girl who furnished the theme for so many of those jests.

She seemed indefatigable. Later and later it grew but still she danced on, her color higher, her laughter louder. The king grew uproarious, his hand became unsteady; Wyatt saw the wine spill in the glass that he held on high to pledge his love. The torches began to flare out, and the candles sank sputtering, and night's shadows, held so long at bay, seemed creeping in now from the corners, determined to be dispossessed no longer. Standing unobserved under the musicians' gallery, Wyatt saw Henry and Anne circling past through the leaping light and shade . . . they were laughing together and Anne, breathless, her bosom rising and falling, half leaned upon the king. As they came past him Wyatt saw the king strain her closer and, stooping, press a kiss on the white throat where his green jewels gleamed.

It seemed to Wyatt that his very heart shed tears. He went stumbling out the nearest door that let him into a space that Henry was having cleared for gardens. The remnants of the homes of the petty burghers which had been torn down to make room for these extensions were piled about in mounds of rubbish; in some places the ground had been dug to admit of the planting of hardy bulbs and plants. A fine powdering of snow covered all the unsightliness with lovely harmony.

The crisp coolness of the air, the immaculate whiteness all about him, was a grateful difference from the noisy rout within, whose shouts fell yet on Wyatt's ears. He walked away from the palace across the frozen ground, drawing in deep breaths of the invigorating air. It seemed a remedy for the state he was in. He shivered but took strange pleasure in his sense of chill. . . . He looked up at the skies. They were paling with the first gray light of dawn: the stars were withdrawn, the east seemed trembling with premonitions of light. It was half after three. He noted this, unknowingly. He was saying to himself, tremblingly again and again, " She is

THE FAVOR OF KINGS

lost." He realized then that he had never before really believed this. But that kiss. . . . He wished that there was a place that he could go and weep his heart out.

It was bitingly cold and he turned at last to reënter the palace for his cloak, and at the door he met the king's party coming forth, Henry laughing in uproarious mirth at Anne's clear, high-toned sally. Some impulse took him swiftly to them: he felt that he must see her once more, see her in her beauty and dead innocence.

He pushed swiftly past the link boys with their wavering torches, to where she stood among her sleepy ladies, drawing her furry wrap about her.

" Good night, cousin."

She turned quickly to him. It was astonishing how lightly the fatigues of the night had touched the clearness of that exquisite skin. There was scarcely a shadow under her eyes, her cheeks were bright with astounding vitality. She was like a spirit of day among effigies of sleepy night. She held out her hand, and a sudden kindliness melted the pettish frost of her voice as she saw his haggard face and sorry eyes. She clasped his hand with an earnest, " Good night, Tom."

As Wyatt took that hand a strange thing happened to him. He gazed for the first time that night straight into her eyes that met his own with a faint wonder at the passion of his look, but shone serene, muddied with no consciousness of guilt. They were the eyes of the maiden Anne, high of courage, instinct with unsurrendered pride, and in that moment all that an instant before had been his certainties became to Wyatt only base and false suspicions. Henry's betrothed Anne might be, but incredible as the world viewed it, she was no more. He drew a deep breath and the kiss that he pressed on her bared hand was of deep, trembling fervor. The girl thought

224

that it was of sad desire, and she pitied him and blamed herself for her early petulance with him that night. But it was not so. The poet was kissing Anne's soul. . . . And with a heart strangely lightened for all its loneliness and forebodings he took himself on his way, smiling whimsically at the impulse that stirred his soul to prayer.

After all, as Anne had long ago told him in that very palace, there was something in him that would have protected her even from himself.

CHAPTER XXI

HOPE DEFERRED

BUT even a heart as young and buoyant as Anne's cannot hope on forever, undismayed by constant denial, and when the Earl of Wiltshire failed in his mission, when all through the next spring and summer he was unable to wring one word of decisive compromise from pope or emperor, and when every avenue of hope was blocked, the girl's spirits plunged headlong from one extreme to the other.

"Anne of England," she mocked ironically, looking out on her life with disillusioned eyes that saw only a great blackness ahead; and the knowledge whipped her that in the same palace, not many rods away, Catherine was sitting at her interminable embroidery, rejoicing at the news, calmly confident of her position, scornful of her rival. Anne could feel that scorn.

She quivered.

And down at York was Wolsey, waiting like some dreadful spider, for his hour to come again. Wolsey! How she hated him! But for him —!

Anne did not wish herself the wife of Percy; she was wrested and detached from that old chapter in her life, but she bore the man who had wrested her from it an unconquerable grudge.

And more recently how he had stood in her way! But for his sly counsels of caution, and the pope, and the legatine court, she firmly believed she would already have been queen. But he had refused to pronounce the divorce, and had let Charles be roused to opposition so that now the emperor was like a challenged man who must sustain the honor of his family, and as the pope was in the emperor's power, small hope was there for an English cause!

And if Wolsey should return to power! Astonishing how her uncle and father shivered at that thought! They knew well of his implacable resentment.

Yet what good did the cardinal's disgrace do her after all? She was as far from her goal as ever, farther, for those who had been her supporters had decidedly cooled to the divorce project now that their own ends were accomplished and they occupied the positions they had long coveted. Even her uncle was secretly indifferent and her father lukewarm, while Suffolk was so enraged by her elevation above his wife, at that banquet last December, that he was openly hostile.

Ah, what a poor deluded little fool she had been, she thought bitterly one dreary morning, leaning on the low wall about the terrace at Windsor and staring out over the pleasant country with unseeing eyes. What was she, after all? . . . In her dreams she had been reigning as a queen, but in good truth she was nothing but a disappointed girl of whom much scandal was spoken, a name that was the jest of five courts, the betrothed of a man whose wife was still undivorced, a pitiful dreamer cheating herself with visions while life flowed swiftly past. What would it do with her? Where would it take her? — Where?

She did not hide from herself the keenest of her fears — Henry's discouragement. Hitherto he had encouraged and comforted her at every fresh disappointment. Now he was baffled and dispirited, she read under his bluster and she felt she could lean on him no more but must encourage and inspire his energies.

Well, she would do so! Her passionate egotism refused to tolerate any answer to the problem of her life except that vision of her dreams. She *would* be crowned.

She repeated this vehemently to herself and her spirit responded to her call for endurance. Let her look the worst in the face, but let her not despair! She felt in herself a stiffening of resolve, a glowing of heroic qualities.

She turned, eager to put her resolves into action, to find the crafty smile of Sir Nicholas Carewe upon her.

" What, alone, dear Lady Anne? "

" And would be," she gave back lightly.

He looked her full in the face an instant, his eyes like guarded fires. A wry smile stirred his thin lips.

" I have never pleased you, cousin," he said slowly.

Anne surveyed him with malicious humor, " No, dear Nicholas, thou never hast," she returned with sweet candor.

" Wilt thou never forgive mine early trespass? " he asked with a show of humble anxiety.

Anne's manner stiffened. " I know not what you mean."

" How little you thought then you'd e'er forget! . . . A lady's memory is a short-lived thing! I refer to my too zealous indiscretion in the matter of the now Earl of Northumberland." His eyes watched her, narrowing.

She felt his gaze like something palpable. How strangely jealous he was of that past, she thought; how he tried to stab her with it! What a torment was his passion for her. It had ridden him like a demon through the years.

" Oh, *that!* " said Anne as if he had been referring to

the merest trifle. " That . . . why truly, Nicholas, I owe
you thanks there, after all. If I had gained my will
there, I would be now buried in Northumberland's estate,
my housewife's keys dangling at my belt — instead of
which, here am I mounting to a far higher destiny.
Lord, what an angel in disguise thou wast, and I thought
thee but a spying fool! How we are mistook in our
friends!" Her edged laughter whipped mercilessly
round him.

" Forsooth, thou hast a high destiny," he said with
peculiar emphasis. " Dost truly think thou wilt ever
mount to it?"

" Yes, dear Nicholas, if I have to mount on the necks
of mine opposers. . . . So look that thine be not among
them," and with a ripple of chill menace in her delicate
laughter she made her way on to her apartments.

Carewe stood looking after her, an unguarded ferocity
in his features. He seethed with impotent anger against
the girl and impotent desire for her. He would have
given that which he considered his soul to have had her
in his power. " I'd tame her — I'd sweat her," he
grunted between his teeth. . . . When she laughed and
he saw the little muscles rippling under the white satin
of her throat he had felt an insane longing to still them
with his fingers, to crush them, gripping that slender
stalk of a neck until she should cry out, entreat, beseech.
. . . His thwarted love, debased and despoiled of all that
had ever given it finer and higher impulses, racked him
with the craving to possess and conquer her, body and
spirit; knowing the hopelessness of it all, he yet spent
time inventing situations when she would be utterly in
his power, utterly his. . . .

" Oh, I must, I *must* go on," Anne was whispering
passionately to her heart.

THE FAVOR OF KINGS

From that day a change was worked in the girl. She no longer felt that her coronation was a beautiful, impending, inevitable thing, just around the corner of events, which the next change of fortune would sweep towards her: she realized it was the price of battle and she must wage that battle alone. There were frightful odds against her. Frightful. And she had nothing to face them with but Henry's favor, and she knew that there were rivals ready to dispute that favor desperately on the first hint of its slackening.

Anne threw herself heart and soul into the difficult game. Her ambitions obsessed her. Her delight in the dances and masques and hunts, whose gayeties had so absorbed her in the past, became secondary to her appreciation of them as distractions for Henry. She saw how much of the cardinal's success had depended on his keeping the king amused, and she gave herself up to revels, merrymaking, singing, dancing, jesting, with all the exuberant vitality of her three and twenty years. But she could not lose herself in these things at once. She remembered feverishly under all the present hilarity that she was playing for high stakes, and grew a little thin and trifles irritated her as never before.

Her anxiety concerning the cardinal increased. She felt he was gaining ground. She was sure that he was intriguing with Eustache Chapuis, the Spanish Ambassador who had succeeded Mendoza, against her, and Henry's information from the English agents at Rome reported that he was in incessant correspondence with officials there. It was pretty evident from the pope's speeches that Wolsey had written him strongly against Anne. Norfolk and Wiltshire were harassed with a secret dread of his machinations. Their anxieties came to a head when it was discovered that Wolsey was attempting now to reach the king directly and intrigue against his ministers; believing that Henry was impatient with the incapabilities of his advisers and was at a loss whither to turn, he sent agents who were secretly to offer the king the services of his archbishop. If these messengers had reached Henry and found him in a capricious mood the anxieties of Anne's relations would have been very well founded.

But the messengers had their own anxieties. They knew that the king was extremely unreliable in all his dealings and it would have been quite in accord with some of his other performances if he had disclosed their secret messages to his council and turned them over to its tender mercies. So they turned informers themselves and revealed their errand to the Duke of Norfolk.

He was immeasurably alarmed. This was proof of all he had dreaded. And nobody knew what other nets that wily and restless man was spinning from his archbishopric! In a panic the party against him set itself to find out, and by arresting Agostino, one of Wolsey's agents, and wringing a confession from him of intrigues with the French and Spanish ambassador and the pope, they secured enough fuel to fire the king's resentment again and orders were hastily given for his arrest on the charge of treason.

It was an astounding evidence to Anne of the irony of existence that it should fall to Henry Percy, Earl of Northumberland, to arrest the cardinal. One of those luckless lovers he had so ruthlessly frustrated was the instrument of his disgrace and the other of his arrest! Life was a very curious thing. . . .

Yet it was only the dramatic quality in the event that made its appeal to her; she felt avenged and avenged in a climatic fashion, and her blood thrilled again to the spectacular nature of her career. Surely her life was strange!

But though she thought herself at twenty-three very old and experienced in the prodigious fantasies of existence, she appreciated none of the inevitable sadnesses of that fall she had assisted in precipitating; she felt the contrast but not the pathos of the cardinal's condition. When she heard how he had wept with his faithful usher, Cavendish, she listened with incredulous scorn. That was not the way to bear disaster! Weeping with his servants —! Or perhaps he but feigned to weep. She suspected him of any duplicity. He was her enemy; he still menaced her and hers, even though arrested. For Henry had declared that he should be tried for his treason in London, and Heaven, to whom all things were presumably revealed, alone knew what would ensue when the king and the cardinal were brought face to face again. . . . There would be more tears on Wolsey's part, perhaps, eloquent speeches, artfully extolling the king, bringing to mind the long years of their association, their friendship, and then suddenly Henry, fired by his passion for the spectacular, would spring to the side of the weeping man who would sink to his knees. . . . Henry would raise him. . . . Oh, Anne's vivid imagination saw the performance very clearly in the watches of some sleepless hours. And Norfolk and Wiltshire were seeing it, too. They urged her to stiffen Henry against the cardinal. But Anne was already aware of the subtle and disconcerting traits of Henry's capriciousness. He might swallow coarse flattery wholesale and yet he was the shrewdest man in the world to know when he was being delicately approached; he appeared to divine in advance the position that he was to be manipulated to take and would sheer off absolutely from it. So Anne felt that it was better to wait for the event.

But the event never came. Instead an old man, taken ill on his way to trial at London, was hurried to the monastery gates at Leicester.

"Father Abbott," he said, as weakly he tottered from his mule, "I come to lay my bones among you."

And three days later, on the twenty-ninth of November, he turned his graying face to the wall.

"If I had served my God as I have served my king," the words came gasping from his lips, "He would not thus have given me over in my old age."

He did not speak again.

And the news was borne to Lady Anne Rochford that the man who had crossed her path with such disaster to them both, the man who had frustrated her young love and destined her for a passing toy, the man who had impeded her ambition and concentrated on her ruin, had passed beyond all power of troubling her. He who had imposed his will on England more imperiously than any within its borders, who had been more hated, more feared, and more flattered than any other, was gone forever from the theater of his activities.

To Anne it was a supremest blessing. She knew from the very poignancy of relief how harassing had been that constant edge of uneasiness. Now it was gone. Her old enemy was no more. Dead! . . . "From that inn no guest returneth," ran the old song and the girl sang it in gay relief. The mysterious cessation of the human spirit she accepted with literal incuriosity. He was dead; that was all. He could trouble her no longer.

And that night the Earl of Wiltshire, in the exuberance of his relief, gave an uproarious masque which portrayed the cardinal's progress through hell.

233

CHAPTER XXII

THE MARCHIONESS OF PEMBROKE

IF on that windy March day, when Anne Boleyn, with Henry on the hill, had looked over Epping forest to far away London spires and beheld in ambitious vision the acclaiming city greeting her as queen, she could have seen how tortuous and baffling was the ascent that she must climb towards her dream city, she might have taken a longer moment's thought before she flung Henry her high-confidenced yes. Could she have seen the uneasy hours, the anxious plans, the sharp reversals of hope she was to know! Every corner turned seemed but to reveal a new corner. Fate had always some new, tricksy card to play against her.

Nearly five years and a half had passed since that day in Epping forest, and it was two years since Wolsey had died, and still Anne's position remained practically the same, a strange pinnacle of anomalous triumph and thwarted hope. In her moments of despondency she told herself that she had not advanced one inch. She had scored tremendously, to be sure, she had remained at court in spite of all the European agitation against her and all the pope's fulminations, and Catherine and Mary had been sent away, but after all, that was merely holding her own and the throne seemed as far away as ever.

And now as she sat at the king's side one September night in 1532 at a banquet given in honor, not alas! of her coronation, but of her elevation to the title of

THE MARCHIONESS

Marchioness of Pembroke, she knew that the throng which smiled so deferentially upon her was busy with wonder over the meaning of this honor which had been conferred upon her. Was it a fresh step toward the crown — or did it mark the end of her ambitions? Only the newly made marchioness herself could have told and her smiling lips did not part over the information.

To her father's suavely insinuating, "I am glad, dear Anne, at your wisdom in contenting yourself with this safe title," she returned a mild, "I am so glad at your gladness," which aroused, but did not answer the Earl of Wiltshire's uneasy suspicions concerning his unquiet daughter.

To Carewe she was more enigmatic still. "A fair resting place, dear marchioness," he had smiled, and she smiled back, "A resting place, indeed."

"'Twill be rest for the journey on, she meaneth," interpreted Helen Sackville, who had overheard this, to the old Dowager Duchess of Norfolk and Wyatt, who were sitting at table near. "She will be stopped by no sop of marchioness."

"'Tis a good enow sop," returned the old duchess, her eyes twinkling. "A thousand pounds in land and a royal present of jewels taken from the queen."

"The queen," Wyatt repeated absently. "Poor old soul, where is she?"

"Let our dear marchioness hear you say that —!" Helen laughed. "Why the lady is at Saint Albans still, for all I've heard, scribbling away to the pope and the emperor. . . . Do you think Anne will e'er stop at marchioness? Do you think she will e'er let Queen Catherine come back to court? Then you know not our Lady Arrogance!"

"Fate is not always of our patterning," Wyatt reminded her. "Anne may not hap to shape her destiny to her liking more than the rest of us."

The old duchess gave the young poet a kindly quizzical look. "Still sighing, Tom?"

"There be many in like case," he laughed back, and his eyes rested on the tall, thin figure of the Earl of Northumberland crossing the hall. The young earl looked older than his years and the lines of disappointment were deep about his features. The three watched as an acquaintance accosted him; Northumberland's manner was perfunctory but absent, and with a vague wave of his hand he passed on. He seemed to come to rest nowhere, roaming ceaselessly from group to group though he was not seen to approach that one where Anne was holding court.

"Another moth," the poet said lightly while the duchess murmured, "Henry the Unlucky. . . . He dares not pluck up spirit to accost her — he is still afraid of that late plot —"

Wyatt raised his brows. "Plot?"

"Good Lord, where have you been mooning, Tom, that you have heard not? 'Twas a month ago — mayhap two — just at the close of Warham's life. It seemeth that earl there cannot abide the wife that his father forced upon him and has no more to do with her than he has with me, if account be true! And when one night she came pattering to his chambers and reproached him with neglect, he turned roundly on her and declared she was no wife of his and he owed her no duty, that he had long ago been betrothed to Anne Boleyn and no other bonds would hold. La, la, the lady countess was in a fine to-to! She wrote it all to her father, thinking to obtain her freedom from such matrimony, and also thinking that her father would be glad to put a stone in the

path of the king and Anne, for everyone knoweth that
Shrewsbury is not the complaisant courtier that his words
appear. But Shrewsbury is no fool and his head and
shoulders are not yet eager to part company. He attempted no deception but showed the letter to Norfolk,
who showed it to his niece, who showed it at once to the
king, and with her usual high-handedness Anne denied it
flatly and called on Northumberland to deny it too. All
of which on oath he very properly did, so the Countess of
Northumberland has still a cold and absent husband and
there is no precontract between our sovereign and his
marchioness. . . . So you had not heard that tale?"

"Oh, the weakling, the thrice damned weakling!"
Wyatt muttered, with a hard look at the earl.

The duchess snorted. "Marry, what would you have
him do — go run his head into the lion's mouth with
his babble of precontract? Henry would snap off that
head on some pretext or other, be sure of that, and then
would Anne be free again. Weakling indeed! What
wouldst thou have done?"

"My all to save her."

"Save her — from a crown? Tom Wyatt, thou art
a madman. Take this fresh flagon here and drown thy
sorrows in drink!"

"Drinking to the new marchioness?" said a thick voice
behind them, and Sir Nicholas Carewe lounged to the
table where the three were sitting. "Here, boy, another
flagon — we'll all join that toast, eh, ladies? To the
Marchioness of Pembroke *and her heirs!*" holding his
glass on high.

Wyatt's finely arched brows drew together in unconquerable disdain of the ribald jester. Carewe saw it and
laughed loudly. "Zounds, Tom, be not so squeamish!
The king himself hath drunk that toast three times

237

already. . . . Aye, and the lady herself, I'll warrant
you."

"To be sure she hath," Wyatt answered evenly, a set
smile on his handsome lips. "We all drink to it, then —
to the Marchioness of Pembroke and her heirs — the
future kings of England!"

"Eh, not so fast, not so fast! Thy imagination out-
strips the circumstance, dear poet. Those heirs will be
no heirs of England! Marked you the patent of creation,
bequeathing the title to her heirs male, and leaving out
those words, 'lawfully begotten,' that are wont to be
used? Ho, ho, ho, ho," Carewe hiccoughed, "'twas a
pertinent omission, a most pertinent omission. I think
Our Lady Kite will fly in lower skies hereafter."

"And I think thy health would scarce improve an she
heard thee so name her."

"Babble it to her then," Carewe gave impudently back
and like a flash Wyatt's hand flew out and struck Carewe
across the mouth.

"That for thy words!" Then as Carewe reached for
his blade, "Thou canst not draw here," Wyatt reminded
him. "Come outside — your venomed blood will be the
cooler for a little letting."

"Outside it is — ho, ho, a worthy quarrel — the good
name of the heirs of Pembroke!"

Helen clutched at the duchess's sleeve. "We must
stop them," she gasped and the duchess, looking up, for
Helen was a tall girl, saw that her thin face was ashen.
"Carewe is a devil with his sword."

"So there sits the wind?" queried the old lady with
an interest not unspiced with malice. "Tut, tut, we cannot stop them. If Nicholas is the old Nick himself, why
Tom is two devils in his present mood. Lord, his love
for Anne is like a fever in his blood — it never cools.

THE MARCHIONESS

Think you ever to console him, girl, for our dark marchioness?"

Helen made a sharp effort at recovery. "I am like to," she gave back with her mocking smile.

"Thou art like to, indeed," the old duchess acceded with a frankness not unkindly. "Poor girl, I have oft wondered what you bleak-visaged maids got out of life; you play in your youth that part of onlooker which we play in old age — and without our memories to feed you. . . . And so you must needs set your hopes upon a star — our Wyatt there. Ah, well a day! If you wish to serve Wyatt, tell the tale of this clash to our lady yonder and win him a smile for it."

Helen Sackville's light eyes sparkled with an indescribable glint. "That is indeed the best I can do for him," she said.

"Pluck up — you see he reappears and not a whit the worse," the duchess cried presently in a tone of relief that denied the nonchalance of her former air. "I trust you have not run him through?" she whispered to the young man who reappeared beside her.

"The devil take him for a drunken fool!" Wyatt retorted viciously. "He had made but one lunge when I sent his sword flying and he stumbled and went flat on his face — I cannot spit a brawler in a ditch! His fellows are washing him up — he'll be in for the dance later, I'll be bound."

The old lady laughed gayly at his angry accents. "Be philosophical, Tom — another time you may be drunk yourself and not so nice of honor! 'Twas but a straw of a quarrel anyway. You cannot go about running through all those who prophesy that the heirs of Pembroke will not be the heirs of England. . . . I am one of

239

them myself," she finished hardily, looking him determinedly in the face, and then she let fall slowly, " And so, I doubt not, is our fair marchioness herself."

Wyatt dropped his eyes from that significant look which seemed resolved to drive the truth home to his repugnant senses.

He thought, as he made his way across the hall where the servants were beginning to take up the tables in clearance for the dance, how bitter a trickster life was to lavish all else but the heart's desire, without which the rest was as nothing.

He had an impulse to vent his despairs on Anne, to taunt her, to implore her, to do any of a thousand follies, but when presently he was dancing with her he held his tongue. Any word that he could utter seemed strangely impotent in the face of that glittering assurance of hers.

Suddenly Anne stopped. " Your arm ! " She put a hand on it. " 'Tis wet — 'tis blood ! "

" It hath not soiled thee ? "

Her look flashed over his, seeing for the first time how white his face and how tense the lines about the ironic smile. " Come hither at once," she imperiously commanded, and hurried into the anteroom that lay between the great hall and a small privy garden. Sir Francis Weston sat there at dice with a page. " Fresh water," said Anne briefly and they vanished.

" Now roll up thy sleeve — who was it did this ? "

" 'Tis but a scratch," he protested and indeed the wound that her hands revealed was not a great matter though a painful one. " Dear cousin Nicholas and I had a brief spat," he grinned, and she returned, " Now I love thee for that ! " and set about bathing it with the water which young Weston brought, who vanished again with a cheery wink at Wyatt. She bound her handkerchief about the arm and tied it in place with three or four long dark hairs of hers, drawn from her heavy curls. " Now dance no more," she commanded.

Wyatt stood looking down at the dark hairs with an indescribable expression. Then he smiled. " What would Henry say to this? "

" It matters little! " She tossed her head in buoyant confidence. " What was the quarrel on? "

" The good name of the heirs of Pembroke," he let fall slowly.

The hot blood rushed into her cheeks; she reared her head with a gesture of proud challenge. " That matter needs no sword to defend it," she flashed.

" No, cousin? " he said sadly taunting, yielding to the impulse to turn on her some of the bitterness she had given to him. " No, cousin? "

" The crown and scepter will do that! "

" The years pass and you are as far from that crown as ever."

" Not so . . . how can you say that? Why, I was never so near as now."

" Perhaps you mistake the coronet of Pembroke for the crown? "

Her nostrils quivered. " I mistake nothing! I tell thee, it is almost reached."

" Why so you said when Wolsey died. . . . That is two years gone by."

" And so it would have been if Warham, that mad archbishop of Canterbury, had not turned from us in his last sickness and refused to pronounce on the case! Who could have foreseen — why he was with us hand in glove at first! But now he is gone and the *next* archbishop —" she paused significantly, her eyes dilating with the triumph she pictured.

"Oh, yes, Cranmer," Wyatt supplied with an impatient gesture with his well arm. "You build on him, but as soon as he is installed he will cool like the others and shirk the responsibility of taking the head of England's cases from the pope."

"Nay, *he* will not cool."

"Oh, you dream, you dream!" said Wyatt thickly. The wine he had drunk, the pain he was suffering, combined to raise him to a pitch of strange excitement. "You are stuffed full of dreams by your sly new secretary, Cromwell. An you can find a priest to wed you, what of the king? Will he dare it, think you —"

"I can make him dare," said Anne and a significant smile touched her eyes and lips as she faced the poet's angry questions.

Wyatt, as he gazed on that proud face, was suddenly maddened with a sense of its changes; he remembered the ball, years before, where he had suffered so at thoughts of her dishonor and where one look into her eyes had reassured him past all doubt, her eyes that now sparkled with such daring implications. She would play now for higher stakes than any she had risked in the past, those defiant eyes told him; they did not shrink before the accusing look he turned on her, they challenged arrogantly, and her reckless smile deepened.

"O God!" said Wyatt in a sudden voice of fury and he clasped her about the waist. "I know what is in thy mind!"

She stared at him, her two hands struggling with his clasped ones. "Leave me go, Wyatt. Art thou mad? . . . I hate to injure that cut arm — but leave me go. . . . Tom, art thou drunk?"

"With more than wine," he said savagely. "Leave thee go! That had always been thy plea of me and I have been the fool to grant it. Never now — I have let thee go too long. What if I be married — is not Henry so and am not I the truer lover? He will devour thee, Anne, and then cast thee aside! I will wear and cherish thee . . . but I will not let thee go." His voice came pantingly for she was struggling with fury. Wyatt was a strong man and now his strength was inflamed. He held her close.

"Fool!" she flung at him. "Henry comes — hear you not his voice? Thou art undone — free me, I demand!"

"Never; I will hold you and cry that you are mine. He will leave you then. . . . I will save you —"

"You will destroy yourself — and me!"

She was in terror. Henry's laughter was on the other side of the door. Now it was pushed open.

That instant Anne stiffened in Wyatt's arms. Her head fell back on his shoulder, her hands dangled limply. He was grasping her in amazement when the king's eyes fell upon the tableau.

"In Heaven's name!" cried Henry.

"Water," came faintly from Anne's lips. Henry's sister, Mary, the Duchess of Suffolk, rushed to the silver ewer on the table, reddened with Wyatt's blood and stared on it in distraction, while Henry sprang to the girl's side. She wavered forward and half shifted her weight to his outstretched arms. "It is — nothing," she murmured, raising her eyes with a palpable effort to the king who clasped her and called for water and wine and Dr. Butts in tipsy confusion. "I was but giddy — the sight of blood on Wyatt's arms — it overcame me. Call the physician for *him*," and then from under her lowered lids her eyes swiftly darted a triumphant and commanding message at the bewildered Wyatt.

His enlightenment was vivid. He shook himself as if

awakening from a dream and with a dreary return to the resignation of everyday, " I will remove my bloodied arm," he said, in a strangely tired voice. " I but trust, your Highness, that I have been the cause of no serious indisposition to Lady Pembroke."

" It is past," Anne murmured.

" Doth it not seem to you," said the Duke of Suffolk in a harsh undertone to young Weston who had hurried into the room at the noise of the commotion, " that a long time elapsed before the lady was so overcome? She had time to grow used to that bloodied arm! Certes, it was near a quarter hour ago when I saw you going into that chamber with that ewer."

" You mistake, my lord," Sir Francis said, " it was but a moment ago."

The duke's eyes snapped. He smiled jeeringly.

" Thy rich bride, then, hath not displaced thy former — shrine?"

" Shrine, my lord, is a good word," said the young man in a trembling voice, " for the reverence that I bear the Lady Anne."

" Well prated," uttered the duke and turned on his heel.

" I am better," Anne declared presently, and began to dry concernedly her water-splashed gown. " Dance but the next dance with me, Hal, and I am cured."

" Nay, rest here with me —" the king began thickly.

Drunk! Drunker than Wyatt, she said to herself with a shiver of repugnance, while outwardly she smiled and shook her head, insisting on the public room and the dance. She had saved Wyatt from the consequence of his folly, now she must save herself from Henry's.

Truly the Marchioness of Pembroke had cause for that deepening line between her arching brows, and the mocking jangle of her laughter.

CHAPTER XXIII

THE LAST CARD

SHE knew well why Henry had omitted those words from her patent of title. She knew what he was more and more demanding of her and she, and she alone, knew how increasingly difficult denial was becoming.

Every time the wretched battle was fought out between them she surrendered something — something of pride, something of resolution. Sometimes she half promised, under the strength of his insistence, sometimes she half named a day, but on the morrow — stopping her ears with her pretty fingers — she would protest that he had dreamed, that he was in his cups, that she had ne'er breathed such a scandalous word! La, la, had he no notion of her virtue after all these years? But such subterfuges ceased to avail her and her continual refusals irritated the king to dangerous estrangement. His wild roisterings in disguise through the town grew more and more frequent and though his masquerades were cloaked and hidden from the girl, the report of them found their way to her and terrified her with keen forebodings.

His reproaches increased. And there came one day when he flamed to passionate anger and flung out of her presence, hurling back words of rage and fury. Never had he so turned upon her.

There was strange fear in the heart of the Marchioness of Pembroke as she leaned back against the cushions of the casement. She had come, she thought, trembling, to the crossroads. . . . Her resources were almost at an end.

"Love me?" he had scoffed, his face livid. "You would not risk for my love what other women lavish on a groom of the chambers . . . is it my crown alone you love?"

His anger, she knew, had been the anger of a thwarted will; it marked the stress of his desire for her, but it marked, too, the end of his patience with her cajoleries. His words had swept round her like a blustering wind; she had been shaken, not at his reproaches, but at the menace of the attitude they betrayed. He was infuriated, desperate . . . he was going to console himself. . . . Well, to-morrow would see him back, repentant, but what of the morrow after that when it was all to do over again? . . . This was not the way she could afford to quarrel with him; Henry's pride and self-love were engaged as well as his passion and he was not a man who brooked denial long. For six years now he had taken it from her, but he was souring . . . if he grew indifferent . . . if she lost him! The girl shivered — then she threw the thought away as too absurd. Henry indifferent! . . . But they could not go on like this forever.

As she sat there alone in the room, her chin in her hand, her dark eyes heavy with anxieties, the thought that had slipped some time ago, shamefaced and sly, into the back of her mind edged more and more into the open. She had mockingly faced Wyatt with the hint of it at the ball last September — but that was a vastly different matter from acting upon it. But now what if she did? What if she played her last card — her precious card — *herself!*

It was strangely, sadly significant of the callousness

of the life she knew, that the desperate concern of this woman now on the brink of self betrayal was with the political expediency of her course. Would it wreck or make her ambition? Feverishly she revolved the aspect of her affairs.

Cranmer was to be Archbishop of Canterbury in Warham's place — Warham who had turned so against them in his last days and had checked them so long. Cranmer was a devoted adherent of hers, yet should his loyalty to the royal wishes ever flag, there was a way, as she had hinted to Wyatt, to spur it. For Cranmer had contracted a secret marriage, as so many of the English parochial clergy did, and should he now, after accepting this high position, where the Romish rule of celibacy could be severely enforced, oppose the king, Henry could pretend to discover the marriage and pack him off to the Tower. So on all counts Cranmer could be depended upon.

And then there was Cromwell, that Cromwell who had flashed so comet-like above the other satellites at court. Cardinal Wolsey had first made the man who had been, until he entered the cardinal's service, a small London attorney and money lender, and upon the cardinal's disgrace, Cromwell had managed to make himself. He had interceded for his former master and made many friends for himself by the distribution of the cardinal's pensions; he had hastened to secure the patronage of the Duke of Norfolk and by shrewd and indefatigable efforts he had come into the royal notice. From Wolsey, Cromwell had learned the lesson of service well, and he applied every wit in his hard, bullet head to furthering the king's desires. And since Anne was the chief of these desires he concentrated upon serving her. Anne felt she might rely upon his intrepid support. "I'll unmake him an he hang back," she breathed to herself. So with these men to aid her and Warham's opposition gone, the way was clearer in England than she had seen it in long years. If only Henry, smarting from the pope's defections, could be made to give the decision over to England! "He will," she pondered, "an I dare —"

Her face grew sharp and defiant. Her mouth fixed and seemed to tighten, her eyes stared out belligerently on the empty room. "I dare not," she whispered to herself, and then in a strangled voice, "I dare!"

She grew aware at last that her clasped hands were clutching each other so tightly that the rings were cutting into the flesh. She drew off the ring from the sharpest cut. It was one of Henry's earliest gifts to her, a plain gold band with, "Thy virtue is thy honor," graved within it. What a man for pious sentiments, she thought mockingly, her lips curling in disdain. Her virtue — God alone knew how she had hugged that comfort to her smarting pride against the secret sneers she divined about her. Yet now. . . . The ring slipped from her fingers and rolled out across the floor. A bit of rush blocked it and it toppled and dropped through an open knot hole. The augury seemed to her complete. She laughed — and then something, like a hand upon her throat, seemed to strangle the laughter at its source and she quivered back among the cushions, her hands hiding her face like some poor shamed thing.

That year the Christmas revels were gayer than ever and King Henry was scarce an instant to be parted from his marchioness.

The dark dawn of the twenty-fifth of January saw a little group of people slipping into an unfrequented attic in the west turret of Whitehall. They were the

THE LAST CARD

king's most confidential attendants, two ladies from the suite of the Marchioness of Pembroke, and an excited old dowager duchess trembling with cold and elation. An Augustinian friar stood by the altar and before him knelt the king of England and a slender girl whose dark hair fell in an obscuring shower about her. Against its ebony her face was the pallor of snow, but her eyes were glowing with hot ecstasy. The hand that Henry clasped was cold but it did not tremble, and she repeated the vows with silvery distinctness. . . . The friar pronounced them man and wife.

As Anne rose the blood rushed into her face; it glowed rosier and rosier like the dawn and her eyes were luminous as she flung a look about that hushed and awestruck gathering as glancing as the light. "At last!" her soul was whispering within her.

With many urgent whispers and reiterated cautions the company stole out as secretly as it had entered to meet again at breakfast with as excellent an air of unconsciousness as could be assumed.

"Let but a breath of this out," warned the Earl of Wiltshire to his reckless son, now the Viscount Rochford, "and we'll have the devil on us! All depends upon Cranmer being made archbishop and the pope hath not yet ratified that. And let him but suspect that Cranmer is a king's man and that Henry stands in urgent need of his archbishop's aid and there will be no ratifying."

"Meanwhile," replied the young Viscount Rochford with a grin, "the nuncio from the pope is here endeavoring to have Henry arrange to submit to the authority of the Holy See! He hath not an inkling of the matter. Oh, for once England hath pulled the wool over papal eyes. We have scored in truth."

249

THE FAVOR OF KINGS

" Wait till 'tis out," Wiltshire foreboded.

But even Wiltshire's courage had risen with the amazing event. Anne was actually married! And nobody could say that he, Wiltshire, had urged the marriage, rather it had taken place in spite of him. Anne and Henry between them had carried things with a high hand and he had become the father-in-law of a king. With a smile of paternal pride he realized that this marriage had been always in Anne's mind and that she had effected it single-handed — except for the aid of Henry's infatuation. What a man she would have made! But would she? No, he amended, she was feminine to her finger tips, she could bewitch, enthrall, command, but she would never have bent to the obsequious flattery that the men at court must yield. She was best a woman.

For some weeks the secret was fairly well kept while the way was being paved for its reception, but hints of it began presently to transpire. Anne lived in almost royal state and at a great dinner that she gave, the end of February, Henry called jovially down the board to the Dowager Duchess of Norfolk, bidding her observe all the rich plate that belonged to Anne and asking if she were not a good match? The witticism flew like wildfire through a court already alight with curiosity, and it was no great surprise, a fortnight later, to hear a sermon in the king's own chapel, in which the priest earnestly exhorted his sovereign to eschew the abominable sin in which he lived with Catherine of Aragon and marry now a good and virtuous woman, even if she were of a lower degree than his own! Somers, the king's jester, parodied the sermon for a week, and Patch, Wolsey's old fool, mouthed bitter jests.

By now the pope had ratified the appointment of

250

THE LAST CARD

Cranmer as Archbishop of Canterbury and the veil of secrecy was wearing thin. Anne's brother was hurried off to France to smooth matters over there as much as possible and enlist France's aid, but France was indignant over the way Henry had broken his promise to Francis not to " innovate " anything until another conference between the pope and Francis had taken place, and George's too independent assurance made something of a breach.

Meanwhile Henry was carrying things at home with a high hand. The middle of March a bill was introduced in Parliament settling the supreme authority in matrimonial cases on the primate and, in certain cases, on the convocation of the clergy. After three weeks' contest, the bill was carried by the Houses which had been carefully packed by the royal ministers. In the meantime convocation had been assembled and, by excusing certain of the clergy and requesting them to give their proxies to others who could be depended upon to do the king's will, a heavy majority was obtained for the decision that the king's first marriage was invalid.

Everything was now prepared for the lifting of the curtain and yet, with all this foreword, it was still with a curious sense of shock that the courtiers, hearing the trumpeters pealing one Saturday in April and baring their heads in expectation of the king, saw Anne Boleyn enter the hall with stately bearing, an assumption of haughty unconsciousness in her face, her purple velvet train borne by the Countess of Richmond, Norfolk's daughter and wife of the king's illegitimate son. After her stepped her maids of honor, pale Helen Sackville and dark Amy Gaynesford, Mary Wyatt, blushing from sheer pleasure, and Jane Seymour, demurely casting down her eyes.

THE FAVOR OF KINGS

Anne walked slowly with high held head, the thrill of triumph coursing through her blood. This was her answer to cautioning friends and sneering enemies! She was queen at last!

Norris, straightening from his bow, was visited with a sudden recollection. He nudged Brereton. " D'ye mind a day in this very hall when we saw Anne pass in the tail of the other's procession, stark mad over some news from Henry Percy? " he whispered.

Brereton shook his head, his eyes following Anne's royal progress down the great room with worshiping loyalty.

" By the mass, but you look as proud as she," Norris smiled.

" Good sooth, I am," the big fellow admitted simply. " I have had great heaviness of mind about her but now methinks her troubles are all passed."

" Thou faithful watch dog! " Norris gave his friend's arm an affectionate squeeze. " Nay, you need loose no more sleep over the fortunes of fair Anne Boleyn. Go to planning instead where to raise the ducats for your fine feathers for the coronation that's to be next month."

CHAPTER XXIV

HAPPIEST OF WOMEN

AT Ampthill a fine rain was falling, veiling the landscape like a curtain of gray from the eyes of the three women who were seated at the windows. There were no signs of life to be seen from those windows, nothing but the slowly widening puddles in the road and the rim of the woods, looming indistinguishable and strange through the drizzling mist, but the women had been seated there for hours in the inaction which had grown habitual with them through the years.

They did not talk much; they were aware to the dreariest limits of ennui of the workings of each other's minds. For so long they had lived at such close quarters, mental and physical, that no element of surprise or interest was left to them in each other.

They had at present a pretext for their presence at the windows; they were awaiting the return of a page, the nephew of Lady Wallop, the youngest of the three women. They had not much expectation of him until the next day or the next, for he would find London only too attractive after his inoccupation here, and it was with genuine surprise that they suddenly glimpsed his young figure on horseback galloping recklessly through the puddles.

His advent was like a sudden stone in a motionless brook; they ringed him in circling confusion.

THE FAVOR OF KINGS

"The news, lad? What's been done?"

Old Donna Blanche clutched his shoulder with an eager hand. "Is she crowned? Oh, is she crowned?"

"Hush, her Highness is sleeping," another interposed. "Wake her not — belike this be too much for her ears. Let us have it first. Come, boy, what learned you? Is she crowned?"

"Crowned she is," gave back the page and at the consternation that fell upon them, the sharp intake of breaths, the rolling of eyes towards heaven, he was visibly elated at the importance of his news. "I reached the town as the lady was coming up the river to the Tower," he went on, "and there were two hundred boats in her train, all splendidly hung and bedizened and she had for barge — what think you? — none other than that of her own Grace!"

"What, the queen's own barge?"

"Oh, shame, shame!"

"They say the king had given it to her and the queen's arms were taken away and her own put on top —"

"Her own!" Lady Wallop fell to laughing. "A fine invention, those arms — of a piece with the rest of the business."

"The popinjay!" The donna's chin was trembling. "Would none other suit her but she must lay her foul, Lutheran hands on that one? . . . Did not the people cry out against it, lad?"

"There were not so many that knew, it being so splendidly bedecked," the boy answered innocently, "but those that did know thought it great shame," he assured her, seeing her rage was somehow increased by his answer. "It was very wonderfully overhung with tissue of gold and of silver and draped with

254

shining clothes and made softly within by many cushions —"

"Aye, aye — many cushions for that sweet body of hers! May it burn in hell a thousand years and may mine eyes be given to feast upon that sight."

"Amen!" echoed another. "Go on, what else saw you of this most Christian coronation?"

"Why — there were two hundred boats, I am telling you, madame. From Greenwich to the Tower the river was a gleam of fine scarlet and purple and cloths of gold and silver, flags flying and trumpets sounding, and at the Tower she was received with great booming of cannon. There was feasting and revelry the whole night long, and all the next day while she lay at the Tower. That day I did discharge me of thine errands, giving one letter to Chapuis and another to the man ye said at the Sign of the Cat and Fiddle, and I made thy purchases. The city was busy making ready to receive the lady on the next day, and the householders were very angry at the expense for a tax had been laid upon them all. Only the Spanish merchants had been excused from preparing some sort of entertainment and the French envied them, saying that they were paying dear for their popularity with the lady. . . . Well, on that day, which was Saturday, she entered the city in great procession and there were fine preparations, flags and carpets hung from windows and barriers erected to keep off the crowds — everyone made holiday."

"A worthy cause."

The Spanish woman's grim interjection checked the boy's enthusiasm. He had forgotten himself in the narration, now as he went on he tried to infuse a becoming bitterness into his account.

"Yes, madame, and so muttered many people as she

255

rode into the city. Nan Bullen is no queen of ours, they said, nathless they were all out in the streets to see her pass. The procession was headed by a dozen or so great French merchants who were residents of the city — it was whispered no knights would come over from France for the purpose being uncertain yet politically — but the merchants made a marvelous fine showing all in purple velvet with the lady's device on their sleeves —"

"A fine jest, that device," Lady Wallop broke in, "for she chose one at random that was the motto of her bitter foes — *Ainsi sera, groigne qui groigne!*"

"Nay, aunt, she hath chosen another," the boy corrected. "I know not how long ago but 'tis all over London now. 'Happiest of Women,' it is. '*La Plus Heureuse,*' as she writ it in French. The gentlemen all bore it in some fashion. After the merchants rode English noblemen and gentlemen according to their degree, and then the Lord Chancellor with the Venetian Ambassador, and then the primate with Bailly de Troye. And after these came the lady's litter carried by two white mules and draped most lavish with white satin. There was a canopy of cloth of gold borne over her head and at one side rode the Duke of Suffolk and at the other Sir William Howard, in the stead of his brother, the Duke of Norfolk, who hath been sent to France. The lady herself —" and in spite of himself the boy's eyes glistened with the remembered sight, "sat in this open litter, bowing and smiling on everyone. She struck the eye in a blaze of white and scarlet —"

"White and gold *I* wore," came a measured voice behind them. Catherine stood in the doorway. Her face was set in the stiff, unrevealing lines with which she tried to fortify it against the curious, but her eyes betrayed the consuming fire of the spirit within.

"Continue, boy," she commanded dryly the discomfited page. "Continue. How say you was attired this 'Happiest of Women'?"

"In a surcoat of white tissue, so please your Grace," the boy stammered, "with an ermine edge and crimson velvet beneath set stiff with gems. She made a vain show of her hair letting it fall over her like a mantle —"

"She to be married in her hair — like a maid!" said Catherine.

"And on her brow she wore a coronet of diamonds, with other diamonds about her throat and on her breast a jewel of monstrous size of red stones of particular beauty."

"Aye? She scarcely missed my poor remainders then? Strange that the king should even have sent unto me — Proceed, Master Wallop."

"Why — why after — that one — came many ladies in cloth of gold and velvet riding on hackneys, and in a chariot rode the old Dowager Duchess of Norfolk and the mother of the lady. And from the Tower they took their way by Fenchurch and Gracechurch to Leadenhall and on by Cheapside, Ludgate, Fleet Street and the Strand to Whitehall."

"You speak, I think, of York Place?" Catherine could never bear to hear the name which Anne and Henry had rechristened the cardinal's palace. She had hated Wolsey as keenly as had ever Anne, but in this she took sides with him.

"Yes, your Grace, York Place."

"A fine procession, truly."

"But one that gave the people small joy," the page eagerly assured the fallen queen. "Although many

257

huzzahed and cheered there were some who did not and among the women not a few murmured and cried out, ' Nan Bullen,' and ' Shame, shame '— some even so loudly that it must have reached her ears though her smiles ceased not."

" Cry out? Why do they not turn on the vile creature," said Lady Wallop fiercely, " and drag her from her litter in her abominable finery and tear those diamonds from her hair? Oh, if I had her I would mark her well with these ten fingers "— and Catherine's partisan crooked a suggestive claw —" so that King Henry would never leave another kiss there! The double-fingered scum! The unclean Lutheran! The shame of all Christendom! "

" They did what they dared," the page urged. " They plagued her in what ways they could. Many back in the crowd uncapped not and her fool saw it and cried out they must have scurvy heads! At Gracechurch corner where the merchants of the Steelyard had been obliged by the Lord Mayor to erect a fine pageant they did revenge themselves for the expense they had been put to. The pageant was fine enow, an image of Mount Parnassus, on the top of which sat Apollo with the Muses, and the fountain ran with Rhenish wines to the great pleasure of all who were allowed to drink of it, and when the lady's litter halted before it, all the Muses sang verses in her praise. But as the lady smiled and read the epigrams in her honor with which the mount was decked, on a sudden her brow grew black and she bade her escort be on. She had marked the Imperial eagle, with the emblems of your Grace's house, at the summit of the mount and down obscure, at the very bottom, were wrought the arms her father pretends to. No doubt but that she smoked thereat, but there is naught, they say, she can do to those German merchants for it is of a truth that the arms of the emperor are higher than those of Wiltshire."

"Aye, is it so?" quoth Catherine with heavy sarcasm.

The lad looked bewildered. He had a talent for direct narrative, but the subtilities of things escaped him. With the idea that he had somehow offended, he offered propitiatingly, "They may deck her way with cloth of gold, they cannot with English smiles, I heard said."

"By some woman?"

"Aye."

"Continue, I pray you. What else was there to this goodly entertainment?"

"It was all much alike. At divers corners came out children dressed as angels, singing songs and reciting verses in the lady's praise to puff up further her vain spirit." The trick of speech the lad had caught from these women went quaintly with his eager face, naïvely thrilled by these wonders he affected to disdain. "But as I said, madame, some did what they could to thwart her. At Leadenhall the merchants of the staple had another pageant and on it sat Saint Anne and Mary Cleophas with four children, one of whom stepped forward and delivered a long oration, in which she said," and the boy began to grin knowingly, "that as from Saint Anne had sprung a fruitful tree so might that be true of this Anne, and as the good Saint Anne never had but the one child, a daughter, our Holy Virgin, why the wish was not to the lady's liking. It must have gone hard to smile on that child! From Leadenhall and Cornfield she went and at the cross at Cheapside waited the Lord Mayor and his men to do her honor and the mas-

ter baker rode forward with a speech and handed her a
purse —"

" A thousand marks in gold therein. I know that
custom."

" And therein she showed herself a mean creature of
low degree," cried the boy, " for it was noted that she
kept the purse, and the crowd murmured and told how
the good Queen Catherine had given hers to the captain
of the guard to divide among the halberdiers and
lackeys —"

" I could not read the future then," said Catherine,
a wry smile twisting her mouth. " I could not see how
I should now lack for gold to clothe me and my poor
faithful servants. . . . I thought all my troubles past.
God knows there had been plenty of them! How long
ago it is, twenty-four years, since I went that road that
she is traveling to-day — but it will not be so long ere
she follows in my steps, follows dishonored and uncrowned. *I* know the man. I was — I *am* his wife.
And what he hath is like a millstone about his neck
till he can cast it off. He was ever changing. . . .
Go on, boy. Why are you stopped? Was I speaking
aloud? Go on."

" I saw little else, madame. At Westminster it was
said the king met the lady on the threshold and said —"

" Well? "

" ' How like you this, Sweetheart? ' " faltered the
boy, " and I had it that she tossed her head and made
answer, ' I saw many uncapped by the way.' 'Tis said
she takes all that he does as no more than her due.
. . . This morning the lady came on foot into the Abbey
to her coronation followed by all that throng, most
splendidly attired. I pressed as close as I could but
'twas so jammed I could only hang hither and yon on

its skirts. Those in front whispered what was doing. They said it was a grand sight." The boy's tone was unconsciously wistful. " The ceremonies were very fine."

" I remember them," the queen informed him. " A pity you saw them not — but you may live to see another, if matters go on so merrily in England. And so they crowned her . . . crowned her. She is queen at last. Queen Anne. . . . *Queen!*"

All the imprisoned anger, the heartache and the hatred of those seven long years blazed suddenly on Catherine's voice and transfigured her heavy face with passion.

" So she is Queen of England," she said, " and you —" she flung a shaking hand at her attendants, " you are all to remember that I am no more than the Princess of Wales — widow of a boy these thirty-one years deceased — and all that hath been since, all these ceremonies of marriage and of wifehood, my coronation and my reign, are no more than phantoms of a dream that are to be forgotten! I must be styled no longer queen — so say those pious ministers who came unto us last month, but rather princess. . . . A learned court — O Heaven, have you no bolt to fly at them! — has sat in solemn judgment on my good name and Cranmer hath pronounced that I was never wife! Oh, it is an infamy too vile for credence — ten years agone I would have smiled at such a phantasy. . . . Yet it is naught to me, it is naught! Whate'er they do is naught! They are not my judges — there is none can judge save him, the pope, in whom I trust — but oh, why is he dumb so long? Why hath he not succored me in my distress? I have waited, I have waited — will nothing stir him? But though all desert me I will never yield." She stopped suddenly, her mouth working, then turned abruptly and walked back to her chamber, drawing shut the door.

In a life of many bitter moments there had been none bitterer than this. . . . Anne was crowned queen. Long ago Catherine had yielded to that younger woman place and power and had become a shadow queen, fighting desperately for her crowned rights and dignities, now after the long anguish and struggle they had accomplished their purpose and taken even the crown away from her to place on that younger, fairer head. How clearly she could see that crowning. . . . Catherine sank heavily to her knees on the steps of the altar in her room, holding up her clasped hands as if to ward off this blow that was come upon her. She tried to move her lips in prayer but she knew not what she was saying. Between her and the crucifix there swam a vision of that head, bending with such delicate grace to receive that crown which had been hers. She could see the glint of diamonds on that slender neck, the flash of the sumptuous silks, could hear them rustle as Anne rose and turning, faced the crowded Abbey with such radiant, smiling eyes — as queen!

Queen! A dreadful pain was stabbing at the older woman's heart. She felt choking, suffocating. She fought for breath, torturing herself with that one word — queen. All that her insolent rival had boasted had come to pass. It was unbelievable, it was unthinkable. For years Catherine had schooled herself not to think it, had refused to face such a possibility, insisting passionately that Christendom would not tolerate such a mockery, that the pope would rebuke this defiance and reinstate his dutiful daughter, but now it seemed that

HAPPIEST OF WOMEN

Christendom was blind and deaf and the pope's promises were less than vapor. Poor deluded fool that she had been to think that right and justice counted for aught in this world against self interest! She had lost — lost. She said it over to herself in a dazed way, her very brain refusing dully to accept the meaning of this thing which had come upon her. It was as if she were sinking under assassins' knives while refusing to believe the fact of the assassination. To-morrow she might goad up her spirit, to-morrow she might fight afresh, but now she was stricken and prostrate. Anne was queen.

And to her crucifix she whispered chokingly, " Happiest of Women! "

CHAPTER XXV

THE CHILD

TO Anne it seemed at last that her goal had been won and all dangers passed, and such annoyances as the people's opposition could prick her with were but a feather's weight against the measure of her joyousness. The happiest of women moved through the days of her coronation as through a dream, elate and radiant, smiling at the world with gay, proud eyes.

After the coronation there had been a great banquet in Westminster Hall with the new queen in solemn state. The haughtiest ladies of the land sat at her feet, beneath the table, to do her more honor, and the highest peers of England acted as butlers and servants. Dish after dish was brought to her on golden platters, served by earls and dukes on horseback, and after each had served his dish he spurred his horse about the hall beneath the admiring throngs in the gallery, while the building echoed with cheers for the new Majesty.

The title on the lips that accosted her was balm to the young queen. "Your Majesty," "Your Highness" — how she thrilled to the sound of them! Even in the irony of Carewe's inflection she found a sweetness that made her smile his bitterness away. The knave had loved her so long — and she was so utterly out of his reach! That, too, accounted for the sadness of Wyatt's smiles as she pressed his hand with a triumphant,

THE CHILD

"What said I, cousin?" There had reached her, on the morning of her coronation, a cluster of white roses still fresh with dew, and in their midst she had found these verses,

> Forget not yet the tried intent
> Of such a truth as I have meant;
> My great travail so gladly spent,
>   Forget not yet!
>
> Forget not yet when first began
> The weary life ye know, since when
> The suit, the service, none can tell;
>   Forget not yet!
>
> Forget not yet the great assays,
> The cruel wrong, the scornful ways,
> The painful patience in delays,
>   Forget not yet!
>
> Forget not! Oh, forget not this! —
> How long ago hath been, and is,
> The love that never meant amiss —
>   Forget not yet!
>
> Forget not then thine own approved,
> The which so constant hath thee loved,
> Whose steadfast faith yet never moved;
>   Forget not this.

" 'Tis hard that one person's joy should be another's woe," mused Anne as she thrust the verses under very careful lock and key, but her fleet pang of sympathy was soon smothered in the ecstasy of those enchanted days.

But the magic change that Anne expected the coronation to make in her position did not take place. She was queen and yet things appeared much the same as

265

before. Her pinnacle had been gained but it was a slippery pinnacle and there was the same alert holding on to be done. The country people did not swallow the fact of her queenship as readily as did the immediate court. They were less influenced by political policies, by niceties of jurisdiction; they knew only that Catherine had been queen for over twenty years and that now in old age she was in retirement while another wore the crown, and when Catherine was removed from Ampthill to Bugden the peasants crowded around her, cheering and crying that they would have no queen but her.

Anne was piqued that Henry passed this over without punishment and she found the behavior of the Easterlings, the Hanseatic merchants, her old enemies, more odious still. For they anchored their fleet directly opposite Greenwich palace and invited Chapuis, the Spanish ambassador on board, and under pretext of his honor they hoisted the Imperial eagle, fired cannon, feasted and made a tremendous demonstration.

" Punish them," urged Anne angrily.

" It can't be done," Cromwell had pacifically pointed out. More and more, through Anne's favor, that unresting Cromwell had gathered the reins of state into his able hands. " The fleet is strongly manned and as the Steelyard is still armed the Germans may prove stronger than the king. . . . Take no notice, your Highness. Demonstrations soon wear away."

And so Anne moved from Greenwich to Windsor out of reach of their annoyances.

The marriage and coronation had brought its chain of political difficulties with it. King Francis, however secretly pleased he might be at the marriage, wished Henry to go on defending his cause at Rome, during which endless time Henry would have had to rely more and more on support from Francis and would really have sunk to the level of a client of France. When England took things into her own hands, and the sentence of divorce was pronounced by the archbishopcal court, Francis was angry and the French party, even at the English court, felt that Anne's faction had behaved most cavalierly and grew hostile to the new queen.

The pope was furious; he proceeded very promptly against Henry and cited him, in the person of his ambassador, to appear to the Rota. Henry retaliated by appealing to the next free council, an act strictly forbidden by the rules of the church.

Such vigor on Henry's part was possible through the absence of Norfolk — on the personally ungrateful errand of defending his king's interests with the French, an errand which Norfolk rightly suspected had been presented him through Anne's and Cromwell's desire to get him out of the country and check his influence. The pope was very naturally inflamed at this defiance and there was no need to urge him to proceed now; he made as great haste as possible. Eager to stir up enemies against Henry he was ready to promise Calais to Francis to induce him to take the field against England with the emperor, and he urged the advisability of the Princess Mary's being married to the Earl of Surrey, the son of the Duke of Norfolk, thus to alienate that party from Anne and overthrow Henry. To be sure the Earl of Surrey had a wife living but the pope was ready enough to pronounce annulment in that case. But as the pope's advisers were uncertain as to the success of these plans, he proceeded to do what lay in his immediate power, declared the proceedings of Cranmer null and void, commanded Cranmer, Henry, and Anne to undo all that had been done in the last six weeks, and took an affirmative vote from the cardinals declaring that the pope really had the right to dispense for a marriage with a deceased brother's widow.

Back and forth hurried messengers to Henry from Francis, to Francis from Henry; Anne's brother and Bryan, her cousin, were constantly in the saddle. When France's aid appeared lost, Cromwell struck out an independent policy for England and sent messengers to Germany and to the Dukes of Bavaria who were hostile to the Imperial power, to try to arrange for aid for England there.

Of all these comings and goings, these plots and counter plots, the woman who was their cause was in ignorance. She rested at Greenwich — now that the Easterlings had sailed away — and as the hope of the English succession was with her, all that could possibly be of disturbance to her was avoided.

And though she surmised the uneasiness of the political situation she did not divine its extreme agitation and she was not alarmed. She had foreseen a " fuss " as she had merrily phrased it but she was assured that it would all blow over once there was an heir in England.

She did not dare let herself consider the possibility of the child being a girl. She concealed, even from herself, a fear of that consequence. She knew that Henry refused to contemplate such a disappointment for even a moment. Every soothsayer, every fortune teller, and he consulted many, assured him of the success of his hopes; the very stars predicted the birth of his prince, they declared, and his natural optimism was fed to certainty. It must be a boy, it *must,* Anne used

THE CHILD

to whisper passionately to herself, as the slow, damp days of that summer crept by in uncongenial inactivity for her alert spirit.

Unconsciously she had come to feel, though she would not admit it openly to herself, how her hold on Henry depended more and more on her hope of a boy instead of her personal attractions. Those attractions had waned, to be sure, as that hope had gained; she was pale, listless, hollow-eyed. But she was to be the mother of England's future king. There lay her strength for all time. And as the crisis neared her excitement tightened to tension.

She could not ride out and she watched wistfully from her windows the parties that set out daily. She seemed so little to be missed. . . . There was always some woman at the king's side, now. At first Anne smiled, thinking his attentions no more than the restless activities of his insatiable vanity, but her pride was touched.

And one day, Henry, entering her presence for the first time in three days, found an angry-eyed woman, bitterly indignant. She had suffered, in those days, a new, intolerable resentment. She had been neglected. She had been jealous. All the court knew that Henry had been with other women, drinking and carousing.

To Anne it had been lightning from a clear sky. Her vanity, the vanity of a beautiful and supremely successful woman, was pierced to the quick, her pride was intolerably outraged. She, Anne Boleyn, *Queen* Anne, neglected! To be sure, there had been the rumors during the long period of her engagement of sundry sly carousals on Henry's part, but the girl had ignored them all as random and unworthy excursions of all that was unworthiest in him, and the women who were the heroines of these adventures were unknown, uncared for creatures, mere accidents of the moment, unaware themselves of the identity of their companion.

But this was different. These were court women, peeresses of the realm. And he was her husband, he had vowed her an absolute fidelity. Everything that was wife in her suffered.

She flashed her anger and resentment at him with the vehement sincerity that always characterized her outbreaks.

"Did you think I would not hear?" she demanded.

The king scowled at his boots and for an instant made no answer. Then he muttered, without looking at her, "I care not what ye hear."

Anne caught her breath. This — to her!

"You care not?" she echoed, her voice rising on an incredulous note.

Henry shrugged.

"You do not care," she repeated, her breath quickening, "that I know that you have been untrue to the vows you have made me? That I know how you have deceived me ere I have been a wife a year, how you have been false to yourself and to me when things are as they are —" her voice broke, but again he made no answer, only pursing his lips and staring past her with irritating indifference.

And as she saw his face it seemed to her the face of a stranger. How full his lips were, how sunken his small eyes in his flesh! She had known he was growing stouter through the years, but she had not stopped and observed that stoutness; she had merely added it unconsciously to the image she possessed of Henry. Now she saw that the change had shattered that image; he was not the lover she had known; his youth, his strength,

THE CHILD

his charm had all been crushed by that bulk of flesh which had descended upon him so smotheringly. He seemed to her enormous, unwholesome. The spirit seemed to have wasted and died inside that great body of his and only the body remained, with its desires and appetites. She felt a terrific antagonism possess her to this insentient mass of flesh.

And Henry, glancing sidewise at her, after a pause, from under his drooping lids, observed with dissatisfaction how unlovely and pale she was and how ill her anger became her. And his spite flickered up under his sullenness that she dared to rail at him and to oppose her claim on him to the gratification of his pleasures.

"You'd best say no more," he muttered.

"Say no more?" She mocked his words contemptuously. "Do you think I am going to submit to this in silence? Do you think I will endure it?"

He gave her a look of malice. "Your betters have done so."

"My betters!" was all Anne could say for a moment. She was terribly angry. Such a taunt from Henry. Her betters! "And you call yourself my husband," she said indistinctly.

"Aye, so I call myself." His emphasis was vindictive. "But not so do many and I bid you remember that if I have raised you it is in my power to lower you as quickly as I have raised you."

That was thunder after the lightning.

Anne struggled to her feet. "Try it!" she flung at him. "Make yourself the mock of England with your wiving and unwiving! . . . How can you lower me? I am your wedded wife — your crowned queen. What you have done you cannot undo."

"Be not so sure," came from him sullenly. He was

271

no match for her in declamation, but his retorts were terrifying in their menace.

Anne felt her strength deserting her. She was ill and weak and at the terrible disadvantage of her ill-health and unloveliness. She was afraid of what she would do next. There was a lump in her throat; the tears were just inside her eyelids. She would have despised herself for breaking down, but she feared she was on the verge, and, summoning her strength, she pushed past her husband and shut the door of her room most ungently between them.

And when, next day at mass, she and Henry met, she gave no sign of recognition, and he, after the first surprised stare, followed her example.

For three days there was no communication between them. But at that game Anne held the cards. She was to be mother of England's prince and she must not be alarmed. When Henry's temper subsided he must conciliate her for the sake of their child. If she thought of the difference of that victory from one gained personally, she did not let her mind dwell upon its significance.

And so on the fourth day, when a fine basket of fruit came from the king, she sent back a civil message of thanks, and when Henry was shortly afterwards announced she greeted him as if nothing had happened. Almost as if nothing had happened. There was a little frost in her manner that did not thaw until he crossed the room to where she lay on the couch and stooped to pass his hand caressingly over her hair. Her hair, at least, was unchanged in its loveliness.

"Come, Anne," he said coaxingly.

She caught at the stroking hand and the next moment he bent over her. For one instant, as he kissed her,

THE CHILD

she had a renewed perception of the thickness and gross-
ness of those lips, the next, it was swept away before
her old time tenderness for him. In the need of his
comfort she clung pathetically to him and the tears her
weakness could not prevent slipped out under her lids.

"Come, Anne," he rebuked gently, kissing them away.
"Thou must not so excite thyself."

"'Twas thou excited me," she returned. "Thou wast
so — so bitter hard. To think that thou —"

"Thou must not provoke me, Anne," and then Henry
slid away from the dangerous topic. "Come, a mere
trifle —'tis all over now and all as it was before?"

Her eyes were wistful as they searched his. "Is all
as it was before, Harry?"

"Why in verity it is. Now try to sleep."

"Thou art not going to stay?"

"Oh — dost thou need me? I have a conference —"

"Go to thy conference," and she gave a smile. "And
thank thee for the fruit. It was very sweet." He kissed
her and made off. She could not help seeing that he
had the air of making his escape from the sick room.

She forced herself, in those hard days, to take what
she called a reasonable view of this. She had expected
too much, she sharply reminded herself. Men were
men; they craved amusement; privilege and not duty
appealed to them. And Henry had known nothing but
indulgence since he was old enough to reach a hand.
Once she was well all would be as before. Aye, even
better, for there would be the prince. The prince!

There came a day when Anne, struggling through the
mists and shadows of her pain, turned her grayed face
to the physician bending over her.

"The prince?" she whispered.

THE FAVOR OF KINGS

The physician murmured, " God hath sent your Grace a princess."

Anne closed her eyes. A sea of misery swept over her. Her sick consciousness lost itself in those depths. This was the end — this was the answer of fate. A daughter! A girl! Another princess. . . . She knew a dull anguish. How Catherine would rejoice! She thought of Henry and she thought of his disappointment with fear. He would be angry. . . .

Suddenly she commanded, " Bring me my child," and she looked long and earnestly, in a yearning of grief, at the tiny, scarlet features. Oh, God, why was it not a boy, why was it not a boy! She repeated it over and over again in agony all through the hot hours, yet when Henry came into the chamber, a smile set stolidly upon his face, she had the spirit to smile at him and, drawing the coverlet away from the little bundle at her side, to whisper, " Our daughter."

And as she said the word something warm and unimaginably tender seemed to flood her chagrined and lacerated heart and the little bundle became inexpressibly dear.

" Well and strong," Anne added, still with that brave smile. " She will have strong brothers," and something of the dauntlessness of her courage found an echo in her husband's face as he stooped and kissed her.

But all through the hot days that Anne lay there a terrible bitterness assailed her. Outside were booming cannon and sounding trumpets, the bonfires and huzzas of rejoicing, but the queen knew that these manifestations were a hollow pretense on the part of her friends while her enemies vented in them their secret satisfaction that the child was a girl. The battle was still to be fought, and fought now for two.

CHAPTER XXVI

A RIVAL FLOUTED

THERE was no doubt that the little Princess Elizabeth, however flagrant her offense in being a princess, was as engaging a bit of royalty as could be imagined, a fat, chubby, cuddly creature all dimples and adorable creases. She had the Tudor coloring, fair skinned, blue-eyed, with curls that were Henry's own yellow reddened to chestnut, and she had the Tudor willfulness that she maintained with a strength of lung penetrating far beyond the royal apartments. What a little prince she would have made! How that prince would have won the people!

The very image of Henry at her age, so the old wives who had attended the king's infancy declared, and they recounted doting tales of Henry's young charms to which Anne gave an inattentive wonder that anyone so gross and vulgar could ever have been a dear miracle of a baby. She could not picture Henry rosy and sweet, sucking his thumb. . . . She could not picture him again as she had first known him. All that was young and frank in him seemed done to death in that mountain of flesh.

Anne's feeling for her child was the most intense that had ever come into her stormy life. It was a passion utterly unforeseen and uncontemplated — in her dreams of the child-to-be the child had meant nothing except to her ambition; he was the prince who was to hush the last murmur against her, to cement forever the bond between herself and the king. He was to be her unassailable defense.

None of this had come to pass. She had been cruelly disappointed. The girl had brought confusion and distress upon her, she was something to protect and not to give protection, yet Anne's love went out to her in redoubled tenderness and her anger against their opponents burned with a hotter flame. . . . She thought of the Princess Mary with tightening lips and hardening heart as the menace of her child, the enemy of this helpless, clinging little thing that nestled against her heart. If there were to be no princes — and for all Anne's spoken assurance she drew that secret fear from Henry's diseased and corrupted frame — it must be Elizabeth, not Mary, who should sit upon England's throne. If Elizabeth were left in Mary's care — ! When that thought stung her, Anne strained her baby spasmodically to her breast and her heart beat in anguished dread. Her fierce wish could have struck both Catherine and Mary dead at her feet. Mary was seventeen now and beginning to be reckoned with; she had been filled by her mother with a defiant hatred of the supplanter and referred to Anne always by the vilest of names. If Mary had submitted to the divorce, Henry would have granted her right as a legitimate heiress, but now, angered at her determined opposition and incessant appeals to the Spanish minister and to Rome, he had determined to deprive her,— so perhaps it was as well that she had been so defiant, thought Anne. But she must submit now, she must realize how hopeless her contentions were! For they were hopeless as long as Anne could hold the king, and this holding of the king was the thought that filled the young queen's mind as she lay in the state bed

A RIVAL FLOUTED

at Windsor through the gray September days, one arm cuddling the tiny bundle at her side.

She faced facts with hard, disillusioned eyes. Henry had had a tremendous passion for her, that had been inflamed by denial; his vanity, his desire, and his obstinacy had all been enlisted in that momentous struggle which had resulted in her coronation. That passion was satisfied. She had brought chagrin and disappointment and vexation to him. Her body was no mystery now to yield its secret. She had given him her all. Already his caprices had veered in a dozen different directions. And she saw that it was her part now to re-create in him the illusion of her mystery and his desire. She must bewitch afresh, reënchant, reënthrall; stripped of all zest and romance she must play the game again from the very beginning and against new and alarming odds. Reigning as queen was not the easy thing her dazzled eyes had pictured! . . . And yet she was queen, she sharply reminded herself; for seven years she had fought the fight to that throne; she would fight now from it to the last!

She must make sure of Henry. The foreign tangle, bad as it was, held no such menace for her as the king's flirtations. Just now — the whisper reached her before Elizabeth was a week old — there was a certain blonde in favor, a cousin of Sir Nicholas Carewe, before whom the court was fawning.

And so while ministers were planning messages and counter messages, plots and counterplots, Anne on her sick bed, planned a gown, a rich, flowing, shimmering, crimson robe like a flame. And like a flame she descended in it, one fête night, into the midst of a surprised and slightly startled court, accustomed to the absence of its ailing queen, for except for her tottering presence at the child's christening when five days old, Anne had kept her chambers.

There was no sign of illness about her now; her body had gathered strength from her spirit and she bore herself triumphantly, feeling that she was again the self of old, before her motherhood had claimed her, erect, alert, confident, unconquerable.

The evening was half over before she saw the thing that she had come to see. The company, broken into small groups, had fallen from its perfunctory addresses into intimate chat. The Duke of Norfolk stood trifling with one of the queen's household, Elizabeth Holland, and as Anne's eyes roamed past them she saw Suffolk pass through a draped doorway with another of her maids, while his young wife stood watching from across the room. He was typical of the times, that Suffolk, thought Anne with curling lips — Henry's sister had not been in her grave ten weeks before Suffolk had married again, and married the betrothed of his son, and now here he was already neglecting her for another! The next moment Anne saw Suffolk's son approach the girl who had been his sweetheart and was now his stepmother, and with half guilty looks about, the two shrank closer into the shadow of the overhanging gallery.

But it was not this play, this tragic farce, that Anne had interest in. Her eyes slipped past these groups, past a knot of the king's gentlemen, Norris and Brereton and Weston and George, egging on two jesters, Patch and Somers, to a trial of wits, to where the king himself stood at the far end of the hall. He was talking rapidly with a confidential air. The woman who listened to him, now smiling up at him, now sighing down into her fan, was the cousin of Sir Nicholas Carewe.

Anne turned to where a short, heavy man lounged,

slightly apart from the others, watching the kaleidoscopic
scene with inscrutable sharp eyes, and made a quick gesture. The man, who was Thomas Cromwell, the all-
important secretary, hurried to her side with that awk-
ward, uneven gait which matched his cumbersome frame.

"Your arm, sir." The queen spoke with unconscious
sharpness born of a gathering distrust. She had heard
how, when Elizabeth was but a few days old, Cromwell
had ridden out to fly his hawks and met, certainly by appointment, Chapuis, the Spanish Ambassador and how
the two had long talked. It was certain that the secretary was considering changing his allegiance, now the
hope of a prince had failed. Well, he should see if her
star was on the wane!

She pressed the tips of her fingers on his arm and
as she directed their steps to the oblivious king he gave
her a sudden look of inquiry, but said nothing.

"Ah, good even — I have not seen you before, Mistress Carewe." Anne's voice with its bell-like quality of
sweetness and clearness cut unexpectedly into the tête-
à-tête.

The instinct which made Henry dissemble in any confusion caused him to turn to Anne with a smile on his
lips and she gave him a most vivid one in return, a saucy,
swift little smile that heralded mischief, and then her
look, bright and glittering as steel, played over the
woman before her, scathing, while it registered, the
charms she presented. The woman was plump and very
fair; the delicate pallor of her skin was whitened by
powder to a degree that contrasted strikingly with the
scarlet of her lips. They were as red as Anne's gown.
Her light blue eyes held a look of satirical suspicion as
she smilingly replied, " I have already had the pleasure
of making my compliments to your Grace this night."

THE FAVOR OF KINGS

"So? I did not recollect thee."

"Perhaps," came the malicious suggestion, "your Grace's memory is not yet fully recovered. I trust you are feeling well?"

"Vastly well, mistress, vastly well. I would I could think the same of you, but your pallor prevents me. Are you not faint?"

"Nay, your Grace."

"Tut! You are bravely feigning health. Why you are as white as a chalk — you should have a dash of cold water to restore your natural complexion! Thy face is too sickly for thy word's credit. Why, thou art fairly green. Is she not, my lord?" Anne put unexpectedly to Henry in a tone of insistent solicitude, and Henry, taken unawares, could only gaze at the angry woman at whom his wife was pointing her fan.

"I fear thou hast too much exerted thyself," went on Anne's mocking tones, edged with indescribable irony. "Master Secretary, give you your arm to escort this lady to the fresh air — she hath need of it," she commanded, and as her speechless rival took her enforced departure with the silent secretary, Anne turned swiftly to Henry to forestall any intention he might have of accompanying them. She shook her fan coquettishly at him.

"Ah, fie, fie on thee, Harry! Tell me not that this is the very she that rumor hath been linking to thy name? I protest my vanity thought better of thy royal taste!" Her blithe audacity held Henry dumb, staring at her uncertainly as she flashed on, "La, sir, do you call that fair? Where are thy eyes? 'Tis a china mug — when it grins 'twill crack, the colors are laid on so thick! La, how she glowered when I said 'water' to her!" Anne's laugh rang out infectiously; the dim-

"'Tut! You are bravely feigning health.'"

ple in her cheek — so long lost during her illness —
flashed again into being.

Henry, conscious that he was being treated like a
school boy being weaned from a dangerous pastime,
half minded to resist and show his spunk, but tickled in
spite of himself by her sweeping assurance, found his
vanity subtly flattered by a quality in that smile. It
reminded him again how irresistible he was when fair
women went battling for him, and, tasting that sweet,
he yielded Anne a smile in return, half grudgingly at
first, but deepening unconsciously as it rested on her.
She was the very spirit of conquest in that red gown,
clinging like a flame to her slenderness, the diamonds
flashing on her dark hair like the starshine of the night
outside.

That smile, she knew, was her captured pennant, and
the wine of victory ran through her. "Why, sir," she
laughed, still shaking her fan at her husband, "if thou
must leave me, let it be for nothing that will do such
discredit to thy royal standards. Remember thou art
a lesson to this court. Where else should taste be upheld save in the king? . . . Try that tall brunette over
there. She hath at least some hair of her own. I vow
I could summon a qualm or so about her, but as for this
— this lady China-Mug I could not squeeze out a proper
wifely tear!"

Again Anne laughed and Henry joined her in a sudden shout and leaned forward and pinched her arm, in
one of his veering reversals of humor.

"By the Rood, an thou lookest like that, thou wilt
never have cause for tears!" he vowed.

"I believe thee!" Anne tossed her head airily and
the diamonds glistened like falling spray. "My mirror
told me as much before thee!"

THE FAVOR OF KINGS

" But did not tell thee as will I," he breathed into her ear.

Ah, how easy, her confident vanity gayly reassured her, how easy it all was for her, after all! . . . And how easy it was later, when they were alone in her chamber, to fully complete that victory and bind him to her with those charms she knew so well how to exert! Kisses, flattery, love words, adoration unstinted — she knew the way very well. She had only to force her reluctant arms into a tender clasp, only to play traitor to that terrible shrinking in herself from what he called his love, only to betray her cold lips and unwilling flesh. Never again for her now the old veil of romance and tender illusion. Life was mercilessly clear. Never again those maiden-misted dreams! —

But this was the price. She paid it for her crown, for the redemption of her pride and the exultation of her spirit. She paid for her daughter's heritage. Many women paid it for less. . . . So she told herself when the king slept and she lay wide-eyed at his side, staring into the darkness.

In the morning the decree went forth that Mary Tudor must no longer be known as Princess, but as Lady Mary. Elizabeth was the only princess in England. As soon as might be Henry proposed to have Parliament ratify this and pass a definite Act of Succession.

When Elizabeth was three months old it was considered high time for her to have an establishment of her own according to all royal precedent. Anne had dreaded this time and she would have opposed it but for fear of lessening Elizabeth's position as a princess by leaving unfulfilled any of her prerogatives.

So the mother stifled the cravings of her reawakened heart and the three-months' baby went to Hatfield in

charge of Mrs. Shelton, Anne's aunt, accompanied by a
long and stately retinue. And to Hatfield, also, went
Lady Mary, to be attached to her tiny sister's establishment. It seemed to Anne and Henry that if Mary were
in constant daily association with Elizabeth and the evi-
dences of her position that she would understand the
baselessness of her own hopes and accept her assigned
rôle. And it was in the back of Anne's mind that Mary
might perhaps succumb to the little sister's attraction.
It seemed to her impossible that anyone should long
withstand her and enroll themselves against her. But
if Mary continued obdurate she was in reliable hands at
Hatfield, and any attempt to escape to the continent and
there gather a hostile force with which to invade England — rumors of this constantly circulated about the
court — could be more easily frustrated.

Mary indeed continued obdurate. She made that
journey to Hatfield by force; she had to be shoved into
her litter by the Duke of Norfolk and the feat of han-
dling a kicking seventeen year old girl roundly taxed the
small duke's physical prowess.

"I'd have wrung her neck for a murran," he reported
viciously to his niece.

"I'd do it for love," Anne retorted. "Lord, each
day brings its rumor about her. Now she is to be smug-
gled out of the country and head an opposing army —
now is she dying by poison or torture and at my hands!
Chapuis is most eager to make her the cause of war. He
is constantly writing the emperor those inflaming accounts,
stirring him up, shaking all the red rags of lies at him
he can manufacture. I learned to-day of a dispatch of
his that proclaims his great fear for Catherine's life and
retails her straits at Kimbolton. She is in no straits at
all. The place is not immense, but it is pleasant enough,

and if she have not all the money in the world, that is her own fault — Parliament stands ready to pay it to her as Princess Dowager. But she will have all or nothing."

The mention of Catherine always brought an edge of rancor to Anne's tone. She remained silent now, staring out with hard eyes; then she drew an unconscious sigh of great weariness. "Would she were gone," she said. "Till then I have no peace of mind."

This secret anxiety that lurked in Anne's heart, ceaselessly gnawing with fine, sharp teeth, was brought again into light by an episode in February. Mary had been particularly troublesome of late; it was found that plans for her escape were all laid and only frustrated by the vigilance of Cromwell's agents — the indefatigable secretary had long been laying the foundations of that spy system that was to terrorize his enemies — and if Mary once escaped to the continent she could be used by all England's enemies as a rallying cry. Charles might demand England in her name — she might be wedded to some prince who would essay to establish her claims for his benefit — there was no limit, in fact, to the things which the imagination of English statesmen saw might be done with Mary. Irascible at his messenger's failures with her Henry himself set suddenly out for Hatfield one day, resolving to try the persuasion of his personal influence.

When Anne learned of his departure she went white. It was a thing she had feared — this meeting of father and daughter. She knew how Mary had often tried to bring this to pass. Henry had been fond of her, he had used to make an excessive show of it, and while this fondness had not prevented his venting his spite upon her, while it was entirely inoperative in separation, once

they met, once Mary wept and made a show of submission to touch the facile sentiment in him that moved so
lightly upon the surface, a gusty tide swayed back and
forth by an erratic moon, there was no knowing to what
length of reconciliation Henry would go. The pair
would weep, kiss, clasp — Anne's fear could see it all.

"Ride!" she shot at Norris and Weston, the two in-
separables who had brought her the news of the king's
departure. "Ride like the wind and overtake his
Majesty. Do you so that on no account he sees the
prin — the Lady Mary."

Norris cocked the quizzical eyes of intimacy at her.

"Now how shall we put that to him?"

"Why as you can best devise for the moment. Say
aught you like. Say"— Anne bit her lip —" say that
I, hearing of his purpose, fell into such low and desperate spirits that you rode at once to acquaint him and
dissuade him from the project. Beseech him to look
only upon the Princess Elizabeth. Say that I beseech
him an ye like. If that works not, say that I command."

Her sense of urgency spoke in her face and voice, and
the very arrogance of her imperativeness. And until
the return of the party she paced about her rooms in restless and uneasy apprehension. She was more than ever
convinced of her foresight in sending that message when
she heard from Norris the full account of the king's
visit. True to the request which overtook him, he made
no effort to see Mary, but as he was leaving, after view-
ing the infant Elizabeth — who most regrettably was suffering from colic and screamed the air blue — his eldest
daughter appeared on the terrace above him, kneeling,
as if to ask his blessing. He had waved his hand to her
and it had seemed as if he were on the point of returning, but checked himself, and rode off. It was noticed

that there were tears in his eyes and that evening he spoke to the French Ambassador about his daughter, with affectionate praise.

"For her obedience?" Anne queried scornfully.

"Her accomplishments," Norris smiled.

"Aye, her accomplishments? I had not heard of these before," Anne sniffed.

But her conscience pinched her as she jeered. Something of her natural sense of fairness, yet uncorrupted by her hatred, whispered to her that Mary was behaving exactly as she herself would behave in her place. Would she ever own any other woman her mother's successor? Would she own any child of that union her own supplanter? Anne tried to tell herself that under the circumstances she would have the sense to do so and not ceaselessly provoke an inevitable opposition, but that secret whisper in her was not hushed. Her vivid imagination flashed across her mind a sudden picture of the life that the seventeen year old girl was leading, apart from her mother, attached to the household of her rival sister, possessed with bitterness and rebellion. So stirred by sudden kindly resolve, the flowering of that seed of mother love in her heart, Anne rode out to Hatfield, some weeks later, to effect a reconciliation.

"Tell the Lady Mary," she said to Jane Seymour, who had accompanied her, "tell her that if she will but be friendly and kind I will be friendly and kind to her and work things better for her at court and with her father. . . . I would be glad to see her, tell her."

Then Anne hurried to the chamber of her little daughter, and, drawing off her riding gauntlets, gathered the sleeping child hungrily in her arms. What change there was, she thought, observing almost jealously the progress of the weeks with that young life. How Elizabeth's hair had grown! She passed her hand over the ringlets and then buried her face in the soft creases of the little neck, all warm and damp from sleep, with the hungry passion of her starved maternity. Elizabeth woke lazily, unclosing big blue eyes like bits of sky and adorably smiled.

Jane Seymour appeared at the door.

" Well? " questioned the queen.

The girl hesitated, and gave her mistress a soft glance as if to beseech her not to connect the unwelcome mouthpiece in any way with the message. Then she cast down her eyes. Jane had a quiverful of these mild tricks that she spread about her, adorning her somewhat uninspiring speech. In a soft voice she repeated:

" The Lady Mary bade me say that she would be most grateful if the king's mistress did aught to soften the king's heart to her."

Anne bent lower over her baby. She felt the hot blood rush to her cheeks, betraying her helpless anger.

" Go back and tell her that the queen of England is minded to be a friend to her an she show herself one. Now has she the mending of her circumstances in her hands."

In a few moments Jane again presented herself.

" The Lady Mary replied that she knew of no queen in England but the good Queen Catherine, her mother, who was indeed a good friend to her. If the king's mistress had any good will to her she could show the same by stripping herself of her pretensions," repeated Jane in her pretty, precise tones, with a manner that conveyed more than ever her sense of extreme grief and shock at being in any way associated with this repugnant sentiments. Yet Anne found the girl's masked gaze distasteful.

THE FAVOR OF KINGS

A dangerous flame burned in her cheeks. She gave an angry laugh.

" She said — Well, thus endeth our endeavor. We have other ways of dealing with her than by beseechment! She can look to herself now. I'll down that Spanish blood! An she shows her teeth so to you," Anne turned sharply to her aunt, " look you, you can box her ears an you list. I'll have no more favors shown her."

The next month Parliament passed the Act of Succession which settled the inheritance to the crown upon the children of Anne, and which contained a clause that enacted that all adult subjects should be sworn to observe this act. And the same month came the sentence from the consistory of cardinals at Rome, given after a long and fruitless attempt to induce Henry to submit the case to a court of cardinals in Europe, which proclaimed that the dispensation of Pope Julius was perfectly valid and that the marriage with Catherine was legal! The gauntlet had been thrown and the second queen who had so lightly thought her goal gained when that crown had been placed upon her head perceived herself in an interminable struggle. But the pope and all Europe were as nothing to her if only she could keep her place in Henry's affection.

CHAPTER XXVII

THE WRITING ON THE WALL

THE months passed. They were months of feastings and revelry at court, a feverish merry-making where Anne seemed sometimes to herself to be in a very treadmill of dancing. She lived lightly, from moment to moment, shutting out the future from her mind with a furious concentration of hope.

" She prayeth nightly for a prince," Mary Wyatt confided sadly to Helen as the two sat sewing one rainy afternoon.

" Nightly?" Helen gave back. " She prayeth that prayer hourly, I'll warrant, aye, every instant in every jaded bone of her."

There was a certain grimness in her tone that Mary noticed. Her lip curved in gentle pity for Anne. The years had made little change with her; she had remained the same, sweet, gentle girl, her lines of thought unaltered, but a little deepened, her habits more settled, her goodness verging sometimes on pretty primness. The court had left her unspoiled. She accepted it literally, with literal simplicity, and had passed through it diffidently, as she passed through life, holding Anne's train.

" A prince would save her," went on Helen, " even as a prince would have saved Catherine. But Anne hath not so many years to wait. She must haste. Spain is her deadly enemy and its fiery emperor is egging on the new pope — peace to Clement's ashes! I fear choler over our second queen hastened his demise — and France, seeming to expostulate, is doing little but look on — in truth, I think the three powers are but all shuffling and looking on and hesitating to see what new thing the morrow will bring forth in Anne's fortunes. For when Henry tires, and his humors are well known,— why then they think he will undo all that he has done of a schism and then there will be no more need of threats and bulls and fulminations."

"And will he?" asked Mary humbly as of a seeress.

Helen shook her head. "It is my mind that he will ne'er retreat from any pinnacle he hath perched on. Parliament hath declared him head of the Church of England and that he will cling to however he discard his queens — But if Anne had a son he would grapple him to him as with hoops of steel and then would her dangers be passed. And the powers, seeing him so fixed, would accept his mind and vie for that son's hand. It is a very irony of fate which withholds from Anne the boys that every thatched roof cottage bursts with."

"She taketh it very hard," the girl sighed. "Those who know her not say she is light — they would not say so an they had seen her as I have."

"Nay, she is not light," Helen agreed.

Mary clasped her hands in her earnestness. "She sitteth silent in the garden, hour by hour, among the dogs. . . . And how much she distributeth in alms! I pray God that he send her a son," she said.

"Pray on — she needeth it," Helen advised dryly. Helen was the same, only a little leaner, a little dryer, a little more caustic than of old.

Mary sat silent a moment, thinking. Again she sighed. "It is not so fine to be a queen after all is said," she mused. "Indeed, I think she would have been happier as a simple maid."

Helen eyed her quizzically. "Do you, indeed? . . . Now I suppose thou art thinking of Percy of Northumberland. Thou wast ever the maid for a love sigh, though thou art so shy with thy own Lee —"

"Nay," Mary denied. "He could not have made her happy, I think. That was but a girl's fancy. . . . I think," she said softly, "that if my brother had been free, there would have been no Percy Northumberland nor — nor anyone else," she finished, with another quick look about to reassure herself that they were alone.

A queer look came to Helen's face.

"He hath always loved her," Mary went on. "He told me once how he first saw her on her return from France and the sight of her went to his heart and ever lodged there. It has always been the same. I know that he has hoped on through the years — thinking that something might happen to break off this match and that he might be free — his wife has such ill health — and that his chance would come. I will ne'er forget how he felt when she was crowned. Wyatt does not ope his heart to the world, but I have always known it. And I know that it aches now. He is anxious about Anne. He told me that he would give his right arm if it would bring her her heart's desire."

"Wyatt is a noble soul." The irony of Helen's voice seemed strangely muffled. She looked old and weary. "There is — there is much love amiss in this world," she said dryly.

"I thought he was perchance taking some thought of little Margaret," Mary went on. "I know 'tis not the same, but 'twould lighten him."

"Margaret Shelton?"

THE FAVOR OF KINGS

"Yes. He taketh her to dance a good deal, I note, and maketh much of her."

Helen laughed, rather disagreeably. "Think again, Mary. For me, I do not think our little cousin was imported from Hatfield, with the country dew still in her eyes, to beguile thy brother's leisure moments. Her Highness needed her nearer home." And as Mary only stared uncomprehendingly Helen sharply elucidated, "She is for the king's consumption."

Mary's eyes widened, filling with surprise. Then she shook her head very positively. "How strange you talk, Helen. Why, how can you think — do you mean that Mrs. Shelton — the Duke of Norfolk — but Anne must understand. She would not let them overreach her like that. You know how she will brook no rival."

"Mrs. Shelton — Duke of Norfolk!" repeated Helen scoffingly. "Nay, indeed Anne is not being overreached. Our pretty little country cousin is no rival, but a tool."

It was some time before Mary understood. Helen went on to throw explanation at her.

"Could the Norfolks have foisted the girl on Anne if she had not wisted? Didn't she herself exploit her? When Anne and the king came back from that trip about the country this summer how did things stand? And do what Anne could, she could keep him no longer from that girl that Nicholas Carewe eggs on to seek his Majesty. And if she kept in power — Lord knows where she and all the Boleyn faction would be! I tell thee things were black and Anne was not well — and she let Margaret come and gave thanks, I'll vow, when her freshness caught the king's taste. Have you not noticed how frequent he is of late? Did you suppose it was Anne again? Anne sits by perhaps, but 'tis the girl he's ogling, and Mistress Carewe hath clean toppled out of his memory. The girl will not last long — she is a little shallow piece, all giggles and pretty airs, but by then Anne will be fresh matter to him again and she will have kept him in her party."

"But the girl —" the pitying heart of Mary Wyatt protested.

"Oh, the girl!" Helen swept that pity summarily away. "She will not break her heart over the matter; she is tickled nigh to death at the notice and fuss she is receiving. She'll have her day and marry some young gallant — Norris, our handsome widower, has an eye on her now. She is a soft piece, like Mary Carey."

Mary Carey, Anne's sister, a widow for some six years now, had lately married again and there was some haste to have the ceremony catch up with her good name — if indeed she had any left.

"Whom was't she married?" Mary Wyatt murmured after a pause.

"Some officer — an unknown, for she hath a talent for obscurity that Anne doth not share. Mary is all whispers and twilight; Anne is for the sunshine."

Mary looked thoughtful; but it was not at this summing up. She was considering Helen gravely.

"I have oft wondered at you, Helen," she said gently, "that your own heart hath never been touched. You speak ever so disdainfully of the affection's weakness. You seem to stand and look on. I have thought that perhaps some man would some day change you, but you are never pricked."

Helen laughed harshly. "Perhaps I am in secret nursing mine own love wound," she mocked. "Perchance an undying desire possesseth me. Perchance I have given all in vain. Is not that a tale to bring your lamb's tears?"

21   293

Mary shook her head wisely. " Nay, then, you would be different," she said. " You would have more compassion on the sufferings of others."

"Would I?" said Helen, with her sharp-edged smile.

Helen had spoken truly. Margaret Shelton had been a tool, a bright decoy, keeping Henry in the ranks of his wife's friends. That Anne should stoop to employ such means, that her pride should lend itself to such assistance, showed a strange change from the Anne of other days.

She bore herself as proudly and lightly as ever, her wit struck as audacious sparks, her laughter rang as free, but it was laughter with a defiant echo, and the big eyes that looked out from the thinned oval of her cheeks were bright with a feverish fire. She was a person constantly on the alert, constantly expecting some summons, on the *qui vive* of attention. When she was in her rooms or believed herself alone in the gardens, she sat for long time with gripped hands and locked lips, her eyes fixed, turning over plan after plan in her restless mind.

She carried anxiety about with her, like a fox in her vitals.

And then came the day when she drew the freest breath that she had known in years, when she felt suddenly like a prisoner who steps out-of-doors, his chains undone, when it seemed to her that at last the corner of her long lane had been turned and that pinnacle which she had been at such trouble to attain was finally hers in undisputed possession. The woman whom she had displaced, whose life had been one constant strife with her and hers, ceased suddenly to be. She had been ailing for some time; so near her end did she believe herself at one time to be that Chapuis, the Spanish Ambassador, rode out and spent four days with her. But as she then appeared so recovered and in such cheerful spirits he had returned. But two days later she failed again, fell into a heavy doze, and on a Friday morning, the seventh of January, 1536, she passed peacefully away.

Catherine of Aragon was gone.

Anne said it over and over to herself, with almost incredulous gladness. She was gone. Never in her life had Anne known such a sensation of relief; by its very poignancy she appreciated how keen had been her apprehensions. She remembered how welcome once had been the news of Wolsey's death; that emotion, by the side of this intensity, appeared childish. What had she known then of actual fear and trouble, she asked rather scornfully of that other Anne she summoned to vision. She recalled a girl, proud-eyed, impatient for the crown, and she shook her head contemptuously at that girl's cares and crosses. What a slight, inexperienced creature she was, after all! How little she knew life, life as this older woman knew it. There were only nine years between those selves, but nine times nine of bitter experience. She had never thought of herself as very inexperienced, very young and childlike; indeed she had felt a superb confidence in her own immense adequacy to all intricacies, but now she looked back on that younger Anne as something pitiably fresh and virginal, dancing with sun-dazzled eyes. How she had striven! How she had suffered! How she had — sunk. . . . She had done things from which that light-hearted Anne would have shrunk in horror. She thought of Margaret Shelton . . . and of herself and Henry. . . . Well, the worst was over now. That other who had disputed her queenship and her wifehood was gone the way there is no returning and her shadow would rest no more upon that throne. She

THE FAVOR OF KINGS

was undisputed queen. Surely, now, the powers would make no more difficulties about their marriage.

Starting up, Anne gave breathless orders to her ladies. They should wear their prettiest gowns; no mourning, yellow — the color of rejoicing.

"We will have no lies here, she said stoutly, clasping on her jewels.

Henry, too, when he came to dine with her was in fine attire. He was jocular and called for more than even his usual allowance of wine; in a burst of uproarious relief he toasted Catherine's progress through hell.

A sudden reaction swept through Anne. She sat still, her glass untasted. She had never been very close to death, but its solemn mystery had made a strong appeal to her imagination. At Henry's words she had a sudden vision of that silent room at Kimbolton where the Spanish women were on their knees, and of the sheeted mass upon the bed. Clearly as if it were before her she saw that scene. Somewhere a bell tolled slowly, dismally, and she could not have told whether it were ringing in truth or in this fancied scene. She remembered, not seeking the memory, that the man who offered this toast had been the husband of that sheeted dead, had kissed her lips, had clasped her children. Like an icy wave a swift and terrible impression went through her. She shuddered, the room darkened and seemed to totter about her. Her wine glass dropped and fell, pouring the wine like blood in a thin stream; she swayed and her ladies kept her from falling. In an instant she opened her eyes. Henry had come swiftly about the table and was bending over her. She received from him a horrible impression of reddened flesh and liquor-laden breath, of something panting and soulless and wolfish. She tried to smile, but she shivered.

"A swift and terrible impression went through her."

THE WRITING ON THE WALL

" It is nothing," she said, and drew her hand from
his hot grasp. " It is — but my condition."

On the 29th of January there was laid to rest in Peterborough Cathedral a woman whom the ceremonial de-
scribed as the Widow of the late Prince Arthur of England. Therefore, the Spanish Ambassador declined to
be present and the body was followed only by those attendants who had shared its long exile and misfortune.

Anne Boleyn could not put from her mind the thought
of the ceremony which was going on. She was unfeign-
edly thankful at Catherine's death. She would not for
worlds have restored her to life or her former position
and she had not the slightest intention of dwelling morbidly on the details of her final rites. She had no love
for horrors. But she could not keep her fancy from
playing about this. She could imagine the finalities of
the service and the ring of feet on the hollow-vaulted
stones of the cathedral. She thought of death with wonder and awe. It was a very mysterious thing. She
thought that it was strange that this was really the last
of Catherine, and somehow an unbidden, repudiated pity
for Catherine, the woman who had worn her crown and
who was being now put away in a distant aisle of Peterborough, stole through her. She tried to lay it by firing
her resentment with a memory of the wrongs Catherine
had done her, but she remained curiously cold. The
woman could not be blamed for clutching the crown she
had worn so long. She had been a fool to do it, that
was plain; she had embittered her own condition and
wrecked her daughter's hopes by maintaining that lost
cause of her rights; she had been clearly in the wrong,
of course, and should have recognized and been grateful, Anne felt, that she had been so long allowed to wear

the crown that had never been rightfully hers. Yet it had been natural, natural, Anne's rebellious mind could not but feel, and Anne went suddenly back to those old days to wake a deep-rooted hate. She recalled that terrible day when she had pled and Catherine had scorned, and her anger woke again, even against the dead and self-pity stirred. Yet the next instant her truant thought swerved; she wondered ironically at her own despair, and smiled with dry eyes at those tears that had poured for Henry Percy. She recalled the erratic, aloof and unconfiding man who too late had entered into the earldom of Northumberland and she wondered fleetingly what had been his inner life. And as that old scene came back to her, the queen's chamber, the embroidery frames by the window, and the meek-faced ladies, she thought how amazing life was, and how unforeseen and dramatic its contrasts. How little that queen, bending over her embroidery in placid meditation, dreamed that the maid of honor at her knees would one day wrest that crown from her and wear it in her stead — would move as queen about those very rooms while she herself was being lowered into a vault at Peterborough prepared for the widow of Prince Arthur! Life was strange. Anne mused on the common fact, as if she herself had discovered it. . . . But that maid of honor, she reflected, had paid well for that crown. How she had waited, had striven and planned and fallen back only to strive again — and always laughing, always with an unconquered mien. Yes, she had paid. . . .

To escape from the thoughts that hummed unbidden in her consciousness, like a swarm of bees, Anne rose and moved restlessly about her chambers. The continual presence of her attendants irked her; she felt the need of being alone, and slipped away from them.

THE WRITING ON THE WALL

At the end of the chain of rooms a tiny ante-room, five-sided, was tucked into the space between the reception chamber and the corridor, a place where waiting courtiers might kick their heels while their betters discussed matters within. Anne threw open the door into this room suddenly and what she saw there, bathed in the glow of a ruddy fire, held her chained a moment on the threshold.

Sprawled in a great chair was her husband, one stalwart arm clasping the waist of a woman on his knees, who leaned lightly away from him, a playful smile on her small, demure features. The woman was Jane Seymour.

In the tense silence that followed the smile dropped, like a flung garment, from Jane's face, and fright and malice and smug assurance looked out her little eyes as both she and Henry hung, in motionless discomfiture, on the queen's white and staring countenance. Then Anne's voice rose in a ghastly rattle of laughter.

"O God, O God!" she cried, gasping wildly in a shrill mockery of mirth, "O God, *my* maid of honor!"

With a shaking of superstitious terror she looked at them and it was a very vision of the quicksands on which the tinsel edifice of her life was built, those quicksands which had closed so remorselessly over her predecessor. Was this the hand of God — His Writing on the Wall?

It seemed as if her very soul shuddered within her, while about her the room grew first blood-red and then a darkness. Still eerily laughing, she made a staggering step to the door.

"Oh, rise not, I beg of you . . . such needless mummery of respect!" fell chokingly from her — for a movement had stirred that pair in the chair — then with arms

299

outstretched she fled totteringly back through the ante-
rooms.

And again there came back to them the wail of her
laughter and the bitter cry, "O God! *my* maid of
honor!"

The little form of the dead prince, so prematurely
brought into the world that day, had been huddled un-
ceremoniously into a final resting place. Anne was lying
in the great bed, so slight a form that the clothes scarcely
marked her presence. Her eyes, turned past the group
of ladies who sat lamenting about her, rested on the
square of out-of-doors that the casement framed. Amy
Gaynesford and Mary Wyatt were tearfully whispering
together, Helen sat in dreary silence, while Margaret
Shelton, plunged into the midst of such solemn misfor-
tunes, did her young best to act the proper sympathy with
lowered voice and appropriate sighs.

Anne did not speak to them and something in the gaze
of those dark eyes hushed their own words and held
them from addressing her. Straight past them she
gazed and out of the window where joyous little white
clouds were scudding along a sky of deepest blue. Down
in the court a dog was joyously barking; someone dear
to his doggish heart had come in sight. The pigeons
cooed under the eaves. From beyond the closed doors
came a subdued hum of voices, like bees in clover. A
wry smile sped across Anne's pain-drawn features, and
the sight unlocked the tongues about her. Her stepmother came hastily with creaking footsteps to her side.

"Do you want aught, dearie?"

Anne shook her head, her eyes half closing with
weariness. And then Mary Wyatt burst out crying, honest childish sobs that filled the room. "O Holy Virgin,

THE WRITING ON THE WALL

O Holy Virgin," she iterated chokingly. The old Dowager Duchess of Norfolk who loved Anne like a daughter
suddenly broke the control of years, and caught her
breath in a whimpering sigh, openly wiping her eyes.
Like a flash Anne's eyes unclosed. " Weep not," she
said, and a spark of her old imperious will made itself
felt through the weak voice. " Nay, weep not. There
might have been disputes about this child — being a child
of Catherine's lifetime. There can be no question about
the next!" Her spirit was tremendous. Yet strangely
it did not cheer them; they felt her indomitable flash of
courage but it saddened rather than enheartened them;
it was like some lost cause fluttering its pennant before
overwhelming odds. Helen rose suddenly and left the
room.

The king came at last to the door. Anne shifted
quickly on her pillow; one hand went restlessly to her
disordered hair. Her lips tightened; a steady smile
curved them. Henry went abruptly to her bedside; she
looked up at him and the smile rested on her lips like
some butterfly pinned on a mask of agony. She had
not seen him since she had closed the door of that ante-
room, and she had seen him then with Jane Seymour on
his knees. There was a frightful menace now in his
look; he was furiously angry; he felt himself cheated
and outraged and he could wreak his rage on no one but
that prostrate woman before him who had thus dashed
his hopes of a son. His lips curled away from his teeth.
His nostrils dilated with his uneven breathing. Then he
turned away as abruptly as he had come.

" When you get up I will talk to you," he flung from
between his teeth.

At the door the dowager duchess made bold to put
herself swiftly in his way.

THE FAVOR OF KINGS

"It was a son, your Majesty," she said in a low voice that was meant to appear enheartening and that held a quiver of entreaty. "The next will also be a son!"

Henry flung a malignantly sullen look at the aged woman. "She will get no more sons by me," he muttered and banged the door.

CHAPTER XXVIII

RUMORS

"THE Spaniard and Lady Exeter are talking together, and each time they ope their lips they bite at my poor name like this," and the queen, her bare white elbows on the dark edge of the casement from which she looked down into the courtyard of Greenwich Castle, bit at the peach she held to her scarlet lips. "An a cat have nine lives, I vow I must e'en have nine and ninety characters," she murmured, "for I still seem to have one left to be scratched at, no matter how many are destroyed."

"Your Majesty should take more care," observed Jane Seymour in her soft, practical tones. "Indiscretion opens the door for calumny."

"Aye, but even the careful are not always so safe from slander! This is an evil world, Jane, and there are evil tongues, even here at court! The most careful are not spared. Why — you will ne'er believe it! — but rumor hath brought us strange tales even of thy careful self!"

Anne looked across at Jane from the window seat where she had luxuriously disposed herself, bright malice in her dark eyes, in the curve of her gay lips. Never once in the months that had passed since that January day had Anne openly attacked her maid for that scene with the king but her nipping wit had often played about the allusion in fitful enmity. She did not fear the girl now; that sudden panic and superstitious terror which had possessed her on first seeing Jane ensconced as a rival in the king's affections had fled on Henry's stout assurance that the demonstrativeness which his wife had witnessed had been but the impulse of a moment, when he had been too much in his cups, leaving only a mocking disdain for the placid little prig, as she termed her, whose suave flattery, she bitterly surmised in spite of Henry's assurances, was being voraciously swallowed by his glutton vanity.

"Monstrous tales, Jane," she repeated gravely. "I could have believed them of any of the court than of you, so trusty, so full of little saws of virtue. . . . You must take *more* care. . . . I trust you sent the purse back?"

Jane, thus baited, had not the steel to strike sparks with. Her pale face turned reddish, she pursed up her lips, half primly, with a look of conscious forbearance always irritating to her mistress.

"I hope I have in no wise laid mine own acts open to censure," she said at last, as Anne was plainly waiting for an answer.

"Oh, I believe you, girl — never defend yourself so blushingly! I believe you — but 'tis an evil world, and care is not enough for calumny — no, not even for the least attractive of us, Jane."

A smothered laughter rippled among the ladies but they were not easy in mind; when Anne's tongue ran in this wise there was no knowing where it would prick next. But the window drew her again.

"Aye, courtesy and pass on, my lady. Mark how the Spaniard smiles! Chapuis is monstrous pleased of a sudden. And how fine he is in his velvet doublet picked out with gold. Nay, on a day like this, with the wind so soft and so full of wood blossoms, I cannot more than

RUMORS

half hate my enemies as is my Christian duty to do.
Aye, but how he hates me. Marry, if all who wished
me ill were in procession to Canterbury they would be
the longest pilgrimage that Becket's tomb hath e'er
seen!"

She stretched lazily, rising to her feet. "My jewels,
girls. 'Twill be a brave tourney to-day to welcome the
May and I must be gowned and adorned for these fine
people."

"It may be that your Majesty's disdain hath pricked
the Spaniard. He is a vain man and thinks himself a
wondrous fine one," spoke up Mary suddenly, wondering
how to slip her counsel into inoffensive words. "But it
would resound much to your Grace's credit and ease and
to the amusement of the court to gain the Spaniard now
by a moment's affability."

"Oh, I will be affable enough," Anne promised.
"Now that this countrywoman is out of the way he can
bend the knee to me with a clear conscience, and I am
in the mood, now, to be affable to the very devil himself,
an I met him on a May morning. Oh, I love spring.
It was ever the time of year for me. Wyatt wrote me
a verse on't, matching me with the season — my sweets
with its sweets, my favor with the inconstant breeze.
'Twas a pretty thing. Ah, never give the whole heart
to a lover. Save it for a friend."

Anne came slowly from the window, the brightness
that the day had brought fading from her face. Absently
she lent herself to the deft hands of her tire women; a
sudden cloud seemed to have enveloped her. When
her attendants were finished, with scarcely a glance at
their work, she sent all from the room but Helen and
Mary.

"Tell me," she demanded imperiously, "struck I truth

305

in what I said to Jane? My page hath told me there was a purse sent — and from your glances while I spoke I saw ye knew the matter better than I. Come, out with it. Mary, for love of me, let me not lack knowledge, and Helen, for love of thy tongue, spare me no hard truths."

Mary began. She was plainly distressed. "There was a purse, so please your Majesty."

"It doth not please my Majesty at all," Anne told her with dry humor where lurked no mirth. "Well, how many sovereigns sent that most generous sovereign?"

"A goodly number," Helen reported. "'Twas well filled, and a letter came with it. It was a good chance for Jane's virtue. . . . 'Tis said Carewe and Seymour have been practicing her in modest arts, stuffing her mouth with well-sounding, maidenly phrases. So down she went on her knees, handing back unopened the king's letter after she had bedewed it with grateful tears, beseeching the gentleman who had brought it to return it to the king and to implore him in her name to remember that she was a gentle-woman sprung from a good and honorable stock, free from any taint whatever."

"O Virgin Mary!" murmured Anne, her eyes uprolled.

"She went on, with more tears, to say that she had no greater treasure in the world than her honor —"

"She would do well to keep the purse then, if that be all —"

"And that not even fear of death would make her forget it. If the king wished to make her a present let it be when God should send her some good and honest husband."

"God will have to look sharp to find one in England. . . . Well, 'twas a fine show," Anne commented. "Did it please his Majesty? He loveth ever a show — even of virtue."

"Aye, he praised her," Mary murmured; "said she had done well."

"And henceforward," struck in Helen's mocking tones, "that the luster of her good repute might not be breathed on, he swore to speak to her only in presence of her relatives. . . . Our shrinking Jane! So now my lord Cromwell hath been dispossessed of a room in the palace and the father and mother of this new star are there lodged. 'Tis the room, I mean, that is accessible by the secret staircase by the king's room. So our most scrupulous delicacy will entail no loss upon our *honest* love." Helen laughed in scornful mirth, her eyes on the queen.

Anne's quick color was burning in her thin cheeks, her eyes bright and hard, her nostrils dilating with the anger that shook her but on which for once she shut her lips.

"She that was on his knees!" was all she flung out and it was the first time she had opened her mouth on that to anyone but Henry.

"My thanks for your kind and true report," she added and her air dismissed them. Yet at the door she called them back.

"Heard ye what gentleman of the king's brought her that purse? 'Twas not Norris or Weston or Brereton, or one of my friends that should have told me?"

"Nay, 'twas a new fellow — a young equerry that Carewe recommended to his Grace but last week. 'Tis said he hath gained much in favor and Norris and Weston are not so well advised of the king's mind."

"Ah!" Anne nodded her head thoughtfully.

At the door again Mary turned back with timid encouragement. "'Tis not thought the lady hath yielded aught," she began, when Anne threw out with a fierceness that told of the strain within, " God grant she would ! "

Then as they raised the curtain before the door, she motioned them again to wait.

" You spoke of his *honest* love, Helen ? "

" The word was not mine own," the girl answered with an inflection of irony. " 'Twas the expression that his Majesty made use of." She let her eyes rest fixedly on Anne's face as she saw the other did not heed her but was staring off somewhere into space. Mary stood looking down into her locked fingers.

Then with a short laugh Anne roused and, turning to meet their gaze, she forced a smile of insolent security.

" Can there be two queens in England ? " she proudly asked.

A short pause before Helen's answer came, low and smooth-tongued.

" There hath been, your Highness."

The women's eyes crossed; in Anne's anger and arrogance cloaking a strange something that fluttered obscurely in their depths ; nothing but pale green-gray surface to Helen's. Then Anne's answer came, sharp as a sword thrust.

" There shall not be again ! "

In a moment she added, " And lest I be not the one I pray you, Helen, of your great love to be my taster from henceforward. Now, go. . . . I will come presently."

" How could you speak to her so ? " the gentle Mary questioned, in reproof and awe, as the door closed behind them.

Helen smiled grimly. " She needeth to be roused. Your tongues would drug her with flattery. She is a woman dancing on a fire. So far her garments are but scorched —"

" What did she mean," the. other girl pondered, " by crying out so sharp, ' God grant she would '? "

" Ha! Know you not how the king wearies of what he possesseth? An hour's possession palls — but a chase keepeth him afield forever. 'Tis a game my lady played herself for some seven year — this one does not mean to play it so long, belike. The king hath more experience; he hath learned through his success, and this time he hath no such dangerous opponent as the emperor's aunt — Nay, Cromwell will try to find some way for him if Jane prove steadfast, and Carewe will see to it that she does — her Highness had best look out," she finished abruptly as the other ladies in waiting neared them.

His honest love — that was the phrase which kept echoing over and over again in Anne's mind. It grated ominously upon her. She was defiant of rumors of her abandonment or divorce or displacement but this pricked through her surface hardihood. It was not Jane, the implement, she feared, but the unresting venom of the men who were striking at her through Jane; Oxford, Norfolk, her uncle, Suffolk, Carewe, were all leaders of that long procession she had pictured so laughingly a few moments ago. They had all been her friends, or called themselves such, in the past when her favor could help them up the slippery ladder of their ambitions, but when she had achieved her own success and dominated them, their envy had turned them to secret hatred, and, now that the king's fancy veered, they were all hand in glove with the new favorite from whom rewards might now be expected, urging her on, surrounding the king with opportunity, and spreading themselves and their incessant activities, like an impervious net, between Anne and the king. It had been weeks since she had seen the king alone. She knew what men to thank for it. . . . Now it appeared, she had more to thank them for — they were teaching Jane coyness and ambition, and Henry assurance.

What did it mean? . . . She stood wrapped in thought, then at a knock on the door she threw back her head and straightened her shoulders as if flinging off a perching imp of care.

"Viscount Rochford," said Mary's voice.

George entered slowly and looked back at the door under the curtain to be sure that it was fast before he advanced into the room. Then he came forward and stood leaning on the back of a carved chair, dangling his small plumed cap in his hand and staring down into that with a frown in dark contrast with his holiday attire.

Anne looked sharply at him. "Well, George, what brings you now? I thought you well on your way to the tourney."

"I want a word with you, sister. What is Cromwell up to?"

"Cromwell? His same tricks of state, mayhap!"

"'Tis something out of the usual, I'll be bound, by the bustling and sly winks and headshakes. A while agone he was at outs with Henry and now he has won back to confidence, close as a shift, and he's forever at parley, too, with Norfolk and Exeter who hate us, aye, and Carewe's in it, too — the damned beast!" George broke off to exclaim bitterly. "That he should have that Order of the Garter in my stead! Od's blood, Anne, why could ye not keep the king agreeable enough for that?"

RUMORS

Anne began to pace up and down the room, her scarlet gown swishing around her nervous feet.

" I ? " she tossed back at him. " Marry, blame all your own mischances upon me. You had had some falling out yourself with Henry —"

" I swear I had *not!* I was honey itself. But he took that chance of putting his spite upon you —"

" 'Tis like you to think so," Anne cried exasperated. " Prithee may not some tricksy word of thine own have undone thee? You never know on what Henry's spite rests ! "

Her brother shrugged sulkily. In his pettishness there was such a touch of youthfulness, he looked so like an angry boy with his scowling brow under his careful curls, that the flash of resentment died in Anne and was succeeded by a look of tolerant affection.

" Ah, well," she said, " what if it were I to blame — it is not my fault. I cannot gauge all Henry's humors. Lord, I was furious enough. To slight thee and honor that Nicholas Carewe! " She drew an angry breath. " The scandal-monger," she brought out, again pacing the room; " the scandal-monger, the spreader of lies, the buzzard of all good fame ! Nicholas Carewe ! I would liefer it were the knave Cromwell or Exeter or the fiery Spaniard than that black bird of ill omen ! "

" You may well say ill omen," said her brother with a touch of grimness. " I think this bodes us no good."

" The puppy ! " she snapped. " I should have had his head long since."

" You should, for now the puppy hath grown a set of teeth. There are strange tales afloat. Everywhere are rumors —"

" I know them of old. The king is cooling — la ! " she gave a contemptuous laugh. " Those tales are old

311

enough to have beards. And never one of them fathered a fact."

His eyes followed her with a trace of anger. "It is all well enough for you to throw them off so, but I think we are in an ill way. Our uncle has grown to hate us. Now we stand in his path, and many are with him. And you are too far out with Henry."

"Out with Henry?" she scoffed. "La, George, I shall be in again before ye cry Jack Robinson! It is the same talk I have heard so much. Look how it was after that — that poor little dead child of mine was born last January. Was not Henry in such a rage that 'twas said he would never enter my door again? Was I not supposed to be as good as dead and buried and forgotten and the willows blooming over my grave? Ha! Was your sister so downed? I was up ere my legs could well carry me and what I lacked for color I borrowed of a clever rouge and I held court with my head high. And I praised the king's hunting till he was red with joy. Do I know the rule to win him? Only spread the jam and he will swallow whatever bitter may lie beneath."

"Well, you do not spread it often enough, then. If it is so easy to win, why cannot ye keep him won?" her brother taunted. "Ye have it ever to do over again. Look how that fool of Wolsey's reviled you in open court!"

Anne's lips trembled. That memory pierced her like a knife. She saw the painted face, the lean fantastic form of Patch and his jibing words intoned through his nose — the words that called both her and her daughter the foulest names women can wear. Anne's breath came stormily, though she controlled her voice.

"One cannot prevent the words of a fool! Henry was furious. The fellow was obliged to hide."

RUMORS

"Yes, and where hid he? With Nicholas Carewe," George ground out with an angry oath.

Anne struck the table a sudden blow that sent her bracelets clanking. "Carewe again? Oh, what a score have I against him!"

"If Henry was so angry why did he not punish the fellow when he showed his head again?"

"Because Henry does nothing when his blood hath cooled," Anne bitterly owned. "You must heat him to get deeds. His humor, as doubtless ye have observed, George, is subject to change."

"I would for God's sake that you would change it again to our favor. Or at least away from that Seymour jade."

"Jane! Poof!" Anne laughed with a bravado her heart did not share. "She is nothing —"

"She is nothing good for us," Rockford sullenly persisted. "And I know your Gracious Highness is not so easy, either. Remember how you railed when you found her wearing a portrait of the king about her neck!"

"Oh, tut, a moment's spleen." Anne's pride made light of her own jealousy. "His fancy will pass, I tell you. It will pass," she insisted.

"Heaven send so soon — when hast thou seen him alone?"

"Thou knowest it hath not been of late. They ever keep him off — come, out with it, George. What fear is in thy head?"

"Such fears as are bred by the last treaty."

"The treaty?" Anne repeated. "Why there has been none signed. There was talk of one — but Henry balked at the terms."

"Let me tell you it was no terms that Henry balked at but the presumption that he had been in the wrong

313

and had ill treated Charles. His vanity holds him fast
there. For his pride's sake he will rest not till the emperor hath made full acknowledgment that there hath
been no ill done. Cromwell is very insistent on this
treaty with Spain. He labored with him near all Easter
day and he and Audeley were in tears when it was all
for naught. Three days later when the Privy Council,
on their knees to a man like a row of flowers, urged the
Spanish alliance, do you know what Henry said? 'I
had rather lose my crown than admit I have done
wrong!'"

"Why, what is there in that? It looketh good to me,
as supporting me."

"Wait. Cromwell took to his bed from sorrow. The
Council was in great straits. The Spaniard wrote his
arm off to his master, recommending Charles to leave
Henry to his obstinacy, to come to terms with France,
and let the pope issue his bull of deposition."

"How know you what he wrote?"

"Sure he told one that told another and mine own
wife taunted me with it as we met — as we ever meet —
by chance."

"Marry, what of it?" Anne urged impatiently. "We
have had bulls and briefs these three years past so they
are become our daily bread."

"Aye, but this one has a little leaven in it that will
e'en leaven the loaf for you, sister." Leaning closer
Rochford uttered with slow emphasis, "Neither Francis
nor Charles is to regard as legitimate any child the king
might have either by — thou knowest the word they use
for thee, 'tis the same the jester shrieked — or by any
other woman whom he might marry during thy lifetime,
unless by dispensation from the pope — which Henry will
never seek."

RUMORS

"What logic is that?" Anne scornfully flung back. "Either I am the king's wife or I am not. If they say I am not why will they not regard as legitimate his marrying another?"

"Logic is not the weapon of the powers."

Anne shut her mouth on some retort, staring at her brother under knit brows. His eyes were fixed on her and under their searching her own face did not waver.

"H'm," she said at last coolly, "I think the Princess Elizabeth will sleep as sound for all that."

"Perchance thou art missing the point."

"Oh, no." She laughed disdainfully. "I see. 'Twill not be enough for Henry to put me away — he must e'en pack the earth over me." She laughed again.

"It is not so excellent a jest as it may appear, my lady," he warned her bitterly. "You had better have a royal taster — or win Henry back."

"Why 'tis really a compliment, brother. See you, that they know I am never defeated till I am out of breath for good and all. As long as I live they know I would be taken back." She threw back her head proudly and fixed a look of haughty confidence on her brother. "They know no matter how they separate us, that I am never outdone. My day would come. I would win him again."

"Win him now."

"Why — so I shall. There is no need for you to twang on that like a harp with one string. Have I lost him so far? Tut, because in a moment of spleen he gave the garter to thy rival thou art not to suppose that he is lost. The matter is not so difficult if only I can see him but once alone. Have I changed so since the day he crowned me queen?"

She drew herself up, turning her proud face to him

in arrogant bravado, daring inspection, a smile curving her lips, a light of daring and of triumph in her sparkling eyes. She made so splendid a figure, the great ruby rising and falling at her throat with her scornful breath, the diamonds flashing in her dark hair like fireflies in a net, the hair that seemed almost too great a weight for that small head and delicate neck to bear, so vivid an embodiment of all that was regal and imperious and enchanting that Rochford's features relaxed their grim tension.

"Aye, you are fair enough," he admitted. "But you will need more than bright eyes and light feet to keep your place."

"You talk like a fool, brother," she retorted composedly. "Are we mice in a trap? Am I Queen of England or am I not? If I have the wit to make me queen, and God knows it was shrewd work all those years, then have I not the wit to keep me once I have worn the crown? Come, come, you are dreaming, man. You have been drinking too many horns — your nerves are on edge." Anne had talked herself into good humor and confidence. The admiration she had read in his grudging, brotherly eyes strengthened her sense of security.

"It is no dream," retorted her brother sullenly, "that Cromwell in his rage at Henry for outstanding him about the treaty, breathed into the Spaniard's ears — who breathed it to a woman who breathed it to me! — that Henry's obstinacy placed them in a pretty fix and it was necessary to appease the Papacy, and other things being so, the time had come for him to set the match to the powder. He said you would be out of the saddle in three days."

Anne answered his apprehensive emphasis with a laugh.

RUMORS

"We'll match his powder with some of our own," she declared. "A fine confection secured from France. So think no more about it. You shall see me hereafter at Henry's side all soft words and honeyed devotion. You are right — I have perchance scamped my bounden duty and been too honest in my pride — I'll make amends and wear a heavier yoke." She sighed in weariness, then turned to the clock upon the fireplace. "If I can but see him to-day at the tourney! Run along now, brother, I must not begin by being late."

George hesitated a moment, then instead of going, he came a little closer to her; a curious diffidence seemed to hedge his speech.

"Hath not Carewe made love to you?" he muttered as he looked down at his hat.

Anne sniffed. "It hath been a constant practice of his."

"Nay, but — I mean of late. Made he not some advances? I remember that thou didst say something, to me, Anne —"

"Why, yes, I told thee. The knave had the assurance to come to me craving an appointment." Her face grew dark. A contemptuous curve twisted her lips into a line of disdain. "He was as mad as a March hare. I would have ruined him with Henry with it but Henry was in the mood to turn on me for listening — and then, even as I hate the knave, I cannot undo him with what he cannot help."

"Did he threaten thee?"

"He always threatens."

George looked at her out of dark and wary eyes.

"Couldst thou not conciliate him with a — a show of consent?" he muttered. "Nay, I mean no real harm," for he saw the flash in Anne's face, "but —

317

grant him soft words — or — or — well, you need not scorn him so witheringly as thou hast always done."

"So I am to go to school to you, brother, for soft ways of rejecting dishonor?" Anne said under her breath. She looked at her brother and in the shamed and defiant glance that refused to meet hers but flitted past like a thing of darkness she read the dark thing that was at the back of her brother's mind, which even his lips refused to bring into the light. She caught her breath; for a moment there was silence.

"You are indeed unnerved," she said quietly. "Dost thou think I will pander with that knave? Soft words! He hath no desire for *words*." She grew calm again quickly after that sudden flash. "George, thou art simple. Should I put my head into the lion's mouth? And were I so lost to pride and honor, so craven with fear, that I should make appointments to that evil knave, how long before he or another would not apprise Henry of the fact — and declare that he had but been making test of mine integrity or else pack the blame on another's shoulders? Am I a fool that I would give mine enemies one jot or tittle of truth against me?"

"You talk as if I — I said naught," declared George hastily.

She gave him a look of dreadful sadness. "Thy fear spoke, George. . . . Now go, and trouble thyself no longer. It is a day of sun and good cheer. Before night thou shalt see thy sister in new estate."

CHAPTER XXIX

A BLOW IN THE DARK

MAY DAY was a day of such sweet spring loveliness, of such bright gayeties of sun and breeze and bird song, that the anxious heart Anne guarded with her constant smiles became insensibly lightened. As she sat at the tourney in her chair of state, under the royal cloth of gold, the stir of life and laughter about her, the pageant of color and motion, with its richly dressed throngs, its waving pennants and sun-flooded field where the light sparkled on the glittering accouterments of knights and horses, all served to engage her mood and banish all that was uneasy and apprehensive.

Impossible to be dismal on a day like this! Impossible that dark things should happen! Leaning forward, at some crisis in the encounter, she caught Henry's glance and sent a swift smile at him over her ladies' heads; he smiled back. What hope that shifty, evasive curve of his lips begot! She flouted the last remnant of her anxiety. What had she to fear? She would regain him yet. If only she could see him alone . . . that was the essential and that was exactly what her enemies took such bitter care to prevent, surrounding him on all sides from her, leading him hither and yon on his new love quests, opposing a continual barrier of distraction and revelry. But her time would come . . . it must come . . . she would *make* it come!

THE FAVOR OF KINGS

Rochford and Norris were the challengers that day
and they were performing miracles of valor. As Norris,
after three times splintering the lances of their succes-
sive opponents, was riding triumphantly past the royal
stands, bowing to the applause and acclaim, the queen's
handkerchief slipped from her hand and fluttered to the
ground. Norris raised it skillfully on his lance and Anne
caught it from its point. At that moment she was aware
of a disturbance in the king's stand; Henry had risen
from his place and was preparing to depart.

Her heart sank and sharp disappointment gripped
her as she realized that their chance of meeting was in-
definitely receding. In helpless chagrin she watched him
mount and ride off attended only by Norris, who had
hastily laid aside his mail at the command to accompany
his sovereign; from a page she learned that they were
returning to London. The sunshine went out of the
day; the sports, continued by Rochford, left alone to
defend the lists, proceeded half-heartedly for a few
moments, then Anne, too, rose and returned to Greenwich Castle with her ladies. The gentlemen were making haste to follow the king. Norfolk and Paulet, however, and a small group of their satellites, appeared to
be remaining; as Anne entered the castle she saw them
standing talking closely together in a court. She found
something more than usually significant in their aloof
and confidential demeanor, and the glances of secure arrogance that they cast upon her in her passing seemed to
hint at withheld knowledge. . . .

At ten that night there arrived at Greenwich a breathless and disheveled rider. It was Roland Bulkley, a
lawyer of Gray's Inn. He asked to be shown at once
to the queen and Anne kept him waiting but a few minutes. She knew him for a devoted friend.

A BLOW IN THE DARK

She received him alone with Madge Shelton, clad in a silver-gray dressing gown, her heavy hair hanging in disordered curls about her. Her eyes, so darkly large in her thinned face, expressed a sharper anxiety than she knew.

Bulkley had dropped on one knee to deliver his errand; he was out of breath and his face was streaked with sweat and dust. "There be strange doings in London," he panted out; "methought your Grace should know with all speed. So I —"

"You come from my brother?" she shot at him.

"Nay —"

"No harm has touched him?"

"None to my knowledge."

"Ah!" she drew a breath of relief. "Say on then and put me quickly out of mine impatience."

"Your Highness, it is sad, sad tidings. This night was Master Norris committed to the Tower."

"Norris?" she echoed blankly. "Norris? . . . Why, man, thou art raving. I myself saw him ride off as usual with the king this afternoon."

"He is in the Tower," the lawyer sadly insisted.

"The Tower? Why — why — for why?" He shook his head, still kneeling at her feet. "Oh, speak on. There must be rumor flying. What is said — what is whispered? Is there no reason known?"

"Naught is known. All are in wonderment. And Mark Smeton hath also been sent there."

"What, to the Tower? Mark, my little player? Why, this is madness — what hath the lad done? Come, rise — what means it?"

Bulkley rose slowly to his feet, shaking his head dejectedly at her questions. She stood and stared at him, racking her mind for an explanation.

321

THE FAVOR OF KINGS

"I have heard whispered — though 'tis but rumor," the lawyer presented hesitantly, " that 'tis for some sort of complicity with your Grace."

"Complicity? Complicity? For God's sake, what talk is this?"

But he could not say. He had heard only excited murmurs of a plot — some said against the queen, some that the queen had share in it. That was all he knew, but his alarm was infinite.

"A plot," Anne repeated, as if the sound of the word would help her wits. She tried to keep calm, to think clearly and very quickly, but her darting surmises could strike out no path of explanation. It was a blow in the dark. Norris — and Smeton . . . why those two? A most unlikely pair to be involved together in a plot; a hireling musician and the king's intimate, one of the foremost gentlemen at court. Norris in the Tower! It was incredible . . . other incredibilities would follow in its train. What did it all mean?

She shuddered in a nameless foreboding. She remembered the king's hasty departure and Norfolk's ill-omened eyes upon her and her flesh pricked. She began to walk very rapidly up and down the room, gripping her hands against an hysterical temptation to wring them in her helpless distress. For she was utterly helpless. She was being conspired against; her friends and dependants were being arrested and flung into the Tower and she was isolated at Greenwich, unable to know what was being done, unable to communicate with her adherents, unable to' reach the king.

Bulkley was powerless. He was only a lawyer of Gray's Inn. And his brother, Sir Richard, an intimate friend of Norris's, was absent in North Wales where he was knight chamberlain.

A BLOW IN THE DARK

"I will write my brother at once," he said, "and meantime I will back to London to see if there be news."

The smile that Anne gave him at parting was beautiful even in her distress. She had never wavered in her steady kindness to her friends and it touched her now that one of the least of them should be so ready to pay that loving debt. And it augured that the others for whom she had done so much would rally swiftly to her. There was Weston and Brereton and Page and Cranmer among those on whom she felt she could absolutely depend; and chief of all, her brother. But if she were struck at would not the blow include her brother, also? And what was it? What was impending?

The terrible vagueness of her fear barbed its anguish. She had such a field of dread to choose from! She paced up and down, remembering her brother's warnings, facing one supposition after another. The thing that pierced her with the wildest apprehension was the king's passion for Jane Seymour. His *honest* love, he had said!

"They want my life," she said to herself again and again, throughout that dragging, intolerable night. Each hour racked her with suspense. The morning, she felt, would bring the facts; she dreaded and longed for its menacing disclosures.

Her ladies were weeping about her. Tearfully they urged flight. There were ships in the river, they said; let her take to one of them and put at once for sea.

"To what harbor?" Anne demanded, flinging wide her arms. "Would France or Spain grant me asylum — I, that have laughed Europe to scorn? And why should I fly? Would it not admit whatever thing they are planning against me?"

"What mattereth what you admit! They are seeking

your ruin — go, go, for the love of heaven," Mary frantically besought.

" I cannot and I will not — and I will not an I can,"
Anne gave back. " I am no coward. We will see what
thing the morning brings us."

What the morning brought was an order for the queen
to appear before a number of a council of special commissioners to answer to charges of high treason against
her. She had never heard before of these special commissioners who, it appears, had been secretly appointed
two weeks before, to investigate any treason in the
realm. She found them represented by Norfolk and
Paulet and Sir William Fitzwilliam who had arrived at
Greenwich during the evening. So this, then, was what
Norfolk's eyes had boded!

It was noon when she emerged from her encounter
with that council and she presented to her waiting ladies
a face so pale, an aspect so charged with anger and disdain and secret terror, that their worst fears of the night
seemed realized. She made a wild gesture to them.

" Pack up. Pack up. I am off to the Tower."

" To the Tower?" their stammering tongues gave back.

" Aye, I am under arrest, it seemeth. . . . It would not
be enough for these vile panderers," she flung out passionately, " to rid me from Henry's path in any quiet
or seemly way — with poison or assassination. No!
The world would suspect him — his deeds would pro-
claim his complicity. They must needs make me mine
own executioner. . . . He is to wed again, girls."

" Wed?" Mary's quivering lips just formed the
sound.

" Aye. The lady is my maid of honor. Our modest
Jane; our prudish preacher. Our sly Slip-up-the-Back
Stairs!"

A BLOW IN THE DARK

"Did the council —" Madge was beginning in bewilderment.

"Tell me this?" Anne laughed harshly. "No, my love, they made no mention of his Majesty's intentions. It was hardly needed — I know him so well! I can see a church door by daylight. They did but acquaint me with mine own misdeeds. My God, do you know what they accused me of? Oh, it is past belief! You will be amazed at what hath gone on under your noses and you never knew! According to the honorable gentlemen in there, I have been wrongdoing with Norris and Smeton — yes, Smeton, that hireling fellow, and another — they did not tell his name. Perhaps they have not decided on him yet. They said they knew all and I had best confess. . . . Is it not a shrewd plot? Is it not well devised? An unworthy queen — to the Tower with her! She hath deceived the king — off with her head! Poor king — how he hath been deceived! He must console himself if he can — and how well that there is another lady at hand! Let him wed and trust this time to be rewarded for his noble faith. . . . Oh, God, was it not enough to strike me down but they must strike down my honor, too? *I* play the fool with those men! Had I the will to do so, the world knows I have the wit to keep my will from it! The fiends, the liars! They know they are liars! And they handled me cruelly — my uncle there, with the sneer on his false face, he would not listen to me, crying out, "Tut, tut, tut," as if I had been a kitchen wench! Fitzwilliam — he that I have helped make — would not meet my eyes; he drummed on the table pretending to be absent in mind. Paulet — yes, he showed me courtesy, but then he would bow a lady to the rack. . . . They *know* they are liars! And this is a vile plot. A plot — ah, now I know why

325

that knave Cromwell was returned to favor! His was the brain that devised this. No wonder Henry smiled on him again. He first made his way by aiding crown a woman — now let him hold his place by beheading her. Oh, why did I not make his head tumble long ago when I had the power! I have been too slack. I knew him all along. He had bragged smugly to me oft of his lack of scruple. He would sell the corpse of his mother. What is a woman to him? A woman — the poorest thing in England — Do I rave? Mary, you look frozen into a mask of fear. Bestir yourself, I shall need gowns and night shifts at the Tower. Make my bag. What, Helen, no word, even from you? And not one laugh to mock me? *I* can laugh! . . . Yea, and I shall cry my innocence till they stop my mouth with clay. I will defy them to the end." She faced her women with the defiant mien that she had fronted her defamers; then her eyes blazing, their fiery indignation seemed to fix suddenly on some point in the distance beyond them; they dilated and filled with terror. She drew a breath that was a groan. "*Elizabeth,*" she said in a voice of anguish.

At two o'clock the tide served to convey her to the Tower and Anne stepped into the royal barge in company with Norfolk, Oxford, Lord Sandys, and a detachment of the guard. Her ladies were not permitted to accompany her. She sat alone, erect, disdainful, in that boat load of men, only once unclosing her lips on the journey. Then it was to ask that she should see the king. Norfolk replied with a contemptuous negative.

The banks along the riverside were crowded with the populace who had heard the news and rushed to see its truth for themselves, but Anne was very little conscious of the thousand eyes; she had the sensations of a per-

son on a lofty height; her head swam, the world was very
far off and fantastically unreal. Her thoughts flitted
in and out of her mind like rooks through a ruined bel-
fry. Now she thought of the barge, and the first time
she had used it, going to her coronation, with Catherine's
arms broken off it to give place to her own — her own.
"Happiest of Women!" She wondered if Jane would
wrench hers away in turn and perch a crest of her own
on that prow. She thought of Catherine and was glad
that she had died before she had seen such humiliation
come upon her supplanter. She looked at the cushions
and remembered the day she had first seen that particular satin damask — on the long tables at Whitehall when
she and Henry had gone to view Wolsey's treasures.
Norris had been the king's only attendant . . . she could
see Henry now, with one hand lightly on Norris's shoulder . . . she could see his eyes smile into hers. How
little she had thought that day — ! Where was Henry
now? Was he in London? What was happening
there? She feared for her brother, in his ardent loyalty
to her — she feared, too, for her father, for though he
could not be said to love her yet there was some affection and he was her father. She thought of her friends,
her real friends, and what they might be able to do to
help her, but here was Norris, whom she had reckoned
the stanchest and most influential already in the Tower
and threatened by the same sword that hung over her
head. A shrewd plot she thought, while the frenzied
terror of its possibilities chilled the blood about her
heart — to implicate the very one who would have
struggled to free her! She wondered in anguish who
could be that third man whom the council had myste-
riously accused without naming — her fears pointed to
Wyatt. Report had always linked them. Yet he had

been so little at court of late and so little with her — surely none could tangle him in this. She thought of Brereton and Weston and Cranmer and Richard Bulkley and the ways in which they might aid her but she thought of them without hope, for the mind that had devised this terrible infamy to bring her low would as surely devise some further schemes to render those friends powerless. Her agony of helplessness deepened tragically in her as comprehension of her position more and more impressed itself upon her. She was at the mercy of men utterly unscrupulous, men who had seen fellow creatures racked, without turning a hair, utterly immoral, unprincipled, who boasted no higher aim than gratifying a monarch's whim, who knew no higher law than expediency. They had nothing to gain by protecting her and everything to lose; it would be disaster or death to oppose the king's passion, backed as it was now by Cromwell's ruthless connivings. She had too great a knowledge of the peers of England to hope anything from their justice.

At five the barge had reached the Tower and paused at the Traitor's Gate. A clock inside boomed out the hour as the doors opened. The guard disembarked, forming a narrow line for Anne to pass through. Sir William Paulet extended a hand to her to assist her from the boat but she refused it; she felt a tremor in her own that her pride refused to have discovered. Her knees were trembling; it was by a supreme effort of the will that she rose and passed between the guarding files into what was to be her prison. The councilors followed.

Sir William Kingston received them, and consigning their royal charge to him, the three noblemen bowed and withdrew. Anne gazed after their departing figures; she

A BLOW IN THE DARK

watched the closing of the heavy door behind them, barring out the light of day, leaving her in a gloom that intensified the grim and forbidding aspect of the place. The chill of the stone beneath her feet struck the cold of fear into her. It rang hollow under her tread as she advanced in the direction to which Kingston was silently beckoning her. Her heart failed as she remembered that this man, her jailer, was a devoted adherent of Mary, and ghastly visions of loathsome cells rose before her. She tried to command her voice to put a quiet question but it quivered over the words.

" Art thou taking me to — a dungeon? "

Kingston shook his head. He was looking at her with some curiosity for it was interesting to see this high lady in such straits. He had heartily hated her since the execution of his friend Sir Thomas More, who had been one of those beheaded for refusing to acknowledge the Act of Supremacy and for whose death he had believed her responsible, yet in that moment his rancor was unconsciously disarmed by her pallid face, shining white through the dimness, and her trembling effort at self-control.

" No, madame," he said gruffly, " to your own lodging, where you lay at your coronation."

A bitter smile parted Anne's lips. " It is too good for me, is it not? " she murmured with her old sardonic inflection, and she flung back her head and burst into sudden loud laughter. Kingston had opened the door that led from the Traitor's Entrance to the main portions of the building. She remembered how the last time she had come to the Tower the king had met her with a kiss and she sank now on the stairway that led to her old chambers. " My coronation — my coronation," she gasped, " Oh, my God, could there have been a more exquisite torture — a more ironic jest! Oh, thou hast a sense of humor, Master Kingston, or did another devise this for thee? My coronation!" Her laughter grew hysterical; it echoed wildly with a hollow ring through those stone halls. She could not control herself, she rocked to and fro, her whole body quivering with her outbursts of laughter. The strain had been too much for her nerves; the terrible suspense and shock had played upon them like an instrument. "My coro—" she uttered chokingly, and her laughter stopped. She felt wild sobs bursting in her bosom; unborn tears and cries seemed to be strangling her in her throat. She fought them frantically, struggling to regain control. She got to her feet, her limbs still trembling under her, and gave one wild look about that hall which she had seen in such happier circumstances. "Ah, wherefore am I here?" she whispered.

In the same blank way she gazed about her remembered room and bowed slightly to the four gentle women who, with Lady Kingston, were deputed to wait upon her. Then as the governor of the Tower was leaving her, she seemed to rally her wits and called him quickly back. She asked to have the sacrament brought to her prayer closet, and "With it upon my lips," she said, "I shall protest my innocence of having ever wronged my lord. I am the king's true wedded wife . . . Mr. Kingston, do you know wherefore I am here?"

"Nay," Kingston told her.

"When saw you the king?"

"I saw him not since I saw him in the tiltyard."

"Mr. Kingston, I pray you tell me where my lord Rochford is?"

"I saw him before dinner in the court," Kingston evaded curtly and was turning away again.

A BLOW IN THE DARK

She took a step nearer, his manner inflaming her distrust. Her haggard eyes searched his half-averted face as if to drag truth from it. "When saw you my brother?"

"I saw him last at York Place," was all Kingston would say. An aversion to further scenes — perhaps a wasteful emotion of pity for the queen — made him shirk the task of enlightening her further.

"Oh, I hear say that I shall be accused with three men," she flared out, "and I can say no more than — nay! Oh, Norris, they said that thou hadst accused me! Thou art here in the Tower — thou and I may die together . . . and Mark, thou, too, art here . . . Oh, my mother, thou wilt die for sorrow!" She checked her outburst and turned sharply upon Kingston again. "Mr. Kingston, shall I die without justice?"

"The poorest subject the king hath has that," he replied, and shut the door behind him on the bitter incredulity of her flouting laughter.

CHAPTER XXX

THE TOWER

THE disaster which had swept over her, as sudden and blasting as a stroke of lightning, seemed almost too great for her shocked brain to conceive. One day a queen, reigning in the midst of her court, and the next a prisoner in the Tower, her life conspired against! Her senses reeled under the staggering horror. She was in a chaos of burning anger, of fear, of terror and of dazed bewilderment.

And the attendants who closed in about her had been assigned, not from her friends but from her enemies, and the two that had been long the most maliciously disposed to her, her aunt, the wife of Sir Edward Boleyn, and Mrs. Coseyns, wife of the master of her horse, carried espionage of her through every hour of the day and night, sleeping on a pallet on the foot of her bed so that she was forever denied the comfort of privacy and the poor solace of breaking down. And all day long there were five pairs of eyes upon her in a smug satisfaction that marked, God knows what, of petty feminine revenge, and five tongues artfully endeavoring to entangle her into damaging admissions.

They pushed insult as far as they dared, parading their disbelief of her innocence with sly headshakes, upraised brows, incredulous smiles and pertinent innuendoes. And Anne, caged and baited, pacing up and down between them in her distracted agony, answered them now with proud silence, now with frantic outpourings of angry denial.

"Lies, lies!" she said fiercely as the aunt — a sister-in-law of Anne's father, a hawk-nosed, mean-mouthed woman, for whom Anne had ever shown a disdainful disregard, repeated an accusation.

Lady Boleyn pursed up her lips and Mrs. Coseyns smiled unbearably. "So they are all lies," she murmured. For ten years she had fawned upon Anne, hating her poisonously for her outspoken frankness and reckless pride and now for once she was expanding in the relief of hinting at her true colors. "Why then on Saturday did Norris tell thy almoner thou wast a good woman?"

"Why should he not tell my almoner so?" Anne demanded passionately. "Thou knowest that my enemies for years have tried to fill the court with evil slanders. It is the part of my friends to deny them. . . . I bade Norris do so, as one who stood close to our person." . . .

"Very close," came significantly from Lady Boleyn.

Anne checked the wild impulse to retort. She remembered that these women were no more malicious than the others of the court and she read sincerity in the suspicion of their eyes and the little tossings of their heads. Her whole body burned as she realized their eager belief of these monstrous things.

"He knew the truth," she said as calmly as she could. "He came oft to our rooms for he is to marry my pretty cousin, Madge Shelton."

"Methinks he hath been a long time marrying this pretty cousin," Mrs. Coseyns insinuated. "His wife was long dead. . . . Was it not known to your Grace that he was said to come for another's sake?"

"Oh, you have been listening to some jest of Weston's — you know he was ever a gay talker," Anne cried impatiently. "It was common flattery for him to say that the suitors of my maids wooed them to be in my presence — 'tis the incense offered a queen. Why, you would not take a light jest so hard — it would do great harm to the innocent gentleman." A deep concern throbbed in Anne's voice as she thought of Norris, gay, debonair Norris, whose friendship had never wavered through all her wavering, uncertain years, now in this very Tower, in fear of death, for her. Oh, it was pitiful! "And as for Smeton," she went on, her voice supplicating in its earnestness to reach these hard old women and win them to belief, "why I have never given him so much as a kind word. He sayeth the same, surely. . . . 'Twas not three days ago he was peevish at some command of mine and I told him he must not look to have me treat him as if he were gentle born. ' I know,' quoth he, ' a look sufficeth me.' You know the boy had a proud stomach! . . . To arrest *him!* I could laugh if my heart were not so heavy. . . . But perhaps the king does it but to try me."

So Anne's tongue ran, as her thoughts darted hither and yon like lost swallows over the unknown fields of dread, now defending herself in eager argument and explanation to these women to whom three days before she would have scorned to condescend, now railing in passionate resentment and despairing surmise. It was for her brother she feared the most.

"They will not dare not to cage him," she miserably foreboded, and it was with no cry of surprise that she learned at last that Rochford was in the Tower and had been there since noon of the day that she had been brought there. She could not discover that anything was charged against him except complicity with her supposed misdeeds.

THE TOWER

Presently she was informed that Brereton, Wyatt, Weston and Page had been added to the prisoners.

"So many?" she said with a melancholy smile. "Must so many be destroyed?"

In these arrests was revealed the scope of the action against her; the inclusive sweep of that scythe which was mowing her down. None of her faction who would have hindered or avenged her death were to be left. Her brother and all his intimates were entangled; some extra charges had evidently been trumped up to include them all. Wyatt, she feared, would be made that third alleged lover at whom the council had hinted. From her experience she was sure that threats and menaces were being used to intimidate those friends still at large. Of her father's fate she remained in ignorance. Once she thought she heard his voice in the halls; Kingston denied it but that was not conclusive.

The commissioners did not visit her further. Kingston shirked talking to her, leaving her to his wife who bustled about the royal apartments in complacent importance. Anne had absolutely no word of what was being prepared against her, nor of what she might expect from one hour to another; her greatest terror was of some mockery of a trial behind the barred doors from which no syllable of her defense would penetrate to the world without. She lived in that terror from one hideous minute to another, starting at every opening of the door. She did not unlock her lips on her anguish now; she began to perceive that these women had been put there about her to report and twist her every word into some damaging admission, to create evidence that they were only too ready to manufacture from her least reference. She tried to hide her grief from their hateful eyes with a desperate effort at composure but as

335

she lay on her cot at night, with Lady Boleyn and Mrs. Coseyns sleeping away at the foot of it, her tears fell silently hour after hour into the pillow, not the hot passionate drops of rebellion, but those cold, slow tears of hopeless misery which despair alone wrings from a breaking heart.

She was on her knees, in the relaxing privacy of her prayer closet, her lips moving in an urgent plea to the God of justice to come to her aid, when Lady Kingston entered to announce that there was someone in the outer chamber who would speak with her upon the king's business.

" What name? " said Anne rising in eagerness, with a rush of hope.

The name was a knell.

" Sir Nicholas Carewe."

" I will be with him in a moment."

She paused, nerving herself to the evil she foreboded in this arrival. Her vanity strengthened her; she shook out her gown, brushing up her hair, and summoning a smile she swept into the outer room.

Nothing in her life had been so stinging to her pride as it was now to face the triumphant gleam under Carewe's insolent lids, and that mocking sneer on his thin lips. He bowed to her with an exaggerated deference and murmured in tones of assumed commiseration, " I fear I interrupt your Majesty's devotions? "

" Oh, I am not in such great need thereof as some wherewith I am acquainted," Anne quickly retorted. Her pulses were beating faster as she faced him; her blood sang its old reckless song of hardy defiance.

" 'Tis well to say them ere it is too late," was his gentle reminder.

"A ripe thought for yourself to dwell upon," her prompt rejoinder came.

"But one whereof I have not so much need as some wherewith I speak," he taunted.

"You have grown nimble of wit — a great change from your former habit."

"There have been many changes since your day, cousin." He paused and with a look he reminded Lady Kingston of his former request for privacy and she withdrew with the four ladies in her train. Sir Nicholas sauntered to the door behind her, closed it carefully, listening to the retreating footsteps, and then returned to Anne, jauntily smiling. He was dressed as for a fête.

"Your errand, sir?" she reminded him. "Do you indeed come from the king?"

"I do indeed come from the king. And he doth indeed commend himself to you and he bids you, by my word of mouth, redeem yourself from this grievous situation in which you now find yourself to the great confusion of his Grace's hope and the scandal of the whole realm."

Carewe delivered himself of the harangue in a singsong nasal manner, his glittering eyes mocking her, that sinister smile still curling his lips.

"And how am I so to redeem myself?"

"He biddeth thee confess the truth. Thou hast nothing to gain by denial. All is known and ascertained — if not all —" and the smile deepened —"at least enough to part that fair head of yours from your neck. Denial, I say therefore, is vain and but bringeth public shame. The king is well advised of your doings. And yet such is his extraordinary mercy and clemency that he is minded to save your life and shield you from the consequences of your own acts if you will but be open and own the truth. He biddeth you to confess."

"And if I confess this truth, then will my life be most certainly spared?"

"It will be spared."

"How may that be, if I should confess to being the vile woman that my accusers declare?"

"All things are possible to his Grace's mercy. . . . He will be kind so you do not anger him by denial."

"And my life will be spared," Anne repeated. "Why then, Nicholas, I am indeed safe for I will straightway confess that very truth which he seeks to know. And the truth is — that I am innocent in the sight of God and man of these infamous charges that have been laid upon me, that never have I been unfaithful to him in word or act, and that those poor gentlemen who are now imprisoned are not the ones who ever solicited me so to betray my wifely honor."

Her tone was barbed with peculiar meaning; Carewe gave a thin laugh.

"This then is the truth which thou mayst bear back to him — the truth, hear you, whereunto I will stake my soul with the sacrament upon my lips. I am innocent. And so I have told the truth and I have his princely promise to spare my life.

"The truth!" jeered Carewe. "Thou art a lying fool to persist in this defiance. I have told you all is discovered. Norris and Weston —"

"Of what can Weston be accused?"

"Of what, indeed! He is tarred with the same brush. . . . Ah, you are touched!"

Anne repressed her bitter surprise. "I know well," she declared, "that Norris and Weston are proclaiming their innocence and mine."

THE TOWER

"Thy musician hath already confessed."

"Confessed? To what?"

"I thought that would prick you. Why to — you know the word, dear cousin. The seventh commandment is framed to forbid it."

"He hath confessed?" Anne repeated.

"Aye, fully. Dates and places. Lord, he hath been three times a sinner, I am told."

"Mark Smeton!" Anne's tone was a blaze of contempt. "You mean that he has been threatened for fear of his life to do this vile thing — or else tortured. Ah!" As she saw from the gleam in Carewe's face that she had struck the mark, "He hath been *tortured!*"

"Belike," Carewe indifferently gave back. "A knotted rope tightened about the head works wonders in greasing the tongue! The rack, too, performeth miracles. A pity they do not employ it in another case." He gave her a terrible and evil look that showed the ceaseless fire burning under the man's assumption of sneering ease.

"A knotted rope, the rack!" Anne repeated, wildly. "Why the poor little fool — he hath a horror of pain. And so he confessed — why so did that Sebastiano Montecuculi confess that he had poisoned the Dauphin of France and it was afterwards found that the dauphin had not been poisoned at all! No one believes what the rack wrings out!"

"Believe it or not," grinned Carewe, "it is enough to sign death warrants on. You see how lies the land. He hath confessed; mayhap the others will follow — they may have so done already for aught I know or care. My business is with yourself. Will you own the truth?"

24   339

"Why I have done so. Ye dare not feign to disbelieve me."

"And so you are innocent?"

"I am innocent, indeed."

"You lie," came violently from him. "You lie, you jade, you —" He heaped vile epithets upon her, his passion leaping its barriers. "You, innocent! Aye, so was Mary Magdalen! So was Cleopatra pure! Why the most defiled outcast that walks these streets of London is clean compared to your besotted filth. You have been steeped in sinning over head and ears."

He approached her threateningly, the smile gone, his lips drawn back over his teeth as the wild beast within him raged out at her.

She did not shrink from him; she met his glare with that old mockery of look, that amused glint of contempt, that had always been her keenest weapon against his fury.

"Well, if I have sinned you have at least this comfort," she tossed carelessly at him in a voice grown suddenly cool and sweet, "that it hath never been with you, dear Nicholas."

The sharpness of that thrust, the unquenched flame of the spirit in the woman he had come to crush, caught Carewe strangely off his guard. "Thank God," was all he could find to say for a moment, as he groped for words, keen annihilating words, that would beat down and dominate her arrogance. He tried to choke back the signs of the rage that overmastered him. "It would have been the safer for you," he got out, with grim significance.

Her eyes traveled slowly, thoughtfully, the length of his figure and came to rest again on his passion-scarred face.

THE TOWER

"Truly," she owned, letting a soft, regretful sigh escape, "it would have been the safer. No one would ever suspect me of taking such a lover. . . . But it would have been a hard price for safety," and her flouting laughter burst out at him.

He flung her a venomous look and turned to the door. "Laugh on," he jeered. "You have not so long a time to hear that voice of thine!"

"No? It is to be silenced, then? . . . And to think it will have to go without having once said any of those sweet things you have so urged on it to say! Never once a yes, from me, dear Nicholas! Never aught but floutings! It is very sad, is it not?"

"By God!" he choked out, "I'd like to behead you with these hands!"

"Fie! I would ne'er let you as near me as that."

She was facing him with her hands clasped negligently behind her head, her beautiful figure was drawn up to its full height. It was a pose of insolent, studied disdain; an unconquerable mockery curled her lips, and glowed in the bright darkness of her eyes. She had forgotten the fears of life and death; she was answering with oblivious passion to the one demand upon her for courage and contempt. It was superb; a bitter admiration stabbed Carewe as he saw that even in that hour of his triumph her spirit was as unsurrendered to him as that body he had so long coveted. He suffered, and he suffered with an anguish compounded of all the venom of his nature. He could gloat ghoulishly upon her danger, he had plotted and connived at her death, but he had never wanted her as now when she was escaping him forever.

CHAPTER XXXI

A LETTER AND TWO SONGS

THE chamber of state was in darkness save for the candles on the table where Anne sat writing. In the shadow-hidden pallet at the foot of the immense bed her two jailers had fallen into slumber and their heavy breathing was the only sound in the room except the occasional scratching drive of Anne's quill. The letter was to her husband. She wrote:

"Your Grace's anger and my imprisonment are things so strange unto me, as what to write or what to excuse I am altogether ignorant. Whereas you sent unto me (willing me to confess a truth and so obtain favor) by such an one as you know to be mine ancient, professed enemy; I no sooner received this message by him than I rightly conceived your meaning; and if, as you say, confessing a truth may indeed procure my safety, I shall with all willingness and duty perform your command.

"But let not your Grace ever imagine that your poor wife will ever be brought to acknowledge a fault, where not so much as a thought thereof preceded. And, to speak a truth, never prince had wife more loyal in all duty, and in all true affection, than you have ever found in Anne Boleyn, with which name and place I could willingly have contented myself, if God and your Grace's pleasure had been so pleased. Neither did I at any

342

A LETTER AND TWO SONGS

time so far forget myself in my exaltation or received
Queenship, but that I always looked for such an alteration as now I find; for, the ground of my preferment
being on no surer foundation than your Grace's fancy,
the least alteration, I knew, was well and sufficient to
draw that fancy to some other subject. You have
chosen me, from a low estate, to be your queen and companion, far beyond my desert or desire. If then you
found me worthy of such honor, good your Grace, let
not any light fancy or bad counsel of my enemies with-
draw your princely favor from me; neither let that stain,
that unworthy stain of a disloyal heart toward your good
Grace, ever cast so foul a blot on your most dutiful wife
and the infant princess, your daughter. Try me, good
king, but let me have a lawful trial, and let not my
sworn enemies sit as my accusers and judges; yes, let
me receive an open trial for my truth shall fear no open
shame; then shall you see, either mine innocency cleared,
your suspicion and conscience satisfied, the ignominy
and slander of the world stopped, or my guilt openly
declared. So that, whatsoever God or you may determine of me, your Grace may be freed from an open
censure; and mine offense being lawfully proved. Your
Grace is at liberty — both before God and man, not only
to execute worthy punishment on me as an unlawful
wife, but to follow your affection, already settled for
that party, for whose sake I now am as I am, whose
name I could some good while since have pointed unto;
your Grace being not ignorant of my suspicion therein."

She paused, her breast rising and falling with the
passionate breath. Then, her eyes shining with un-
daunted courage she went on:

343

THE FAVOR OF KINGS

"But, if you have already determined of me, and that not only my death, but an infamous slander must bring you the enjoying of your desired happiness; then I desire of God, that he will pardon your great sin therein, and likewise mine enemies, the instruments thereof; and that he will not call you to a strict account for your unprincely and cruel usage of me, at his general judgment seat, where both you and myself must shortly appear, and in whose judgment, I doubt not (whatever the world may think of me), mine innocence shall be openly known, and sufficiently cleared."

Again she paused and the light died out of her eyes and they filled with a look of unutterable pain. Her hand trembled on this last paragraph.

"My last and only request shall be, that myself may only bear the burden of your Grace's displeasure, and that it may not touch the innocent souls of those poor gentlemen, who (as I understand), are likewise in strait imprisonment for my sake. If ever I have found favor in your sight; if ever the name of Anne Boleyn hath been pleasing in your ears, then let me obtain this request; and I will so leave not to trouble your Grace any further; with mine earnest prayers to the Trinity to have your Grace in his good keeping, and to direct you in all your actions,

"Your most loving and ever faithful wife,

"ANNE BOLEYN.

"From my doleful prison in the Tower, this sixth of May."

The quill slipped from her fingers and she sat silent, in bitter meditation. Slowly she grew aware of the

A LETTER AND TWO SONGS

plaintive strains of a lute that were floating softly down to her through the night air from some open window. She knew the melody and Wyatt's manner of playing, and her thoughts went pitifully up to him as he played there in the dark. She felt a sudden wistful craving to see him, to speak to him and say those kind things which she had never said. . . . She stole to the window and knelt there resting her cheek on the cold ledge as she listened. He had composed that very melody for some verses that he had written her and she repeated them silently to herself now as the sad cadences sank about her.

> My lute awake! perform the last
> Labor that thou and I shall waste,
> The end that I have now begun;
> For when this song is said and past,
> My lute, be still, for I have done.

The candles flickered and went out as she knelt there, sad beyond all words and yet faintly comforted by that sweet music falling from one whose thoughts must be of her. . . .

Suddenly the delicate strains were lost in a noisy outbreak of song from directly beneath her window, and rising, she looked down on a chain of gayly-lighted barges moving over the dark surface of the river, filled with hilarious revelers. She pressed her face against the bars trying to distinguish the figures in the flare of the torches; through the music she heard loud voices and roistering shouts from one barge to another.

> Drink, drink, the canakin clink —

Lady Boleyn and Mrs. Coseyns roused.

"Rest you, ladies," said Anne, stepping back from the

window with a smile lost to them in the darkness of the room. " 'Tis but the king returning from his revels."

Although she lay awake a long time listening the lute did not sound again. Just so, she thought, had the king's din drowned out Wyatt's delicate strains in her life. . . . Then she thought of the letter that she had penned to that oblivious reveler beneath her window and a desolation too deep for tears possessed her. . . . If ever the name of Anne Boleyn had been pleasing to his ears! . . . One wife he had given over to indignity and isolation, and now another he flung to shame and death.

One noon she learned that Wyatt and Sir Richard Page had been released. A flash of hope shot through her only to be succeeded by an increased despair as she realized that this sorting out of the innocent from the guilty made her brother's position and that of his companions more desperate. Evidently they were retained as guilty. But of what were they accusing George? — complicity in all this supposed wrongdoing, she concluded. But she was profoundly grateful for Wyatt's escape; she had been afraid that his past intimacy with her might entangle him, though he had absented himself from court for so many years now that it would appear difficult to connect their names. She surmised that Page's powerful relations, the Fitzwilliams and Russells, had secured his immunity.

It is useless to record the terrible gusts of anger that shook her, as the hours went by, cooped there in that room with those spying women. She paced up and down, up and down, forgetting sometimes those spies about her in the driving extremity of her impotent rage.

346

A LETTER AND TWO SONGS

She knew a wrath that she had never known. She had thought she was in straits before, thought she was helpless, pitiable, but this, this was helplessness and misery such as her darkest thought had never fathomed. Not to be able to lift one finger in her own defense! Not to be able to aid her brother! He and Elizabeth were the two dearest beings on earth to her, and one lay under fear of death and the other — what would be Elizabeth's fate if the mother were taken from her? Who would fight for her? . . . Well, Parliament had decreed that she was the next heir; it would take some time, even if her mother were done away with, to go back from all that, and Henry's stubbornness would dislike to undo what he had so persistently labored to effect. His stubbornness was probably the reason why he had not ridded himself of Anne by the more simple expediency of divorce. There would have been small opposition in her case; she had no emperor uncle to menace on her behalf. . . . And then she caught her breath as she remembered that agreement of the powers, that no woman would be recognized as Henry's wife during her own lifetime. And Jane would fear her living. Of course she must die! And as no one was more adept at such matters than Cromwell, the able secretary had come into favor again by devising this method of relief for his master. Why it was simple as sighing! And yet it could not be. There must be some way out. Perhaps her father — but the days went by, full of dragging hours yet too swift after all in passing, and no ray of light appeared.

Yet however Anne's reason might array these powerful facts against her, and admit the extreme improbability of any chance of escape, however she might say to herself that she expected nothing but the worst, hope lived unquenched in every drop of her blood. Reason had nothing to do with it. It was simply incredible that she should die. She was so alive. These disasters happened to other people, to old men, to others, but never to young women of scarce twenty-nine so quick with life.

Two weeks had almost dragged out their course and then one morning Anne's feverishly alert hearing caught the distant sounds of bustle and the clanging of heavy doors. She listened, her heart seeming to stop beating, but the steps did not approach and the sounds died away. From Lady Kingston she learned that Norris and Brereton and Weston and Smeton had gone to Westminster to their trial.

" And I and my brother? "

" To-morrow."

CHAPTER XXXII

THE TRIAL

TO avoid the crowds that would block the streets to see the queen taken to her trial, it was determined to have the case heard in the hall of the Tower itself. Seats and platforms and barriers were hastily erected during the night and by morning — it was the morning of the fifteenth of May — the peers who were to sit on the jury commenced to arrive. But early as they came they found the way blocked by a huge concourse of people that had been gathering solidly during the hours before dawn. The green enclosure within the walls was densely packed with those who had fought their way into the foremost ranks, while without the entrance, wedged with humanity, a mob of all sorts and conditions of men and women struggled and pushed to advance within.

Excitement had run riot in London since the queen's arrest and the condemnation of the four commoners, three days before, had stirred it to deeper intensity. For the first time the exact accusations had been made public, and while it would not have been hard for a scandal-breathing populace to accept the story of Anne's guilt, in moderation, the very thickness of the mud that was plastered on, the lack of any evidence but hearsay and the confession of a tortured boy, the dauntless and unswerving denial of the three young gentlemen, produced its inevitable effect. And more potent still were

349

the rumors of Henry's new wedding clothes that were under way. How very pat Anne's guilt was falling for him! Quite as pat as a scruple of conscience that had pricked him some ten years previous. And the London people who had sided against Anne in that first question of conscience rallied about her now, helplessly indignant and pitiful. And so there were low mutterings in the crowd that surged and pressed against the doors, and many black looks at the peers who passed within to their work of judgment.

Within the hall the peers had assembled upon the platform built for them, a curiously constrained body of men who, in general, appeared to avoid each other's glances and were at some pains to assume an elaborate appearance of ease. But here and there were eyes alight with malice or revenge. Suffolk smiled continually, an arrogant, cruel smile, that foretasted triumph. Near him sat Anne's father, very quiet and contained at the first glance, but the second found something subtly aged and shrunken beneath the suave exterior. Heaven knows the thoughts that filled that secret and calculating mind as he sat there with eyes fixed and averted from the furtive, wondering glances of his neighbors — it would be strange indeed if no agitation at the fate of his son and daughter invaded his anxious speculations as to his standing with the new régime! When the trumpets sounded, announcing with ironic pomp, that Anne, Queen of England, was entering the court, Wiltshire's gaze dropped to the floor; he did not raise it for some time.

Anne came between Sir William Kingston and Sir Edward Walsingham, with Lady Kingston and Lady Boleyn following after. She walked slowly, with high-held head, a little pale, but with a mien as serene and

THE TRIAL

undisturbed as if she were going to some great honor,
so the courtiers whispered. With a condescending
graciousness she bowed to the jury of peers, and her
eyes lingered quietly for a moment on the face of her
uncle, the High Steward, in his raised chair beneath
a canopy of state, and cold and vindictive as the small
man was, he did not meet her glance, but stooped and
began whispering to Lord Chancellor Audeley, who sat
beside him and who had presided over the trial of the
commoners on the twelfth. On the other side sat Sir
John Allen, the Lord Mayor, visibly uneasy and perturbed, who had attended, at the king's request, with a
deputation of aldermen, wardens, and members of the
principal crafts of London. Behind the barriers
crowded members of the court and any others who had
obtained entrance.

Anne seated herself in the armchair provided for her,
arranging her heavy, ermine-bordered robes with careful attention. The hum of tongues that had lowered at
her entrance sprang up again louder than ever, and she
raised her head to meet the curious eyes upon her with
the composure that came from the tensity of her pride
and courage. Her mind had never been more clearly
alert and vigorous. Hopeless as she could not but know
any defense of hers to be before those men who had assembled to fulfill the formalities of sentencing her to
death, every vestige of spirit in her was resolved upon
fighting to the last.

The whispered conferences and murmurings ceased
as Sir Christopher Hale, the king's attorney, rose to
commence the argument on behalf of the crown. He
was a man of fine presence and fine voice, capable of
manly strength of utterance and of expressing a most
varied range of feeling. Anne remembered as she lis-

tened now intently to him — for this was the first knowledge she had of the accusations against her — how she had once said he could let his voice tremble and sob over his phrases while he was wondering what he would have for dinner. He was putting the whole of his eloquence now into the case, denouncing, with telling emphasis, this woman whom the king had loved and believed in, whom he had raised from her low estate to be the sharer of his throne and the mother of his child, and how, after he had heaped honor after honor upon her, she had betrayed his faith and the faith of England, so indissolubly bound up in the person of its sovereigns, and had plunged into such vicious excesses that language itself halted in the description. Thereupon his language flowed steadily on. The queen, he declared, had solicited and corrupted three of the gentlemen of the king's court, men about his person whom he had trusted as his brothers, and another, a favorite musician of the court, and she had held repeated criminal intercourse with her brother, Lord Rochford.

A shock went through Anne as she heard that infamous charge; her body trembled slightly and then she held herself still. Hale was going on and on. There was no depth, he solemnly declared, to her depravity. She had conspired to bring about the king's death, agreeing to marry one of her lovers afterwards; she had given a locket to Norris in a conspiracy to have the late Princess Dowager, Catherine, poisoned and her daughter, the Lady Mary, also. She had spoken contemptuously of the king, of his literary productions, and of the way he dressed, showing clearly that she was altogether tired of him.

Cromwell seconded the efforts of Hale. He was not so eloquent a speaker, but there was terrific insistency in his address. And all the time Anne listened intently, noting each point and framing each refutation, while all the while it seemed to her so bizarre and unreal that she was sitting here on trial for her life against such charges. Nothing in her whole experience had ever seemed so strange and dream-like as her presence here in this dark stone chamber, her jailers at her side, the voice of her accusers thundering about her and those rows of hostile faces before her. Her mind told her that there was no hope, no faintest dawn of it, but this message of her mind was ineffectual and meaningless to the vivid life that coursed through her veins. Die? And under such vile charges? Every drop of blood and every whit of spirit in her were in brave allegiance to defeat this wretched conspiracy. And when she rose to meet her accusers she had never in her life been more intensely collected, more alertly on her guard. Before she spoke she let her glance pass for the first time about the throng of onlookers at the other end of the hall, meeting for the briefest second the eyes that were gazing up at her with such widely ranging expressions. She felt she saw her stepmother's tear-swollen face under a heavy veil, and next her the old dowager duchess, shrunken and pale like a figure of ivory, and then she saw Lady Exeter and the Duchess of Norfolk and Lady Carewe alight with bitter revenge — face after face of the women and men with whom she had jested and made merry through the long years of her ascendency, and again the feeling of the strangeness of her presence here and of the night-marish quality of the whole thing gripped her intensely. Then she turned toward the peers.

" I hardly know," she said, speaking in a quiet voice that penetrated with its peculiar singing quality to the farthest corner of the hushed hall, " whether to begin, this, my defense, with those charges of my unwifely criticism of the king's literary productions or of the conspiracy to poison the Lady Mary. . . . Ye have amassed so much of accusation! . . . These things are so strange to me that I scarce know how to speak of them, but," she paused and her look passed slowly from man to man of that jury, " I do declare my absolute innocence of each and every one of all these infamous charges. . . . I have never exchanged a word or a deed of love with any man save my husband, my liege lord, the king."

Cromwell was on his feet instantly, " Do you deny, madame, that you have given a locket to Henry Norris and certain money to Sir Francis Weston ? "

" I can not and I do not," she replied with spirit. " There is no evil in that doing — I would have given you a locket if I had deemed you worthy such a token from your queen. It was given openly as a token of royal pleasure and you can no more construe into that blameless act a shred of love or a plot to poison my husband, the king, or the king's daughter, than I can construe a pair of gloves I once gave you, my lord, into a plot to murder my mother. The world knows this. You but bring such childish trifles as evidence against me here because there is none other evidence that you can bring. . . . You have said unto me that I did play the sinner when my infant daughter, the Princess Elizabeth, was not a month in age. Why ye know yourselves, those that were at the court then, that I was scarce upon my feet at that time and that, but for the day of her christening, I never left my room nor the society of my ladies."

Again Cromwell's voice thundered at her. " Where

were ye then, madam, on this night, the sixth of October, which Mark Smeton hath sworn on his oath was one when he had meeting with you?"

"The sixth of October? Master Cromwell, that is over seven months ago and I do protest that my memory cannot now without thought recall whether I slept or read or played. Nor I do believe is there one among you —" and she faced the jury —" nor you yourself, sir secretary, who can name offhand, being taken so unawares, how any certain night, seven months gone by, was passed — unless that night be some sort of special occasion to him as this night ye name was not. But I do vow that it was spent in the society of my ladies, in womanly and modest undertakings, nor did any moment of it afford displeasure to my lord, the king. And as for the oath of Mark Smeton — wrung from him on rack, my lords — what credence is there in that? Will ye not give heed to the stout protests of those three good gentlemen, who even under the offer of pardon, would not admit so infamous a slander to themselves and to their queen? The word of three gentlemen, my lords, against —"

"But the confession of one criminal," boomed Hale's fine voice.

"One witness is not enough, sirs, to convict a person of high treason," she gave back.

"In your case, it is sufficient," spoke Cromwell with sharp emphasis.

"Nay, but there you speak the truth!" she flashed. "Any hearsay, any witness, however untrustworthy, will do to condemn me . . . but I put it to you, sirs, on your conscience as Christian gentlemen and knights of honor, to consider whether the tortured oath of a lowborn lad can stand against the declaration of these gentlemen, who have refused, even under promise of their lives, to confess so vile a lie. That these gentlemen came often to our rooms cannot be denied nor have I thought to do so — it were strange that a queen were neglected at the court! And that they are my particular friends is indeed the truth — being the intimates of my good lord I did naturally honor them — that is why they have been singled out for to lend the color and semblance of truth to this vile aspersion. What others than my friends would serve? But I have never seen these gentlemen save in the presence of my ladies, nor have I been advised of the nature of these accusations and the charges that ye confront me now with, nor allowed to procure my witnesses to confirm the honesty of my words, and to account for each questioned hour.

"As to my relations with my brother — what you say as evidence is that once he was alone with me for a considerable time and that I have always given signs of fondness to him. I ask you, my lords, when has it ever been the custom in England that a brother may not spend time with his sister, nor remain in the room together? I have ne'er heard denial of the goodness of such usage either here or in foreign countries. It hath always been held right and sweet for brother and sister to love one another. Is there a wife of yours who hath not at some hour been alone with her own brother? Is she then a sinner? Ye see what child's talk this is! And as to those accusations ye have read out of unsigned letters, handed in to these juries by those, my enemies, who under the dark shield of namelessness have thrust these lying daggers at me, why I will but ask you, sirs, what credence you dare place in such unsigned and unsupported statements?"

"'Tis for you to disprove, madam, not for these lawful accusers to support," the king's attorney reminded her sternly.

"My lawful accusers!" Anne's eyes were a blaze of contempt. Her voice did not raise its pitch, but it rang with redoubled intensity. "They are lies, pure and simple, handed in by enemies vowed to my destruction. Never in my life have I said those false things that are written here. I deny that I have e'er spoken contemptuously of my lord, the king, or of his writings, and I ask you to confront me here face to face with those that dare say otherwise. And I ask of you, my lord, to bring before me, according to English law, that Mark Smeton, this 'confessor,' who hath spoken such infamy of me. To my face he dare not repeat it!"

That appeared to be also the opinion of the court, for after a brief instant's interrogation, her plea was denied. At this she blanched a trifle, understanding in such injustice the absolute determination of her death. "An ye call this English justice!" she said. "My lords, even a peasant woman would not be so cruelly handled! But I am not here to rail at you, but to make manifest my absolute innocency. Ye have said that a certain locket, given to Henry Norris, was in token of a conspiracy to poison his Grace, my husband. This locket was given in last November, 1535. I ask you to turn back your minds to the then condition of my affairs and of the affairs of England at that time. My predecessor, the Princess Dowager, was in excellent health. I held a contested throne by virtue of my lord and king's protection. Were his strong support once removed what would have been my condition? As pitiable, my lords, as to-day I find it, when the malice of mine avowed enemies has turned that support from me! With the king gone, you wot well that there would have been that instant uprising in favor of Catherine and her daughter, which her supporters have endeavored unceasingly to bring about with the king alive. I would have been able to offer but scant resistance. Master Cromwell would have turned against me; Master Kingston," and she glanced for a moment at the man, "whom I do know for a loyal friend to that deceased lady, would have shut the doors of that fortress, the Tower, in my face, and the jailers of Kimbolton and Hatfield would have been the first to try and obtain forgiveness by raising the banner of Catherine and of Mary. I would have had all Spain and all the Holy See against me, and more than half, I fear, of England. Would I have dared to hope that I could reign alone upon that throne to which the kindness of my lord hath raised me? Such a rash and presumptuous thought hath never visited my breast! I ask you to consider these things truly, my lords. Weigh them well, and you will see how baseless and of what light credence are these slanders of my enemies. And, at that time, when you have said I was conspiring against my husband, know you not I was hoping to have a son to my husband, if which thing had happened I would have been the safest wife in England and the happiest of women — as was indeed my motto upon a time not so long passed. At that day I was deemed worthy of the crown of England, and I say unto you, good my lords, that I have never betrayed that trust, but have striven to fulfill my duties that I might appear before my lord husband on earth and God, our judge in the world to come, with a conscience innocent of all offense. That I have been given to laughter and mirth hath perchance yielded cause for this malice of mine enemies, now manifest, to find an entrance. I deemed myself above all suspicion or reproach, so sure was I of mine own faithfulness and integrity towards the trust that had been reposed in me. Nay, hear me," she uttered, in imperious command as Cromwell made a motion to interrupt, "this is the truth and from it I will not depart though my body should be torn in pieces — I am innocent of all you have accused me and I stand before you the most foully wronged lady in the domain. . . . I ask you to consider on what light babble these accusations rest! I have given a locket to Norris, and therefore, you say, I have conspired the king's death — I have shown you how little reason, aside from the grief of my true love and duty to my prince, I would have to rejoice in that death! I have been alone with my brother, who is a dear brother to me and whom I love as a sister, therefore we have been wrongdoers! And I say unto you that all this slander, this talk of evil-doing, of conspiring against the king, of making sport of his person and his works, hath all arisen in the minds of my sworn enemies, whom ye dare not confront me with, and that not a syllable thereof hath proceeded from us.

"As to having tried to poison the Lady Mary — God knows I have made many proffers of friendship and it is not my fault but the fault of those who have ill advised and inflamed her mind that we are not in accord as mother and daughter this day. And as to that other charge, that this discovery, as you name it, of my ill-doing hath grieved the king's Majesty and brought his health into sad danger, I cannot think that you are serious in this nor will any credit your words who have heard the music and the merrymaking that have sounded from the king's barge as his Grace hath passed on the river these many nights of my strange imprisonment."

At that a hum of voices sounded from the back of

the hall, a swelling undertone of agreement. Few among
that crowd but had heard those sounds of revelry, few
were unacquainted with the tales of the king's latest infatuation, and the tide of popular feeling, so long against
Anne, the usurper, the second queen, surged now in
helpless sympathy to the woman who stood there, unfriended and unflinching, in the most gallant fight that
ever championed a lost cause. Hale was quickly on
his feet, but Anne made a denying gesture towards him,
and took a step nearer the peers.

" My lords, I have answered all that which you have
accused me," she said slowly. " You have given me no
time to prepare defense, have denied me counsel and witnesses, and I was not sure indeed of what you were ac-
counting me guilty until I was brought hither, but I have
answered you out of the mouth of innocence, and so
I rest my case. God, He knoweth all hearts. He knoweth that I speak the truth. I take Him for my witness
that I am innocent of all that ye have accused me."

There was a long silence when that clear voice ceased,
and then the hum of undertones swelled again about
the hall. Anne took one quick look out over those
crowding faces and then her steady eyes rested on the
faces of the peers turned somewhat uncertainly towards
each other. She read in those frowning and calculating
looks what they had come there to do. She saw Cromwell sitting quietly and gazing at her. If he had been
perturbed, bustling about — but no, he sat there un-
alarmed and lost himself in that strange absorption. It
was as if he saw her in a new and blinding light and she
read a frank and curious admiration on the man's hard
and cruel face.

She saw the Lord Mayor shaking his head with sadness — that honest Lord Mayor who afterwards blurted

forth that he could observe nothing in the proceedings against her, but that they were resolved to be rid of her, and then her keen eyes turned again to that dreadful jury.

Her uncle drew on the black cap. Anne rose to receive her sentence. Not even those nearest to her could detect the quiver of the features when she heard pronounced that Anne, Queen of England, had been found guilty of high treason, and was to be beheaded or burned at the king's pleasure. Very quietly she asked leave to say a few words.

"I am ready for death — my innocence doth not fear it," she said in unfaltering clearness, "but what doth grieve me sadly is that those poor gentlemen, who are innocent of all that is charged to them, should suffer on my account. . . . I ask a short time to be prepared for death."

One of the peers rose uncertainly to his feet and moved towards the door. It was Percy of Northumberland, and Anne, for the first time taking note of his presence there, thought numbly how strange it was, among all this strangeness, that he should be sitting in judgment upon her. Ten years ago, a girl of nineteen, she had cried her heart out for him. Well, she had Wolsey to thank for that, and Catherine, those two old enemies whom she was so shortly to join. . . . At the door Percy turned back on her a strange look. She had met his eyes many times at court, but always between them had been that screen of artificiality; now there was something poignant and awful in his revealing gaze. She had heard that he was ill, slowly dying of some nervous disorder. She gave him a faint smile, and in that moment she remembered what her lips had long forgotten, the first touch of his mouth on hers. . . . Well, she was soon to receive the kisses of another lover, that cold and ultimate possessor, Death.

These thoughts all flashed through her mind like one thought; then she saw that her jailers had resumed their positions at her side to reëscort her to the Tower. Just at the doorway she passed George being brought in for his trial and the eyes of brother and sister met in a swift, deep look. He was erect, smiling, disdainful. He had not one trace of hope now and an insouciant defiance was painted on his debonair features. The jig was up, his smile seemed ironically to say. They had never been so completely united as in that final and speechless second. Anne's heart went out to him in a surge of tenderness and pride. She smiled as she left the room.

CHAPTER XXXIII

THE NUMBERED HOURS

DEATH! Anne repeated it over and over to herself as she sat at her casement that night overlooking the Thames. She could not sleep, but a sense of fatigue after the storm of the day had laid hold of her and she felt inert and unwilling to move. Her tired body seemed a cage to her throbbing mind. In the next room slept Mary Wyatt and Helen and Madge and Amy, for she had been granted the company of her own maids now there was no longer the necessity for putting spies about her person.

Death! Anne sat there trying to prepare her mind for that stupendous event, as she had requested time to do, and all the while she was thinking how fantastic and unreal it all was. A night wind from the north was blowing and she heard beneath her the swishing of the little waves against the gray stones of her prison and breathed the warm, languorous smell of reedy river waters. It brought to her mind the remembrance of the days she had spent upon that river, of exquisite green shores where the trees hung breathless over their still reflections and of deep, emerald pools where the silver fish poised in their swift flights. With an impatient effort she wrenched her wayward mind from these futile wanderings to fix it on that thought of death.

She could not realize that thought, but it was coming to her, she repeated, death on a scaffold, for she had been told that owing to the king's leniency, her sentence would not be the stake. She would be beheaded. She put her hand to her neck as if to assure herself of the fact. There was where the sword would fall. She tried to vizualize the scene. She saw herself mounting the scaffold, she saw the black-clad executioner and the worn and blood-stained block where she must kneel — but even such dire images did not make that scene real to her, but it appeared like part of another's life on which she, Anne Boleyn, was gazing.

She thought of the beyond, the unknown bourne to which that final moment on the scaffold would send her journeying. She had always had faith in a hereafter, or rather she had assumed that she had, in that unquestioning and literal acceptance which youth gives to those shadowy affairs of so distant a date. But now death was actually upon her. And after death — what? If death should be all —! The thought of the absolute cessation of the human spirit roused in her an incredulous and passionate denial. It could not be all! It could not! Of what avail was life, its strivings, its griefs and sufferings, if death ended all, like a huge snuffer over a flickering candle? Did such wrongs as hers descend into the grave with the poor body, to be covered by the earth, unredressed by any higher judgment? Did such dissolute monsters as Henry caper through their satyr lives to sleep in an eternal peace? It could not be! Her desperate need of higher justice compelled its own belief; she felt that life without this ultimate summing up was chaos unthinkable. Surely God would requite her for all she had suffered here . . . would reveal her innocence . . . would confound her enemies . . . her stricken heart dwelt on that thought. At His Throne all would be made clear. . . .

THE NUMBERED HOURS

She roused from the passionate comfort of that thought to remind herself that there was yet much to do to prepare herself; she must make ready her soul, and repent of those matters that needed repentance. She tried to turn her thoughts back through her years, and search them with remorseless clearness, but her thoughts evaded her and slipped into straying by-paths of her own. Disconnected visions passed hazily through her mind in fitful waywardness; she saw good Madame Simonette, her governess, crying at the foot of a tree she had rashly scaled; she saw herself trying on her coronation robes and the dazzling white and scarlet of the image that laughed back at her from her glass; she remembered the first touch of her baby's hand on her breast. And with that memory came the only pang of fear that assailed her. Her baby, Elizabeth! *In what measure ye mete it shall be measured unto you again.* . . . She heard it as if it had been spoken — and she thought of the day she had surprised Henry and Jane — then she thought of the Lady Mary. Aye, she had done wrong there. The girl had driven her to bitterness with her disdainful pipe of "the king's mistress," . . . but would she not have done the same? Would she not have had her own daughter do the same? There was something fine in that haughty and unintimidated Spanish blood to which Anne had yielded secret admiration through her spite — and now a sad and helpless remorse possessed her at the irritation and bitterness she had expended upon the dispossessed little princess, a remorse that was quickened by a terrified foreboding of the retaliation upon her own child. Oh, she had sinned there! But let it not be visited upon Elizabeth, her innocent baby! Let her bear it all — surely, in the agony of this ignoble death she was bearing it all!

THE FAVOR OF KINGS

But fear had touched her and she began to pray feverishly, pleading with Heaven to save her baby from the
anger of her elder sister and her enemies. Then she
prayed for her brother, for the courage and comfort of his
soul. She wondered how he was passing the night and
if she could get permission to see him on the morrow
for the last time — the last time. . . .

She covered her face with her hands, but she could
not weep. She remembered her brother as she had seen
him that day, erect and proud, meeting his fate with
dauntless scorn. She had heard that he had· defended
himself so well that the betting had been ten to one for
his acquittal. It was a losing wager, for Cromwell intended none of that faction to escape. He himself was
to marry Jane Seymour's sister. For a few moments
her thoughts went back almost wonderingly to the man
who had undone her. And she had never really feared
him. . . . Now he loomed before her as a monster, subtle, shrewd, unscrupulous, a cunning, wary spider, weaving, weaving, with his round bright eyes darting in incessant watch over his precious interests. Her downfall
had been a fine stroke for him; he had by the same blow
removed the woman who was blocking his Imperial
policy, and cleared the path for the king's new favorite,
which was also the path of his own personal interests.
. . . Anne thought of Jane and wondered at the tides of
hope and vanity and ambition that must have flooded
that narrow breast. What thoughts were locked behind
the unrevealing features of that woman who had helped
attire her on that fatal May Day!

Then her thoughts came back to her brother again.
It seemed to her if she could only see him, could only
cast herself upon his neck, that this stone in her side
would melt and she could weep again. Their tears

would mingle as in childhood. . . . Was he alone now
in this dark hour of his despair or had he the sad solace
of his doomed companions? Her heart went out to them
all in aching pity; even to poor Smeton, her craven musician. It was so cruel, so cruel to crush them all with
this calumny — Norris, for whom little Madge Shelton had cried herself to sleep, and Weston, whose young
wife must be wrung with grief, and honest Brereton, her
" faithful watch dog," as she had called him. A straying
gleam of memory brought a sudden picture of those
three, arms linked about each other, glasses on high towards the king, joyously toasting with him his sweetheart, fair Anne Boleyn. Her friendship had cost them
dear, thought the woman in the Tower.

She believed herself done with hope forever, yet she
was to know once more the rack of its suspense. That
next morning Cranmer came to her, Cranmer the archbishop she had made, and whose allegiance she had so
widely counted upon. Now he told her of his sympathy
and his helplessness — how he had written anxiously to
the king protesting his belief in her, but how the fear
of the king had forced his outward acquiescence. Now,
he assured her, he found a way to save her. Henry desired a divorce. Despairing of Heaven's sending him
a son, he had resolved to make the Duke of Richmond
his heir — Norfolk, whose daughter had married Richmond had been influential doubtless in the matter. Well,
to do this, he wished to make Elizabeth illegitimate.
How could he? He refused to admit himself in the
wrong and his marriage invalid on account of Catherine,
but sought to invalidate it for some other reason. The
old matter of the precontract between Percy and Anne
had been brought up, but the very day after the con-

demnation of the four men Northumberland had sworn upon the sacrament that no precontract existed.

The wary earl had no notion of contradicting his former oath and laying himself open to a charge of treason. But would not Anne admit that contract — on consideration that her life was spared?

"My life!" said Anne with a weary note of contempt, and yet the blood that had seemed congealed in her veins like frozen ice, seemed to quiver and flow again in the involuntary resurgence of her youth. But she shook her head.

"Percy shall ne'er go hang for me," she vowed.

Cranmer besought her in vain, pleading her desperate straits.

"Nay, ye need urge me no more," she declared, "I will ne'er undo Northumberland. But there is another reason I will own to,— an you can promise me that life will come of it. Life! I had not thought I cared to live, but now it seems that something in me is still eager to draw breath and look up at the sky — be it in that wilderness of the New Country across the seas which that Genoese, Columbus, sailed to. Yes, I will make the bargain — my life for my unwiving. For if the king is set on making out his daughter illegitimate — 'tis the same boat that all the rest are in! — he will do so in spite of me, take oath upon 't. But that sickly lad of his will never reign — and then will come my child's chance. . . . But, oh, Cranmer, I have grown fearful that thrones are not such pinnacles of fortunes! You will be friendly to my child? . . . The reason? Why, turn your mind back, my lord, to some dalliances of Henry before I was betrothed to him, and ye may surmise a reason for invalidating this marriage of mine that I procured with so great weariness and now undo with

but a little breath. . . . Do you recall my sister Mary?
She was very fair."

Cranmer nodded. "But had not his Highness a dispensation for — for that degree of consanguinity?"

"Aye, but Rome is not the fountain head of our conscience any more. If I wished to contest, true, I would have a shrewd case, but I will not contest but so much as may make my safety worth my concession. I will own I knew of this affair, and then the knowledge, by *both* parties, of an opposing reason, maketh the offspring illegitimate. Will that satisfy them, Master Cranmer? And shall I sure go free?"

He promised it, and the will to live sprang up in her in pitiful eagerness. She told her maids of Cranmer's assurance that she would probably be sent in exile to the Low Countries and upheld her spirit with the ring of her words. She made new plans, dreamed new hopes of a quiet life somewhere — of books and flowers — and perhaps again the sight of her child —

She might have spared herself the pains.

She seemed scarcely to have fallen asleep that night before a noise roused her. The room was gray with the first faint lightening of dawn, and the casement framed a patch of lilac sky. The noise came again — a crash of board and then a regular click-clack of businesslike regularity. She went to the window on the west and in the dim light she saw the figures of men at work in the courtyard below. They were building something — and the dreadful truth flashed through her. They were making a scaffold. Was she to die at once?

Lady Kingston, entering some two hours later, when the sun was flooding the room with light, and finding Anne, ready-gowned, in pallid readiness, informed her that this was not yet for her, but for the men who were to die.

"Beneath my window?" said Anne with ghastly eyes.

The people had come in great numbers. They poured in before the workmen had finished their job, men and women and even children, animated with the tingling excitement of the execution. They streamed in increasing throng. Anne heard the babble of their incessant talk, the medley of laughter and banter and inquiry and gossip that filled the air. It was a memorable occasion for them. Those children, that they had roused from their beds to come, would long remember it and tell their children's children of the day they had seen die five lovers of a guilty queen. Smeton was to be hanged, being of ignoble birth. The other four were to be beheaded.

The sun, that shone so brilliantly at first, slipped away behind a thin cloud, and left the morning but faintly luminous, with the milky opaqueness of an opal, flashing an occasional spark of brightness. One such ray slipped out and briefly gilded the heads of the condemned men as Anne, kneeling at her window through the endless hours, saw them led out to die. They were led punctiliously in the order of their rank, her brother in advance. Something seemed to stir and quiver in Anne's side as if her heart felt the stab of a mortal wound, then she was quiet, very quiet, in a still and frozen calm. She saw the men mount the scaffold, and stand beside that menacing figure that leaned, with rolled-up sleeves, upon an ax. She saw the composure with which the four gentlemen surveyed this figure and then turned to face the mob before them. She became aware of the faces of curious onlookers appearing along the Tower wall, peering in between the spikes, uncanny apparitions like bodyless heads set in a row with the grin of life surprised still upon their lips. She saw young Smeton shrink back and cover his face at the sight of the gallows arm that was to dispatch him when the gentlemen's affairs had been concluded.

After a brief colloquy between the figures on the scaffold Anne saw her brother step forth. There was a tightening of the indescribable tension throughout her rigid body, but Anne felt nothing more. She seemed encased in stone. Her brother was speaking but the wind blew the words away and only occasional sentences reached her ears. She knew there was little he could say; for a condemned man to protest his innocence and denounce the king's justice was to invite torture instead of beheading, a confiscation of all his goods, and the wreaking of the king's displeasure upon his family.

" Not to preach . . . but to die," came George's voice, " desiring all, and especially masters of the court that ye will trust in God especially and not in the vanities of this world; for if I had done so I think I had been alive as ye be now. . . . Forgive me whom I have offended . . . as I forgive all . . . God save the king," he concluded mechanically.

The executioner stepped forward. He said something and George knelt. And never once looked up and said farewell, the sister thought in her dumb agony. They had refused her permission to see him yesterday night. . . . The executioner raised his ax. . . . She did not stir or quiver at the hideous scene. She could not move or shed a tear. She could not even hide her face. She became vaguely aware of Mary and Helen crouching beside her, with muffled sobs, of Madge swooning at their feet, but she could not turn a head to them; her eyes were tense upon that thinning group.

26   371

THE FAVOR OF KINGS

She saw Weston step to his place and wave his hand down at a young woman who held up a little child. It was his wife and son. It seemed but yesterday that Anne had seen them wed. And now — how soon it was all over!

It was a nightmare of blood — those strong young men stepping forward in their youth and strength, that swinging ax — and then those headless trunks, blood-spurting necks, and those severed heads rolling on the greasy boards. . . .

At last she raised her eyes to the women who were bending over her. It was all finished.

"Their souls are gone straight to heaven," said Anne slowly in a voice from which all color of life was extinct.

She roused, at Kingston's entry, to face him with, "And not one word of admission, not at the last! . . . And Smeton, that poor rack-wrung lad — did he not acquit me of the infamy he had laid upon me?"

"He said naught, madame," Kingston replied.

It seemed that her white cheek turned whiter. She laid her hand upon her heart. "Alas, my lord, I fear his soul will suffer for it."

That afternoon she was told that her case had been tried at Lambeth and Cranmer had pronounced an annulment. There was no word of pardon, and what poor assurance she had secretly clung to was extinguished in a blaze of bitter comprehension.

The advocates, to whom Cranmer had urged her to assign her cause, had betrayed her through too ready yielding. Had they stood out, the king might have been forced to come to terms with her, but they were royal officials, eager to please their sovereign. Had not

THE NUMBERED HOURS

Thomas Cromwell frankly stated that, "The duty of politicians is to penetrate the disguise which sovereigns are accustomed to throw over their real inclinations, and to devise the most specious expedients by which they may gratify appetites without appearing to outrage morality or religion." And here these politicians had no disguise of Henry's appetites to penetrate. They promptly yielded and with their case went Anne's last hope, for though she was pronounced now to have been no lawful wife of Henry's, and so could not be logically sentenced for betraying a husband who denied the relationship, logic had no voice in the affair.

Kingston informed her that the execution was fixed for the morning of the eighteenth.

"Why, 'tis to-morrow!" she repeated incredulously.

She was very merry at dinner.

"Lord, Lord, the long faces," she cried, gazing about on her ladies. "Ye are the girls whose cheer I craved and now look on yourselves! Why do ye weep? There is no more to fear. And think what strange history you are seeing! There will be ballads and tales writ about me — Wyatt will make some, I warrant. I shall not lack for a name — tell my chroniclers that I proffer them Queen Anne Sans-Tête — Queen Lackhead, that is, Madge. You never knew your French. . . . Is there no more o' the pigeon? Think —'tis the last that I shall eat."

In eerie gayety her laughter rang out and her talk rattled on with desperate jest, yet when the meal was over, she went quickly from them to her prayer closet and knelt there alone, pressing her hands over the throbbing temples.

"O God, O God," she whispered, "it is true — it is real . . . I must die." She repeated it over and over,

373

closing her eyes as if to shut out the horrid pictures that swam in blood before her. Phrases and words of grief floated through her mind and fixed themselves into lines. Presently her ladies heard the sound of a lute from her chamber and entering, discovered her at the window, softly singing.

" 'Tis a verse of my own making," she told them dreamily. " Listen; you may not hear me sing again."

> Oh, Death! rock me asleep,
>   Bring on my quiet rest,
> Let pass my very guiltless ghost
>   Out of my careful breast.
> Ring out the doleful knell,
> Let its sound my death tell,—
>   For I must die,
>   There is no remedy,
>   For now I die!
>
> My pains who can express?
>   Alas they are so strong,
> My dolour will not suffer strength
>   My life for to prolong!
> Alone in prison strange,
>   I wail my destiny;
>   Woe worth this cruel hap, that I
>   Should taste this misery!
>
> Farewell my pleasures past,
>   Welcome my present pain,
> I feel my torments so increase
>   That life cannot remain.
> Sound now the passing bell,
> Rung is my doleful knell,
> For its sound my death doth tell;
>   Death doth draw nigh,
>   Sound the knell dolefully,
>   For now I die!

THE NUMBERED HOURS

And again, she sang,

> Defiled is my name full sore,
>   Through cruel spite and false report;
> That I may say for evermore
>   Farewell to joy, adieu comfort.

She continued playing slow, bell-like dirge notes on her lute, staring absently out the window. It was open and the night had grown misty. A rising wind played with her hair which she had allowed that night to fall as she used in the days when she was maid of honor.

"It bloweth chill upon you," Mary said anxiously and Anne laughed.

"What matter?"

Mary looked confused. What matter indeed, how chill the wind blew on Anne or how much cold she grew now? Anne laughed on sharply and then sobered, "Is it not strange," she said, frowning thoughtfully as if trying to reason out a curious puzzle within herself, "that to-morrow you will be here and you, Helen and Madge, all alive somewhere, combing your hair, looking out that a chill wind blow not too sharply upon you and I, I, this Happiest of Women, shall be — where?"

"In heaven," said Mary Wyatt in a trembling voice.

Anne smiled gravely at her. "Why so I truly think myself. I have had but faults, not crimes, and this martyrdom should atone for much more than can ever be truthfully laid to me. If there is a heaven I think I shall win to it. And if there be nothing — for these thoughts come to those who are about to die — why then I shall know nothing and sleep on with the dust in the earth's keeping."

"Say not such things, Anne," begged Mary, crossing herself. "Not at this time."

THE FAVOR OF KINGS

"Little trembler! If you shiver so at a word how will you have courage to stand beside me on the scaffold? Besides, if the thought is in the heart doth not the Lord know all hearts and doth he not read it and respect more an open speech than a hypocritical silence? But no, I have no doubt. I think there must be another world for this is so full of wrong and sin that another world must there be to place things right and undo the work of this. And again I feel that I must go on, somewhere." She put her hand on her heart. "It beats so strong," she said. She raised her hand. "Hush!"

Faint notes of music were floating up to them from the dark of the spring night. Barges were passing on the water, laden with pleasure seekers. The strings of lutes were gayly twanged, voices rose high in jovial measures. Anne knew the voices — her own had chimed with them many such a night. It was a song of the king's composition, the one to which Anne had danced some ten years ago.

> Pastance with good company,
> I love, and shall until I die. —

Oh, poignant memory! She saw the feast of Cardinal Wolsey's, the lights and colors, the brilliant throngs,— and before them all, aglow with the triumph of her dance, a girl in a sky blue gown, sparkling with silver stars. Anne remembered how she had embroidered away at those stars. She thought of her first dance with the king that night, and all the vanities and conquests that quickened her young blood and made up the sensation she called life and happiness. How little she had dreamed that night of being queen — how little of a queen dethroned, condemned to die!

A medley of strange memories enwrapped her as she

376

sat at the barred window while a rollicking chorus floated
in the air about her, her husband's voice ringing over
all — a bizarre confusion of unsummoned scenes. She
saw Henry as he had appeared in the garden at Hever
with the sunlight on his fringe of hair and beard, and
again on that wind swept hill in Epping forest when she
had first promised to be his queen. She saw his face as
he had welcomed her at the Tower, the day of her coronation procession in London, smiling on her and kissing her
before all the crowd. In strange review passed the many
days and nights of their association — his passionate
words of love, the kisses, the touch of his hands. She
remembered how often he had clasped them about her
neck, turning her face up to him. She had not dreamed
then of a ruder clasp! And now he was going to marry
Jane. He passed beneath her window, singing. She
doubted if he meant it for an affront. He had probably
not remembered her existence. The spring was in his
blood, his old diseased, ulcerous blood, and he was singing of his new love, thrilling of the lust of the new conquest. Passion was all of which he was capable. She
remembered what she had wrung from her ladies — the
story of the new white satin clothes, trimmed with gold,
his wedding clothes that he was to don the next day. Incredible . . . callous . . . satyr of life. . . . And he had
written a play on Anne's infidelities and execution that
he was reading to his court! It did not seem possible.
Her motto danced mockingly before her eyes — Happiest
of Women.

At length she went to bed. "I had best or my limbs
may tremble in spite of me," she acceded to her ladies'
prayers for her to rest herself, but no sleep could visit
that agitated and excited mind. Somewhere in the early
morning Helen woke to see Anne sitting in bed, very pale

and ghostly looking in the light of the single chamber candle, the shadows of the blown curtains swaying over her like birds of ill omen.

Helen rose quickly to know if she might do anything for her.

"Yes, be thyself, dear Helen," Anne laughed under her breath. "Doth it not seem a shame to waste these hours that are the last my mortal tongue can have to wag in converse, in trying to sleep? Let us talk. Let us open our hearts to each other. I always liked the stiff crust of thine. What shall we tell each other? Let us cast all pretense aside. See, this time to-morrow morning I shall be unable to betray thee."

Helen crept softly into bed with her. Mary lay asleep, the light in her face revealing the traces of her tears.

"After all, what is there to say?" Helen said drearily.

"There must be many things. Bethink thee that after this sun hath risen one may ask of me in vain."

Helen turned her light gray eyes upon her. "Didst thou ever love the king?"

"Love is a strange word, Helen. I loved the shadow of the king once. But what I loved was a figment of my mind, a dream of my dazed fancy. But thou — Helen, dost thou not love Wyatt?"

Helen gave a wan smile. "Why should you care to ask? . . . In heaven all is revealed."

"Then why should I wait a day? A few hours make no difference. I do think ye have."

"Indeed, ye think truly."

Anne considered it in silence. "Why then you have had a tragedy of your own, poor girl . . . I wonder not — Wyatt is beyond all others it was e'er our lot to know — Oh, I would, I would that when I came from France he had been free —"

THE NUMBERED HOURS

" Free," gave back Helen in a voice tense with feeling.
" What were freedom or honor or those things that men
name virtues if I could have won him! You tossed him
aside, as one forbidden. My God, how gladly I would
have sacrificed all, *all* for him."

Anne was silent a moment. Then she shook her head.
" You may yet hope," she said. " For you all things are
not ending."

" Hope," whispered the other girl ironically. " His
heart will be buried with you, Anne. He is a man possessed. He hath talked with me before I came here,
because he knew that I was true to you, and said over
and over that he would give his life for the chance of
raising a rescue expedition. He said to me that if all
were hopeless and the end came that he would not let you
lie under the stones here in a dishonored grave. He will
come and steal you, he said, and carry you by night to a
place in Blickling or Hever Churchyard."

Anne shivered. " I wonder if you can guess how
strange my flesh creeps to hear you speak of me as under
the stones, when here I sit in my flesh so strong and well.
Helen, 'tis a strange thought that to-morrow night this
gown will lie here as it was, but I — I shall be no more.
The lumber that we call into being, the gear that serves
us, is of more lasting stuff."

The girls were silent. At length Anne prepared to
rise. " Call mine almoner. If there is strength in prayer
I will seek it. I would put my mind upon high things."

From two o'clock she remained in prayer, trying steadily to compose herself, to face the great ordeal with an
inner calmness as well as the outer fortitude of pride.

In the morning she sent for Kingston and asked him
to be present while she received the sacrament. The
communion was celebrated and both before and after re-

ceiving the host she declared upon the salvation of her soul that she had never been unfaithful to the king and was guiltless of the crimes laid to her charge. Kingston was uneasy under the pitiful ceremony.

"What is the good?" he muttered. In his heart he did not believe her guilty — to him, the man of obedience, it did not matter. The only thing that mattered was that she was going to die and that he must see to the arrangements.

Then she returned to the chamber with her maids. She had dressed herself in a low cut gown, and looped her hair away from her neck. So she sat among the four who were to accompany her to the last.

"Thou had best not come, Mary," she said kindly. "It will be a sad sight for thee."

Mary looked at her with tear-stained eyes. "I shall not weep, dear Anne, and trouble thee. But I shall not leave thee," she said. And Mary sat as quietly as Anne in the room, with folded hands and set lips, waiting, waiting. Her look dwelt upon Anne in passionate love; when their eyes met she smiled, a brave little smile to show that she was strong and ready. It seemed to Anne she could endure no more.

At ten o'clock, she sent for Lady Kingston, unable to wait longer in silence. She was not to die before noon, Lady Kingston declared and Anne rose restlessly, and asked to have Kingston himself come to her.

"Mr. Kingston," she uttered, "I hear I shall not die afore noon, and I am very sorry therefore, for I thought to be dead by this time and past my pain."

"The pain should be very little," said Kingston with his crude attempt at consolation, "it is so subtle."

She burst out laughing, "I have heard the executioner is very good and I have a little neck." Still laughing

softly in the face of the astonished man she clasped her
two hands about it.

" I have seen men and also women executed," wrote
the governor of the Tower in the letter to Cromwell,
" and they have been in great sorrow, but to my knowledge this lady hath much joy and pleasure in death."

Time dragged on. No notice for the execution was
given. The swordsman, a Frenchman from Calais, who
had a great reputation for dexterity, had been chosen and
it was reported that he was delayed. Again, Lady Kingston said that the people were too excited; it was told
abroad that the lady was to die that day and numbers
had come to witness it; it was better to wait till they
dispersed. There would be few admitted.

To Anne's taut nerves, tuned to this funeral calm, the
delay was torture. She began to pace restlessly back and
forth, in bitter longing to have the terrible ordeal over
with and done. Now her thoughts rushed to meet it,
picturing each step that she must take up that grim scaffold where she had seen her brother die, playing morbidly
with the thought of her last moment; now they strayed
back over the past and she caught herself irrelevently remembering how blue were Elizabeth's eyes and how deep
her dimples. She folded against her breast the arms that
ached to feel that baby weight in them once more, while
she tried to keep at bay the unnerving terrors of her
fears for her little one. She was leaving her defenseless
— with a shameful stain upon her mother's name. What
would become of her? Would Mary wreak her hate on
her?

At last she sent for Lady Kingston, and commanding
her to follow, led her into the great presence chamber.
She shut the door and locked it, and then turning to the
lady, who stood surprised but tolerant of some new com-

munication, "Sit upon the seat of state," Anne said quickly.

Lady Kingston protested. "It is my duty to stand, and not sit at all in your presence, much less sit upon that seat which is the seat of you, the queen."

"Ah, madame, that title is gone," Anne smiled wearily. "I am a condemned person and by law have no estate left me in this life but for clearing of my conscience. I pray you sit down."

"Well," Lady Kingston quizzically returned, "I have often played the fool in my youth and to fulfill your command, I will do it once more in mine age," and thereupon she marched to the chair of state, ascended the two steps, seated herself on the chair, with an ironic upward glance at the cloth of state hanging about her.

But Anne had no humor in her at that moment. She was desperately in earnest, and schooling her spirit to a scene of penance, she deliberately knelt. She had not knelt since she had received the crown upon her head, three years ago that very month. She could not help remembering that torturing fact, fixed as her mind was upon its act of reparation.

"I charge you," she said in deep earnest, "as in the presence of God and His angels, and as you will answer before them when all should appear to judgment, that you will so fall down before the Lady Mary's grace, and in like manner ask her forgiveness for the wrongs I have done her. Till that is accomplished my conscience will not be quiet."

"Well, well . . . then will I," Lady Kingston made answer and rose with alacrity from the elevation where she felt herself vastly out of place, "but there will few believe me when I tell this tale," she added under her breath.

THE NUMBERED HOURS

The day was interminable to Anne's strained nerves. After that scene in the presence chamber her mercurial spirits rose in extravagant levity and she chatted in desperate merriment, laughing and joking of old times. She gave her maids her dresses, and then wondered if they would be allowed to keep them —" Or will Queen Jane wish them — she hath ever admired this blue so!" She talked of her mother and sent many messages.

And so through the night. It was impossible for her to sleep.

"Do I keep you up?" she asked once. "Well, you — and in troth I — shall sleep sound enow by the morrow and so make all well."

CHAPTER XXXIV

THE END

SHE had breakfasted next morning when Kingston approached her and stated that the hour was set. She heard him with a curious tightening of the nerves, as if the instrument of her body were being tuned for its last performance upon earth.

Kingston handed her a purse, telling her that according to custom she was to distribute those twenty pounds in alms before her death. Then Anne hastened to make ready.

Shortly before nine he returned, and Anne and her four ladies, with dumb looks of parting, strained hand clasps and the touch of cold lips on cold cheeks, formed in line and followed him. In the hall they paused while he ordered his men in position and Anne, glancing down, found that she was pressing against an old elm chest used there for keeping arrows. It had been changed from its old place and stood open now, the cover removed. Anne pointed to it with an ironic smile.

" Could you do no better for your queen? "

Kingston apologized. " There being no better provided and time pressing —"

" It will serve," said Anne. She gave a swift, half-fearful glance at the empty chest as she brushed past it. In a few moments it would be filled! Her poor head and disfigured body, the lips, the limbs that Henry had

384

THE END

caressed and wrapped with such soft luxury would be huddled into this rough chest. . . . There was a terrible smile on her mouth as she stepped into the doorway and faced the sun-flooded courtyard.

Only a few privileged spectators were present, for too many mutterings against her fate had been heard among the people and some manifestation was feared. The platform, that stood in the center of the green enclosure, was so low that the figures upon it could not be seen from without the walls, and outside a file of soldiers were keeping the crowds that had haunted the place away. Anne heard their voices.

She had paused in the Tower doorway, looking out on the scene, her eyes passing slowly with no sign of recognition, save the ironic deepening of that mocking smile, over the faces of the courtiers who had come to see her die. She stood before them with a mien of exaltation; it seemed to them that never had they seen the queen in such radiance of beauty. She wore a gown of black damask, with a deep white cape falling from the neck which was low cut. Her hair was raised high on her head, and adorned with a small headdress of black and silver — one that would in no wise obstruct matters, she had murmured in its selection. She stood etched in black and white save for the feverish brilliance of her cheeks that animated her with a bloom that held some quality of secret terror for the onlookers. Her very lack of fear was fearful in one so full of life and all its loveliness.

As Kingston still delayed over some last order, she turned to the captain of the guard, erect and ill at ease beside her, and with a sudden gesture unhooked a trinket from her chain and passed it to him.

" That is the first gift that the king e'er gave me," she

385

said, and as young Gwyn, with an embarrassed word of
thanks was clasping it dumbly, his honest eyes speaking
the pity that was forbidden his tongue, she murmured,
" You will observe there is a serpent in the handle."

She was silent a moment and then spoke again, very
clearly, though in a quiet voice. " Commend me to his
Majesty and say that he hath been ever constant in his
career of advancing me. From a private gentlewoman
he made me a marchioness, and from a marchioness, a
queen, and now he hath left no higher degree of honor,
he gives mine innocency the crown of martyrdom."

The words echoed curiously about the silent group.
Then Kingston hurriedly gave the order to advance, and
with a firm step Anne went on.

On the scaffold she turned to Kingston. " I entreat
you not to haste the signal for my death till I have
spoken that which is on my mind to." Kingston bowed.
He looked ill at ease.

She turned and faced the little group before her. She
saw Cromwell regarding her with steady attention and
noticed that he was in particularly fine array. Doubtless
he was to hurry back to join Henry at his wedding feast.
She wondered how soon he was to marry Jane Seymour's
sister and become the king's brother-in-law. Strange
events! There was Suffolk, the king's other brother-in-
law, beside him. Well, it was not so difficult to be the
king's brother-in-law as it had been. There might be
several more of them if this continued.

A step creaked behind her. She cast a swift, uncontrollable glance over her shoulder, dreading that the executioner would stealthily strike her down. Hastily she
began to speak and a tense hush fell upon that little
courtyard, over that strange gathering of the most powerful men in England who had come to see a queen die for

THE END

that of which they, more than all men living, knew that she had never done.

"Masters, I am come hither to die according to law," she began in her clear, penetrating tones with their singing, carrying quality which made men keep them long in memory, "for by the law I am indeed to die and therefore I will speak nothing against it. I am come hither to accuse no man," and her glance for a moment rested on Cromwell's face, staring fixedly up at her, "nor to speak anything whereof I am accused as I know full well that aught that I could say in my defense doth not appertain unto you and that I could draw no hope of life from the same. . . . But I come here only to die . . . and to yield myself unto the will of my lord, the king. I pray God to save the king and to send him long to reign over you,"— again there was a slight pause, then the people, too accustomed to hearing the king extolled by those whom he had sent to the scaffold, suddenly caught their breath at the delicately mocking inflection of those clear tones as they went on smoothly with no word that a censor might disapprove but with a ripple of indescribable irony, "the most godly, noble, and gentle prince there is! If any person will meddle with my cause I require them to judge the best," she added with sudden vehemence, and then slowly and softly, her gaze passing over those set, upturned faces. "Thus I take my leave of the world and of you." The quiet voice ceased.

With a fleeting glance at that waiting figure, the bared sword in its hand, she turned to her ladies. The girls were powerless to aid her. Their hearts were breaking with the smile she gave them. Then, refusing to have her eyes bound, she knelt down, and as she knelt she leaned and whispered to Mary, " Tell Wyatt I send my love to him too late."

THE FAVOR OF KINGS

She put her head on the block. She felt the pulse of her throat beat frenziedly against it. She heard the creak of the executioner's shoes, and her brilliant eyes, looking back over her shoulder in irresistible fascination, saw the man pause, as he met her glance, and his arm drop to his side.

She forced herself to stare steadily ahead. " *In manus tuas,*" she breathed.

The executioner slipped out of his shoes. He motioned an assistant to approach the queen from the other side. Anne, hearing that man draw near, turned her eyes involuntarily in his direction.

From the other side the swordsman stole suddenly upon her.

Then, stooping, he lifted by the long dark hair and held aloft before them the dangling head of Anne, who had been Queen of England.

(1)

THE END